PRAISE FOR GOOD ENOUGH FOR A PRINCESS

An enchanting romance between Crown Princess Adeline and Charlie Brewer, a single father , with no noble pedigree. We learn that we need to look to God for help for life's troubles.

— LINDA R.

Charlie has a fender bender with a beautiful young woman one night. Addie just seems to grab a place in his heart right off the bat. But there's these 2 guys always hanging around her. What's up with that? Addie is not used to dating American men but Charlie just strikes a cord in her heart. She knows nothing can ever come of it, though, her being who she is. She tries so hard to put Charlie out of her mind but he just refuses to leave! This is an inspirational romance novel. The characters, both of them, consult God regularly and strive to live their lives in a way that is pleasing to Him.

— SUSAN S.

Yet another 5-star rating for this amazingly talented author, Carol Moncado. Addie and Charlie crash into each other. She is the Princess of his dreams (literally) and he is the her knight in shining armor...she has a royal title, he does not. Will it ever work out for them to really be together?! This book shows how God can work things that seem totally impossible out. A Must Read!

— RH

Good Enough for a Princess

Carol Moncado

USA Today Bestselling Author

CANDID
Publications

DEDICATION

To the Brit Crits
Joanna, Jessica, Kristy, Jen, Stacey

For always believing in me.
For doing life with me.
For crying with me.
For rejoicing with me.
For making me be better and stronger than I ever believed I
could be.

Charlie Brewer pushed the hood of his heavy winter coat back with one gloved hand. A fender bender? Really? Like he didn't have anything else to do? Like get home to... Screaming interrupted his thoughts. He rapped on the window and prayed for it to stop. "Ma'am. Are you okay?" Stinging bits of ice pelted his face and peppered the car as he prayed she wasn't hurt.

Abruptly, her mouth clamped shut.

Bits of sleet pelted his face as he knocked again. "Are you okay?"

The girl looked up and the first thing he noticed was her big hazel eyes, filled to overflowing with tears.

"Are you okay?" Broken records had nothing on him. He cupped his hands and peered in the window. She didn't look hurt. He flinched. Except maybe for the gash on her forehead.

She nodded but didn't say anything and didn't roll down the window.

"I need to give you my contact information."

The window creaked down half an inch or so.

"No. I do not need your information. I will take care of my own vehicle, thank you." Even with the frantic note in her voice, he knew it would be almost melodic in a calmer situation. The window scratched its way back up and slid into the rubber casing. He tried to take a deep breath but the frigid air pierced his lungs. "Let me buy you a cup of coffee. You'll need a tow. Your wheel well is all messed up and you've got two flat tires."

She bit her bottom lip as her eyes flickered to the café across the parking lot. The look in her eyes suddenly reminded him of a scared little girl.

With both hands held up, Charlie tried to look less threatening than he must have when she first saw him with his hood up and face shadowed. He gave the best smile he could with frozen cheeks. "I promise I'm a good guy."

Finally, with a nod, she grabbed her purse from the front seat of the SUV, and turned the engine off. She reached for the handle on the inside of the driver's door. It didn't budge.

Bright lights caught him in the eye. A semi-truck passed a little too close for Charlie's comfort. If she had that door open and slipped...

"This side," he hollered at her and pulled on the handle.

She nodded and climbed across the center console while he pulled again.

Frozen shut.

Ice continued to fall, sliding down the back of his neck and into his shirt. If he wasn't already frozen through, that would have done it.

"You push from that side," Charlie yelled. "I'll pull."

Another nod and she pushed with one hand but it didn't move. He closed his eyes and breathed a quick prayer. "Put your shoulder into it."

Tears flowed, but she pushed against the door with her shoulder as he pulled. The door popped free and she tumbled out.

He caught her by the elbow to steady her on her feet, caught off-guard by the whiff of sunshine in her hair. "Are you okay?"

She nodded, her chin quivered just a little and Charlie gentled his hold on her. "I am. Thank you, sir."

There was something in her voice, or maybe her perfect posture, that brought visions of Mary Poppins to mind. He shrugged them off and closed her car door behind her. With a slow steady pace, he continued to hold her arm as started toward the inviting warmth of the café.

Warmth? Yes. He couldn't feel his nose anymore.

"You do not need to help me." The dismissive note in her voice bothered him until she jerked her arm away.

And slipped, wobbled, then righted herself. But she didn't fall.

Charlie contained his smirk and a dutiful bow. "I'm sure I don't, miss, but I'd feel much better if you'd allow me. I already crashed into your car. If I let you get hurt in the parking lot, I'd never forgive myself."

She sighed. A puff of white air blew out in front of her but she didn't pull away again. The thirty-second walk took nearly five minutes. Slow, half-steps, muscles tensed, toes bunched inside his boots trying to grip the slippery surface on top of the asphalt. They finally made it to the door. Hot air and the smell of sizzling bacon blasted him.

"Have a seat anywhere, kids!" a woman's voice called.

Charlie turned toward a row of booths along the front window. "After you?"

The woman pulled the knit cap off her head. Golden brown curls tumbled around her shoulders. She looked around carefully before walking all the way to the far end and sliding in the seat against the wall.

He sat across from her and held out a hand. "I'm Charlie."

One corner of her mouth twitched up before she shook his hand. "Adeline."

3

"A pleasure to meet you, Adeline. I just wish it was under other circumstances."

"Agreed. A car accident..." A flash of awareness crossed her face and she set her large black bag on the table. She flipped open one flap and dug around. "Where is it?" she muttered as she searched. Somehow, even that action seemed delicate. She wasn't from here.

"What are you looking for?"

"My phone. I need to call..." She stopped abruptly, gaze traveling to the café window. "Do we need to move the vehicles?"

Charlie shook his head. "We're far enough out of the main lane and the cars are stuck together. We'll have to wait for a tow. It could be a while." He pulled out his own phone to call roadside assistance.

"Should we call 911?" Adeline asked as she took a sleek black phone out of her purse. He tried to control an eyebrow quirk but failed. There were cell phones. There were nice smart phones. There were really nice smart phones. Then there was this one.

"No. They're on emergency status only. As long as no one's hurt, you deal with it yourself."

"Of course," She whispered and stared at her phone for a long moment. "I do not have a card for roadside assistance. Perhaps you could ask your service to send an extra tow truck for my vehicle?"

Something in the way she asked made him wonder if she'd ever called for auto help. The tilt of her chin and honest curiosity in her eyes reminded him of the children's fairytales he used to read. Did fairies come into the real world during ice storms? "I'll take care of it." It made him feel protective. Almost manly. When was the last time he'd felt the need to protect a woman? Ever? He found the right entry and pressed the screen. After listening and going through the process, he finally got a real person. Holding up one finger to Adeline, he stood and walked toward the front door to explain the situation.

Crown Princess Adeline Julianne Elizabeth of Montevaro relived the sickening crunch of metal as her car slid to a stop in the ditch outside. She could still feel the steering wheel as she'd gripped it, trying to keep the tears, and the panic, at bay. Her unsuccessful attempts now showed on her face, she was certain. Red, blotchy eyes. Tear-stained cheeks. Moisture still leaking out from time to time. Her mother would be mortified.

She knew when she left the house an accident could happen. No one ever dreamed of letting the Crown Princess learn to drive on ice, of all things. But she had taken matters into her own hands. Adeline, the girl who never did anything wrong, who always did what was expected of her, had slipped away from her security detail, taken the safer of the two vehicles at her disposal, and left. All because she wanted a few moments of freedom before the ice storm settled in.

A shaking hand had pushed the hair back from one side of her face as she ran through her mental checklist.

No airbag deployment. Good.

Pain in her head meant she likely hit the steering wheel. Bad.

Slow speed at time of impact. Good.

Impact. Bad.

As long as she did not have a concussion or bruising from the steering wheel or seat belt, she would be able to convince Mark and Todd she was fine. They would read her the riot act. Debate long and hard about calling her father. Eventually, they would call their superiors, debate some more and, sooner or later, her father would find out. She had rested her head on the steering wheel. He did not need the additional stress. The last two times she visited Montevaro, her father had seemed off. She feared what he would tell her when she returned home for good in a few months.

She had contemplated digging her cell phone out and giving a preemptive call. Cut them off at the pass. Reassure Mark she was rattled but fine and his relief would overwhelm his anger and concern.

She took a deep, shuddering breath and dug her phone back out of her purse. Addie closed her eyes and finally turned her phone back on. Three times, her finger slipped off the "on" button. It went through its start-up procedure and buzzed with missed calls and text messages. Every one of them came from Mark, Todd, or the house. Before she could listen to any of the twenty voice mails, the phone rang again.

With a deep breath and a whispered prayer, she pressed "answer." "Hello?"

Mark's bellow did not help her headache. "Where are you?"

She sighed. "At the Serenity Landing diner on Highway 60 about two miles from town."

"What are you doing there?" His voice softened slightly as she heard the garage door open in the background.

Just saying the words made her wince. "I was in an accident."

His bellow returned. "What?"

"I am fine, Mark. A gentleman ran into the back of the SUV. He helped me out of the vehicle and to the restaurant. He is calling tow trucks right now."

"We're on our way." His words were clipped and nearly cut off by the sound of a slamming car door.

Once the connection severed, Addie set the phone on the table and rested her face in her hands, biting back the groan threatening to escape her throat.

"Tow trucks will be here when they get here." Charlie scooted into the seat across from her. "We're way down on the list since we're not on a major highway. We're somewhere safe and warm, we're not blocking traffic, and no one's hurt."

"I will likely be gone long before they get here." She put her phone in the side pocket of her purse and snapped the flap closed.

"At least let me buy you that cup of coffee." He turned to look for a waitress.

Addie looked at Charlie for a moment before deciding she could trust him. Something about his curly, dirty blond hair and mocha eyes convinced her to give a curt not. "Very well."

The waitress, stereotypical for a restaurant of this kind, bustled up. "Sorry, kids." She handed them each a menu. "What can I get ya?"

With a smile, Addie looked at her. "Hello, Melony."

A wide grin split Melony's face. "Well, hey there! How are ya, sugar? Where's Mark and Todd? What're they thinkin' lettin' ya out here in this weather?"

Addie nodded toward the street. "Mr. Brewer and I had a bit of an accident. We are fine. Mark and Todd will be here shortly." She tucked her hair behind her ear. "Could I get a cup of tea?"

Melony gasped. "You're bleeding." She grabbed a napkin, sending a fork and spoon clattering to the floor.

"I am fine, Melony. I promise."

"Nonsense." Charlie watched as Melony pressed the napkin against Adeline's forehead. "You need to go to the hospital."

"No. Mark and Todd will be here soon. Mark has medic training. If I need stitches, he can do it." The girl took over holding the napkin to her own head, leaving Charlie wondering who Mark and Todd were and why she seemed both annoyed and comforted by the idea of the two men.

Her brothers maybe?

But if they were on their way, he needed to get to know her and fast. Because he'd never met a woman who intrigued him so much from the first moment he heard her speak. Was it the accent? The lilting tone? He didn't know but he wanted to find out. Charlie turned his best smile up to the waitress. "Melony, is it?"

The dark curls bounced up and down as she nodded. "Sure is."

"Melony, would you get Adeline that cup of tea? I'd love some coffee if you've got it. Do you still have breakfast?" He'd driven by the diner many times but had never stopped. Most of these places had breakfast all day, didn't they?

"Sure do, hon. Twenty-four seven. Why don't you two decide what you want and I'll get those drinks?" She looked pointedly at Adeline. "Keep pressure on that."

More than anything Charlie wanted to reach out and brush the hair back, away from the cut in the otherwise smooth skin. He tilted sideways and pulled a handkerchief out of the pocket of his pants. He dipped it in the water glass Melony had set there. Half-standing, he leaned over the table. "Let me see?"

Adeline nodded and pulled the napkin away. "It feels as though the bleeding has stopped."

The cut didn't look good, but it didn't look too bad either. "Here." With slow movements, he did his best to wipe off the dried blood. "I think you'll be okay."

"Thank you, Charlie." Her eyelashes lifted enough for him to see the gold-flecked hazel of her eyes then moved downward again.

He finished cleaning around the wound, refolded his handkerchief, and held it to her head. "You might still want to hold that, though."

Her fingertips brushed his hand as she reached up, sending chills, the good kind, down his spine. "Thank you, again."

He settled back in his seat. "You're not from around here, are you?"

The silky brown hair shifted as she shook her head. "No. I am not."

"Where are you from?"

Melony set two steaming cups in front of them. "Just like you like it."

"You are a queen among women, Melony." Her voice drew Charlie further in.

"Don't you know it?" Melony winked, covering one of her pale green eyes. Charlie couldn't help but compare them to Adeline's. Though they were both primarily green, they were as different as the Amazon rain forest and split-pea soup. "Now, what can I get you to eat?"

Charlie ordered pancakes and bacon. Adeline decided on her "usual," whatever that was.

Once Melony headed for the kitchen, Adeline resumed their conversation. "Have you ever heard of a country called Montevaro?"

With his brow furrowed, Charlie tried to think, but came up mostly blank. "I think I have but that's all I can say."

One corner of her mouth tipped upward. "It is a small nation, sandwiched between Mevendia, Switzerland, and Italy."

"Mevendia?"

"Yes. It is even smaller than we are, on the southeastern border of Switzerland. We have cultural and historical ties with Mevendia and Ravenzario. Ravenzario is..."

"Two islands off the coast of Italy and France in the Mediter-ranean. I think I visited there as a kid."

Adeline nodded. "Yes."

"And you're from Montevaro, is it?"

She nodded. "Yes. Three of us were chosen to come here and study International Relations at Serenity Landing University."

"Chosen?" He quirked an eyebrow at her. "Did you do the best on some sort of test?"

This time the smile was a bit more full-fledged but still didn't reach her eyes. "Something along those lines, yes."

"I'm sorry I hit you, but I'm glad you're here so I could meet you." Deep inside, he cringed. That sounded like such a line.

"You did not hit me, Charlie. You hit my vehicle. And given the weather conditions, it could hardly be considered your fault."

"Still. I'm glad we've met. But what exactly does one study in international relations?"

"The relationship between countries. The relationship between countries and all kinds of different organizations: intergovernmental organizations, nongovernmental organizations, multinational corporations. Things like that."

"So will you work for the State Department of your country?" Charlie wrapped his hands around the mug to warm his fingers and sipped his coffee.

"We do not have a state department like America's, so no. But yes, I will be involved in foreign relations between Montevaro and any number of other entities."

"Is it interesting?" He didn't see how it could be, but different strokes for different folks and all.

She gave a bit of a half shrug. "It is not uninteresting. International relations is the family business."

Family business? Like the Kennedys? Or what was the local family he saw in the tabloids while stuck in the checkout lane? The last name was Langley, he thought, because it always made him think of the CIA.

"So it's expected of you."

"Something like that."

Melony chose that moment to come back and set their food in front of them. "Here ya go. If you need anything else, just holler."

They ate in silence for a few minutes until lights flashed across them. Charlie looked outside. A dark sedan with tinted windows pulled up.

Adeline set the rest of her sandwich on her plate and picked her napkin up from her lap. "That is my ride. Thank you again for your assistance."

Charlie chuckled. "I hit you. It's the least I could do to offer to help."

She reached for her gloves and hat before setting them back down and reaching into her purse. "Here is my card if you need to reach me." She left it on the table.

The door jangled open behind him and he heard boots stomping.

"Adeline, let's go."

Turning his head, he saw a giant hulk of a man standing near them.

"Of course." She slid out of the booth and stood.

Charlie followed suit.

"Thank you again, Mr. Brewer."

He took a deep breath, ignored the man towering over him, and plunged in. "Can I call you? Once this storm blows over?"

Adeline smiled, this time showing perfect rows of pearly white teeth. "I suppose that would be all right."

Charlie watched as she and the man walked toward the front door. He wondered if he'd see her again. The thunderous expression on the face of the man in front of him said, "no."

2

Addie sat in the back of the sedan and waited for the yelling to start. Mark maneuvered the car out of the parking lot and onto Highway 60. Slick roads caused the normally short drive to the house to take at least twice as long as it should have.

Once he turned onto the winding drive leading to the house in a semi-rural neighborhood, Addie leaned over and peered up out the window. "Are those branches going to fall, Mark?"

"We've taken care of them, Your Highness." Addie winced at the sign of how mad she had made him. "Any that fall shouldn't land on the road."

"And if a tree were to fall?"

"We have chainsaws and a four-wheeler."

And an SUV. She whispered a prayer the damage would be minimal and it would be repaired quickly in the event they were to need it.

The first thing she felt when she climbed out of the car was the chill in the garage. Todd said winter was his favorite time of year because when you ran out of soda you could just get one out of the garage and it would already be cold. Not so in the summer. Walking into the kitchen, she tossed her purse on the counter and turned, arms folded across her chest, as she watched Mark shut and lock the door behind him. All three locks. No matter they were in a safe, upscale neighborhood. Locks abounded.

"Well?" She quirked an eyebrow at him.

"Well, what, Your Highness?"

"Aren't you going to yell at me?"

Mark shook his head slowly. "No, Addie. I'm not. There's no point. You know the rules. You knew what you were doing when you violated those rules. My yelling at you won't help you know the rules any better. I want to know why, but I also know I can't *make* you tell me anything you don't want to."

Addie's stiff posture relaxed against the counter behind her. "I am sorry, Mark. You are right. I do know the rules. I know I blatantly flaunted them. And I know you and Todd could lose your jobs if I were to get hurt."

Mark moved closer to her, staring down with his coal black eyes. "It's not my job I'm worried about. It's you and you know that. What if it had been one of the big tractor trailer rigs instead of that little thing?"

"I know."

He checked her eyes and asked a series of questions about her well-being. Mark turned and pulled the First Aid kit out of the cabinet. "It doesn't look like you have a concussion. Now, let me stitch up that wound. I don't think you need to go to the hospital, especially in this weather. I'll do my best to leave the smallest scar I can." After putting some numbing cream on it, he started stitching.

Fifteen minutes later, he was done and she downed a few pain killers to take the edge off. Addie hopped up on the tan granite top of the island. "Don't you want to know where I went?"

"Do you want to tell me?"

"I had dinner at C's Bakery and Bistro. I just wanted a bit of time to be away from here before we were stuck for several days. That is all. I did not think the storm was supposed to hit until later and I was done by the time I realized it had already started." She put her hand on his arm as he walked by. "I am sorry."

When he turned, she was nearly on eye level. "You should have called."

She gave a quick nod. "How will Todd get home?"

"I don't know yet. But I do know you won't be leaving the house until the roads are completely cleaned off. Do I make myself clear?"

"Crystal." She hopped down. "I am going to bed. Please let me know if there's anything you need."

"Very well."

Addie walked up the wide curved staircase to the left of the front door. At the top, she turned, took two steps and went into the master suite she had called home for the last five and a half years. She squished the Frieze carpet between her toes as she headed for the bathroom. Time for a hot bath, warm pajamas, and bed.

But first she had to get the man with sandy blond hair and brown eyes out of her head.

Charlie flipped the card over and over in his hand. Every few turns, he'd stop, stare at her name and phone number, then start flipping it again.

"You should call her."

He looked up to see his cousin and roommate leaning against the door frame, arms folded across his chest.

"You didn't see her, Dan. She's way out of my league." He flipped the card onto the table.

"CeCe thinks you're hot, so this girl can't be that far out of your ability to catch." Dan used a twist of the wrist to turn the chair around, straddling it backwards.

Charlie snorted. "Your fiancée is a true judge of who's good-looking. You see who she's marrying, right?" Dan grinned. "And it wasn't just that she's beautiful. You should have seen her SUV and the car that picked her up. Way nicer than anything I could ever afford, even without..." He tilted his head toward the back of the apartment. "And the way she talked. Accent. Well-educated. Well-bred. Some sort of upper crust, nobility in England type thing except she's not from England. She's from a little country I've never heard of."

He picked up the card and stared at it for a minute longer. "It's not gonna happen." Even though she said he could call, he wouldn't.

Even thinking about getting involved with someone where there was no real future wasn't a smart idea. Especially since it wasn't just him.

"Adeline?"

Addie stood, brushing her hands against her slacks as she did.

The lady nodded at her. "This way please." Addie's shoes clicked on torn linoleum through a maze of hallways, past rooms filled with teens doing homework, until they stopped in front of an office. "After you."

Addie sat in one of the hard plastic chairs across the cheap wood laminate desk from the director of The Club. The cluttered desk reminded Addie of the protocol secretary's desk in his private office in Montevaro. The most organized, precise, exacting person she had ever met but his desk, the one few people ever saw, was a mess. The one in his official office remained pristine, but not in the background. His desk was massive, more ornate, and made of solid cherry, but otherwise it possessed an eerily similar quality to this one.

Mrs. Ginny Hart picked up a stack of papers, resting them on top of an already teetering pile of folders. She set another folder down in the now-clear spot. "As I told you before Miss Montevaro we keep everything completely confidential. We ask that you refrain from telling the girls you'll be working with much about yourself while not asking them for information. Many of our girls come from difficult, though generally loving, home situations. Most have single parents. Most of your girls have single fathers struggling to make the best out of the hand they were dealt. As I'm sure you can understand, fathers simply need help as their daughters grow up. That's where we come in. We have groups and one-on-one sessions to help these dads learn how to talk to their daughters about adolescence, boys, and things like that. One thing we do every spring is a father-daughter banquet. That's where you'll come in. Etiquette is something few girls are taught today and we want to teach them. I dare say we've never had someone with your credentials offer to help."

Addie smiled gently. "There are few women out there with my credentials. I am very happy I saw your notice. My last volunteer effort came to an end a few months ago and I have been searching for the right place to donate my time for the remainder of my stay in the States. I am under instructions from my security team to remind you that no one, not even your closest associates, can know my identity."

"Of course."

"Do you have the schedule for me?"

She opened the folder and handed Addie a sheet. "We want to work with your schedule as much as possible, but there are a few dates that may be difficult for us to change. I've highlighted those. The others are our regularly scheduled meetings. There is some leeway there but we need as much notice as you can give us."

Addie scanned the dates. "I do not see any obvious conflicts, though I will need to check my official schedule. I will get back to you if there is a problem."

Mrs. Hart pushed back from the desk. "If you'll follow me, I'll show you the facilities."

Addie pressed her foot back into the four-inch heels she foolishly decided to wear. The clickety sound on the cheap floor grated on her every nerve. She should wear quieter shoes when she came back. Something more sensible.

They walked through metal double doors into a fair sized, multipurpose room.

"This is where we'll hold our banquet."

It took everything in Addie not to judge. The utilitarian carpet was held together by duct tape in so many places, the floor appeared to be gun-metal gray. The walls had been white once upon a time. Now they bore stains and marks of pencils and crayons and who knew what else. The underlying scent of something she could not place had been nearly obliterated by a citrus-based cleaner.

Mrs. Hart gestured to the brown, wood-paneled screen above the counter on the other side of the room. "They'll make the meal in the kitchen and some of the boys from our program will act as waiters. The girls return the favor in the fall with the mother-son banquet."

"I am sure it will be quite lovely." Addie drew in a deep breath. "What will you do for decorations?"

Mrs. Hart began speaking about streamers and balloons, while Addie's mind went a whole different direction. She had things to ponder before saying anything to the director. They spent about fifteen minutes touring the facilities before Addie took her leave.

"Thank you again, Adeline, for everything."

Addie started to respond but was stopped by a girl bouncing through the door.

"Hi, Mrs. Hart!"

A genuine smile crossed the director's face. "Hello, Lindsey. There's someone I want you to meet. This is..."

"Addie." She jumped in, not wanting to bother with her full name and held her hand out.

"I'm Lindsey."

Mrs. Hart smiled at them. "Addie is going to help you girls with etiquette this year."

Lindsey's eyes lit up. "Really? I thought we were going to have to figure it all out with help from the older girls 'cause you didn't have anyone."

Mrs. Hart put an arm around the girl's shoulders. "Miss Addie is an answer to prayer. God sent her at just the right time."

"I cannot say that anyone has ever called me an answer to prayer before." Addie smiled as she pulled on her gloves. "I must be going. I will see both of you next week."

She walked out to where the car was waiting for her. It had taken months for her to convince Todd and Mark to let her open her own door, at least most of the time. She hated people thinking she was different or special while she was here. She liked her anonymity. As soon as her seatbelt was buckled, Todd drove off and Addie pulled out her cell phone.

It took a minute for the international call to go through, but before they reached the first stoplight she was talking to the protocol secretary about what she would need.

It had been over a week since the accident, but Charlie finally had his car back. He hoped Adeline had hers back as well, though there had been no further contact with the woman. All of his dealings had been with the insurance company or the man who'd stayed when she left.

Dan dropped his keys into the bowl on the table by the front door. "We gotta talk, dude."

Charlie clicked the TV off with the remote. "What's up?"

"CeCe and I are getting married in May. I'll be moving out."

Charlie grinned as his stomach dropped. "That's great! I'm glad you guys finally set a date." It meant he'd be on the prowl for another roommate sooner rather than later. He'd thought they were going for a Christmas wedding and he'd have more time.

Dan flopped into the recliner. "Maybe it's time for you to get your own place."

He lifted one shoulder in a half-hearted shrug. "We'll see. I want to stay in town. I can't afford the two-bedroom apartment, but I can afford a three-bedroom with a roommate."

"You'll have your Master's degree by then. Won't you be able to get a better job?"

"Maybe. There's no guarantee of that these days. You know that. And I don't want to move to a bigger city where I might have a better shot. Your parents are here, Ellie's only a couple hours away, and..."

Dan held up a hand. "I know why you don't want to leave, though I don't think I'd count my little sister. We've gone over the reasons about a million times."

"Since we were sixteen," Charlie confirmed. They'd hashed it out time and again, but one mistake changed everything for Charlie when he was a sophomore in high school. It changed the path he'd been on, headed for possible baseball scholarships to some of the country's top colleges. The new path included living in a decent, if not fabulous, apartment with two other people at a time when most of his friends were like Dan. Just settling down, getting married, and starting to talk about when to have a family.

Those decisions were already made for Charlie. He wouldn't change anything. Unless he could and still have essentially the same outcome. But changing things was impossible. He'd do his best at whatever job he had to put food on the table and have a warm place to sleep.

"You're gonna have to think about the future though, Charlie." Dan leaned forward with his elbows on his knees. "I know you want to stay here, or close to here, but if you can't find a job that will let you provide what you need, maybe it'll be time to look elsewhere." A glint appeared in his eyes. "Like maybe a small country in Europe. Where did you say she was from?"

Charlie blew out a frustrated breath. "I don't remember. I didn't look it up and there's no point in calling her. She's way beyond anyone I would ever have a chance with. Not just because of the whole disparity in social strata I'm pretty sure exists, but what would a girl like that want with my baggage when she could have someone without it?"

Dan grew quiet until Charlie wasn't sure he would reply. He had to strain to hear his cousin's words. "CeCe has baggage that makes yours look like a carry-on. So don't tell me there's no girl out there who would love you and all of yours. It's part of what makes you who you are. And CeCe's is what makes her the person she is today. I love her and I wouldn't have it any other way. Do I hate the pain from her past? Absolutely. But I love her today. Here. Now. And that pain is part of what made her so strong and resilient. Would you take it all back? Do things differently? Say no when your parents gave you that ultimatum?"

Charlie furrowed his fingers through his hair. "Of course not. I wish I'd played college ball. Maybe gone on to play professionally. If I could have figured out a way to make it happen without trading everything else, I would have been in heaven. But my priorities changed and I'll live with the decisions I made."

"And there's a woman out there who will be glad you did. Who's to say this gal isn't her?"

Charlie still had a hard time believing he'd been brazen enough to ask her if he *could* call her and more surprised when she seemed open to the idea. But would he actually ask her out?

"If you don't at least try, you'll regret it." Dan's quiet words spoke the truth and Charlie knew it. They'd been best friends since preschool. Dan knew him better than anyone. He'd told Dan before he told anyone else about what happened when he was sixteen.

"I know." With a resigned sigh, he acquiesced. "I'll call her tomorrow."

Footsteps pounded on the walk outside the door.

Dan grinned. "She's home. Ask her what she thinks about you dating."

The door flung open and Charlie couldn't help but smile at the look on his girl's face. "Have a good time?"

She slammed the door shut before jumping and twisting so she landed on Charlie, trusting him to catch her. "I did. Mrs. Hart introduced me to the new etiquette lady so we'll get to learn for real before the banquet."

"That's great." He brushed her dark, honey blond hair off her face. "I'm glad. I can't wait."

She kissed his cheek and bounded back up. "Me either." A "love you, Dad" trailed behind her as she went to her room.

Charlie covered his face with both hands and groaned. The after school program was free, but the clothes and banquet tickets weren't. How would he tell her he didn't think they could afford to go? He didn't have a suit or a dress for her to wear, and didn't know anyone who did. They usually got stuff at a discount from one of the resale shops, but it still wasn't cheap. Maybe he could pick up some extra work or find a kid who needed a baseball coach to get into shape before the season started. With the increase in auto insurance he was sure to see after the accident, he'd be scraping by at best.

"She needs a mom, Charlie." Dan stood and headed for the back of the apartment. "You know that better than I do. Call her."

Without giving himself time to talk himself out of it, Charlie reached for his phone.

3

"**I**s this seat taken?" Jonathan William Langley-Cranston the Fourth turned his best smile on the beautiful foreigner.

Addie looked up at him and shook her head. "No, please have a seat."

He flipped the chair around and straddled it, his backpack resting on one of the other chairs at the small table. "Are you ready for this test?"

With a shake of her head, Addie closed her book. "I have never felt less prepared for a test in my life."

He gave her another of his million-watt smiles, the ones that put him on every "most beautiful person" list in the country. "I'm with you. Who gives a test the second class meeting, even if it's a once a week class so the first meeting counted as two?" The complaint held some reality, but he would do well on the test. He always did. His parents expected nothing less and were more than a bit irritated the woman across from him bested him regularly.

He didn't care so much, not when his competition was so beautiful. How had she not made some of those lists? She kept a lower profile than he did, but then, she didn't have his pedigree. If Jonathan was given his choice in the matter, he wouldn't be in the news as much as he was. But if he really wanted to stay out of it, he wouldn't take a supermodel on a date in Manhattan on New Year's Eve.

Addie's voice pulled him out of his thoughts. "A professor who taught the first part of the course the semester before would give a test so quickly. Especially since everyone in the class took the first half of the course with him. I am half surprised Professor Putane did not give us the test last week."

"If there hadn't been an ice storm the night before, he might have." Jonathan hung his elbows off the top of the chair and rested his chin on his wrists where they crossed. "Are your roomies joining you for a study session?" He liked the two men well enough, but they took over-protective to a whole new level. Since he first met Addie nearly six years earlier, the three of them had been closer than Alvin and the Chipmunks.

"Mark and Todd had another study session earlier today with their group and had an errand to run this afternoon. They should be here before class starts."

Good. Meant he had some time alone with her. She'd always intrigued him, but they'd been assigned to work together on a project in the fall and he'd gotten to know her a bit. While he was in New York over break, he found himself missing her. Would he actually decide to ask her out on a date? Instinctively, he'd known since they first met when he was eighteen that she was different. A relationship with her would be different.

He opened his mouth to ask her about her plans for Friday night, but was interrupted by his buzzing cell phone. A glance at the screen made him groan. "Sorry, Addie, but I need to take this." She nodded her understanding as he pushed the "answer" button. "Phil, what's up?" Jonathan stood and walked to the window several feet away as he waited to hear his little brother's answer.

The gray clouds hung low over the Ozarks, threatening

another winter storm, but if the weather reports were to be believed, it wouldn't start until later in the evening.

"I need money."

The words didn't surprise Jonathan. His little brother was known for his proclivities. "How much?"

The number, well more than the ten thousand he'd asked for last time, also didn't surprise Jonathan, but it did disappoint him. "No, Phil. We talked about this at Christmas. I'm not giving you anymore money."

"You're not giving it to me. It's a loan. I'll pay you back when I get access to my trust fund."

"You already owe me half your trust fund, bud." An exaggeration but not by much. "I'm not going to enable you anymore. If you need money, you need to get it somewhere else. Mom and Dad give you the same allowance the rest of us got at your age and we didn't blow through it in no time flat. Talk to them."

"They won't give me any more and you know it. Neither will Catherine."

"Sorry, Phil. Guess it's time for tough love, but no more from me." Behind him, Jonathan heard Addie answer her phone. "I've gotta go. I'm studying for a test." Close enough to the truth.

"Is she hot?"

For some reason, the term bothered Jonathan when it came from his brother. He'd given voice to the same opinion about Addie, but from Philip... His little brother was known as a player for a reason. Addie was... different.

"Goodbye, Phil." Without giving it a second thought, Jonathan ended the call. He'd known this day would come, but he'd hoped it wouldn't be so soon. His shoulders slumped as he stared over the brown hills. His brother would have to hit rock bottom before he bounced back up and Phil wasn't there yet. Jonathan hated going to God only when he needed something, but now he whispered a prayer that his brother would hit bottom and still be alive to recover.

Turning, he took a deep breath and squared his shoulders, returning to his seat across from Addie.

Was she blushing? Her bottom lip was stuck in her teeth as she nodded into the phone. "I would love to have dinner on Friday, Charlie." Whoever Charlie was said something, with Addie shaking her head. "No. I will meet you at the restaurant." Another pause. "Yes, I know where it is." A "see you then" and "looking forward to it" later, she hung up.

"My apologies, Jonathan." A definite blush crept up her cheeks as she set the phone on the table.

Was he too late? "Big date?"

She nodded. "Big? I do not think I would call it a big date, but a date, yes."

Whatever else Jonathan was, he wouldn't ask out a woman who was seeing another man. He'd bide his time and see if this new relationship, if that's what it was, amounted to anything. If not, then Jonathan would ask her to dinner. Wine and dine her and see if anything developed between them. Flipping open his International Trade Agreements textbook, he turned the conversation back to the matter of the test.

Parent-teacher meetings weren't usually something Samantha Dean looked forward to, but this one felt different. She couldn't explain why, after all these years, the thought of seeing Charlie Brewer fascinated her. Sure, there had been that little crush from the ages of twelve to sixteen, but that was before she found out he'd slept with Tricia and gotten her best friend pregnant.

It wasn't like he'd been dating Samantha at the time. He and Tricia had been an item for some time, but it wasn't until Tricia started showing that Samantha - the one Tricia shared *everything* with - found out about the one time together that led to Charlie and Tricia's break-up even before she took the pregnancy test. When Tricia finally told Samantha what happened one night in the back of his parents' SUV, she also admitted to making an appointment for an abortion. Only Charlie's insistence that he'd be an involved dad stopped her. Samantha had been just as shocked as everyone else when Tricia and her parents had packed up and vanished overnight, leaving baby Lindsey with Charlie.

The knowledge of that night, though Tricia had always insisted it had only been the once, had been enough to knock Charlie off the pedestal Samantha had put him on.

But now... All year, Samantha had seen what an amazing dad Charlie had become. She loved Lindsey more than she should as her teacher. She'd found herself being extra careful not to play favorites, but Samantha was afraid everyone knew anyway.

A quick rap on the door startled her out of her musings. Samantha looked up in time to see Charlie walk in. "Charlie, hi! Is Lindsey with you?" She stood and walked toward him, extending a hand. Tingles spread up her arm as he shook it.

"No. She's at The Club. Believe it or not, there's someone there who's supplanted you as her favorite for the moment, Sam." That crooked grin should be illegal. "Some gal is helping them with their etiquette. Linds thinks she's pretty awesome."

Samantha laughed as her gut twisted. "Addie, I think it is. Several of the girls have mentioned her. Said she talks like a snooty European but is nicer than they expected." Mentioning something another girl had whispered in confidence wasn't very nice of her and Sam hated herself for it.

"Don't know about the snooty thing, but Lindsey adores her." He took a seat in one of the too-small desk chairs. "So, how's my girl doing, Miss Dean?"

The only thing that bugged her more than being called "Sam" as a reminder of her tomboy days, was someone she'd known since first grade calling her "Miss Dean."

"It's Samantha, Chuck." She snuck the barb in, smiling to herself as he winced. "Sorry." Her snarky streak shouldn't get the better of her so often. "But how long have we known each other? I knew Tricia for crying out loud."

At the mention of Lindsey's birth mother, Charlie's visage contorted into a grimace, pain skittering across his otherwise handsome face. *Smooth, Sam. Remind him of the woman who abandoned them.*

"Sorry again." She took a deep breath. "Let's move on. Lindsey's doing great. She's a wonderful girl. You've done a great job with her, Charlie, really."

Charlie shook his head. "Whatever wonderfulness there is in my daughter isn't because of me. It's only by the grace of God that I haven't already screwed her up beyond recognition."

Samantha laced her fingers together and rested her arms on her desk, leaning forward slightly. But not too far. The mention of God reminded her Charlie wasn't the same guy she used to know. Showing cleavage wasn't the way to get him interested. "I work with all kinds of kids. In just five years as a fourth grade teacher, I've seen abuse that would make your toes curl. Lindsey is one of the happiest, most well-adjusted kids I've ever seen. Whether you want to take credit or not, your daughter is a joy to be around. If you weren't doing such a good job being both father and mother to her, she wouldn't be."

A snort shot out of him. "Yeah. I'm a great mother. Thank God for my aunt and cousin is all I have to say there."

She had to choose her next words carefully. Drop hints without being too obvious. "Have you thought about that? Dated a woman and let it turn serious?"

"Not in years." His mocha eyes lit up, though. "But I think that may be about to change."

Could he mean...? Samantha didn't let her hopes rise too high...

"I have a date tonight."

...before they were dashed against the rocks. "A date?" Hopefully, the words didn't sound like a croak to Charlie's ears.

"Yeah. I met this woman last week. We had coffee and dinner after I ran into her car during that ice storm. We have a date tonight."

Samantha hated how her heart curled in on itself. "You like her?"

"So far, yes." He shrugged. "We're big giant steps ahead of ourselves to think Lindsey might have a step-mom someday, much less someone who might want to adopt her, but yeah. I like her."

"Tricia would let someone else adopt her?" The words escaped before Samantha realized it.

Charlie's crestfallen face made her want to take it back. "You haven't had much contact with Tricia since she left, have you?" he asked.

Samantha shook her head. "A few emails here and there. A friend request sent on Facebook, but never a reply."

"She signed away her rights when Lindsey was two." Were those tears in his eyes? "That's the last time I heard from her - the only time I heard from her except the note saying they were moving and giving me custody the week after they left. Lindsey doesn't know about the letter from the lawyer. She just knows her mom isn't around."

"She won't hear it from me."

"Thanks." Charlie took the papers she'd set in front of him. "Our time's up, isn't it?"

How quickly time flew when you realized your hopes were being dashed. "It is. But you can call me anytime, you know."

Charlie smiled at her and gave her a one-armed hug as they walked toward the door. "Yep. I know."

Samantha watched his back as he walked toward the exit, grateful she didn't have a meeting for half an hour. Listening to him whistle as he headed to his date was almost enough to drive a girl to ice cream.

Almost.

Oh, who was she kidding? Samantha opened her mini-fridge and pulled an emergency pint of Hiland Dairy Cookie Overload out. This day definitely called for ice cream.

Addie twisted her fingers together in the waiting area at C's Bakery and Bistro. How long had it been since she had been on a real date? Ever?

She had been to balls and other formal events with escorts her parents arranged. Men as close to her social standing as she was likely to find in Montevaro and even some minor nobility from other European countries. But she'd never gone out with a man just because *she* liked him. Because *she* wanted to.

She did not know what it was, but she seemed to put off some sort of "stay away" vibe.

Or maybe it was her two ever-present shadows. Both men were at least five years older than she was and already held degrees in other fields, but were conversant enough in international relations to make them believable as students in her courses. Only the president of Serenity Landing University knew who she really was and she worked hard to keep it that way. Certain things she simply could not change. She knew she spoke more formally than the others around her. They wrote it off to her European upbringing, but it was more than that.

Between all that and her shadows accompanying every move for the last five and a half years, no one had asked her out. This was different, yet they insisted on accompanying her. They'd sit nearby, not with her and Charlie, but close enough. Charlie had wanted to pick her up but that was out of the question. She knew there had been a background check done and he had passed it. At her insistence, Mark had not told her what it revealed about Charlie or his past.

Whatever she found out about him, Addie wanted him to be the one to tell her.

The bells over the door jangled and she looked up to see the brown eyes that had haunted her dreams for more than a week.

She smiled at him. "Good evening, Charlie."

"Good evening, Adeline."

Her insides winced, but for the time being, she felt it was best to keep that slight bit of formality between them.

"Have you been here long?"

She shook her head. "No. Not long at all."

The hostess pulled two menus from the stand. "Are you ready?"

Charlie nodded and held a hand out for Addie to precede him.

Once they were seated, she tried to think of what to say but could not think of a thing.

"Did you get your car back yet?"

Out of the corner of her eye, Addie saw Mark and Todd settle in at the table across from them but behind Charlie. "Yes. Yesterday. Thank you for taking care of it that night."

"It was the least I could do."

Awkward silence settled between them as they looked at the menu. The waitress relieved the tension somewhat as she took their orders - and flirted shamelessly with Charlie.

To his credit, he did not flirt back.

Once the waitress left, Addie was determined to get past the awkward stage. "Charlie, you never told me what you do."

"I'm a student, too. Working on my Master's degree in Accounting and Business through Mizzou on the Serenity Landing University campus."

Her brows knit together. "At Serenity Landing University? I was certain they only housed the International Relations program. In fact, many of the core courses outside of my major, I had to take through an agreement with the community college. Is Mizzou not several hours from here?"

He nodded. "You're right. But the University of Missouri, Mizzou, has satellite campuses and uses the campus of other schools for those of us too far away to attend the main campus. Serenity Landing's campus is one of the Business locations."

"It is not a very large campus. It is a wonder we have not seen each other."

Charlie shook his head. "Most of my classes are hybrids. Most of it's done online but we meet once a week or once every other week, depending on the course, and then usually at night when the building's deserted."

"I see. Do you work during the day then?"

"I do. I'm a department manager at Serenity Landing Hardware and Home Store."

Unease filled her insides. His blue collar status did not surprise her, but it did leave disappointment settling deep inside. She liked Charlie so far. She really did. But would her parents, and Parliament, approve of her dating, much less eventually marrying, someone from the working class? She had never agreed with the long-standing tradition of royalty marrying nobility from Montevaro, one of the other countries in the Royal Commonwealth of Belles Montagnes, or another friendly country, but she was expected to abide by it.

They were less than thirty minutes into their first date and already she wondered if she would have to call it off because of her position and what was expected of her.

Charlie's hand resting on hers caused her head to shoot up. Not just because it was so unexpected but because of the warmth and electricity it sent spiraling up her arm.

"Where'd you go?" he asked softly.

Her eyes flitted to the other table and Mark's frowning face. "My apologies, Charlie. Other thoughts occupied my mind for a moment. Tell me. What does a department manager do at a store such as that?"

He launched into a description of his day dealing with customers and their paint needs. She did her best to stay interested but had a hard time keeping her mind from crossing the ocean, back into the Alps, where her parents surely wore disapproving looks on their faces.

The waitress arrived with their dinner just in time for Addie to plaster a smile on and ask about his studies as they ate.

She said a quiet prayer over the food and another one for the strength to make the decision she knew she would have to make sooner rather than later.

4

Charlie hadn't talked about himself so much in a long time, if ever. He tried to ask Adeline about her studies and what she did with her time since she didn't seem to have a job, but every time she deftly turned the conversation back to him and his life.

He managed not to mention Lindsey, but just barely. He never mentioned her on a first date. Rarely by the fifth unless it was someone who already knew her. But he wasn't going to bring his daughter into a relationship that had no future. He learned the hard way a time or two when she was still pretty young.

Instead, he found himself talking about his mother's work as an anthropologist studying parts of ancient Europe. He paid the check without looking at it first, something he never did. But when he stood and turned to help her with her coat, he caught sight of the two men she said were her roommates.

What was that about?

He rested his hand on the small of her back and walked her out the front door and to the SUV he recognized from the other night.

"Can I call you again?"

The same shadow he noticed earlier crossed her face again but she nodded. "Yes. You may."

She climbed into the driver's seat and he shut the door behind her. He moved back to the sidewalk and watched her drive off. Right behind her as she turned onto the highway was the car she'd ridden off in after her roommates showed up at the café.

Something wasn't quite right, but he couldn't put his finger on what it was.

Charlie turned and went to his own car. He hadn't kissed Adeline, but it was early enough he'd get to give his favorite girl a kiss before she went to bed.

The next morning, he fixed that same girl a bowl of cereal with milk and sat on the bar stool next to her while she ate.

"How'd your date go?"

He shrugged. "It went fine."

"But you like this girl, don't you?"

For ten, she was insightful. "What makes you say that?"

Lindsey shrugged. "Dunno. You just seemed different when you mentioned her than most of the time when you talk about a date."

"We had dinner and I walked her to her car."

His daughter's hazel eyes twinkled. "Did you kiss her?"

"Nope. Not even on the cheek."

She stirred her cereal and stared into it for a minute. "Did you tell her about me?"

Charlie reached out and brushed her hair back over her shoulder. "No. Until I know if I like her enough to tell her..."

"I know." She poked at her cereal a bit more. "I just wish..."

He leaned over and pressed a kiss to the side of her head. "I do, too."

"My mom...?" The question hung unfinished between them.

Moving to stand behind her, he put his hands on her shoulders. Charlie closed his eyes and breathed a prayer. "I don't know where she is. I haven't seen her since not long after you were born and she left you with me."

"You've never heard from her?"

"Not in a long time." More than anything, he wished he could give his daughter a mother. More than he wanted to find someone to spend his life with, he wanted to help his daughter fill that mom-sized hole. Finding both would be preferable, of course, but he ached most for his daughter.

He knew some days she wished her birth mother would come back into their lives but Charlie knew how unlikely that was. He'd never had the heart to tell Linds.

"I'm okay, Daddy. Promise." She looked up and gave him a tremulous smile. "We'll find the right person someday."

Charlie wished he had her faith. "I'm sure you're right."

"So are you going to call her again?"

With a slow nod, he moved back to his seat. "I think so."

"Mrs. Hart, I do hope you do not feel I am stepping on your toes. That certainly is not my intent." Addie sat in the same chair in the office, legs tilted to the side and crossed at the ankle as she handed the folder over.

Mrs. Hart looked puzzled but opened the folder and looked at the papers inside. "What is this, Miss Montevaro?"

"A very preliminary proposal. I need you to work with me to get the final numbers."

"To do what exactly?"

Addie gave her a demure smile. "I want to do some renovations on your facilities, to benefit the group as a whole, but the families in particular. Let me share my thoughts and you tell me if it sounds reasonable." She launched into her ideas, including updates and upgrades, with the families doing as much of the work as possible under the supervision of experts. "For every dollar they save in labor that I would have paid to a contractor, I will give two to operating costs. And for every hour they work, I will give the equivalent of minimum wage toward their attire for the banquet. They give the receipts to you for reimbursement. If they have a balance remaining, they can use it towards other things for that night like hair or pedicures. If they choose not to or still have money left, it will go to a college fund for the child."

Mrs. Hart's eyes grew wider with each sentence. "Are you serious? You'd do all this?"

"Absolutely."

The director's voice held a warning tone. "It won't be cheap."

"I am aware of that. My family and I donate large sums to many charities every year and I have some discretion over a certain amount of those funds. This is what I choose to do with it this year."

"I don't know what to say."

"Thank you will suffice and then we need to get to work if we are going to have this done in time for the banquet."

A tear streaked down Mrs. Hart's cheek as she swiveled in her chair. She gave one of the filing cabinet drawers a tug. With a creak, it pulled out. Mrs. Hart dug through the folders until she found whatever she was looking for. She held it toward Addie.

"What is this?" Addie asked as she flipped the cover open.

"My dream file. I update it every year or so. Call around to find out how much all that stuff will cost, just in case we have a sudden influx of money. We never have, but the information in there is about six months old, so it should give us a good basis to start from."

Addie nodded as she scanned the pages, noticing one thing that was missing. "Please be sure to include office supplies and updated furniture for this office and the others as well."

More tears streaked their way down the woman's cheeks. "I don't know what to say."

Curious, Addie pressed. "Why do you not have those things on the list already? It is obvious you need new filing cabinets and a desk and better chairs."

Mrs. Hart swiped at one cheek then the other. "Because I never dreamed there would be enough money to recarpet the multipurpose room much less redo the office."

"I am glad I can help." Addie stood. "I will take this with me and look it over. Perhaps we can meet about an hour before our first etiquette lesson with the young ladies?"

"That sounds perfect." Together they walked to the outer office. "Thank you again, Miss Montevaro."

Addie shook her hand. "Please, call me Addie."

"Addie. I can't thank you enough."

"It is my pleasure. Truly."

They spoke for another minute and Addie turned to see Mark waiting patiently for her. He was good to her. Too good. He was her bodyguard, and her friend, but sometimes it seemed like it might be more than that. Almost like family.

Her phone buzzed and she checked the screen. She smiled and looked up at Mark as they walked out the door.

"I have a date tonight."

"Do you understand any this?" Jonathan motioned to the papers spread out between himself and Addie.

She gave him a small grimace. "For the most part, I do. I am still struggling to figure some of it out, though."

Jonathan leaned back in his seat and glanced to the table across the atrium where her two roommates sat. "Did you ever think about doing anything else with your life? Besides government service?"

Addie shook her head, her eyes focused on the paper in front of her and nothing else. "It is expected of me. In this matter, as in several others, I have little choice."

He let out a sympathetic sigh. "I understand. This is why I'll end up with two degrees by the time I'm done. One in International Relations and one in Private Sector Relations." He poured on the sarcasm. "That way I can run the family business *or* be an ambassador to some country I've likely never heard of."

That drew a small smile from Addie. "I doubt someone with such an illustrious family will end up in New Glousterstan or some other place in the far flung reaches of the earth. If you end up in diplomatic service, you will be in Western Europe or one of the more important trade partners in Asia. Perhaps Australia, but never some little country most Americans would be hard pressed to put in the correct hemisphere."

His pen twirled around his fingers like a miniature baton. "You're probably right."

She propped her elbow on the table, her chin resting on her fist. "What do you *want* to do, Jonathan? If you could pick anything in the world."

He leaned back in his chair and stared at the exposed metal rafters two stories above his seat. Absentminded, he tapped his pen against his notebook. "Anything in the world? Rodeo clown." Addie's laugh brought out a mischievous grin from Jonathan. "Seriously, if I can't be a space cowboy, I think I'd want to work with kids. Or run my dad's security firm."

Her nose wrinkled and he imagined himself kissing it. "Securities? That doesn't sound nearly exciting enough."

It was Jonathan's turn to laugh. "No. Security. One of the many things my family owns is a firm that does security for celebrities and traveling diplomats who need additional support or for corporate types working in dangerous countries. I don't know that I'd want to be a security officer with them, but learning how to plan the details, to keep people safe? I think I'd like that."

Izzy's face swam in front of his eyes, but he shut them and

shook his head to will her away. As the oldest of six, protecting came naturally to him. If only he'd been there when she needed him most. But the past was the past. He couldn't change it any more than he could keep the sun from rising. The sudden urge for some Jack Daniels or a shot of tequila nearly propelled him out of his seat, but he managed to stay put. His hand found its way into his pocket where he fingered his token of sobriety. Hard earned. At a young age. Too young. Too driven by pressures from his family. Too... everything.

"Jonathan?" Addie's quiet voice broke through.

His grin fixed itself in place. Never let anyone in. Never let them know how you hurt. It had been ground into him at an even younger age. From the outside looking in, life has to be perfect, the veneer flawless. The one thing Jonathan had ever done to the satisfaction of both of his parents. That they knew nothing of his early struggles with alcohol and his short stint in a rehab facility stood as silent testimony to his success. "Yes?"

"Why do you not do what you want? Talk to your parents? Or start your own security firm?"

The front legs of his chair landed on the tile with a thud. "For the same reason you're here, Addie. You do what's expected of you. Period."

She opened her mouth to say something, but it snapped shut. A moment later, she spoke. "For some there is no choice. For others, it seems as though there is none when God can make a way for the desires of your heart."

God. Right. "I'll pray about it, how's that?" A flashing smile changed the subject. "So tell me how your date went." He didn't want to know. Not really, but anything to get his mind out of the slide it had started down.

The color on her cheeks simply highlighted her natural beauty. Why hadn't he asked her out sooner?

Right.

Because with her, his heart might get involved.

And that was something he never planned to risk again.

Samantha walked in with the second row of students trailing behind her like little ducklings. The fourth grade concert was at eight-thirty. Younger siblings in the audience were getting ants in their pants. Parents were hoping to get their children - all of them - in bed at a reasonable hour, and the kids now walking onto the risers were excited enough the cranky took a backseat. For now.

Walking to her seat in the front row, on the floor of the basketball court, she scanned the crowd looking for the families of her students. Not even to herself did she admit there was one family member in particular she hoped to see. But when her eyes connected with Charlie's, Samantha's heart skipped a small beat.

A slight nod passed between them. She sank into her seat before her knees gave out. When had she started acting like such a school girl? Did she feel his eyes on the back of her head? Or was his gaze glued where it should be? On his daughter.

She sat through the mostly patriotic songs in honor of the upcoming Presidents' Day holiday. They skipped *Star Spangled Banner* and included *God Bless America* and *God Bless the USA*, alongside *Yankee Doodle Dandy* and *Take Me Out to the Ball Game*. Twenty minutes after it started, Assistant Principal Jones, thanked the music teacher and told parents where their children would be for pick-up. Mr. Jones had been Samantha's principal when she was in elementary but had decided he didn't want the pressure a few years earlier, letting Principal Brown take over while he stayed on as the assistant. He loved talking with parents though so Principal Brown let him do the thank yous most of the time.

Samantha made her way to the end of the court, standing underneath the raised basketball goal as her students surrounded her. She gave a number of hugs and high-fives to her students, praising them though she remembered precious little of the actual concert.

With one arm around Lindsey and another around Lindsey's BFF, Megan, Samantha bent slightly to be more on their level as she smiled for pictures. Charlie smiled at the other dad and held up his camera. After another round of pictures, Lindsey insisted on one with just the two of them. By the time they finished, she'd waved good bye to most of the other families.

"How's this kiddo really doing?" Charlie asked her with his arm around his daughter. "She's behaving."

Samantha smiled, this one coming more easily than it would with some other parents. "She's wonderful. Behaving very well. I can't wait to see her project on the Duchess of Cambridge." She'd already seen some of the early research Lindsey had done. There was no doubt it would be one of the best projects this year.

"I just wish I had darker hair so I would look more like her for Night at the Museum," Lindsey whined. The fourth graders would present their projects to their classes, but one night, in a few weeks, they'd have them set up science fair-like and many would come dressed as the people they'd researched.

Charlie pulled her closer and kissed her head. "You're always my princess, kiddo."

Lindsey rolled her eyes causing Samantha to smile. "Not the same, Dad."

With a chuckle, Charlie let her go. She ran off, calling over her shoulder that she'd be right back.

"How are you?" she asked as he tracked his daughter with his eyes.

"Good. You?"

"Can't complain." It wouldn't do any good to whine about teacher's salaries or the tubs of ice cream finding their way into her freezer more often the last couple of years as most of their friends settled down. Lindsey might be the first child of one of Samantha's friends to pass through her classroom, but she certainly wouldn't be the last. "How was your date?" Though she couldn't believe she asked, Samantha had to know.

"It went well. We went out again last weekend and we have plans Saturday."

Three dates in three weeks? "Sounds serious."

"Maybe." Charlie shrugged. "She's not from around here, so there's a lot of reasons why it might not work out."

How small and petty was it of Samantha to wish it wouldn't? "I hope it goes well." Social veneer? Check.

"Thanks."

Lindsey ran back to their sides. She and Charlie said goodbye as Samantha sank against the wall.

"You still wish you had a chance with him?"

Samantha looked up to see the too-good-looking-for-his-own-good PE coach standing there. "Stick a sock in it, Vinny."

He'd been a thorn in her side since she'd turned down his prom invite their senior year of high school. Somehow, they'd ended up in class together every semester of college. Samantha was sure he'd managed to do it on purpose. The other night, the other reason he managed to get under her skin more than any other man, *that* night she shoved out of her mind.

Without another glance toward Vince, Samantha headed out of the gym and toward home.

And ice cream.

Charlie grinned at the look of shock and wonder on Adeline's face.

"We are going ice skating?" He couldn't figure out if she was excited or just surprised.

"I hope that's okay."

"Of course, but it has been many years since I have skated. I do hope I do not embarrass myself."

He couldn't believe he was going to say it, to flirt with her, but he did. "I'll hold your hand and keep you from falling."

"How gallant of you." She gave him a coy smile from under lowered lashes.

Annoyance flooded him. If he wasn't careful, the vein in his forehead would begin to tic. "Do they really have to go with us?" A glance in his rearview mirror showed the SUV trailing them.

"I am afraid so, yes. They are quite protective of me, but have promised to be on their best behavior and stay far enough away they will not overhear us."

"But close enough to rescue you?"

"If the need were to arise."

"Has it ever? Have any of your dates actually done anything that would make them need to rescue you?"

Adeline turned and stared out the passenger window for a moment before answering. "No. They have never felt the need to interrupt a date."

"I'll be sure not to give them any reason to." It was early for a date, but he needed to be home fairly early. He promised Lindsey he'd be home in time to tuck her in. "Ice skating then dinner. I promise to behave."

A few minutes later, he pulled into the parking lot at Jordan Valley Skate Park. He turned the engine off and turned to Adeline. "Ready?"

"As I will ever be." She waited for him to walk around the car and open her door. His hand rested on the small of her back as they walked toward the building. "You know, I have lived here nearly six years and I did not know there was a skating rink."

He gave her his best smile. "You learn something new every day."

It took fifteen minutes of laughing to get their skates on. Adeline knew what she was doing, though she still claimed to be rusty. Glad she dressed warmly enough to skate without her coat on, he held her gloved hand in his as they carefully made their way to the rink.

One girl skated through the middle doing one jump spin thing after another until she stopped and spun fast enough to nauseate him.

"I do all right skating," Adeline told him, "but I always wanted to skate like that."

Charlie put his first skate on the ice, grateful when he didn't slip at all. Normally confident, the first few steps often threw him. Of course, he was usually helping guide a still-learning ten-year-old. Adeline exuded more confidence than he did. She didn't let go of his hand as they took a couple of laps around the rink.

Her crimson knit hat held her hair back but also made it so he could see hints of gold in the dark strands that spilled out of it and over her shoulders.

They neared the end of the rink and began to turn, but Charlie turned too sharp. Adeline gave a little scream as she headed toward the ice and Charlie fell toward her.

He closed his eyes, twisted his body and prayed he wouldn't land on top of the girl with two friends-slash-bodyguards waiting in the wings.

5

The cold of the ice took Addie's breath away as much as the fall itself did, at least until Charlie landed on her, though he immediately moved away. She opened her eyes to see him lying next to her, shock and fear written all over his face. He scrambled to his knee next to her.

"Are you okay, Adeline?" He held his hand out and she grasped it.

"I am fine." It took everything in her to laugh, but she did. Until the pain in her chest made her gasp.

"What's wrong?"

She clamped her hand to the side of her chest. "It hurts."

Addie closed her eyes and tried to breathe a bit more shallow to see if that would stop the sharp pain. It helped some, but not enough.

"Let me help you up and get you to a bench."

The wet cold was beginning to seep through her jeans. Charlie grasped her elbow and helped her to her feet. He held her left hand in his and wrapped his right arm around her waist as they skated slowly toward the nearest opening. By the time they reached it, Todd and Mark were there and took both of her hands, helping her onto the outer surface and away from Charlie

"Where does it hurt?" Mark, ever the efficient medic, asked.

"My ribs." She sat on the bench and closed her eyes. "Every time I breathe it hurts."

Mark's hand gently pressed on the spot and she winced though she managed not to yelp. "I think it's bruised, if not cracked. We're going to take you to the ER to find out for sure."

"Hey." Charlie moved back into her line of sight. "Adeline, I'm sorry you got hurt, but this is *our* date. I'm happy to take you to the emergency room if you needs to go, but I don't think we need those two."

Addie breathed a prayer for the right words. "Charlie, I would be happy to have you accompany me to the hospital." She gave Mark her best "I am in charge" look. "Mark and Todd will follow because that is what they do."

She'd never seen Mark glare at her like he did at that moment, not even after the accident. "Very well."

He started to untie her skates but Charlie stepped in. "Thanks, Mark. I think Adeline and I can take it from here."

Mark opened his mouth to tell him to back off, most likely, but Addie stopped him. "Thank you for your help, Mark, but Charlie's right. He and I can handle it from here."

Her friend and bodyguard stood and stared down at her, nostrils flaring, but he backed off. "We'll follow you there."

Addie nodded knowing it was the biggest concession she would get. Once Mark and Todd were on the other side of the room, she turned back to Charlie. "I am sorry for how they are acting. They are from my country and take my safety very seriously."

Charlie shot a dark look their way. "I'm glad you have someone looking out for you but I can be trusted. I know they don't know that yet, but I can." He knelt in front of her and untied one skate then the other before tugging them off with more care than she could have imagined. Todd had brought her boots over a few minutes earlier. The feeling of Charlie's hand guiding her foot into the boot shaft was an odd one. Not bad, but odd. Despite the chill still permeating the parts of her jeans where she'd been on the ice, her leg warmed from where his hand was on the back of her calf. Her foot slid into place and he zipped up the calf-length boot before turning his attention to the other foot.

By the time she had both boots on, she felt flushed and not just because of the exertion and the pain. She might be the Crown Princess but no one had put her shoes on since she was a little girl.

Charlie smiled at her. A soft smile that made her hope for more of them someday - at least until she breathed in again and the pain hit. "I'll be right back. I'm going to get my shoes and coat and then I'll help you with yours, okay?"

She waited right there as he quickly changed. Before she knew it, he was back at her side helping her with her coat. Mark's and Todd's eyes followed their every move and walked behind them to the door. The look she gave them made sure they stayed back further than they preferred.

Charlie opened the car door for her. She climbed in and tried to get her seatbelt but this time she couldn't stop the yelp. Reaching her hand back to get it was more than she could handle. Once Charlie was seated on the driver's side, she did not have to ask for help. He did not say a word, but leaned over and drew it across her until he could click it into place.

With her eyes still closed, they left.

Charlie did his best to avoid the bumps in the road, choosing the smoothest lane possible whenever he could. The ride was quiet except for the occasional whimper from his passenger.

Fifteen minutes later, he pulled up in front of the emergency room doors. "I'll get a wheelchair." He left the car running and went to get a seat for her.

"Thank you." He didn't know her well, but he could hear the strain in her voice.

Boots crunching in the snow, he wheeled her inside. "I have to go park. Where do you want to wait? I can roll you to the desk."

"No. I'll wait for you."

"I'll hurry." He trotted back to the car, but by the time he parked it her *friends* had already walked inside. What was with those guys? He understood protective, better than most, but they passed the border on ridiculous about halfway back.

When he made it through the sliding glass doors, both men were seated on the other side of the room. The smaller one watched Charlie. The other one never took his eyes off Adeline. Charlie did his best to ignore them both as he pushed the wheelchair toward the check-in desk.

Adeline talked with the lady, a severe looking woman who didn't appear to have any sense of humor whatsoever. Adeline even attempted to make a joke, not a very good one to Charlie's way of thinking, and the lady hadn't even cracked the smallest smile. Instead, the lady handed over a clipboard with several papers and told Adeline to fill them out and turn them in.

Charlie put his hands back on the handles of the wheelchair and pushed Adeline over to a nearby couch. "Is there anything I can help you fill out?"

She winced, but started filling the papers out. "Thank you, but no."

It took her about ten minutes to fill them out and she'd just about finished when a nurse called her. He pushed her back to the counter and looked down. "Do you want me to go with you?"

"Would you mind terribly?" For a fleeting second, she looked like a scared little girl, but the look passed before he could be certain of what he saw. "I really do not want to go alone and since this is our date, I would prefer you to those two."

That made Charlie smile, but the nurse stopped him. "We're just doing triage right now. Weight, blood pressure, that kind of thing. You're welcome to come, but there's not much room."

Charlie looked back down at her. "I guess I'll wait?"

She nodded. "I will be back in a few minutes."

He went back to sit down and whispered a little prayer for her to be okay. It wasn't long before she returned, walking this time. Charlie stood and held her arm to help her sit down. He didn't know how, but he found himself holding her hand as they waited. It was nearly half an hour by his estimation before Adeline's name was called again. This time a male orderly of some kind waited for them with a wheelchair.

The next three hours were a blur of waiting, followed by flurries of activity, followed by more waiting with quiet conversation. Charlie started checking his watch more frequently until he looked at it every minute or so. Finally, he stood. "I need to make a quick phone call. Are you okay for a minute?"

Adeline's eyes were closed and he'd dimmed the lights by turning one set off. "I will be fine."

He pushed the sliding-porch-door-looking panel open and pulled the cell phone out of his pocket to call the number one woman in his life.

Addie was glad for a moment alone. She liked Charlie and his presence but when he stepped outside, she could let her guard down. Let a tear or two fall.

His voice filtered in through the sliding door that had not quite closed. "I'm so sorry, sweetheart."

Sweetheart?!

"I thought I would be home by now..." A pause. "I know. You're ready to go to bed. It's been a big day for you."

Addie's heart thudded heavy in her chest. How had she managed to end up going out with a man who seemed to be living with another woman? Her mind scrambled to come up with some other explanation, but she could not. Perhaps the medications made her thinking more sluggish than normal. Before she could come to any more conclusions or find another possible answer, Charlie came back in the room.

His gentle smile did not seem to be one of a person with a huge secret. Dating her while living with someone else. Instead, the smile made her feel safe. Comfortable. "I'm sorry about that."

"Is everything all right? Did you have somewhere you needed to be?"

She sensed his hesitation. "Everything's fine. I did have something I was supposed to do, but it's fine for me to stay here with you."

"If you have somewhere else to be, Mark and Todd can sit with me. I know that must be why you wanted to have an earlier date this evening."

He did not deny it. "You're right. But when I fell on you and cracked your rib, you became more important than what I had scheduled for later."

Addie started to tell him he could go, but before she could, the nurse walked in.

This nurse was much friendlier than the lady at the front desk. Addie liked her. "We're going to go over your discharge instructions and then you can get out of here." She showed Addie forms and instructions then had her sign them. She handed over a prescription for pain medication for Addie to take as needed then removed the IV.

The medication helped but her side still twinged every time she took a breath. "Will you hand me my things?" She would have to get dressed on her own or... Addie called the nurse back. "Is there someone who can help me get dressed?"

Addie could tell the nurse tried not to glance at Charlie. She had obviously read more into the relationship than there was, but she did not say anything except, "Of course."

Charlie excused himself and Addie finished dressing in minute. "I can get my shoes," she told the nurse. "Thank you very much for your help."

The nurse smiled at her. "My pleasure. I'll get your friend."

With a nod of thanks, she reached her foot toward one boot.

"Hey! I'll help you with that!" Charlie hurried to her side. He moved the chair until he sat directly in front of her.

The warmth of his hand on her ankle shot through her like a bolt of lightning. She was amazed again at how gentle he was as he slid her foot in and zipped up her boot. A minute later, his hand gripped her elbow and steadied her as they walked slowly toward the waiting area. Mark and Todd were at her side seconds after emerging from the doors.

"What did they say?" Mark demanded.

"Bruised. Maybe a slight crack, but I should be just fine in a few weeks. Until then, I am to take it easy." She gave Charlie her best smile. "Mark and Todd can take me home if you need to go."

He shook his head. "No. I'll take you to your car."

And so she ended up back in his car. It was easier than trying to explain to him that she had overheard his conversation. The ride was quiet, with Addie trying not to think about the implications of the phone call.

They reached the parking lot at C's where Charlie cut the engine and shifted in his seat until he was looking at her. "Let me take you out again next Friday. Please? To make up for tonight."

It took everything in her to nod. She would call later in the week and cancel, but for now she just wanted this date to be over with. "That sounds nice." It did. Or it would if she could figure out what other meaning the call could have.

"I'll call you later this week and we can make plans?"

A nod was all she could manage with Mark staring at her from the front steps. Charlie got out, walked around the car and opened her door for her. He was solicitous in his care for her. She gave Mark and Todd a slight nod and they disappeared inside the restaurant.

Charlie must have noticed it. "For two annoying, overprotective guys, they sure pay attention to your instructions."

"They are good to me." It took longer than normal to make it up the steps, but when she did, she turned to him. "Thank you for a lovely time, Charlie."

He gave a snort of laughter. "It would have been lovely if I hadn't hurt you so badly. But thank you for saying so anyway." For a minute, she thought he would lean down and kiss her but instead he moved away. "Good night, Adeline."

She put on a tremulous smile, the best she could manage. "Good night, Charlie." Addie unlocked the car and sat down on the passenger seat. She would not be able to drive home. Charlie shut the door behind her as Mark exited the building. Once he turned the car on, Charlie moved away. Adeline did not watch as they drove off. She could not.

All she really wanted to do is go to bed.

And forget Charlie Brewer ever existed. Something much easier said than done.

"You look especially happy." Jonathan flipped the chair around again, settling in across from Addie without asking first.

A pretty blush again spread up her cheeks as she tucked her phone into her purse. "I suppose I am."

He cocked an eyebrow at her. "You suppose you're happy? Must be the guy."

She looked up at him, her blue eyes deliciously puzzled. "The guy?"

"Yeah. Whoever you had a date with."

Addie winced. "Charlie. Yes, he is wonderful, but I am afraid at the moment, my mood is due more to..."

Mark pulled out a seat and inserted himself into the conversation. "Did you take your medicine, Addie?"

Who did he think he was? Her dad? Why did she put up with it?

Addie nodded. "Yes, Mark. I took my medicine. I was just telling Jonathan it is likely the reason why I look happy."

"You should be home resting." Mark needed to take a chill pill.

"What happened?" Jonathan kept his focus on Addie.

"I went on a date Saturday and ended up in the emergency room when Charlie and I had a little incident on the ice."

Mark snorted. "A little incident? The guy landed on you."

Addie gave Mark a look of reproach. "It was as much my fault as it was his. He did not mean to fall on me or bruise my ribs."

Jonathan winced. "Bruised ribs are no fun. Been there, done that, got the t-shirt."

Addie looked puzzled. That adorable puzzled look Jonathan liked. "There is a t-shirt for broken ribs?"

He couldn't help but chuckle. "Not really. It's an expression. It means I understand because I've been through something similar. I'm sure there are t-shirts that say it, though."

"I see." Jonathan wasn't sure she really did.

"Did Mark and Todd kick the dude to the curb for hurting you?" Seemed like something they would do.

"No. They refused to let me go alone, though, so they followed us to the emergency room to make certain it was nothing more serious."

The guys went on her dates with her? That was ludicrous. Unless...

Something niggled at the back of his brain. Something... It was right there... But he couldn't quite put his finger on it. Almost... but...

"I am on fairly strong pain killers for the next few days, but since we do not have a test and I can tape the lectures for review later, I doubt my diminished mental acuity will have any real effect."

"You should have stayed home." Concern colored Jonathan's words. "At least tell me you didn't drive?"

Addie glanced at Mark. "No. Mark drove." Jonathan wished the intruder would leave the conversation, but since he insisted on tagging along on Addie's dates, Jonathan didn't think it was likely.

"Back to Transnational Security." Something more up his alley. A topic he could discuss forward and backward. "What's the best way to keep kidnappers from getting a hold of their target?"

"Varied routes, last minute schedule changes, incomplete or inaccurate public schedule, heightened security surrounding heightened threats, both visible and invisible." Addie rattled those off with surprising ease.

"Good standard answers, but we're going to have to dig deeper than that and you know it."

Addie shot Mark a look Jonathan couldn't decipher. "You are correct, Jonathan." She pulled her text toward her. "Let us see if we can figure this out."

Half an hour later, they headed into their only class for the night. Jonathan only half paid attention as his mind wandered back to that night. The night he didn't remember in its entirety. It wasn't only because of his likely intoxication, but because of the head trauma. The night that cemented his path in life. He would follow in his father's footsteps. There hadn't been a cover-up per se, but the accident involved a multimillion dollar yacht and a girl's life. His parents could afford to repair the boat and to compensate the family for the medical bills for Izzy's care over the next few weeks.

They didn't know he'd spent those weeks not recovering at a private retreat in the Adirondacks but in a very exclusive rehab facility. He'd checked in under an alias. They hadn't asked questions once the check written by his security guard cleared. It was an account his parents didn't have access to and they'd never known. Or if they had, they'd never mentioned it.

"Mr. Langley-Cranston the Fourth?"

Jonathan dropped the twirling pen as the professor called on him. "Yes, ma'am?"

"Can you tell me the last instance of a royal family member being kidnapped?"

He searched his memory. "Princess Anne?" But that hadn't been a successful attempt. "No." He shook his head. "I don't remember off the top of my head." He should know this.

Addie popped in to save him any further embarrassment. "Prince Jedidiah of Montevaro was kidnapped as a child by his nanny. She later returned him unharmed. It was discovered she had lost a baby to an early miscarriage not long before and suffered a temporary psychotic break. They never left the palace grounds, but were hidden for several days in one of the seldom used turrets. His cries were heard by a maid who was bringing down Christmas decorations as the holidays approached. He was handed back over without incident when his nanny was confronted by the royal guard. The kidnapping attempt of Princess Anne was several years later and thwarted by her own refusal to cooperate and passers-by who protected her at their own peril, including a tabloid journalist. This is in contrast to the supposed influence the paparazzi had on the accident that claimed Princess Anne's former sister-in-law, Princess Diana." The recitation was almost robotic. As though Addie knew all of this by heart and not something she'd studied over the last few weeks.

"Very good."

The class moved on and Jonathan did his best to leave the past where it belonged. The past.

"Go out with me?" Vince leaned against the door of Samantha's classroom. "Just dinner. That's all I'm asking."

She looked at him. His long legs were encased in jeans, his arms folded across his chest still looked as good as they had the last time they went out, their senior year of college. "How many times do I have to tell you no?"

"Until you decide to say yes." He pushed off the door jamb and ambled toward her as she put a stack of math quizzes in her bag. "You said yes before."

"And the last time I said yes, you didn't like my no later," she reminded him. The reason she'd walked back to her dorm. Granted he'd apologized and tried to give her a ride, but she'd refused.

"I'll be a perfect gentleman." He stopped just on the other side of her desk, forcing her to look way up at him. Straight into his eyes. Eyes the color of the sky on a perfect, cloudless day.

"That's what you said last time." Samantha felt her breath catch in her throat. "And the time before that." The one date they'd gone on in high school. "You're oh-for-two in the being a gentleman department."

His indignant reply ripped open wounds long left buried. "Don't blame me for..."

"I can't do this with you, Vince. The answer is no. For now. For tomorrow. For eternity." She slung the bag over her shoulder and shoved her chair out of the way.

As she rounded the corner of her desk and brushed past Vince, he grabbed her arm. Not tight. Not painful. Just enough to make her stop. "I'm not the same guy I was back then, Sammie. You know that. I know that. All I ask for is another chance."

The newly-reopened wounds wouldn't let her answer. Tears filled her eyes and clogged her throat. Mute, she shook her head and ran off. Away from the memories. Away from it all.

She made it to her car before the tears spilled onto her cheeks. How did she let him get under her skin like that? Home. Ice cream.

Her phone buzzing. Samantha glanced at the screen. A text from Charlie. She groaned. She'd signed up to help at The Club. Their benefactor had made it hard for family and friends to refuse to help, not when she was being so incredibly generous. A quick text back that she'd be there in ten and she pulled out of the parking lot. But before she did, she saw Vince standing there, hands shoved deep in his pockets and shoulders slumped as he watched her drive off.

When she reached The Club, Samantha pulled her makeup out of her purse, using it skillfully to cover up the signs of tears and headed inside. The first person she saw wasn't Charlie, but Mrs. Hart, one of her high school teachers. After hugs, Samantha was directed to an area where she could change into work clothes. When she returned, Charlie stood there, torn jeans and painted-in tee a contrast to Vince's put together look.

Charlie's smile appeared genuine as he greeted her. "Hey, Sam. Did Mrs. Hart tell you where you'd be?"

Unable to reply, she shook her head. Charlie called to the director and Samantha found herself in the kitchen next to Lindsey and several other girls she knew by face if not by name.

Time to clean.

Charlie looked at Addie in surprise. "You've never been bowling? Seriously?"

Her dark curls bounced as she shook her head. "No. I am not sure that there is a single bowling place in my entire country."

"It's an alley. A bowling alley."

Adeline gave him a beautiful smile. "I do not believe there is a single bowling alley in my entire country."

"Then next time, we'll have to go bowling."

She nodded. "I would like that." Her lashes lowered slightly. "Will you teach me?"

It warmed his heart to hear her ask. "Absolutely." He leaned closer, his forearms resting on the table. "But do you think we can leave Lenny and Squiggy behind?"

Little lines appeared on her forehead as she thought. "Who?"

"Your shadows. Do they go everywhere with you?"

Another one of those smiles flashed at him. "They do. They are my roommates and my friends. They take my safety very seriously and until you've proven yourself to them, they will not leave me alone with you."

"And how long will that take?"

This time the smile had more of a coy look to it. "Depends on how long you stay around. The more they get to know you, the more likely they are to trust you. If I see you once a week, it will likely be several months before they do." Her next words were gentle. "I will be leaving for home, permanently, in May."

He nodded. "And there is no chance you'd be willing to relocate to the States? Specifically this area, and do your work from here?"

This time the words were sad. "I am sorry, Charlie, but no. I must return home. In this, I have little choice."

Charlie leaned back in his seat and fiddled with his napkin. He came to the same conclusion she likely had, but hadn't wanted to ruin their time together during their other two dinner dates or during the ice skating fiasco. It also explained her reluctance. The words were some of the hardest he'd ever tried to choke out. "In that case, Adeline, I am terribly sorry for taking up too much of your time. If there is no way you could move here, then there is no point in the two of us going out." He sighed. "I'm at a point in my life where, if I'm going to date a woman, it has to be something that *could* have a future. Since that's not the case, I think it's probably best if this is our last date."

He was nearly certain he saw tears in her eyes, but, if so, she blinked them away before he could be certain. "Perhaps we can be friends, then." She gave him the smallest smile he'd seen yet. "I do not have many friends but perhaps we can be that to each other while I am here."

Unwilling to tell her no, Charlie gave a bit of a nod. "Maybe." He glanced at his watch. "May I at least walk you to your car?"

She nodded and he helped her with her coat. When they reached the car door, he leaned over and brushed her cheek with a kiss.

"I do wish we'd been able to get to know each other better, Adeline."

She held his gaze with her own for a long moment. "Me, too."

He took a few steps back. "Until next time..."

"Until next time." She climbed into the car and stared at him for a few seconds until she put the car in reverse and pulled away.

Charlie's heart rested heavy in his chest.

There would be no next time.

6

"Very good." Addie walked behind the row of girls as they sat in chairs pulled up to a long rectangular table. "Now, who can tell me which fork you use for salad?"

"The salad fork," called out Megan, a bit of snark coloring her voice.

Addie managed to hide her smile. "Technically, you are correct, Miss Anderson. However, you did not raise your hand and that is not the answer I am looking for and you well know it." She did her best to keep the reproach gentle, but she was here in the capacity as a teacher, not a friend.

Another girl, three down from Megan raised her hand. "Yes, Miss Brown?"

The girl rattled off the correct answer, showing Addie and the rest of the girls how to tell which fork to use. "Work your way in" was close enough for what they were doing. At a state dinner, it was a bit more complicated, but the likelihood of any of these young women needing the more sophisticated knowledge was slim. She would explain it to them one more time - she already had once - but "outside in" would get them through any social situation they were likely to end up in.

They worked their way through the rest of the cutlery and the assorted drink cups. "If a lady, or gentleman, chooses not to partake of a particular drink being offered, how do you inform the wait staff of this?"

Lindsey's hand shot up.

"Yes, Miss Brewer?"

"You turn the cup or glass over."

"Not if it's already full," Megan snickered.

"Of course not, Miss Anderson." Addie gave that look again. The one she hoped she got right. Megan did not wilt under the look like Addie feared but nodded, knowing she had broken the rules once again. "Very well. We are done for the day. You are doing well, ladies. I commend you. Now, I believe there is a study session in room C. You may walk there with your things, except Miss Anderson. I would like a word."

The girls scurried out, but Megan stayed seated, her head hanging slightly.

"Miss Anderson," Addie said softly. "Can you tell me why I asked you to stay?"

"I know. I need to raise my hand and not blurt out answers."

"Do you just yell the answers at school?"

Megan shrugged. "Sometimes."

"And what does your teacher think?"

"Miss Dean just rolls her eyes and calls on someone else."

"In here, I need you to learn the correct way. That is my whole purpose in being here. Not to stifle you, but to help you channel your energy properly."

Megan just nodded.

Addie lowered herself into the seat next to her. "Is there anything else bothering you?"

Tears spilled down Megan's cheeks. "It's been a rough few weeks Miss Addie. That's all."

"Rough how?"

Halting words fell out of the girl, telling a story of job loss and increasing desperation on the part of her father, taking odd jobs when he could get them, not eating to save food for her and her two siblings when he could not, and desperate to avoid what he called "the dole", but he was not quite that destitute. Yet.

Addie hugged the little girl close, thanking God she had never dealt with that sort of desperation and asking for inspiration and a way to help.

A few minutes later, the sobs slowed to sniffles. "Miss Addie, can I give my dad the money I'm earning here? Instead of using it for the banquet?"

Addie rested her cheek on Megan's hair. "I am afraid not, Megan. The money was donated with very specific guidelines that must be followed. But, tell me, what does your father do for a living?"

If they were in Montevaro, the man would have a job in the palace by nightfall. Any man who refused to eat to make sure his children could, would be a valuable asset in some capacity. Perhaps she could help here, too.

"He'll do just about anything, Miss Addie. He only went to high school. He married my mama when they graduated and had Maile a year later. Mama got sick after my little brother was born and she died a few years ago. He's worked hard for us, but he can't find work nowhere."

Addie knew it was not the time to correct grammar. "Well, then. I suppose computer programmer or CPA is out, but what has he done in the past?"

"Janitorial work most recently. But he's been a landscaper and a greens keeper before."

"Very well." The wheels were turning in Addie's head. "You should go splash some water on your face, sweetie, and join the other girls. I will think about what we *can* do to help your father, even though you cannot use your earnings from here."

"Thank you, Miss Addie."

Another long hug and the girl walked off. Addie tapped her finger on the table for a minute before going to find Mrs. Hart. Surely, there was something to be done.

Another day, another Arby-Q.

Good thing Charlie liked them. The recently opened Arby's gave him an option besides the McDonald's up the street on the days he didn't have time to make his lunch. He gave the teen his order and pulled his wallet out of his pocket when a voice caught his ear.

"I can't believe this." Resignation filled it the next time she spoke. "I left my wallet at school." Samantha stuffed something back in her purse. "I'll have to cancel the order. I'm sorry."

The teen mumbled something semi-accommodating when Charlie stepped in.

"I got it, Sam." He nodded at the kid. "I'll pay for it." Once he paid for both meals, they headed for the only empty table he could see.

"I'll pay you back, Charlie," Samantha promised him. "I can't believe I forgot my wallet."

"Don't worry about it, Sam. It's what friends are for."

She munched on a fry. "We've been friends a long time, haven't we?" He could hear the nostalgia in her voice.

"We were friends for most of school, but I hadn't heard from you in years until Lindsey was assigned to your class this year." The specter of Tricia hovered over the words.

Sam went straight to the heart of the matter. "Do you ever

think about her? Wish things were different?" Charlie didn't have to ask who "her" was.

He twirled his fry in a pile of ketchup as he turned the idea over in his mind. "I hate how much it hurts Lindsey that her own mother didn't want her, but I'm glad I'm not a part-time dad or that Trish didn't give her up for adoption without talking to me or go through with the abortion. Things never would have worked out between us, though. We were too different, wanted different things out of life. She's probably jet setting somewhere with us long forgotten."

"She did dream big, didn't she?"

Charlie nodded. "I always knew I could be happy here. Put down roots and never leave. That's why..." He clamped his mouth shut, the decision he and Adeline had made still fresh in his mind.

"Why what?"

He couldn't not tell her. She'd know if he lied. "It's why it didn't work out with the woman I was dating. She has to move after graduation. I want to stay here. We only went out on four dates, but I liked her. I thought about introducing her to Lindsey, but she won't even consider moving here so..." Charlie shrugged.

"And you're just as stubborn about staying local?"

"You know what my parents are like. I saw them for a couple weeks at Christmas, if I was lucky, and I spent every summer break until Lindsey was born at whatever dig site they happened to be at."

"You know, a lot of kids would have loved it."

"I know, and there was a lot of good to be found in those summers but..." He worked his straw around the ice in his cup. "I always wanted the stability my cousins had. Dan is staying here after he and CeCe get married. Ellie hasn't moved far. She's still in the Ozarks and comes home often. I don't want to drag Lindsey off to Europe on a 'could we be something' for a woman, you know?"

Sam reached out and rested her hand on top of his, squeezing gently. "Maybe you need to a look a little closer to home. Maybe to someone who already knows about Lindsey and loves her?"

He looked up from his sandwich to see the look on her face. "You and me, Sam?" He shook his head. "I don't know."

"I'm not saying propose, goofball." She released his hand and smacked it. "I'm just wondering if a date might be in order. Nothing serious. Maybe take Lindsey to a ball game or something."

That made Charlie chuckle. "It's a bit early for a ball game unless we want to head to Florida for Spring Training."

Sam gave him a coy smile. "Well, now that you mention it, Florida does sound pretty nice."

He shook his head. "I don't know about Florida, but..." Maybe it was time to take the dating plunge. Maybe Adeline had just been a warm up, to get him used to the idea, to get him looking for something permanent. "How about dinner on Friday?"

Sam smiled at him. "Sounds perfect."

"Don't mention it to Lindsey, though, okay? I don't want her to know just yet. Not until we know if there could be something between us."

After a moment's thought, Sam nodded. "Okay. I won't tell her, but you'll have to tell her you're seeing someone eventually."

"I know. But not yet."

His own heart had already broken once in the last week, he didn't need his daughter's to deal with on top of that. Especially not since the woman in question was her teacher for the next four months.

Only years of training, engrained in her to the point it had become first rather than second nature, kept Addie from tapping her foot in time with Mrs. Hart's pencil as they waited for the phone to ring.

It surely would not be the only opportunity for her to help Megan's father find a job.

No amount of training could keep Addie from jumping slightly as the phone jangled. Before it finished the first ring, Mrs. Hart spoke into the handset.

Addie drew on all of her years of practice keeping her face impassive to maintain her outward calm as Mrs. Hart said only, "yes", "mmhmm", and "I see." Finally after what seemed an eternity, the other woman hung up the handset.

And then a grin crossed Mrs. Hart's face. "I was right. My niece is still looking for a janitor and general handyman at Serenity Landing Comedy Club. David will be here soon to pick up Megan and Matthew?"

"Megan told me he would pick her and her brother up in about fifteen minutes." Addie felt a weight lift off her shoulders. Since hearing about the difficulties in Megan's family, she had felt virtually helpless to rectify the situation.

A "bing" sound from the computer drew Mrs. Hart's attention. "Let me print this information out..." Her voice trailed off as she clicked a few buttons and reached for the phone. This time she asked the person working the front desk to send David back when he arrived.

Seconds after Mrs. Hart handed over the still-hot papers to Addie, a knock sounded on the door. Both women swiveled in unison and stood to greet Megan's dad.

He looked from one to the other. "Is there something wrong, Mrs. Hart?"

Mrs. Hart motioned toward the empty chair next to Addie. "Why don't you have a seat, David. There's something I want to talk to you about."

Addie returned to her seat, smiling at the man she had yet to officially meet. He sat next to her his leg bobbing up and down as he waited to hear what they had to say.

"David, this is Addie. She's been working with the girls for the last few weeks."

She held out a hand. He shook it as he nodded. "Megan has told me about you. It's a pleasure."

It took a very close look, but Addie could see stress in his face, in the set of his eyes and shoulders. Hopefully, what Mrs. Hart had to say would help alleviate that.

"The other day, Megan told Addie you had lost your job?" Mrs. Hart asked.

David nodded. "I know I'm behind on payin' ya for the extra time the kids are here, Mrs. Hart, but I promise..."

Mrs. Hart stopped him with a raised hand. "I'm not concerned about that at the moment. Megan also said you're having a hard time finding permanent employment?"

Addie set the papers back on the desk as he nodded. She had never met the man and there was no reason for him to see her as the one working hard to find him a job. She had brought it to the attention of Mrs. Hart, but Mrs. Hart had done all of the work and used her connections to find the opening.

David seemed to put on his best face on. "I have a few leads," he said vaguely. "I'm hopeful."

Mrs. Hart gave a sympathetic smile. "We know what the job market is like and we want to help." She picked up the papers and handed them over. "This is an application and job notice for Serenity Landing Comedy Club."

He stared at the pages in his hand. "A job?" David looked first at Mrs. Hart, then Addie. "A job?" he repeated.

"My niece is good friends with the owner at the comedy club. She's looking for a janitor and general handyman, perhaps some work on sets from time to time. The starting pay for someone with no work experience is on there but actual pay will be negotiated at the time of hire. I can't promise you'll get the job, but the posting hasn't been made public yet so you have a week to be the first applicant. She's happy to give you that long to get your application together and turned in. She won't post the job until you've interviewed as long as it's in a timely manner."

Addie watched as David's Adam's apple worked up and down. She sympathized with his attempt to control his emotions, but knew he'd likely fail.

"Thank you, Mrs. Hart." Sure enough, a tear leaked down his face. "Miss Addie. I don't know what I can say beyond that. My kids have said great things about you both and Lindsey talks non-stop about you, Miss Addie, when she's at our house."

"Both girls are lovely," Addie told him. "I have only met your son once but he seems like a wonderful young man."

"Thank you."

Mrs. Hart stood. "If you need anything, please let me know."

Addie and David both stood as he nodded. "I will. I don't know how to thank you. Really."

Mrs. Hart winked at Addie. "Help us with renovations when you're not working and we'll call it even."

He chuckled as Addie smiled. "You got it."

His step had a bit of a bounce and his countenance was lighter as he left the office. Warmth filled Addie. She loved being able to help. If only she could do more.

Why am I so nervous? Charlie rubbed his hands on his jeans as he sat in his car outside Sam's house. He'd known Sam since he was five. He'd been on double dates with her in high school though he'd never been *her* date. And it wasn't like he hadn't been on dates. He'd gone on a first date - and a second, third and fourth - with Adeline in just the last month. Could that be why he didn't want to get out of the car and ring the bell? Because he still wished he could be with another woman?

He had never fallen in love with Adeline, though he believed he might have if she'd just been willing to consider moving to Serenity Landing. Charlie's phone buzzed and he looked down to see a text.

U COMIN N?

An eyebrow raised. Text speak? Really? She had a phone with a full keyboard, he knew that. Text speak annoyed him to no end. And from a teacher?

JUST A MINUTE, he sent back. He was a few minutes early and he needed them to figure this out. *Okay, God. I'm almost done with my degree. I'm ready to find someone to be serious about. To look to the future with, to be a mother to Lindsey. I don't know if Sam is the girl for me, but it seems pretty obvious Adeline isn't. Help me forget about her?*

With a deep breath, he opened the car door and went up the walk. Before he could knock, Sam flung the door open.

"Hey! How are you?" She stepped to the side to let him in. "Did you have a good day?"

Charlie nodded. "I did. Lindsey is at my aunt and uncle's for their monthly dinner tonight. Usually they do it on a weekend, but they've got stuff going on almost every night this month." He stood in the entryway, fiddling with the keys in his pocket.

"So you can't be out too late?" Did she sound disappointed? He couldn't see her face as she walked toward the kitchen. "Can I get you something to drink?"

"No, thanks. Actually, I'm pretty hungry and I'd like to beat the dinner rush at Mr. Humongo's, if that's okay with you."

Sam came back into the entry. "Sure. That sounds great."

Her black boots made a clicky sound on the tile floor. They looked like nice boots but he figured they wouldn't feel quite as butter soft as... *No!* He had to get Adeline out of his mind. Sam's long legs were encased in skin tight stretch pants of some sort, the kind Lindsey had worn when she was younger, with a long top over them.

Charlie helped her put on a nice brown leather coat and

waited as she locked the door behind her. In minutes, they arrived at the old house converted into a pizza and pasta place. A teenager showed them to a table in what had to have been the front parlor at one point. It was a bit away from the other patrons and slightly darker than the rest of the room, giving it a romantic feel.

He rested his forearms on the table and leaned toward Sam. "So, tell me. What made you decide to be a teacher?" The first step to forgetting about that other person was to figure out what made Sam tick and what they had in common

She shrugged, leaning across the table toward him. "It just seemed to fit. I never really wanted to do anything else. I babysat a lot as an early teen and everyone said I was good at it."

"Why fourth grade though?"

A grin crossed her face. "Old enough to button and zip, not old enough for too much lip. Fourth grade is pushing the second part of that. Second or third is better, but I like fourth grade a lot. It's my fifth year teaching it." Sam reached out with one hand, her finger rubbing light circles on the back of his hand. "What about you? Paint department?"

The waitress arrived at that moment, giving him a bit of reprieve and allowing him to remove his hand from under Sam's.

They ordered their drinks and he leaned back as the waitress walked off. Once they decided at kind of toppings to put on their pizza, Sam asked the question again. "Why Serenity Landing Hardware and Home Store?"

Charlie shrugged. "Mostly because my uncle helped me get a job there not long after Lindsey was born. I've worked my way up. I'm hoping for a different job in my field once I actually have my MBA, but I don't have any leads just yet."

They talked about life in general, including Lindsey a bit, while waiting for dinner to arrive. The meal itself passed in near silence. Once the leftovers were boxed up and Charlie paid the bill, without using the coupon he'd brought because it felt kind of cheap to do so even if it would have saved about five bucks. Sam suggested frozen custard for dessert, even though it was a cold February night. They had heaters near the counter.

Charlie thought she just wanted an excuse to sit close to him for warmth.

Ten minutes later, his suspicions proved correct. He worked on his dish, named after a local radio celebrity - frozen vanilla custard, hot fudge, bananas, and strawberry sauce. The only word he could use for Sam's position was snuggled. Snuggled next to him as she ate her very small cup of chocolate custard.

Small talk continued. He learned about several friends and acquaintances he'd lost touch with over the years. Caught up on weddings, children, and divorces for about half of the two hundred students in his graduating class, plus many from the years before and after him.

"You missed the five-year reunion." Sam set down her half-full cup. "Are you going to the ten year?"

Charlie shrugged. "I've got a while to decide. Probably not." He didn't want to run the risk of running into or being forced to talk about the one person Sam hadn't mentioned.

Tricia.

She bumped her shoulder into his. "Be my date?"

He nearly coughed up the banana bit. "Excuse me?"

"Be my date for the reunion?"

"It's over a year away, Sam. Why don't we talk about it when it gets closer?"

She nodded and rested her head against his shoulder. "We can do that."

They threw their trash away. Charlie drove her back to her house but declined her invitation to come in for a cup of coffee. He did walk her to the door and managed to avoid her blatant attempts to get him to kiss her.

With a quick hand squeeze, he backed off and let her unlock the door. After a soft good night, she locked the door behind her and he escaped.

Escaped.

If that's how he thought about the end of the date, it didn't bode well for the potential future with Sam.

"Very good, ladies. I am proud of you." Addie stood in front of the room of twelve girls. "Mrs. Hart is waiting for you in the recreation room. She has explained how the renovations will work and how it will help you earn your dress and accessories?" They nodded in unison. "Very well. Time to get started."

She followed the girls into the large room where several dads spent the last three weeks tearing down some of the drywall and replacing it. They had been blessed to discover one of them worked in construction and could supervise much of the work. Another worked for a paint store and provided the paint at a considerable discount.

She wore old blue jeans and her oldest sweatshirt and tennis shoes and still she dressed significantly nicer than many of her students on their better days. They were going to spend the next hour cleaning so they could paint later in the week.

"Miss Addie?"

She looked up to see Lindsey standing there. "What can I help you with, Lindsey?" One thing she'd learned at a young age was that people loved it when you called them by name. It made them feel important.

"I just wanted to thank you for helping us."

Addie smiled. "It is my pleasure. I am enjoying my time with you girls." It was the absolute truth. She enjoyed it far more than she expected she would.

Lindsey started to say something but stopped when the door opened behind them. "Daddy!"

The voice stopped Addie's heart in its tracks. "Hey there, princess."

Lindsey bounded up. "Dad, this is Addie. She's teaching us etiquette."

Addie pasted a smile on her face and stood as gracefully as she could. "Do you remember the proper way to introduce someone, Lindsey?"

Lindsey nodded. "Dad, this is Miss Addie. Miss Addie, I'd like you to meet my father, Charlie Brewer."

Addie brushed her hand on her jeans and held it out. "It is a pleasure to see you again, Mr. Brewer."

He took her hand and held it longer than necessary. "You too, Miss Addie. I've heard a lot about you."

"You too, Mr. Brewer. Though I did not know it was you I was hearing about."

"I could say the same." He did not take his eyes off hers. "Could you give us a minute, Linds?"

The girl gave them an odd look but walked off to talk to one of her friends. Charlie still held her hand and it tingled all the way up her arm.

Addie broke the silence. "I did not realize Lindsey is your daughter."

He finally dropped her hand but moved a step closer. "I didn't tell you I had a daughter. How could you know?"

Deep in her heart, she realized, no matter how she ended up feeling about him, they would never work. Her parents and Parliament might accept someone from the working class but not someone with a child. Unless he had been widowed. But he was quite young to have a daughter as old as Lindsey.

Her mind spun with the possibilities. Perhaps Lindsey was a friend's child who he had taken in when she was orphaned. Or...

He stopped her runaway thoughts. "Can I take you todinner tomorrow night? I'd like to talk."

She considered it for a moment then nodded. "Yes. I will meet you at C's at six?"

He leaned in a bit closer. "I look forward to it."

7

The ride to the apartment was quieter than normal as Charlie and Lindsey both contemplated the revelation.

Lindsey broke the silence. "Is Miss Addie the girl you ran your car into, Dad?"

He propped his head up in his fist as his elbow rested next to the window. "Yeah."

"Why didn't you go out with her again? I like her."

"I do too, princess, but she's headed back to her country in a few months. She can't move here and we can't move there. We'd all end up hurting more when she left if she and I started a relationship."

"Why can't we move? If things worked with you guys, why couldn't we move to her country?"

"A lot of reasons. But mostly because we can't."

"Why?" Her voice took on the whiny tone that grated on his every nerve.

"Linds." Even as obstinate as she must be feeling, she heeded the warning. Charlie would take Adeline - Addie - to dinner, talk to her about Lindsey and make certain there was no chance for her to stay in the area, then guard his heart and do his best to guard his daughter's. And figure out how he was going to tell Sam that, even though they'd postponed their second date, he was taking another woman to dinner.

The next night, he sat in the parking lot at C's and tried to convince himself to walk in. To get to know the beautiful woman a little better and break his heart a little more when he walked away.

Her SUV was already there, as was the car her two roommates always rode in. He understood being protective of the women in your life, but those two guys took it to a whole new level.

After staring for an eternity, he finally opened the door and headed inside. The two men followed him with their eyes as he walked toward the table where Adeline - Addie - sat. He did notice they were several tables farther away than they had been the other times they'd gone out.

He sat in the chair across from her, more subdued than on their previous dates. "How are you?" seemed like a safe opener.

"I am well, thank you." Her hands remained folded in her lap even as the waitress set a water in front of her and a Coke in front of him, before saying she would be back in a minute to take their order. "I do hope you do not mind I ordered your drink based on our previous meals together."

Charlie leaned back and gave her his best smile. "You noticed."

Adeline nodded. "Yes. A lady notices those kinds of things about those around her."

"And my daughter tells me you are quite the lady." Her head dipped and her eyes didn't meet his. "She's quite fond of you."

"And I am fond of her. She is a wonderful girl and it is apparent to everyone how much she loves you."

His smile widened. "I guess we're going to get straight to the elephant in the room, then, aren't we?"

"I suppose so." Addie shifted back in her seat and rested her forearms on the table. "Is there a reason why you did not tell me about Lindsey earlier?"

"I generally don't talk about her until I know if there's a possibility of a future with a woman. A way of protecting both of us, but especially a way of protecting Linds. I made that mistake when she was younger. Introducing her too soon to a woman and..." Charlie shrugged. "I got to the point where I didn't."

"Do you date often?"

With one hand he stirred his soda with the straw. "A few times a year. Maybe. It's been five or six years since I've gone on a third date with anyone."

The waitress chose that moment to walk up and take their orders. A few minutes later, it was just the two of them again.

She started right where they left off. "And yet, we have been out more than three times."

One corner of his mouth twitched upward. "True. It's been many years since a woman has intrigued me as much as you, but we came to an impasse."

"I did notice you had not called."

"With you going back to your country, and me and Lindsey staying here, there was no point." He leaned forward and looked directly into her eyes. Beautiful brown-green eyes with specks of gold that somehow matched her dark hair. "I didn't want to hurt any of us." He reached out and twisted a strand of silky hair around his finger as she broke eye contact. "I liked you more than any other woman I've ever dated. I saw more potential between us and I had to protect myself and my daughter." With the hair still wrapped around it, he crooked a finger under her chin and forced her face upward until her eyes once again met his. "I wanted to protect *you.*"

Addie's voice thickened with emotion. "I understand." Her eyes filled with tears, though she blinked rapidly to keep them from falling. "It is quite commendable of you to protect your daughter so thoroughly."

Charlie let the strand of hair slide through his fingers as he moved away. "She's my world. I have to protect her."

Addie took a deep, shuddering breath. "May I ask where her mother is?"

"She left a long time ago. Before Lindsey was born, really."

"How is that possible?"

Shifting forward so he no longer looked at her directly, Charlie picked up his napkin and began shredding it. "I was sixteen. My... girlfriend and I got carried away one night. She got pregnant. Her parents pushed for her to have an abortion. She almost did, but I talked her out of it. Told her I'd take care of the baby. We made those 'we'll be together forever' kind of promises, but no sooner than Lindsey was born..." He shook his head sadly. "Her parents brought Lindsey to my house for my weekend visitation when she was about three-weeks-old. They never came to get her and I never saw them again. I hadn't seen her mother since the hospital. A few years later, I got a letter from a lawyer signing away her parental rights."

He watched her brush a tear from her cheek. "What about your parents? Were they supportive?"

"Sort of. They're gone a lot. Mom's an anthropologist and Dad's an archaeologist. They've been studying ancient Europe since before I was born. My aunt and uncle raised me with my cousins while my folks were gone on their trips. My parents didn't *not* support me but mostly it was my aunt and uncle who helped me and Lindsey. I finished high school and my uncle helped me get my first job afterwards. My aunt helped with daycare. She babysat while I worked and went to college. Once Linds started school, she and I and one of my cousins got an apartment not too far from here. I'm working on my Master's degree and, hopefully, once I'm done this semester and get a better job, we'll be able to afford a house soon."

He leaned back in his chair and gave her a sad smile. "And that, in two minutes or less, is the story of how I became a single father who rarely goes out with a woman more than twice."

Their meals arrived, but Addie didn't begin eating. "You are a good father, Charlie. And I know Lindsey thinks so, too." She gave him a sad smile. "She may forget that for a few years, but she loves you. Of this I am certain."

Charlie finished his bite of sandwich. "Is that how it was with you and your parents?"

She shook her head. "No. My parents and I never went through the 'I hate you' teenage phase, but we were never as close as I wished we were. They too were often busy with their... work." Addie stirred her soup. "Is that why you do not want to move from here? To be near your family? If your parents study ancient Europe, then it seems likely they would be much closer if you moved there?" She gave a delicate half-shrug. "I am not presuming that you and I would ever reach the point where we would consider marriage, but if the potential for marriage is one of the criteria you have for reaching that third date, and your parents are in Europe, why would you not consider the move?"

"Because I wouldn't want to leave my aunt and uncle and cousins. They were my family for all intents and purposes growing up. They need me here more than I need to be closer to my parents. Dan lives here and Ellie works for a minimalist camping tours group a few hours away."

They talked about the weather and other unimportant things until they finished their meal. The waitress took their plates, but still they lingered. Talking about their time growing up in different parts of the world. She seemed to be holding something back, but it was obvious to Charlie, she grew up in a life of privilege. Deep down, he didn't want the meal to end. He would still get to see Addie, get to spend some time with her and get to know her better while they worked on the renovations, but this was the last time he'd get to spend time with her alone - as a woman he could be interested in.

But all too soon the employees were mopping floors and putting chairs up on tables.

"I suppose it is time to go." Addie looked at him from underneath lowered eyelashes.

"I guess so." He helped her put her coat on and followed her out the door. They stood together next to her car. Charlie reached out and trailed a finger down the side of her cheek.

She looked up at him, blinking away tears again. "Thank you for a lovely evening, Charlie. I am glad I will get to know Lindsey and I do hope we can be friends."

"I do, too."

He watched her drive away again, her friends following behind her. This time he knew it wouldn't be the last time he saw her, but he knew he would have to keep his distance.

For all their sakes.

Jonathan tapped his pen against the side of the text book. Addie was already ten minutes late, very unusual. What could be keeping her?

Had he ever been so nervous? Why? He'd dated super models and movie starlets. What was it about Addie that made him wipe his sweaty palms on his pants at the thought of asking her to dinner?

When she entered the small library study room and shut the door behind her, he noticed two things. First, she looked tired. Second, though it was just the two of them, Mark and Todd were digging books out of backpacks at a table clearly visible through the window.

At least they hadn't insisted on studying together.

But he turned his attention back to the gorgeous brunette. "You okay, Addie?"

She nodded but slumped in her seat. "I suppose. But if I was not, there is nothing I can do about any of it."

Jonathan's fingers itched to close the mini-blinds and block the two men out. "Want to talk about it?"

Addie glanced toward the window before leaning forward and resting her forearms on the table. "Perhaps it would be good. I cannot confide in Mark or Todd."

He moved to the other side of her, situating a chair so he was between her and the window. "What's the deal with them anyway? Do they have no life outside of whatever you're doing?"

Manicured nails tipped long, graceful fingers as she fidgeted. The tassel on the side of her purse wouldn't survive much more of this treatment. "They are not just roommates and friends."

The words sank in though she didn't elaborate. Jonathan turned various scenarios over in his head until it hit him. "They're bodyguards." As she nodded miserably, he wondered why he hadn't seen it sooner.

Jonathan leaned forward, his chin resting on his hand. "Why? I don't even have bodyguards most of the time. I have security at the house and a driver sometimes, but unless I'm out in a big city, I don't usually." He also had his conceal and carry license. Just in case. But Addie didn't need to know that.

"Because of who I am, what I will be. Though no one in the States knows, my parents were unwilling to risk my safety so far from home."

"Who are you?"

She fiddled with that tassel for several minutes before answering. "Crown Princess Adeline Julianne Elizabeth of Montevaro, oldest daughter of King Jedidiah and Queen Alexandra, heir to the throne of one of the oldest monarchies in Europe."

Jonathan sank back into his seat. "Wow. I never would have guessed."

"You were not supposed to." She turned earnest hazel eyes his direction. "I know you understand the reasons why no one knows my identity and I trust you to keep them to yourself. I know how the tabloids have treated you the last several years. If I did not know how you felt, I would not have told you."

He nodded. "Of course. No one will hear it from me." They sat there for a few more minutes before he asked another question. "So what's bothering you?"

Addie took a deep breath and blew it out slowly. "Remember the man I have been dating? The one who accidentally broke my ribs?"

Jonathan thought they'd broken up, but he nodded.

"There are three countries in the Royal Commonwealth of Belles Montagnes. Each of the three still have some outdated customs. Ravenzario has the old rules of primogeniture. My distant cousin, Christiana, is queen only because her younger brother died as a small child. In Mevendia, to our north, the royal family has arranged marriages and marriage contracts. In recent generations, they have found someone to marry and then arranged it, but it is still the law."

Arcane, but it seemed royalty often was. "What about Montevaro?" he asked, almost dreading the answer.

"Whoever I marry must meet with the approval of Parliament. It is unlikely they will approve of anyone who is not nobility or the American equivalent." She gave him a small smile. "For about four years, my mother has been insisting I do everything short of asking you on a date. You, Jonathan, are close enough to royalty for my mother and Parliament."

Good to know. Flattering. In a way. Once again, it had nothing to do with *him*, with who *Jonathan* was or would become, but rather his pedigree. One he had memorized by age five. Five U.S. Senators, too many prominent lawyers to count, including his mother, a more distant relation to two U.S. Presidents, both the Queen of England and Prince Philip, Duke of Edinburgh, plus Prince Albert of Monaco and the newest monarch in Europe, King Willem-Alexander of the Netherlands.

Some of the connections were tenuous at best, through "bastard lines" and other junior lines that converged centuries earlier. But the connections did exist. His grandmothers had never failed to make sure the family was aware of the blue blood running through his veins, each one attempting to one up the other in bloodlines. Both had researched the other's family line, just to make sure.

They also took great pleasure in informing each other of the scandals and scoundrels in the other line. He'd lost count of the number of distant relations who had been hanged for horse thieving or wife stealing.

Jonathan gave a slight shake to his head and turned back to the business at hand. "The man doesn't meet any of those requirements?"

"Not even close. His parents are archaeologists. He was raised by his aunt and uncle for the stability. And..." A lone tear streaked down her cheek. "Yesterday, I learned he has a daughter. She is eleven. If he were a widow, perhaps, but..." She shook her head, curls tumbling around her face. "I am afraid if you had a child at sixteen, my mother would have eliminated you from the list of potentials, much less someone who would not meet their stringent requirements in the first place."

While his family - particularly his grandmothers - would prefer he marry someone like Addie, a pedigree as good or better than his own, his parents had made it quite clear he should marry someone who would make him happy. Addie had no such support. He reached out and covered her hand with his own. "I'm sorry, Addie." She squeezed his hand before taking a deep breath.

"Thank you, Jonathan. I have few real friends here in the

States. I know Mark and Todd can be overbearing and overprotective, but..."

He interrupted her. "It's their job. Your safety is their top priority, not your happiness or the happiness of your date."

"Precisely."

Jonathan gave her hand one more squeeze before letting it go. "What do you want?"

He could see her spine stiffen. "I want what is best for my country, for my people. That means I will forget about what could have been with Charlie and finish my studies before hoping I find a man who is an upstanding Christian, approved by Parliament and my parents." She tossed another smile his way, this one an obvious attempt at flirtation. "My mother would have been apoplectic if you would have asked me to dinner."

His chance couldn't be more clear if it jumped up and bit him. "Then let's do it."

Addie's brows pulled closer together. "Do what?"

Jonathan leaned closer. "Have dinner with me."

The princess frowned. "I cannot this evening."

"I can't tonight either. Beast Feast at church. I'll be in a meat coma by eight. What about Saturday?"

Addie stared into his eyes for a long moment. "Yes. Jonathan, I think that would be lovely."

Charlie held open the door for her as they entered Rosita's. Always the gentleman. Always had been.

Once seated, Samantha started the conversation that had never begun in the car. "How's your weekend been?"

He gave a half-nod, half-shrug thing. "Not too bad."

"Anything exciting?" He was hiding something. Maybe hiding

was too strong a word, but definitely keeping something from her.

The menu held his interest far more than she did. "Not really. Worked most of yesterday, picked Lindsey up at The Club, met the infamous Addie, had dinner."

It was in there. Something about the day had thrown him off his game. "Is Addie as wonderful as the girls say? Or did you have a chance to talk with her?"

His face was a study in practiced nonchalance. "Turns out Addie is Adeline, a woman I went on several dates with after I ran into her car the night of that ice storm. Though we'd already agreed nothing would ever come of a relationship between us, we went to dinner so I could explain a bit more why I don't talk about Lindsey and give her a little background so she'll know what makes my daughter tick."

Was that all it had been? Was there more between him and this woman? Did he wish there could be? "You never told me. Why did you both decide it wouldn't work out?" Samantha almost kicked herself for being such a glutton for punishment.

Charlie shrugged. "She refuses to even consider moving here for the long term and I have no intention of moving. Without the possibility of geographic compatibility, there's no point in spending time discovering if there's more to the relationship."

Samantha nodded as her stomach churned. So Charlie liked the woman, but they had incompatible geographic goals in life. She could fix that. "You know I love it here in Serenity Landing." She turned the menu over. "I don't understand why everyone wouldn't want to live here." Before he could defend the saintly Addie, she hurried on. "I'm glad not everyone does or everyone would and what we love about the place would disappear, but give me a small town any day."

Charlie's chuckle sounded a bit forced. "I'm not sure Serenity Landing counts as a small town anymore. We were over fifteen thousand at the last census and will likely double that by the next one."

"I know, but it still has that small town feel. My boss was my principal when I was a kid. Several of the teachers in my building were my teachers in elementary. When I go to the pool in the summer, I know most of the lifeguards, still." Samantha made a mental note to try on her swimsuit and see just how much winter weight she needed to lose before bikini season started. "Every time I go to the store, I see families whose children I've had in class - or who I went to school with." She shook her head. "I wouldn't trade it for anything."

Charlie gave her a genuine grin. "Not even your own palace?"

Samantha spewed her water his direction in a coughing fit. "You remember that?" she finally gasped.

"Yep. You and Tricia were planning for one of you to marry Prince William and you'd both live in Buckingham Palace. You even promised I could take care of your horses."

Did pain flash through his eyes at the mention of Tricia? "We were what? Ten? We would have promoted you eventually." She leaned forward and whispered. "You could have driven the cars."

His chuckle and slight shake of his head told her he'd forgotten about the snotty European. "Thanks. I appreciate it."

The talk turned to other matters, including Lindsey's upcoming project about the woman who'd taken the coveted spot at Prince William's side. The Night at the Museum was coming up and Samantha couldn't wait to see her kids' projects. By the time, Charlie walked her to the door, the woman had to be long forgotten.

But no matter how many hints she dropped or how many times she asked him inside, Charlie still didn't kiss her. Frustrated, Samantha fell against her front door as it closed behind her. Maybe next time.

A noise in the back of the house startled her. She reached for the bat she kept near the front door for just this reason, but when she reached her bathroom, she dropped it. "Vince!"

Expletives sounded as the half-hidden torso jumped and he hit his head on the pipes.

"What are you doing here?"

A glimpse of his washboard stomach grabbed her attention as his shirt shifted and he slid out from under the sink. "I promised you I'd fix the drip under here before it started molding." Vince stood and wiped his hands on a towel as he looked down at her. "How was your date with Chuck?"

Samantha stifled a scream and spun on her heel. "I'm not discussing this with you. How'd you even get in?"

His footsteps told her he followed right behind. "Key hidden under the bunny? Really? I forgot you had a date and came by. When you weren't here, I let myself in. You knew I was coming."

She had. He'd told her Friday he would be by, but when Charlie called to ask about one of Lindsey's assignments then asked her out, she'd pushed Vince to the back of her mind. "Fine. I forgot to tell you I was going out, but how did you know I was with Charlie?"

"Who else would you be with?" She turned in time to see him tuck the towel in his back pocket. "But I'm done, so I'll get my stuff together and get out of your hair." As he walked down the hall, his next words drifted to her. "Glad you and Chuck didn't come in and..." She couldn't hear the end of the sentence but she could imagine.

"We wouldn't have!" she called after him as she went to the kitchen sink, grabbing the empty cup in it. She pushed up on the faucet handle to refill it and take a long, calming drink, but nothing came out. Another stifled scream. He'd turned the water off. It made sense. Now to get him out of here before she killed him.

"Please, Miss Addie?!" Lindsey had her hands clasped together. "Please?"

Addie smiled gently. "A lady does not beg, Lindsey."

"But I'm not a lady. I'm a girl having a birthday party and my dad doesn't know anything about girl birthday parties. Four friends are spending the night and Dad thinks we should *just* watch a movie and have popcorn. But we have to do other stuff, too. And I need a girl to help."

Something twisted inside Addie's stomach. "I never had a slumber party growing up. Not really. A distant cousin stayed with us sometimes but it is not quite the same. I am afraid I will not be much help." Christiana was younger even than Addie's siblings. Ana and Rick were eighteen months younger and Christiana nearly a year younger than them.

"I know what I want to do, but Dad can't help us do hair and nails. Your hair and nails always look great. Please?"

Addie stifled a sigh and barely managed a smile. "Very well. If it is acceptable with your father, I will come and help with hair and nails."

Lindsey launched at her and Addie barely had time to brace herself for the assault. "Thank you, Miss Addie!" The girl's arms were flung so tightly around her, Addie could barely breathe and her ribs began to ache.

"Lindsey!" Charlie's voice reverberated throughout the room. "Don't hurt her!"

His daughter pulled back. "Oh no! Miss Addie did I hurt you? I forgot about your ribs."

The ache intensified a bit, but not too much, as she tried to regain her breath. "I know you did not mean to, Lindsey. And truly, I am mostly feeling much better."

Charlie stood behind Lindsey with his hands on her shoulders. "Are you sure she didn't hurt you?"

Addie arched a brow at him. "She did not hurt me nearly so badly as you did."

He winced. "Good point. So what was that all about?"

Lindsey practically bounced. "Miss Addie said she'd come to my slumber party and help us do hair and nails."

"I said I would *if* your father said it would be fine with him. And I will not be spending the night but I will come for a little while if it is okay."

The girl turned in her seat to look up at her father. "Please, Daddy?"

Addie could tell he was struggling with the decision, but finally he nodded. "If Addie would like to and it isn't a scheduling conflict for her, of course she can come."

"Thankyouthankyouthankyou!" Lindsey's words ran together as she leapt up and threw her arms around him. "You're the best."

Charlie gave her a small smile. Somehow it would have to be okay.

This was it. Addie would be coming to his home in just a few minutes. Charlie wondered if her two *friends* would come with her or if they would let her come alone. He double checked the bathroom the girls would use. Clean. The kitchen. Clean. The living room. Clean. His room. A disaster. But Addie wouldn't be in there for any reason.

The doorbell rang and Lindsey bounded out of her - mostly clean - room. "I got it!" She opened the front door and Addie stood there.

While his daughter greeted her, Charlie let himself just drink in the sight of the woman he'd thought he could fall for. The sweater looked as soft as the kittens his aunt loved while he grew up. It was a red color - similar to one his mother loved. Mulberry maybe? Mom had told him a dozen times it wasn't maroon, but he didn't think mulberry was right - mulberry would be more of a purple color.

What did he know? Sure, he ran the paint department, but that's why he had all the little colored squares. Charlie could name them by sight, but for some reason, the talent didn't transfer to sweaters. He might not be a fashion guru, but even he knew the jeans were high quality and not the purposefully ripped ones many women found popular. Her high-heeled black boots weren't the same ones she'd worn the day they went ice skating, but looked just as butter-soft as the other ones.

When they turned away from the door, Addie had her arm around his daughter's shoulders. The sweater, like the hat when they went skating, looked great with Addie's dark hair. And did her lipstick match the sweater?

Charlie knew he shouldn't be looking at her lipstick close enough to notice, but he couldn't help it. He shook himself mentally and took the few steps to the doorway. "Let me get your coat."

Adeline - Addie - gave him a beautiful smile as he helped her shrug out of it. Had he ever felt such soft leather? Further proof this relationship should never progress past friendship, if that. Her wealth alone put her out of his league.

"Thank you." Her accent provided even more proof. She didn't live in the States and wasn't willing to move. The way she acted, the way she carried herself, all indicated she was high class.

And he wasn't.

But this was going to be a long evening, seeing her in his house, interacting with his daughter, and not wishing for what couldn't be.

There was another knock on the door and Lindsey abandoned them to greet her friends. He talked to the girls' mom for a minute. It would help if he could tell the twins apart. Even at eleven, they tended to dress alike, but in different colors. If he could figure out which one wore what color, maybe...

He wouldn't hold his breath.

Ten minutes later, all four girls had arrived. They disappeared into Lindsey's bedroom, leaving him alone with Addie.

"What may I help you with?" she asked looking around and twisting her fingers together.

Charlie walked toward the kitchen. "We're having homemade pizza for dinner. You can help me get those ready, if you don't mind. I know it's not what you signed up for."

He heard her following him. "I have never made pizza before, but I am happy to help if I can."

Once in the kitchen, he pulled the pizza pans out of the cabinet next to the stove. "We're going to make four bases." He'd borrowed pans from his aunt to have enough. "The girls will make their own half a pizza here in a bit and then we'll bake 'em." The dough was already sitting out in bowls on the counter. Pizza he could make, and make well. It probably wouldn't impress her, but he wasn't trying to. He just had to remember that.

Charlie nodded toward one of the bowls. "Grab one and plop it into the pan on the counter by the fridge." His little kitchen didn't usually bother him, but sometimes he wished for a little more elbow room. With both hands, he pinched his ball of dough into two smaller ones. "You're making a deep dish so just use that whole ball and smush it around."

He tossed the dough back and forth a couple times, dropped it on the tray and started to spread it out. A minute later he was done with his first one.

"How do you do that?" She stood there watching him.

It took everything in him not to laugh. "I worked at a pizza place in high school and the first year or so of college. They gave me two options - get good at it or do dishes. I got good."

She tried to toss the ball of dough from one hand to the other but only succeeded in dropping it into the pan. This time he did laugh.

"Here. Watch." He put a little more flare into the toss now that he knew she was watching. Amazed at his own audacity, he winked at her and began working it into shape in his hands before tossing it into the air in true pizzeria style. Her startled gasp brought him some small bit of satisfaction. He might not be high brow but he could toss a pizza with the best of 'em. Tricks were out of the question. It had been too long and he didn't dare drop the dough. There wasn't any more and he was nearly out of flour anyway. Thirty seconds after he set the dough on the new pan, it was ready to go.

"Wow!" Her voice was breathless.

He shot her a puzzled look. "Have you never seen anyone make pizza before?"

Addie shook her head. "No. Mark, Todd and I order pizza sometimes and every once in a great while we will have frozen pizza, but no, I have never seen anyone make a pizza." She poked tentatively at the dough in her pan.

Charlie smiled at her and moved to her side. "Like this." He tried to get to the pan to show her but his angle was wrong. Moving slightly to stand behind her, he reached around, one arm on either side of her as he worked the dough. Her nearness took his breath away, but when he did breathe in, the only thing he noticed was her. Her scent - some kind of flowers and something else he couldn't define. The tease of her hair against his cheek.

Before he could take it all in, her hands were in the pan with his.

"Like this?"

Between them, it was short work to spread the dough. He didn't breathe again the whole time.

Addie turned her head and looked up at him. With every fiber of his being he wanted to kiss her. Right on the wine-colored lips that matched her sweater. To run his fingers through her hair and find out if it felt as soft between them as it did against his chin.

The sound of a door opening across the apartment broke the spell woven around the two of them and he stepped back, clearing his throat. "Just like that."

"Are we ready to make the pizzas?" Lindsey led the stream of girls into the already too-small space.

Charlie took a steadying breath and turned to wash his hands. "Give us about ten more minutes."

The girls turned and ran back to Lindsey's room, yelling something about the new werewolf movie he wouldn't let his daughter watch.

"Oh my." Addie's quiet words caught his attention. "I do not think I knew what I was getting into."

He leaned a hip against the counter as he dried his hands and flipped the towel over his shoulder. "You can still back out if you want."

"No. I just do not know how you do it." Her gold-flecked eyes fixed on his. "How you deal with pre-teen girls. They can be handful for me sometimes at the center, but I am not their parent and I know they feel great desire to please me and do what they are supposed to. Being a single parent is a challenge I am only now starting to appreciate."

With arms crossed in front of him, he didn't flinch under her continued scrutiny. "It's not easy, but it's not like I have much of a choice. After she came to live with me, the only alternative was adoption and by then she'd stolen my heart. I couldn't have done it so I find a way to make it work. My aunt and uncle have been a huge help and support. So has my cousin, who lives with us but is avoiding this place like the plague until the girls go home."

Her eyes finally released his. "What about your parents?"

He turned away and pushed a couple of buttons on the oven before picking up the last ball of dough and beginning to work it. "I've told you a little about them. My mom is an anthropologist and my dad is an archaeologist. They spend most of their time in Europe, the Middle East or North Africa studying ancient civilizations. When I was old enough for Kindergarten, I moved in with my aunt and uncle during the school year. My folks would be home for a few months at a time and had a house here until a few years ago." At one point, he'd hoped they'd let him live there with Lindsey, but they sold it before he broached the subject.

"That had to be difficult for you growing up."

"It was what it was. When it's the only life you know, it's normal." He picked up two pans. "Would you open the oven?"

She did and he slid all three pies onto the racks.

"Now. Time to make the sauce."

8

Addie felt her eyes go wide. He made his own pizza sauce? "Can you not buy pizza sauce?" she asked, feeling more woefully ignorant than she had in a very long time.

His back was to her as he pulled several things out of the cupboard. "You can buy it, but I make it better." When he turned he winked - winked! - at her again. Twice! She did not think she had been winked at twice in her life! "Can you handle a can opener?"

The question would have been insulting if she had not just failed at spreading pizza dough on her own. "Yes. I can."

"Good." He handed it to her along with a big can of whole, peeled tomatoes. "Open, drain, and then empty into the blender."

It took all of her concentration, but she managed to open the can in a reasonable period of time. She did know enough to use the lid to cover most of the can and just let the liquid dribble out around it and into the sink. Feeling quite proud of herself, she turned but the pride left quickly when she saw how much he had accomplished in the same period of time. A small bowl now held measured amount of... She tipped her head to read the labels of the bottles next to him. Salt, oregano, black pepper and she thought those were already-minced cloves of garlic in the baggie next to the bowl.

"Go ahead and dump it in." He set the glass container next to the sink and she did as she was told.

Charlie took it back and sprinkled the contents of the bowl on top if it before reaching for another bottle - this one a liquid. Extra-virgin olive oil. Followed by red wine vinegar. He set the container into the base, put a lid on it and pushed a button. The kitchen filled with a loud whirring sound that made Addie wince but Charlie seemed unconcerned. A few minutes later, he stopped it, removed the lid, stirred and repeated the process.

By the time the buzzer sounded on the stove timer, he'd declared it ready. He dipped a wooden spoon into the mixture and held it out to her, his hand cupped underneath to make sure none dripped. "Try it," he encouraged.

Addie took a small taste and then a bit bigger one. "Delicious." She stepped back, a bit further away from his physical appeal. "You certainly know what you are doing."

The beeping had gone on long enough to be annoying. Charlie grinned at her as he pulled a pot holder out of a drawer. "I told you I had plenty of practice, but this is a recipe I found online."

The girls came back as he set the three non-deep dish pans on the table. Already there were toppings of all kinds. Lindsey was not new to this and gave instructions. Soon her half was loaded with extra Mozzarella, black olives, pepperoni and green peppers. Addie could not see what the others did. About the time they finished, Charlie pulled the other base out of the oven.

"You said you like deep dish, right?" he asked her.

She nodded, surprised he remembered the comment she had made in passing while in the emergency room several weeks earlier.

"Good. You get half of this one, and I get the other half."

Her eyes grew wide again. "I cannot eat half of that pizza. Can you?"

"Oh, yeah. I might not, but I could. You can take the rest home or one of us will eat it later. But I won't finish making this one until later. After the girls are done. I'm the waiter and chef tonight, after all."

The pizzas went back in the oven and Addie went to the living room with the girls. They went through the different nail polishes and hair magazines they all brought. One of the twins tried to convince her they should put on make-up, too, but Addie put her foot down on that even if the girl had brought some with her. These girls were too young for that - and none of them needed it anyway. They were all beautiful.

Charlie announced the pizzas were finished and the girls flocked into the dining room to eat. Addie got things ready in the living room and when the girls returned twenty minutes later, she showed one how she wanted them to brush their hair out and started doing Lindsey's nails. She would never admit to anyone, but she had spent a fair bit of time on the computer learning how to do some of this. She paid to have manicures and pedicures and to get her hair done, but she would do her best to show the girls. Maybe she should take Lindsey for a mani-pedi for her birthday. Except she would not be taking any of the other girls. Or would she? Maybe they could go as a group a few days before the banquet.

The next ninety minutes passed quickly. All five girls had their fingernails done. They were going to do their toes while they watched a movie in Lindsey's room. She had also done more French braids and twists than she ever had. Since moving to the States, she had learned how to do far more of that than she ever had at home. Why they wanted a French twist before going to bed she did not know, but she had done her best to accommodate their requests.

Finally, she sank onto the couch as Lindsey's door closed behind the girls.

"Worn out?" Charlie stood in the opening between the living room and the kitchen. He crossed one foot over the other and leaned against the wall. When he crossed his arms over his chest and smiled, she had to look away and blink back tears. Why had God seen fit for her to be truly attracted to a man for the first time only to have that man be completely off-limits?

But she nodded anyway. "Yes. I had no idea doing hair and nails could be so taxing. Stylists have new respect from me."

He walked toward her and held out his hands. "Come help me finish making this pizza and then we can eat."

She grasped them and let him help her stand. Once in the kitchen, she realized he already had everything out and waiting again.

"What do you want on your half?"

"Just cheese is fine."

His hand went to his heart as he faked chest pain. "Say it ain't so! A pizza isn't really a pizza without toppings." He waggled his brows her direction. "Nothing that goes in a salad or on a sandwich of course, but toppings galore."

"What do you put on yours?"

Charlie's laugh filled the small kitchen. "After I said all that, I'm going simple tonight. Barbecue chicken." He pointed to the pan. "I even cut the dough in half already. It'll be easier to get apart that way and since I'll put barbecue sauce on my side instead of pizza sauce, I thought it would be better that way." His eyes held a challenge. "Will you at least try it?"

She could not back down. "I will try a bit, but I will not promise to like it."

"That's all I ask."

When the half barbecue chicken, half cheese pizza was back in the oven, Charlie cleaned up the kitchen while she watched. Addie wanted to volunteer to help, but even here, she did not have to at home. When they first arrived, she tried to convince Mark and Todd she should do her fair share. They refused to let her.

The timer sounded as he put the last plate in the dishwasher. Charlie took the pizza out and told her to help herself to a soda from the fridge. Instead, she chose a bottle of water.

They spent dinner talking about favorite meals. Addie did her best to avoid naming things too fancy, though fancy meals with names her friends at school had never heard of were commonplace when she was at home. Still, Charlie did not recognize a number of things she mentioned.

She carried her dishes to the kitchen and wondered if she would be leaving momentarily. Though there could be no future with Charlie, she enjoyed his company and would not mind staying a bit longer.

"Do you need to go?" he asked as he put the last of their dishes in the dishwasher. "Or would you like to stay and watch a movie or something?"

Mark and Todd were at the restaurant across the street, sitting in a position to watch the apartment. What would they think if she made them sit there longer? They would not say anything unless it got to be too late, but she did not like to do things that made their lives more difficult.

A glance at the clock told her she had a bit of time before she had told them to expect her to be done. The earliest she had figured on was ten. They had plenty of time to watch a movie before then and she told Charlie she could stay.

They sat on the couch together and watched a romantic comedy he picked out, saying it was one of his aunt's favorites. Close to each other, but not close enough to be touching. Close enough to have a tantalizing glimpse into the life she longed to have but not close enough to believe it could truly be real.

No. When she married, she would likely marry a man her parents and Parliament could agree was a wise choice. Since she had yet to meet one of those men who she did more than tolerate, her marriage would probably be one of mutual respect and possibly some affection, but no real love.

It was not what she had dreamed of since she was a little girl when she would go into the highest tower of the palace and dream of her prince riding up on a white horse and rescuing her. Even when she grew older and determined to rescue herself, she still wished for a man to come alongside her to love her and help her as she tried to guide her country eventually.

The reality settled over her like a dense fog. If she loved her eventual husband, or if he loved her, was secondary to other considerations. No matter what she wished, her country had to come first.

Addie felt more like Adeline than she ever had while in Serenity Landing. For most of the last five and a half years, there had been two parts to herself. Adeline, the Crown Princess and royalty who lived in a world where no one was "real" and nearly everyone wanted a piece of her or something she could give them. And Addie, the still very formal, but more laid back international student at Serenity Landing University, who still had very few friends but who discovered more of "herself", who she was without the trappings of the palace.

But when she agreed to dinner with Jonathan, he'd told her they were headed for Savarino's, one of Springfield's nicest restaurants. That meant a nice dress and heels along with a good overcoat. She heard the crunch of tires on the drive and, with one last look in the mirror, decided her attire was appropriate.

When she reached the second step from the bottom, the doorbell rang. Todd lay in wait and reached it before she could. A hushed conversation ensued before Jonathan entered the foyer. As she expected, he wore a well-tailored grey suit with a long black overcoat. One part of her mind noted his sharp, highly polished dress shoes while the rest of her focused on his smile.

"Good evening, Adeline." Jonathan bowed slightly at the waist, though she had told him to forgo all of the protocols he would have been expected to follow if they were in Montevaro. At least he had forgone the title with the name.

For whatever reason - and she had every intention of getting it out of Jonathan - Mark and Todd allowed her to go without them. Jonathan's hand rested low on her back as he guided her to the Jaguar still running in the drive. He held her door, as she expected he would, and smoothly shifted into first gear.

"How did you do it?" They had not yet left the driveway before she posed the question.

"Do what?" He flashed a grin her way. "Get the boys to stay home?"

She nodded.

"Simple. The security threats to me at the moment are greater than to you. But they are still minor at worst. I have spent time learning multiple martial arts since I was young and I am more than able to defend both myself and you should the need arise. Given those things and my lack of a security detail, they agreed to let us go unchaperoned."

"Thank you." How long had it been since she had been anywhere without a guard? The accident, of course, but besides that? Ever? There was something freeing about it. If only she and Charlie...

No! She may not have been on many dates with a man of her own choosing but she knew it was bad form to think of another man.

They talked quietly about anything but school until they reached the valet stand. One opened the door for Jonathan. Another opened her door as Jonathan reached it, in time to offer his hand to help her out of the low slung vehicle. Her hand tucked inside his elbow, they made their way into the restaurant. There was no mistaking it for anything but what it was. Made for romance.

Dim lighting, a dance floor, and a strolling violinist created an ambiance she had not found in the Serenity Landing area before this night.

As she anticipated, dinner was exquisite. She declined Jonathan's request to dance, citing her still sore ribs. Conversation easily flowed from one topic to another, finding they had much in common.

By the time they reached her front door, Addie had enjoyed herself, but feared he would try to kiss her. For reasons she could not explain, not even to herself, she was not ready for her first kiss, ever.

"Good night, Princess Adeline." Jonathan's eyes twinkled and he tried, and failed, to keep the corners of his mouth from tugging upward. He leaned over and landed a gentle kiss on her cheek. "Thank you for a lovely evening. I do hope we can do it again sometime soon."

Addie nodded. "I would like that, Jonathan." A moment later, she entered the house, surprised by the lack of male presence. Had both of her shadows decided not to grill her about her evening?

She made it to her room without seeing either one of them. After getting ready for bed, Addie forced herself to assess the evening. All in all, it had been wonderful, nearly perfect even. There were none of the "sparks" romance novels implied she should expect, or like she had felt before. As she slid under the covers, she could think of only one thing wrong with her evening.

Jonathan was not Charlie.

The smell of roasting venison hit Charlie full force when he entered the Grace Community Chapel rec room. Several of the men called hello and he waved back.

The Beast Feast.

What guy could pass that up? Held four times a year, the "no vegetables allowed" policy attracted many of the men from the church and a number from the community at large. As Charlie reached for a thick paper plate, a hand clapped him on the back. He turned to see Pastor Geoff smiling at him.

"Charlie! How've you been?"

The man's gentle spirit always put Charlie at ease. "Pretty good. Just finishing up my MBA and hoping to find something in my field."

"I've missed seeing you in service."

Charlie should have known Pastor would notice. "They've had me working a lot of Sundays lately. I'm supposed to be off the next few weekends, so hopefully..." He reached for the napkins. "I've been listening to the podcasts of last year's series on Kings David and Solomon. Definitely worth a second listen."

"Not the same as being here, though."

"No. It's not, but hopefully I'll be here the next few weeks and once I get a..." He held up one finger on each hand as he tried not to drop the plate and napkins and made finger quotes. "'real' job, it'll be easier to be here regularly."

Rather than circulating, Geoff picked up a plate and fell in line behind Charlie. "How're your folks doing? They haven't been home in a while."

Charlie shrugged. "I haven't talked to them in a while. Last I heard, they were in southeastern Europe hot on the trail of some ancient mystery."

Geoff chuckled. "Hot on the trail? Archeologists?"

"Dad is. Mom's an anthropologist. I'm not sure what it is, but they think they figured out some ancient secret and are excavating in Greece or something. Italy, maybe?" He shrugged. "I'm not really sure. They call when they can, but they tend to keep their work pretty close to the vest until they're ready to share it with the world." He put a thick slice of smoked ham on his plate and reached for the spoon in a crock pot full of chili.

"You do know that's Wes's famous chili right?"

Charlie chuckled. "Guaranteed to put hair on your chest."

Another man pulled Geoff's attention toward the grill and Charlie continued down the line. He exchanged pleasantries with several men he knew, though none he knew well. When he reached the end of the table, his plate was piled high with nearly every kind of meat and wild game imaginable. Looking around, he caught sight of Dan waving him over to a half empty table.

A few minutes later, the round table had only one empty seat. Two of the men were dads of Lindsey's friends. He wasn't sure where he fit. Age wise, he could belong in the college and career group, but for some reason, it had never really taken off at GCC. Neither had a singles group. They had a monthly get together for anyone in college and anyone out of college *and* single *and* under the age of thirty. That wasn't how it was billed, but was the reality. Charlie didn't fit. He hadn't fit in the high school group after Lindsey was born, though the youth pastor did his best. Neither did he now fit in the groups with the other parents. Few of them were single parents and even fewer were parents at sixteen. Men's group was an exception at least for the last couple of years when he finally felt he might belong with the "men."

A plate found its way onto the table next to Charlie. He looked over to see Vince Parker pulling out the chair. Vince had been a couple years ahead of him at Serenity Landing High, but Charlie knew Tricia and Sam had been friends with Vince and his buddies. Chatter flowed easily around the table as the St. Louis Cardinals top prospects were debated, the Kansas City Chiefs dismal season dissected, and the Serenity Landing High Patriots basketball teams chances to win back-to-back state championships.

About the time most of the men finished eating, Pastor Geoff stepped to the microphone on the kids' church stage. "Good evening, gentleman!" He made several announcements, including the date of the next Feast then opened his Bible. "I promise I won't take long, but you had to know I'd take an opportunity to get a little bit of preaching in."

Charlie noticed Vince check out as soon as the Bible appeared. He wasn't a regular attendee but had been invited by his brother, who had been kept home with a sick wife and son at the last minute.

After Geoff finished his short lesson on trusting God to work things out for His glory, Charlie found himself alone at the table with Vince.

Vince cut straight to the heart of things, though Charlie wouldn't have suspected the topic. "So, Charlie, you're dating Sam?"

"We've gone out a couple of times. I don't know I'd classify it as 'dating' just yet. Certainly nothing exclusive." What interest did Vince have? Wasn't he Lindsey's PE teacher? He must see Sam regularly, but this was more than that.

Vince leaned closer. "She's been hurt in the past. Don't be the one to hurt her again." He didn't expound on his statement but pushed back from the table and walked off.

Charlie watched as he did. Something in the way Vince said it made Charlie wonder if the teacher was one of the ones who had hurt Sam in the past. It also made Charlie wonder what Vince's feelings for Sam were at present. Because that wasn't the statement of a man who didn't have a vested interest in the outcome of a woman's relationship.

Dan interrupted Charlie's thoughts. He'd have to figure it out later.

Addie sat in the passenger seat of the Land Rover as Jonathan walked around the front. "I am sorry," she started as he opened her door.

"Don't be," he interrupted before she could go any further. "I've put this thing through worse than parking in grass." He held out a hand and helped her down, her heels sinking in the soft turf. "You had no idea the parking lot would be so full."

"I should have known. Every fourth grader in the building has a project on display tonight." Even though school had been out for several days because of another ice storm that hit the area, it seemed like the entire town of Serenity Landing had shown up. Addie had just been grateful her house had not been one of the many to lose power. It seemed the line of the storm had cut through downtown and further south, but not to the north where she had lived. She did not understand why the line was so abrupt, but Jonathan told her it was not unusual. His home had lost power, but had back-up generators.

With her hand tucked securely in his elbow, they reached the cracked asphalt of the parking lot. Her heart pounded in her chest as she prayed Charlie had not yet arrived. She had overheard Lindsey telling Mrs. Hart he would not get off work until six-thirty and hoped to make it to the last few minutes of the Night at the Museum exhibit. She hoped to avoid seeing him while with Jonathan.

"How many of your girls will be here?" Jonathan pulled open one of the double doors and let her precede him in. Mark and Todd were around, but Addie could not see either one of them.

"Four have projects on display, but several others may be here."

A woman with short, reddish hair stood in the middle of the hallway, welcoming visitors and pointing them the right direction for their child's class. She turned to smile at Addie. "Welcome to Serenity Landing East Elementary. Can I help you find a class?"

"We are looking for Miss Dean, Mrs. Long, and Mrs. Hoodenpyle."

The woman nodded and pointed down the hall. "Mrs. Long and Mrs. Hoodenpyle are in the gym. Miss Dean's class is in the library."

Addie held out her hand. "Thank you very much, Mrs..."

The other woman smiled warmly. "Brown. I'm the principal around here."

"It is a pleasure to meet you, Mrs. Brown. Thank you for your assistance."

Mrs. Brown's eyes narrowed and her gaze flitted from Addie to Jonathan and back. "Pardon my question, but are you Addie by any chance?" At Addie's nod, she went on. "I've heard a fair bit about you from the Club girls and Mrs. Hart. Thank you for your work with them."

"It is my pleasure, truly." After speaking with her for another moment, they headed for the library. Every empty area was filled with displays about famous folks, both living and deceased.

Jonathan stopped at the first display. "Jackie Robinson was one of the greats."

Addie's brows pulled together. "Jackie who? I am afraid the only Jackie I can think of is Jackie Kennedy."

Jonathan chuckled as a boy of around twelve moved took a couple of steps toward them. "Jackie Robinson was the first African-American to play professional baseball."

She could feel a blush cover her face. "Oh." The next few minutes was spent asking the young man, in a baseball uniform with the number "42", questions about Mr. Robinson. Rather, Addie asked and she watched Jonathan try to contain his smirk. Thanking the young man, they moved on. After two more displays - one about Albert Einstein, complete with dry ice smoking, and another about Walt Disney - Addie realized they would have to skip many of them if they were to find the four girls and leave before Charlie arrived. They reached the end of an aisle of books and turned the corner.

There were no displays, but several voices came from inside an open door.

One drifted out. "I thought all of the girls loved the new lady. She's donated a lot of money to The Club and I've noticed several pay better attention in class." Could they be talking about her?

Another voice answered. "Seems like she's made of money so a few thousand to fix up that old building doesn't mean a whole lot." The voice took on an affected, and awful, British accent. At the first words, Addie knew she was being made fun of. "I do hope I don't ruin my nails while I *supervise*." Her heart squeezed in her chest. It was not the first time someone had made fun of her and it would not be the last.

There was no laughter. "Sam, you really shouldn't..."

Jonathan cleared his throat and stepped around the corner. "Pardon me, but could any of you tell me where to find Lindsey Brewer's project?"

One of the women, a lovely brunette in her mid-thirties, stepped out of the room. "Of course. This way." She walked down the aisle. "Are you friends of Lindsey's?"

"Yes." Addie gave only the one word answer, fearful the tremor in her voice would show if she said any more. She felt Jonathan take her hand and squeeze lightly in support as they turned the corner.

Lindsey turned as they approached her corner of the library. "Miss Addie!" She ran over and gave Addie a big hug. "I'm so glad you came!"

The brunette's face paled, but her smile remained pasted in place. "So you're Miss Addie." She held out a hand. "I've heard lovely things about you from Lindsey and the other girls. I'm Mrs. Summers, the librarian."

Addie shook her hand, giving a tight smile. She should be used to women being catty. In school, she had overheard more than her share of conversations about her assumed snobbery. In truth, she had always wanted to have girlfriends her own age, but the few times she opened herself up to it, she found herself hurt, quite deeply more than once. This woman, at least, seemed to have been uncomfortable with the statement made, even if she had not ardently disapproved. "Lovely to meet you, Mrs. Summers."

Lindsey did not give Addie a chance to chat with the other woman, but directed Addie's attention toward her project. "Look at this, Miss Addie. Remember the research you helped me with?"

The young girl chattered excitedly about the Duchess of Cambridge. Addie found her smile becoming more real. She had met Prince William on a number of occasions growing up, though she was several years younger even than Prince Harry. She and both of her siblings had attended the wedding several years earlier, attended a few functions with the Duchess and rejoiced with the rest of the world when their first child, Prince George Alexander Louis, arrived.

While helping Lindsey with the research, Addie took great care not to let her personal acquaintance taint the project. To her relief, Jonathan took over asking questions, drawing Lindsey's attention away from Addie. After several moments, she felt composed enough to ask a question or two of her own, though she already knew the answers. Breathing a sigh of relief, Addie told Lindsey she would see her in a few days and headed for Megan's project on the Queen Elizabeth. Between the two, another young woman had done a project on the Princess of Wales.

"Quite the royal collection," Jonathan murmured, a smirk on his face.

"Yes. Quite."

"Very British."

That brought a smile to her face. Though Montevaro did have a British heritage, few familiar with the countries would mistake one accent for the other.

Megan was occupied talking with several other people about the queen's long reign. Addie and Jonathan decided to visit her other young ladies and then return. Uneasiness filled her as they returned to the library. A glance at the clock in the hallway told her Charlie should still be at work, but one never knew if he would have managed to leave early.

When they reached Megan's display, she was as excited to see Addie as the other girls had been. A few minutes later, as they were finishing discussing the queen with Megan, Addie heard Lindsey's excited squeal. Charlie had arrived.

9

C harlie watched his daughter from a few feet away, a bit nostalgic at the sight of the pipe cleaner tiara sitting on her head. He'd already seen Sam's assessment of the project and he was inclined to agree. She'd done a great job.

He listened as she went through her presentation with another student's family, pride swelling his chest as she answered every question thrown at her. Something else caught his attention and his mood fell when Addie walked into view with another man at her side.

She smiled politely, but he could tell the situation made her as uncomfortable as it did him. "Hello, Charlie."

"It's good to see you, Addie."

He shook hands with the man she introduced only as Jonathan. Something about him looked familiar, though Charlie couldn't quite put his finger on it. After a few awkward words about the weather and the projects, she and Jonathan smiled their good-byes. While he waited for Lindsey to finish talking with her friends' parents, he checked out a few of the other exhibits.

One gave him information he would have preferred to live

without. One of the boys in Lindsey's class had done his presentation on one of America's leading political families. Justin told everyone he spoke with that he'd had a chance to talk to the nephew of the sitting U.S. Senator from North Carolina. When Charlie looked more closely, he realized it was Jonathan, Addie's... friend.

And that ended that. For certain. No way Charlie could compete with someone like Jonathan even if he and Addie were to end up in geographic proximity to each other.

He wandered around for a few more minutes before finding Lindsey in between guests. She told him about some of her friends' parents who had stopped by, but something seemed a bit off. Her eyes didn't have their usual sparkle, but she put up a good front. No one else would notice, except maybe Sam. And with the cold shoulder Lindsey appeared to be giving her teacher, he wondered if she didn't have something to do with it.

As they walked to the car an hour later, he tried to draw it out of her.

"I don't want to talk about it" was the only answer he got. A while later, he sat on her bed for nighttime prayers.

He sat against her headboard, legs stretched out in front of him as she leaned against his shoulder. She wanted to talk, but had to be in her own time. Finally, she spoke.

"I heard Miss Dean say something tonight, Daddy."

Charlie wrapped his arm a little tighter around his daughter. "What did you hear?"

"She said something about Miss Addie being snooty and it didn't surprise her that you broke up with her." Did he hear tears in her voice? "Is it true? Did you break up with Miss Addie because she's snooty?"

So many loaded questions and information in that statement. "First, Addie and I were never really a couple, so there wasn't a break up. We decided not to date each other anymore because she's going back to Europe after graduation and we're staying in

Serenity Landing. Second, has Miss Addie ever been snooty with you?"

Lindsey shook her head against him. "No. She's super nice. She talks real formal and stuff, but she's great. She even helped Mrs. Hart find Megan's dad a job."

"So if Miss Addie's never been snooty with you, there's a couple options. What do you think they are?"

"Well..." A moment passed in silence. "Maybe Miss Dean doesn't like Addie for some reason or maybe Miss Addie said something that Miss Dean took the wrong way?"

"Two good options." He had a couple others, but letting her think it through was a good exercise for her. "Any others?"

"I misunderstood Miss Dean?"

"Possible."

"It's possible it wasn't Miss Dean." Her defensive tone surprised him. "Except I know it was and I know what I heard."

"Okay then. If you heard her right, what do you think you should do?" He didn't know what the right answer was. Maybe Lindsey would come up with it.

"Give Miss Dean the benefit of the doubt or confront her about it are the only two things I could think of."

Good. She'd been thinking through options even before she'd told him. "What do you think?"

Lindsey gave a deep sigh. "Give her the benefit of the doubt."

Charlie kissed the side of her head. "I think that's probably the best plan."

"I'm not wrong, though, Daddy. I know it was her and I know I heard her right." She looked up at him with her big blue eyes, filled with tears. "I heard some other stuff too, but I'm not completely sure it was Miss Dean. It might have been Mrs. Summers, but I don't think so."

"Mrs. Summers is your librarian?" Lindsey nodded. "Why don't you think it was her?

"They sound different. Mrs. Summers has an Australian accent because she grew up in Sydney."

Good point. Very little chance of mixing the two up. They sat there for several more minutes before saying bedtime prayers and Charlie left her room. He pulled the door nearly closed behind him, turning over what Lindsey had said in his mind. It didn't surprise him, unfortunately, that Sam would be snarky though he hadn't a clue why she'd be snarky about Addie. He didn't know Addie well, but he had a feeling she didn't have a snarky bone in her body.

Charlie headed into his own room and went through his bedtime routine. He sat against his headboard, Bible propped open on his raised knees. *Okay, God. I could use some guidance here.*

Half an hour later, he slid under the covers, no closer to an answer than he was before.

Jonathan trotted up the steps to the family home in North Carolina. Though built in the style of an Antebellum home, it was much newer. His family had owned the property since about the time of the American Revolution, but the original home had been destroyed during the Civil War. The next house had been much more humble, until his grandfather built this one several decades earlier.

Not bothering to knock, he walked right into the two story foyer - always pronounced foy-yay, not foy-yer - and wondered where his grandmother would be. In her room or in the sunroom?

The first person he saw wasn't a member of the family at all, but rather his grandmother's secretary of nearly thirty years. "Jonathan! What a pleasant surprise!" The woman squeezed him tight enough to knock out all the air. "Your grandmother will be so pleased!"

He laughed as she moved away. "Hello, Mrs. MacDouglas. How are you?"

"Oh, you know me." She patted his stomach. "I'm just fine. What brings you to this part of the country?"

"I had a long weekend and decided to visit Grandmama. Where is she?" Jonathan picked up an apple and bit into it as they worked their way into the kitchen.

"Upstairs in her bed, convinced she's dying." He didn't see Mrs. MacDouglas roll her eyes but was sure she did.

"Is she?"

"Of course not, but you know how she is."

Jonathan chuckled and walked quickly up the staircase, munching on his apple. He knocked lightly on the door waited for his grandmother call for him to come in. She lay in the middle of a large four poster bed, looking much better than Jonathan would have expected given the weak sound of her voice in the message she left him.

"Good morning, grandmother." He kept his voice cheerful. "How are you this fine morning?"

"Jonathan, is that you?" The lilting sound of her voice floated across the room. She patted the bed. "Sit by me, dear?"

A minute later, he sat on the chenille comforter and held her hand in his. Grandmama was a slight, if formidable, woman. He ran his the pad of his thumbs along the veins covering the bony fingers. Sturdier than she looked, Grandmama often played to her supposed fragility.

They talked for nearly an hour about the weather, the Carolina Panthers, and the upcoming Senate race in North Carolina. He could think of no reason why his uncle wouldn't win reelection but Grandmama always thought of every scenario.

"Promise me, Jonathan?" Her green eyes sparkled with unshed tears.

"Promise you what?"

"Don't be like your cousin. Arthur is no help to his father and his wife refuses to let him put their family on stage for the acceptance speeches or election functions. Jocelyn has done more to hurt our family's image than even your brother."

Jonathan winced. True, Phil kept most of his incidents out of the papers, but a few had snuck through. Arthur though..."Grandmama, she's just trying to protect her family."

She waved one hand through the air. "Posh. Jocelyn simply doesn't like me or my son. She won't outright sabotage the campaign, but she won't lift a finger to help it."

He did his best to be diplomatic. "I know you remember what her father went through when that man stalked him and threatened her." Jocelyn's father was a local weatherman. When a hurricane came through South Carolina, this man had refused to evacuate. When it all ended, his family was dead. In his mind, it was the fault of Jocelyn's father and he came after all of them. It ended quickly and peacefully, but Jocelyn had no intention of putting her family in the spotlight. Just marrying Arthur pushed her level of comfort nearly too far into the spotlight with her two-year-old son.

"Arthur already pays for security. What would it hurt to help out her father-in-law?" Grandmama seemed to sink into the pillows behind her. "I do know he loves her and, despite what all of you think, I do care about your happiness, but reason must come into it as well. You need to marry a girl who will be an asset to our family, not a detriment." She pointed a bony finger at him. "I would imagine your other grandmother feels the same way after what her other grandchildren have done."

What "her other grandchildren have done" was marry wonderful, Christian, middle class men and women who wanted quiet lives, just as his cousins did. Jonathan didn't blame them.

Of course, he was the one dating a princess. And not just any princess, a *Crown Princess*.

What Grandmama would do with that information!

Jonathan refused to share it, though he was tempted. He

started to say something, but his phone buzzed in his pocket. Ignoring it, he focused his attention on the woman next to him.

"Who is that, dear?"

He gave her his best smile. "Doesn't matter. The only woman I want to talk to is right here next to me."

She pashaw'd. "What if it's that lovely Paulson girl? You wouldn't want to ignore her for the likes of me."

At her urging he pulled his phone out and checked his missed calls. Addie. "Nope. Not Ida-Belle Paulson. Someone I can call back later." Addie would have taken him to task for interrupting his time with his grandmother to talk to her, though his grandmother wouldn't see it that way. She would have him drop everything to speak with a princess.

"Are you dating anyone, young man? Is that why you don't want to talk to her?"

"It wasn't her, Grandmama."

"But you wouldn't have talked to her anyway. So are you dating someone?"

Jonathan hesitated, then nodded. "A girl I go to school with. You've never met her. She's from a very old, very well-respected family in Europe and that's all I'm going to say about it unless and until it turns into something more serious." He enjoyed spending time with Addie, but would it develop into something more? Only time would tell.

After another hour with his grandmother, he gave her a kiss on the cheek and squeezed her hand, promising to be a good boy and make her proud - just like he had since he was little. Once back in the Mercedes he borrowed from his uncle, Jonathan called Addie, using the Bluetooth to talk to her for a few minutes and confirm their study session Monday night.

He spent the rest of the day with family, Addie always hovering in the back of his mind. Where were they headed? Grandmama would no doubt approve.

But was he good enough?

Deep down, Jonathan wondered if her family would approve, think he was good enough for a princess. Despite the family tree his grandmothers constantly reminded him of, he had a feeling there was *some* reason he'd be found wanting. If only he knew what it was.

Charlie remained quiet and contemplative as he picked Sam up for another date. Lindsey had spent most of her time in her room, not nearly as chattery as she usually was. When he asked her about it, she just shrugged and said she had a lot on her mind.

"Where are we going?" Sam texted someone and then set her phone on her leg as Charlie pulled out of her driveway.

"I thought we'd go to Serenity Landing Steakhouse for dinner." He liked a good steak as much as the next guy and he knew Sam liked it there.

"Sounds good." Her phone buzzed on her leg and she peeked at it smiling, typing back a message and setting it back.

A conversation of silence filled the car until they reached the eatery. Charlie opened her door for her, was the perfect gentleman his uncle, and to a lesser extent his dad, had raised him to be.

When they made it inside, the wait had reached nearly 45 minutes, but Sam insisted she wanted to wait. Charlie followed her to the far end of the waiting area. The country music meant they had to yell to be heard, keeping their words to a minimum. When a family with three young children, including one still in a car seat, came in, Charlie stood, letting the mom have his seat. The change in position made it impossible for him to talk to Sam. She texted a couple of times, but mostly they both just sat there.

He did notice when she stiffened and followed her gaze to see Vince on the other end.

Vince looked back at her, and if Charlie wasn't mistaken, their eyes locked. The two stared at each other for a good minute before Vince broke the contact. Charlie looked down at Sam to see her staring at the black screen of her phone. He didn't say anything, and neither did she, but after a few minutes, their number popped up on the screen.

Charlie let Sam go ahead of him, following the waitress but declining to pick out his own steak. Once they reached their table in a back corner, the noise had dimmed enough he knew they'd be able to have the talk he'd been thinking about for two days.

"Did you ever date Vince?" Charlie jumped right in, staring at his menu as he spoke.

Sam took a sip of her water and looked out the window. "We've gone on two dates, if that's what you want to know. Once in high school and once in college."

Charlie looked at her over the top of his menu. "I don't remember you dating Vince. I remember you could barely stand him our senior year."

"I couldn't stand him by then. We went out on one date about the time Tricia told all of us about..." Her words ended, but he heard the rest of the sentence anyway. *When Tricia told all of us about the baby.*

And that told him all he needed to know. He couldn't remember much of those first few weeks, trying to talk Tricia out of an abortion and trying to figure out how they were going to be parents while going to high school. Telling his aunt and uncle. Calling his parents. Long, late night conversations with Dan about the mistake he'd made and how he regretted it, but could never regret the coming baby. He still felt that way. Charlie could never regret Lindsey.

In the midst of all of that, he wouldn't have noticed if Tricia's best friend had gone on a date with one of the most popular guys in school. "It didn't go well?"

Sam let out a short bark of laughter. "That's the understatement of the decade."

Charlie broke open a roll and slathered it with apple butter. "Then why'd you go out with him again in college?"

She shrugged. "Seemed like a good idea at the time. It went almost worse than the first one."

"And now he's the PE coach at the school?"

Sam took another sip of water and reached for a roll of her own. "As much as I don't like him, he really is great with the kids. He knows when to push them and when they're doing their best."

"Like all good teachers."

The waitress walked up and they placed their orders. After she brought them their drinks, he asked another question.

"Was there something more between you and Vince?"

Sam leaned on her elbows and stared at him. "What's with the third degree about a guy from high school?"

He gave a quick shrug. "I saw the way he looked at you." Charlie, too, leaned in. "And I saw the way you looked at him. Is there something more with you two?"

Dirty blond hair flew through the air as she gave her head a violent shake. "No. There's never been anything. I haven't kissed him in forever. I wouldn't cheat..."

Charlie held up a hand. "Whoa! I didn't say anything about cheating! And we've never defined our relationship as exclusive, so I don't know that either of us could cheat. You see each other nearly every day during the school year, so even if you only went on those two dates, there certainly could be something between you."

The silence stretched on until their food arrived. It wasn't until half of his sirloin was gone that she spoke again. "There might be some truth to what you're saying. There's *something* between me and Vince. An attraction, maybe. But attraction isn't enough for a relationship. You of all people should know that. He's not a man I want to date, much less spend my life with or have children with." Sam gave the whole speech leaning forward, looking straight into Charlie's eyes.

But Charlie leaned away from her and pushed a bit of steak around on his plate. "I can appreciate that, but, Sam, I don't think I'm that man for you either."

She slumped in her seat. "I can't believe you're saying that. We've only gone out on a couple dates." Sam raised an eyebrow at him. "You haven't even kissed me."

"I don't need to kiss you to know this isn't going to work out." He tried to be gentle with the words. No reason to hurt her any more than he had to. "I think, deep down, you know it, too."

A solitary tear streaked down her cheek. She swiped at it with her hand. "Maybe."

When Sam went back to eating, Charlie did, too. At least until a shadow fell over the table. He looked up to see the man of the hour standing there. "Hey, Vince."

Vince nodded at him, but kept his eyes focused on Sam. "You all right?"

Sam shrugged. "Yeah." She looked over at Charlie. "You ready?"

The bill hadn't arrived, but Charlie pulled his wallet out of his pocket and tossed some cash on the table. "Sure."

Vince didn't move out of his way. "Are you sure, Samantha?"

Something about his words got Sam's attention and she looked straight at him. Charlie watched her nod and take a deep breath. "Would you mind taking me home, Vince?"

It didn't surprise Charlie that she wanted someone else to take her home. It did surprise him Sam would ask Vince.

Vince nodded his agreement. "Sure."

Sam gathered her things and stood, nodding at Charlie. "Thank you, Charlie. I'll talk to you soon."

Charlie nodded and sat there, waiting for them to walk away. Giving Sam plenty of time to get out of the restaurant before he followed. He hadn't brought up the thing about Addie but he took the chance to compare the relationships, such as they were. With

Sam, they went to full service restaurants. He didn't dare suggest something as mundane as ice skating or as low key as Cee's Bakery and Bistro.

But Addie was obviously the one who should, by every right, demand nicer dates. The vehicles she and her roommates drove, the clothes she wore, all spoke of money. But Addie seemed to love the ice skating trip - until he landed on her, of course - and had mentioned the idea of bowling some day at Lindsey's birthday party.

With a sigh, he stood and left the money sitting on the table. He may not have a future with Addie, but he knew he didn't have a future with Sam. Good thing he figured it out before Lindsey got too attached to the idea.

If only she wasn't still hooked on the idea he'd somehow end up with Addie. Because that wasn't going to happen.

Addie used the key Mrs. Hart had given her to let herself into the recreation room. The carpet had yet to be pulled up but it was time to start painting. A few paint stains would not matter since it would be replaced anyway.

If only she knew what to do.

After finding a water leak in the kitchen, it had taken three more weeks to get ready to finally paint.

Weeks where she and Charlie had been unfailingly polite to each other.

Weeks where she had gotten to know both him and his daughter better.

Weeks where she had had great difficulty sleeping because she lay awake wishing there was some way to bridge the gap between what she knew had to be and what she wished could be.

She propped her fists on her hips and looked around, trying to decide what she should do first. Charlie had told her nothing needed to be taped off as the moldings and trim had been removed and would be replaced.

Addie jumped when her cell phone buzzed in her pocket. "Hello?"

"Addie, this is Ginny Hart."

A smile crossed Addie's face. "Hello, Mrs. Hart."

"Did you get my voice mail?"

"No."

"We've canceled the work day. Several of the girls are fighting the flu and we decided it would be best to let them rest. I do hope that's okay with you."

"You are right to do so. I noticed myself three days ago that a number of them did not seem to be feeling well."

Mrs. Hart sighed. "I left messages for everyone, but would you mind staying for a few minutes to see if anyone shows up? If they arrive, will you tell them?"

"Of course."

They spoke for another moment and hung up. Addie looked around and tried to decide if she should call Charlie or not. Before she could decide, the metal door creaked open. She turned to see him walking in. His well-worn, paint splattered blue jeans fit like they were made for him. A faded flannel shirt hung open over a T-shirt that had seen better days.

Charlie looked around. "Where is everyone?"

Addie held up her cell phone. "I just spoke with Mrs. Hart. They canceled the work day because so many of the girls are sick. Where is Lindsey?"

"Sick." He looked around. "Do you want to help me get started? The two of us could knock at least some of it out in a few hours."

"I have never painted anything in my life."

A smile crossed his face and melted her heart. "Then I'll teach you."

He showed her how to open the five gallon bucket, how much

to pour into the pan, and how to put the roller brush on the roller itself.

"I could have figured that out on my own, Charlie." She crossed her arms over her chest. "I am not so completely inept that I could not figure out on my own how to put that together."

He grinned again. "I know."

Addie took the roller from him and brandished it his direction. "Do not make fun of me, Charlie, or I will exact my revenge when you least expect it."

Charlie threw back his head and laughed. The sound wrapped around Addie and pulled her in, just a little further, toward what could never be. "I'd like to see you try." He nodded toward the tray full of paint. "Get paint on the roller and then roll it on the wall."

She eyed him cautiously, but did as he said. With one hand, she pushed her sleeve up. She gripped the roller and dipped it in the paint. With her bottom lip caught in her teeth, she tried to get it to roll, but instead she sloshed paint onto the carpet.

The roller dripped paint onto her shoe as she straightened.

"Need help?" The warm voice in her ear made her jump.

And flip paint toward Charlie.

Another chuckle and he moved behind her. "Let me show you." He covered her hand with his own and they bent to get the roller into the paint. Controlling the handle and the brush, he demonstrated how to cover it. "Let it drop, scrape the drips off..." He did. "...and then put it on the wall in a W."

His breath teased her hair and his arm stretched the length of hers as he showed her how to apply the paint to the wall. After a couple Ws, his grip loosened and let her take over.

"You're a natural."

Addie turned her head and realized just how close he was.

Close enough to kiss.

And he certainly seemed to be looking at her lips more so than her eyes. Would he kiss her? Did she want him to? The butterflies in her stomach said she did.

Instead, Charlie seemed to shake himself and moved away. He opened his mouth then closed it again and cleared his throat. "You're doing great." He picked up a brush about two inches wide. "I'm going to do some cutting in at the corners."

Addie nodded and did her best to do as he had shown her. Two hours later, she had made real progress and her arm was beginning to ache.

"Are you hungry?" Once again, he made her jump. But this time she splattered paint on herself.

She swiped at her face with the back of one hand. "Yes. Would you order pizza? My treat."

"Sure." He set his brush down and pulled his phone out.

They worked steadily until the pizza arrived. Addie cleaned up some of the other things while Charlie cleaned the paint brushes. The roller went into the trash. She sank to the ground against an unpainted wall and pulled the pizza box toward her. Pizza was a rarity in Montevaro, served mainly when American dignitaries were visiting and she ate with their children. But since arriving in the United States, she, Todd and Mark ate it about once a month. The rest of the time they either took turns making dinner, ordered out, or ate ones made by a service.

But right now, after working harder than she normally did, a fully loaded pizza from one of the local pizzarias was just what she needed. She took a big bite and savored the flavors even as the cheese continued to string out. Finally, she resorted to the very un-princess-like use of fingers to break it and feed it into her mouth.

"It's good?" Charlie stood over her, an amused grin on her face, holding out a bottle of water.

She nodded and reached for the bottle. "Thank you," she muttered around her mouthful of food. Also very un-princess-like. But so was having paint splatters everywhere and she surely had plenty of those at the moment.

Charlie sat down next to her, one leg straight in front of him and the other knee up to support his forearm. "You've done well today, Addie. I'm proud of you."

"Thank you."

"I mean it. For someone who's never painted before - and I'm guessing hasn't done much manual labor of any kind - you did fantastic."

"You are right. I have never done anything like this before. The closest I would come is..." She thought for a moment. "I am an accomplished horsewoman, or was before I came to the States. I do not get to ride often while at school. Riding a high spirited horse can be very difficult and taxing on one's arms and legs."

"Then I'm doubly proud of you." Charlie leaned over and bumped her shoulder with his. "Stepping outside your box and helping such a great group while you're at it. I'm very glad, and I would be even without Lindsey." He checked his watch. "I'm going to have to get going. My cousin has an unbreakable date with his fiancée tonight. Something about shopping with his soon-to-be mother-in-law. And I don't want to leave my little girl home alone while she's sick."

"And I am certain she will appreciate you being there for her."

They packed their things up and threw their trash away.

Charlie held the door open for her as they exited the building. He made sure the door locked behind them. "Where are your shadows today? I don't think I've ever seen you without them."

"They had a school project to work on today. Believe me when I say they were not happy about sending me over here by myself. I had to stay locked in the building with whoever was here working and then go directly home where they will be in..." She checked her phone. "...about twenty minutes."

She came to a stop next to her SUV. "Thank you for your assistance today, Charlie."

He started to say something, but his phone rang before he could. He held up one finger and turned away.

10

Charlie rubbed his forehead with the heel of his hand. "Are you sure there's no one else?"

"Sorry, but no. There's no one else and Cal is really, really sick."

He ran a hand through his hair. "Okay. I'll figure something out and be there in an hour or so." It took everything in him to muffle a scream. Lindsey had been so upset she wouldn't be able to make the work day that she insisted he go anyway. But Dan had to leave soon. Maybe he could call his aunt? No. His aunt and uncle would be with Dan and his fiancée. Who else?

"What is wrong?"

He pivoted on one heel to see Addie watching him expectantly. "I have to go to work. Perils of being department boss. Big inventory going on tonight. I was supposed to be there but when Lindsey got sick, I got my assistant to cover for me, but now he's sick, too."

"Who is going to stay with Lindsey?" Addie's brows knit together. "You cannot leave her home by herself when she is sick. I cannot offer to go to your house, but if it would be acceptable, she could come to mine. I have some things I absolutely must get done today, but she is welcome to one of my guest rooms or to the couch."

Charlie turned that over in his mind. "She'll have to stay overnight. I won't get off until about two or three, if I'm lucky."

"That will be fine. There is plenty of room."

"Let me ask her, but I don't see what other choice I've got at the moment." He pressed a couple of buttons on his phone until he connected with Lindsey. She still sounded weak and tired, but was excited about spending time with Addie. Once he was armed with directions to her house, he made sure she got off okay then headed to his apartment to pick Linds up.

When he got there, she was ready to go, but lying on the couch, under her favorite blanket. "Are you sure you're up to this, princess?" Charlie kissed her forehead. Burning up and not time for more medicine.

"I'll be fine, Daddy. I'll just lay around at her house instead of here. Maybe we can watch a couple movies together or something."

"She said she has things to do so don't bother her if she's busy."

"I won't."

Charlie called for his cousin to open up the doors for him and he scooped his little girl into his arms.

"Dad!"

"You're not walking when you feel like this, okay?"

"Fine."

Charlie set Lindsey down as gently as he could in the back seat. He followed the directions on his phone until he pulled onto the tree-lined drive. The low whistle when he saw the house couldn't be helped.

"Nice place?" Lindsey's voice sounded weaker than when they'd left the house.

She likely had her eyes closed still, Charlie realized. "Yeah, sweetie. It is." He brought the car to a stop in front of the main entrance. "Stay here while I go make sure it's still okay." He bounded up the brick staircase and shook his head slightly at the solid wood door surrounded by some kind of glass panes. He didn't recognize what kind it was though. Odd since he worked at a home improvement store.

The doorbell he recognized as a high end brand and the chimes could be heard outside.

A minute later, footsteps sounded and the door was opened by a much cleaner Addie.

"Hello!" Her smile was bright, but she sounded a bit out of breath.

Her hair was wet and curled around her face. "Hi."

Addie looked around. "Where is Lindsey?"

Charlie pointed behind him. "In the car. Are you sure this isn't too much of an imposition?"

"Not at all. Shall we take her to one of the spare bedrooms? There is a television and DVD player and On Demand movies."

He turned and headed down the stairs to the car, returning a minute later with Lindsey in his arms. "Where are we headed?"

Addie moved to the side to let him in. "Upstairs. Left at the top, second door on the right."

Charlie didn't watch to see her follow him, but her footsteps told him she did. He walked into the bedroom, more nicely decorated than any he'd ever been in. The bedding was already turned down and he set Lindsey on the bed. "Are you going to be okay, sweetie?"

She nodded. "I think I'm gonna take a nap if that's okay with Miss Addie."

Addie leaned against the door frame. "It absolutely is fine with me. You rest and if you need anything let me know. I can show you how to use the television later if you want to or bring you something to eat. Whatever you need to do is just fine."

"Thanks, Miss Addie." Lindsey gave a weak smile in her direction.

"My pleasure."

Charlie leaned over and gently kissed his little girl on the forehead. She was still so warm, hot even. "I'll give Miss Addie your medicine along with directions okay?"

Lindsey nodded and rolled onto her side, curling up with her stuffed animal. "Come get me in the morning, Daddy?"

He pulled the covers up around her. "Of course." He brushed her hair back and whispering a prayer for her to feel better.

Addie inclined her head toward the hallway. Charlie followed her, closing the door behind him.

"Thank you again, Addie."

"It is my pleasure. Truly. But I need to know what it is you want me to do with regards to medicine and in what situations."

He handed her a piece of paper with notes on it. When Lindsey had taken her medicine last and when she could take it again. "The night of the accident you said one of your roommates is a paramedic?"

Addie nodded. "Mark will be home shortly. We will call you if we have any questions, but I am sure with this..." She held up the slip. "...we will be just fine."

Charlie stared at her. She seemed utterly confident and completely at ease. "I'm sorry to have to ask you to do this."

She started down the stairs. "Charlie, you need to go to work. Lindsey will likely sleep most of the time. Go. Do your job. Go home and get some rest. Call us in the morning. I will not be going to church regardless so she and you may sleep as late as you would like." When she reached the foyer, Addie turned. "I promise you, everything will be fine."

Plodding down the rest of the steps, Charlie stuck his hands in his pockets. Mostly because what he really wanted to do was reach out and pull Addie into his arms. Deep in that place, way inside, down in the deepest recesses of his gut, he didn't want to leave Lindsey. That she needed him. Or would need him before morning. But he had to go to work, so with a quick prayer, Charlie started for the door.

Standing on the front porch, he turned to look at Addie. "Take care of my little girl?"

Addie smiled. "Like she was my own."

Charlie stepped back toward the house - and Addie. He looked straight into her bright blue eyes. They drew him in and he moved even closer to her. Reaching out, he took his hand in hers and squeezed. "Thank you." A part of him wished she really meant that. That she would take care of Lindsey like she was Addie's own.

He leaned over and gave her a lingering kiss on the cheek before turning, trotting down the stairs, getting into his car and driving away.

With one long brush stroke, Addie put the pink polish on Lindsey's nail. This kind of painting she knew how to do.

"Thank you for letting me come over." Lindsey sat back against the headboard, pillows propped behind her. "Dad wouldn't let me stay home alone when I was so sick and he wouldn't go to work if I didn't have somewhere to go. He needs the job until he graduates."

"He needs it? Has he almost lost it?"

She nodded, her face was devoid of most color as the fever still held her in its grip. "Every time I get sick for a few days or he has to take off work to take me to the doctor or whatever, his boss threatens to fire him."

Addie put the brush back in the bottle and drew it out slowly, removing the excess polish. She took Lindsey's hand in hers and painted two more nails. "Why does he stay, then? If his boss gives him such a difficult time about you, why can he not find a job with more flexibility?"

Lindsey gave a weak shrug. "He wants to do money stuff. He's really, really good with numbers but until he finishes his degree and gets a job in his field, he needs a job that mostly gives him flexibility for school and me. This job gives him that. At least that's what he always told me. But sometimes he does have to work when he doesn't want to, like tonight."

"I am glad he has employment where he is able to take care of you." She set the hand she held down and reached for the other one.

"And I'm glad I get to spend some more time with you. I like you, Addie."

Addie smiled at the girl. "I like you, too, Lindsey."

The hazel eyes flitted downward. "Why can't you and my dad be together?"

"I am going back to my country in May. I cannot stay here and your father does not want to move. That means there is no future for us. I like your father and I hope we can be friends while I am here, but if we were to start dating and then end the relationship in May, all of us would be hurt more than if we never started it in the first place." She set the other hand down on the blanket and reached out to touch Lindsey's forehead with the back of her hand. Still very warm. "Can you understand?"

Lindsey nodded, but Addie could see the tears in her eyes. "I understand, but that doesn't mean I like it."

"I wish things could be different, sweetheart, but they are not." Addie leaned over and pressed a kiss to Lindsey's forehead, blinking back tears of her own. "Lie down and get some sleep. It's bedtime anyway. Your medicine should be taking effect and allow you to rest."

With pink nails held in the air to protect them, Lindsey slid down until she lay flat. Addie pulled the blankets up under her arms and Lindsey laid them down with her fingernails up on top of the covers.

Addie walked to the door and flipped the light off. "Good night, Lindsey. If you need anything, call out. I am right next door. Or pick up the phone and dial one, wait for the beep and then talk. It is an intercom that I will hear."

Lindsey nodded. "I will."

Closing the door behind her, Addie walked to her own room and then to the bathroom, her sore muscles screaming for relief. The hot shower earlier had helped some, but now it was time to indulge in a long, hot, bubble bath.

Charlie tossed his clipboard onto the desk and sank into the chair. He didn't want to look at his watch. It was well after midnight, but he was finally done. His phone vibrated in his pocket. Confused, he pulled it out to see Dan calling.

He flipped it open and leaned back in the seat. "Hey."

"Where's Lindsey? Where are you?" His cousin's voice sounded frantic.

"I had to work after all, but Addie offered to watch her. I took her over there earlier and will go pick her up in the morning after I wake up."

Dan's relief came through in his voice. "Gotcha. I'm headed to bed. Think we got a bunch of wedding stuff sorted out. You're the best man, you know."

"I know."

Dan didn't say goodbye but just hung up.

"Everything done, Brewer?" His boss walked up carrying a number of other clipboards.

Charlie picked his up and held it out. "Yep."

"Thanks for coming in tonight. I know Lindsey is sick but we needed you here."

"I know."

The man's eyes softened. "Get home and check on her. Take tomorrow off. We got it covered."

"Thanks. She's staying with a friend of mine. And one of my friend's roommates is a paramedic so she's in good hands. I'll pick her up after I get some sleep." Charlie yawned and stretched his arms over his head, reaching back until he felt his back pop.

He grabbed his keys off his desk and headed home where he'd sleep like the dead.

Addie sat straight up in bed, gasping for breath. With one shaking hand, she pushed her hair out of her face and tried to figure out why she had woken so suddenly.

And then she heard it.

Crying coming from the other room.

She did not wait to put slippers on but grabbed her robe and ran out of her room toward Lindsey's. Addie did not bother to knock but went straight in. Lindsey lay on the bed, but rolled back and forth in apparent pain.

"Lindsey, what is wrong?" Addie pressed the back of her hand to the girl's forehead. Burning up. She reached for the phone and pressed a single number, waiting impatiently for the beep. "Mark, Lindsey needs you."

Thirty seconds later, he burst into the room. Addie stepped aside, letting Mark sit on the edge of the bed. He spoke quietly to the girl. All Addie could decipher was that Lindsey was in pain and a lot of it.

Mark turned to look at her. "She needs to go to the emergency room. I'm afraid she may have appendicitis."

Addie reached for the phone to call an ambulance, but Mark stopped her.

"There's no time for that. You have about two minutes to get some clothes on while I take her temperature and a couple other things, then we're taking the SUV." He grabbed the phone and called Todd as Addie hurried to change.

She threw on the same jeans she'd worn to paint in and a sweatshirt she pulled out of a drawer. As she tugged on her boots, Todd ran past her room and down the stairs. Mark followed closely behind, Lindsey in his arms. Addie followed and by the time they reached the front door, she'd caught up. Todd pulled up in the SUV. Mark motioned for Addie to get in the front.

The second the doors were shut, Todd accelerated around the circle drive and toward the road. Addie pulled her phone out and found Charlie's number. It rang several times, but there was no answer. Frustrated, she tried again. Two more times.

"He is not answering." Addie set the phone down and pulled her hair back into the ponytail holder she had grabbed on the way out the door.

"We'll try again from the hospital."

The drive seemed to take an eternity, with Lindsey crying in the back seat. Todd screeched to a stop in front of the emergency room doors. Addie jumped out and moved to the rear to help Mark. Once he had Lindsey in his arms again, she redialed Charlie's number.

"Still no answer," she told him as the doors hissed open in front of him.

"Send Todd."

Lindsey hit another button on her phone, passing the message along as Mark came to a stop in front of the triage desk.

"What's wrong, sir?"

"I'm a medic. I'm almost certain she has appendicitis and think it may have burst already."

The nurse hustled around the desk and pressed a hand to

Lindsey's forehead. Then she nodded. "Bring her back here. Are you her father?"

Mark shook his head as Addie followed them. "My roommate is friends with her father. He thought she had the flu but had to work so he left her with us. He's not answering his phone but we sent someone to get him."

Addie hung back as Mark set a whimpering Lindsey on the table in the triage room. Another nurse touched Addie's arm.

"Ma'am? Can you tell us her name? Birthday? Anything to help us see if she's in our system so we'll know if there's anything she's allergic to and her medical history?"

"I can try." She followed the woman to the desk out front. "Her name is Lindsey Brewer and she is eleven. Her birthday was last month. The twenty-fifth maybe?"

The clickety-clack of the keys did little to reassure Addie.

"I think I found her. What is her father's name?"

"Charlie Brewer. They live in an apartment in Serenity Landing. He works at a home improvement store." Tears streaked down her cheeks. "That is all I know."

The nurse smiled at her. "It's enough. I can't tell you anything since you're not on her paperwork, but that's enough information for me to verify this is her and we do have a picture of her on file. We'll be cautious until we can verify it with her father, but I'm sure this is her."

"Thank you."

Mark walked out of the room behind her and took her elbow. "They're taking her back."

Addie looked over her shoulder. "She is all alone."

"They'll call us when we can go see her." Mark stopped next to a plastic couch. "For now, all we can do is wait."

T he banging gradually seeped into Charlie's consciousness.

"I'm coming! I'm coming!" Dan's voice rang throughout the apartment.

Charlie swung his feet over the side of his bed as Dan opened the front door.

The voice drifted through the pre-morning darkness. "I'm looking for Charlie Brewer."

"Who are you?"

"I'm a friend of Addie's. I need to find Lindsey's father."

That was all Charlie needed to hear. He practically ran to the door, into the living room to see Todd standing there. "What's wrong?"

Todd took a step into the room. "We took Lindsey to the emergency room. Mark thinks it's her appendix."

Charlie pivoted and nearly flew back into his room, grabbing his jeans, a flannel shirt and sneakers, before returning to the living room. "Let's go."

Dan put a hand on his shoulder to stop him. "Get dressed first."

Shooting him a glare, Charlie dropped everything before grabbing his jeans and hopping into them. He shoved his feet into his shoes without tying them and stuck one arm in the sleeve of his flannel shirt while he grabbed his coat. "Now can we go?"

Dan shoved him toward the door. "I'll be right behind you."

Charlie followed Todd to the still-running SUV and climbed in the passenger seat. They were moving before he could get his seat belt on. "How is she?"

"I don't know. Mark said he thought it was her appendix. I dropped them off and came to get you because you hadn't answered your phone."

He reached toward his pocket for his phone only to realize he hadn't grabbed it or his wallet. Not that he'd be able to afford the hospital stay without making payments into eternity but he still felt weird without it.

Todd held his phone out. "Call your cousin and have him bring it."

It took Charlie a minute to remember his cousin's phone number. He'd long ago preprogrammed it into his phone so there was no need to dial it. But it came to him and he dialed.

"Hello?" He could hear the confusion in Dan's voice.

"It's me. I forgot my wallet and phone."

"Already got 'em."

Charlie didn't bother to say good-bye but flipped the phone closed and held it out toward Todd. He closed his eyes and gave solid thought to the prayers that had been flying through his head even before he could form coherent words. He stared out into the blackness of the night, broken by the occasional streetlight. It seemed like an eternity before Todd pulled to a stop in front of the emergency room doors. Before the wheels had stopped turning, Charlie had his seatbelt off and struggled to open the still-locked door.

Todd clicked the button and Charlie ran for the hospital. The doors wooshed open in front of him. The first thing he saw was Addie, sitting on one of the ubiquitous vinyl couches. She jumped up when she saw him.

All he had time to do was react as she flung her arms around his neck.

Addie buried her face in Charlie's neck. "I am so glad you are here."

He wrapped his arms around her waist and held her. "How is she?"

"They will not tell us anything since we are not family." She loosened her grip and settled her feet all the way back on the floor. "Mark thought it was appendicitis and the nurses agreed it was possible. I helped them find her in the computer. At least they were pretty sure it was her and then they took her back to a room."

Charlie's arms slipped from around her, but he grabbed her hand and held on tight as he walked to the desk. "I'm looking for my daughter," he said before the nurse could say anything. "Lindsey Brewer."

"Can I see some ID, please?"

Charlie put his other hand, clenched in a fist, on the counter. "I left my wallet at home. My cousin is on his way with it."

The nurse nodded. "This way."

Addie didn't move until Charlie tugged on her hand. "Come on."

Together they followed the nurse back through a maze of corridors and rooms with curtains pulled in front of glass doors.

Whimpers came from the room where they headed. "I want my daddy."

Charlie dropped her hand and moved more quickly toward the sound, speaking before he even entered the room. "I'm here, princess."

"Daddy!"

Addie hung back near the sliding glass door as Charlie rushed to Lindsey's side. It filled her heart to overflowing to see the two of them together. He leaned over the side of her bed, holding her hand. He alternated between brushing her hair back and wiping her tears.

"Excuse me, ma'am."

Addie stepped aside to let the doctor in the room.

"Mr. Brewer?"

Charlie straightened but didn't let go of Lindsey. The doctor talked in tones low enough that Addie couldn't hear.

She heard Charlie answer. "Are you sure?"

The doctor nodded.

Charlie looked at Addie, almost like he was looking at her for confirmation he was doing the right thing, though she had no idea what that was.

"Okay."

The doctor turned just enough Addie could hear him clearly. He put a hand on Lindsey's leg and she could see him squeeze reassuringly. "Someone will bring her the drink in a minute."

Charlie nodded as the doctor left. Addie walked inside. "Drink?"

"They're going to do a CT scan to check her appendix. She has to drink some dye stuff and then wait an hour before they can do it."

Addie rested a hand on Lindsey's leg. "How are you feeling?"

"A little better." She gave a weak smile. "I'm sorry to get you up in the middle of the night."

"Nonsense. I am glad we were there. Mark is a medic and he knew exactly what needed doing."

Charlie brushed Lindsey's hair back. "She's right. I might have waited longer to bring you in because I don't know what I'm talking about and everyone else has the flu. I'm glad you were there."

A nurse chose that moment to walk in. "We got the IV going earlier, but here's some pain medication for Lindsey." She did her checks of ID bracelets and then put the medicine into the IV. "I'll be back in a few minutes with the drink."

Charlie pulled the blanket up a bit higher around Lindsey. "Try to get some rest, kiddo. I'll turn the lights down and I want to talk to Addie outside for a minute, okay?"

Lindsey nodded. "I can feel it in my arm. It's weird."

Addie smiled when Charlie did and watched as he leaned over and kissed his daughter's forehead. "I'll be right outside if you need anything."

Charlie sank against the wall and covered his face with his hands. The feather-light touch of Addie's hand on his arm brought them down.

"Are you all right, Charlie?" The concern in her eyes nearly surpassed the exhaustion he also saw there.

"They're talking about surgery for my baby." He took her hand in his, watching as he linked his fingers with hers. "I know she's not my baby anymore, but this is her first trip to the emergency room. It's scary."

She lifted their joined hands and covered them with her other one. "I have been praying for her and for you. I cannot imagine how difficult it would be to watch your child like this, especially since you were not there when it all started. May I pray for you?"

He nodded, unable to do much of anything else. Addie's quiet words washed over him, helping calm his spirit. At her whispered "amen", he lifted his head and let go of her hand to pull her to him in a long hug. When he'd left Lindsey with her a few hours earlier, he had prayed his daughter wouldn't get too attached. Now it looked like he was the one who would have that problem because this was exactly what he needed.

And so he took a deep breath, rested his hands on her waist. He used slight pressure to separate the two of them. "I'm going to go sit with her." Without thinking about it, he reached up and brushed the hair back out of her face. "Thank you for being here. You must be tired, though. You don't need to stay."

Addie took a slight step away from him. "I would like to stay, if that is all right with you."

"Of course." He thought about saying something else, but the nurse walked up.

"I have the dye for her to drink." She held up a large Styrofoam cup.

Charlie pushed off from the wall and turned into Lindsey's room. The nurse explained how much she was to drink and when. She waited until Lindsey took her first sip then left. Given the look on his daughter's face, it wouldn't be easy for her to drink it all.

It was going to be a long hour.

Addie sank down next to Mark on the vinyl couch and let her head fall backward.

"How is she?" Mark's voice sounded as tired as she felt.

"They are doing a CT Scan now. Charlie went with her. They said it should take about thirty minutes, but they are pretty sure her appendix burst and they will be doing surgery soon. Charlie will text me when they are done." She tugged the ponytail holder out of her hair and put it back up. Her mother would be mortified to see how she looked. No make-up. Sloppy ponytail. Jeans and a sweatshirt that did not match her socks. Not what a Crown Princess was supposed to look like.

"Did they say what kind of time frame they were looking at?"

"No. They will do the CT Scan. If it is what they think, they will send her to a room upstairs on the children's floor and talk to the surgeon. They did not say what kind of timing we would be looking at once they finish the scan."

"We should go home, Adeline." He had to be serious if he used her full name. "You need your rest." Mark leaned forward and turned to look at her. "You worked harder yesterday than I would have liked. Your parents would not be pleased."

Addie glared at him. "My parents are not here and they would appreciate that I want to stay near a friend. If only because it would be good public relations if it ever came out, but that is not why I will be staying."

"Todd and I can overrule you."

"But you will not. And I will not listen if you do. I am going to stay here with Charlie and Lindsey for the time being. I will do my best to get some rest when I can, like now." She closed her eyes. "There will be no more discussion about the matter."

"Very well." She could tell Mark was not happy but for the moment it did not concern her. She would stay where she was needed most and right now it was right here.

Addie thought she dozed just a bit before her phone beeped at her. "Charlie said I can go back but did not say what they found."

Mark sighed. "Very well. Keep us posted."

She walked past the desk where the nurse buzzed her in and tried to remember how to get to Lindsey's room. It only took two wrong turns for her to find the right place. The doctor was talking to Charlie as she slipped through the sliding glass door.

"So, we'll get her moved upstairs and the surgeon will be by to talk to you as soon as he can."

Charlie sat on the bed next his legs stretched out in front of him with Lindsey tucked into his side. "You're sure it's her appendix?" Addie heard relief and concern warring for dominance in his voice.

"Yes, sir." The doctor made a notation on the piece of paper on his clipboard. "I'll have someone come get you as soon as they're ready for you upstairs." He smiled at Addie as he made his way out of the room.

She moved to the side of the bed. "How are you, Lindsey?"

"It hurts less than it did before." The girl closed her eyes, letting a couple of tears leak out.

Charlie extracted himself from Lindsey and motioned for Addie to follow him. When they were in the hallway, he turned to her, running a hand through his hair. "She's on pain medication now and when it burst, the pain actually lessened."

"That is one upside to it bursting, it seems."

"Would you mind to sit with her? I'm going to try to call my folks. They're in..." He rubbed his forehead with the fingers of one hand. "...Italy, I think."

"Of course." Addie went back into the room while Charlie pulled his cell phone out of his pocket and headed for the doors. She sat in the chair next to the bed and took Lindsey's hand in her own. With her eyes closed, she began to pray and did not stop.

Charlie stared at the fingers laced through his own and leaned his head against the one resting on his shoulder. At nearly three in the afternoon, it had been twelve hours since the banging on the door woke him up. He closed his eyes to try and rest while his baby girl had surgery.

"She's been here the whole time?"

He may or may not have dozed off, but his cousin's voice nearly made him jump. Dan sank into the chair next to Charlie. "Yeah. Refused to go home."

"How much longer?"

"I'm not sure. Depends on what they find, I guess."

"And it took them eight hours to get to her... why exactly?"

"This surgeon is the best at this kind of operation but he was in surgery all morning."

"A slightly less qualified but still fully competent surgeon seven hours ago wouldn't have been better?"

Charlie rubbed his eyes with the heels of his free hand. "Don't second guess me right now, Dan. I did what the doctors thought was best. Period. You're not helping."

Dan leaned back and stretched his legs out. "Sorry. It's been a long day."

"How's your grandpa?"

"They think he's going to be okay. Mom and Dad said they'll be over later after he gets settled."

"I understand. I've had Addie here with me. Her roommates are around here somewhere, too."

"She's not family, though."

"I know."

Dan looked pointedly at their joined hands. "Are you sure?"

"There's no future with her, but I'm not going to push her away. She's been here every step of the way today and her support's been rock solid."

"I'm not denying that, but what's Lindsey going to think?"

"Lindsey's in surgery. She won't know about this and I'll be back to keeping my distance once she wakes up fine. Addie's a friend, nothing more." He looked at their hands again and rubbed his thumb over her knuckles. "Maybe if she wasn't moving..."

They sat in silence until Dan broke it a few minutes later. "You'd be closer to your folks in Europe."

"Your parents raised me way more than mine did. They were never here more than three or four months a year, usually less."

"And wouldn't you like to change things? For Lindsey to know her grandparents?"

"I don't want to uproot her from her life here. She has friends, teachers, a church, all sorts of reasons not to move. Drop it."

Dan did and stared at the television hanging near them. "What happened?"

Charlie looked up to see the same story he'd already seen twice since moving to the waiting room. "The First Family is skiing in some little country in Europe while the president is at that summit."

"Ah. Your folks anywhere near there?"

Charlie shrugged the shoulder not being used as a pillow by the most beautiful woman he'd ever seen in real life. "Don't know. They're researching Charlemagne. Again. Somewhere. I think."

"Of course they are."

The pager lying on Charlie's leg vibrated. He jumped and jolted Addie awake.

"Is she done?"

He held up the pager. "I'll go check." With a deep breath and a whispered prayer, he walked to the desk to find out what was happening with his daughter.

Her eyes tracked Charlie as he nearly ran to the information desk before she tried to rub the sleep out of them with stiff fingers. Addie glanced at the television to see if the time was showing on the news station, but it was not. The glimpse of mountains reminded her of Montevaro but the shot only lasted a split-second.

"Good morning."

She turned to see Dan sitting there. At least she thought it was Dan. She'd never met him. "I do know it is not morning."

He held his hand out. "I'm Dan, Charlie's cousin."

"It is a pleasure to meet you." His handshake was firm but not painful. "What time is it?"

"About four. She's been in surgery about an hour."

Addie winced. "And I fear I have been asleep most of that time, have I not?"

Dan shrugged. "I just got here, but I would imagine so. Just being here is what Charlie needed."

"I am glad."

She watched Charlie lean both hands on the counter as the woman behind it looked at some papers. He said something, nodded and turned toward them. As he got closer, she could see relief written all over his face.

"She's out of surgery. The doctor will be out in a few minutes to talk to me and I can go see her in a bit." He sank back down next to her and reached for her hand. "Thank you for being here, Addie."

"I would not be anywhere else."

The feeling of his fingers meshed with hers gave her a sense of rightness she had never felt any other time. Why could he not move to Europe? Or be from Montevaro? And a member of the nobility so her parents and Parliament would give their approval for a relationship between Charlie and herself?

God, why do I feel so much for this man when there can be no future for us? Why did you bring him into my life? For this day? So we would get Lindsey to the hospital in time?

No answers were forthcoming, but Addie did not expect any. In her experience, God did not speak to her directly, but His hand was often visible in her life - it was not always apparent until later where He had been working.

Charlie and Dan talked quietly while Addie stared into space contemplating the relationship. Ten minutes later, Charlie's pager buzzed again. She slid her hand out of his as he stood.

He turned to look at her. "Will you come with me?"

Dan stood next to him and Addie's gaze flitted between them.

"I will stay here with your things." He had two books and an iPad. She had her purse and a laptop bag Todd had brought so she could work on an assignment for class.

"I'll stay, Addie." Todd sat next to her. "Go with him."

She gave her friend and bodyguard a grateful smile before following Charlie and Dan. While in the small meeting room, she tried to stay in the background, but Charlie would have none of it. He wanted her right next to him.

According to the doctor, everything went well. The appendix burst, just as they expected but he thought he was able to get everything. They would keep her for a day or two, depending on how she responded. Charlie would be able to see her in about twenty minutes, after they got her moved and settled into recovery.

Charlie thanked him and they went back to the waiting room. Dan pulled Charlie to the side as Addie went back to the chairs where Mark and Todd waited. They both stood up as she neared.

"You need to go home and get some sleep." Mark crossed his arms over his chest and she knew she would not be able to argue with him. They were both several years older than her and though they were also students, their primary job was her protection and well-being. The three of them had lived together in Serenity Landing for most of the last five and a half years, returning to Montevaro for vacations and between semesters. It was easy to forget they were not her friends - or not *just* her friends.

She nodded wearily. "I will go home for a time and take a nap then come back."

Todd handed her the bag with her laptop in it. "Tell him good-bye. We'll be by the door."

Addie waited until Dan turned away to walk up to Charlie. "I will be back later, Charlie, but I need to go home for a bit. Now that Lindsey is doing well, I have a bit of work I have to get done." It was the absolute truth. She did not mention Todd and Mark were giving her little choice.

Charlie reached toward her and tucked a strand of hair behind her ear. "Thank you for being here this long. You didn't need to."

Her gaze skittered away from his all-too-frank eyes. The emotion there overwhelmed her. "Yes. I did. You are both my friends and she was in my care when this happened."

"It would've happened no matter where she was." His finger pressed on her chin until she looked back up at him. "Don't blame yourself, understand?"

"I do not blame myself, but I do want to make certain she will be fine, in part because she was at my home."

Dan called for Charlie. Charlie held up one finger while he spoke. "I'll call you after we get Lindsey back to her room."

"I will be back later."

Charlie's eyes held her own and did not release them until they flicked a bit lower. The look, so intense she could not breathe, made her want to do something completely out of character. Wrap her arms around him and kiss him senseless.

Dan called again and the moment ended. Charlie gave her one more smile and turned away.

Todd and Mark were quiet until the three of them were safely in the SUV.

"What are you doing, Adeline?" Mark sat in the passenger seat and his voice sounded as tired as he looked.

She bristled at the words. "Going home so I can take a nap like you ordered me to."

"That's not what I'm talking about and you know it. You and Charlie. What are you doing? There can be no future there. You know that. A date or two was one thing, and we decided to let you because you don't get out and have good, clean fun often enough. You've been on very few dates and we thought it would be good for you and you would know not to get attached." Mark turned to look at her. "You and Charlie can never be, Adeline."

Addie closed her eyes and did her best to ignore the prick of tears at the back of them. "I know. My parents and Parliament would never approve."

Todd chose that moment to interject. "So what are you thinking?"

She could hold them back no longer and hot tears trickled down her face. "That I love him."

Charlie shifted uncomfortably in the chair that, supposedly, turned into a bed for him to sleep on when the time came. Lindsey slept in the hospital bed, worn out from the surgery and still feeling the effects of the anesthesia. At least that's what the doctors said. The IV in her arm also had morphine running through it. She looked... weird. Her color was off somehow. Not abnormal, according to the nurse, but still disconcerting.

His book sat unopened on his lap. He'd tried to read during surgery, but to no avail. He couldn't concentrate on the words swimming in front of his eyes while some doctor looked at his daughter's insides.

"Daddy?"

He looked over to see Lindsey's eyes slowly blinking open before closing again. "I'm right here, princess."

A tear leaked out of her eye. He watched it until it disappeared in her hair. What he wouldn't give to make it easier on her. "I'm sorry."

"For what?" He squeezed her hand. "I'm just glad you're okay."

"I know we can't afford this. I don't know who I was near who got me so sick, but I'm sorry."

Charlie stood and turned until he sat on the edge of the bed, careful to avoid hurting her. "Linds." Her eyes stayed closed. "Look at me, sweetheart."

The lashes fluttered and eyes opened. The tears broke Charlie's heart. Her tender spirit was one of the things he loved the most about her, but it also made him worry, especially as she got older. He feared her heart would break more easily than most and he'd spend more time than he cared to think about drying her tears.

He raised her hand until he could kiss the back of it. "Your appendix ruptured. Nothing anyone could have done about it. It'll be fine. Don't worry about it. We have insurance for a reason." The bill would still be astronomical on his budget but there was nothing he could do about it except pray for a job to come through after graduation.

Lindsey looked around the room as much as she could without moving. "Where's Addie?"

"She stayed until surgery ended but she has a project due this week for one of her classes. She'll be back later."

"You really like her, don't you, Dad?"

Charlie did his best to school his features and not show his true feelings. "I like her a lot, punkin, but she's moving in a few months."

"We could move, too. I'd like to live in Europe near Grandma and Grandpa."

It took everything in him not to squish her dreams completely. "I promise I'll think about it, but don't get your hopes up."

A nurse chose that moment to walk in, giving him a bit of a reprieve. "Hi there, Lindsey. Let's take a look at you, okay?"

Lindsey nodded and Charlie moved out of the way, watching as the nurse checked vital signs and peeked at her abdomen. "Everything looks good." She patted Lindsey's shoulder. "I'll be back in a little while. Mr. Brewer, dinner will be here in a bit. Lindsey can have some clear fluids but that's it for now. If she does okay, we'll get her some more later."

"Thank you."

No sooner had the nurse left, than the door opened again. Charlie couldn't see who it was but had to smile at the huge purple teddy bear.

"Where's my girl?" The bear moved and Charlie could see his uncle's smiling face. "How are you, sugar?"

Lindsey gave a weak smile. "Is that for me?"

Uncle Ben shook his head. "Nope. Thought your dad would need a bear to hold onto while he sleeps tonight."

Lindsey started to laugh but it quickly turned to whimpers. "Don't make me laugh, Uncle Ben. It hurts."

"Ben Brewer, leave her alone. She just had surgery." Aunt Cara brushed past her husband. "How are you, sweetie?"

His daughter glared at Ben. "It doesn't hurt when I'm not laughing."

"Then he won't make you laugh anymore." Cara perched delicately on the edge of the bed. "We're sorry we weren't here sooner."

Lindsey, always more concerned about others, shook her head a bit. "How's PopPop?"

Cara brushed Lindsey's hair back. "My father is home already. You are still in the hospital so *you* are the one we should be talking about." PopPop wasn't Lindsey's grandfather by blood, but he'd adopted her just the same, just like all of Aunt Cara's family had done with him.

"I'm glad he's okay. Tell him I love him?"

With a soft smile, Cara squeezed Lindsey's hand. "He knows. He spent most of his time asking about you."

Another knock came as the door pushed open. "Hello?"

Lindsey's eyes lit up as Addie entered the room. "You came!"

Addie smiled at the look on the girl's face. "Of course I came, Lindsey. If I did not have a project due and roommates who insisted I needed a nap, I would never have left."

"So you're the infamous Addie."

She turned to see a couple, a bit older than her own parents standing next to Lindsey's bed.

Lindsey took care of introductions. "Uncle Bob, Aunt Cara, this is Addie. She's teaching us about etiquette at my after-school program and helping with the renovations."

Addie held out her hand first to Aunt Cara then Uncle Bob. "It is a pleasure to meet you both."

Charlie stood up and smiled at her. "Take my seat. I need to stretch anyway."

She nodded at him and sat in the hard vinyl chair. Conversation flowed around her. Charlie leaned against the wall with one shoulder, one foot crossed over the other, toe of one shoe resting on the laminate tile floor. His hands were shoved deep in his pockets and the lines on his face told how tired he must be. But the smile was genuine. The relief evident.

From the outside looking in, they were a wonderful family. Warm. Caring. Different than her own family. Her parents loved her. She had never doubted their love, but they did not have the easy camaraderie found here.

She'd been sitting there for about half an hour, just soaking it all in, when the door opened again. Todd crooked a finger toward her.

Addie excused herself and followed him into the hall. "Yes?"

"We need to go." Something in his demeanor told her this was serious.

"Tell me."

"You are returning home. There's been an accident. As far as we've been told, everyone is fine, though your father is in the hospital. His injuries are not life threatening but you do need to leave for Montevaro as soon as we can."

She stumbled backward, stopping only when she came in contact with the wall. One hand covered her stomach as she tried to keep the growing dread at bay. "You are certain the injuries are not life threatening?"

"That's what we were told."

Before she could reply, the door opened next to her. Charlie poked his head out. "Everything okay?"

Addie shook her head, tears spilling down her cheeks. "My father has been in an accident. They told Todd he will be fine but..."

Charlie's arms were around her before she could finish the sentence. Her shoulders shook but she refused to give into the heart-rending sobs. After a couple of minutes soaking in his strength, she moved away. "Thank you. I must be leaving. I will be returning home as soon as I can."

He took her hand. "Of course. Do you know when you'll be back?"

With a quick shake of her head, Addie squeezed his hand. "No. It will depend on the seriousness of his injuries and what I need to do with regard to..." Her lips clamped shut before she revealed her true identity. "...the family business," she finished instead.

"What about your classes? Will your professors work with you?"

They would. If she had to reveal who she really was, she would, but her goal had always been to get her grades and degree because of her mind, not her last name or position in life. But if they would not work with her, she *could* threaten to make them look bad. Once she graduated, the deal had already been made for them to use her name in conjunction with promotional materials, as long as her family approved it. Until then, she needed to get her classes finished and the grades in.

Charlie watched her expectantly so she pasted on a bright smile. "Yes. I am certain they will."

Laughter rang out from the room behind them. "Lindsey and the other girls will miss you."

"I will miss them, too, but I will do video chats with them if I will be gone very long."

He glanced behind them. "Let me walk you out?"

She shook her head. "No. You need to stay here with Lindsey."

He started toward the end of the long hall where a locked door kept the children's unit safe. "I'll walk you to the elevator at least."

They walked slowly until they reached the doors.

Addie looked up at him, reaching with her free hand to rest it on his cheek. "Thank you for everything, Charlie. I will miss you as well as Lindsey."

Charlie swallowed and looked like he was trying to get himself under control. She could not wait for him to get control of his emotions. Not if his were churning like hers.

"Goodbye, Charlie. I will keep in touch." She put both hands on the door and pushed.

"Don't go yet." Charlie stopped her with a hand on her arm.

Her eyes shimmered with still unshed tears. "I have to. Todd and Mark are waiting just outside. They will be going home with me so I will not be alone for the trip."

It would be hard enough to let her go, but harder still if he didn't say something to her about how he felt.

She gave a timorous half-smile. "Good-bye."

This time the tug on her arm did more than stop her. This time it pulled her to him until he could wrap his arms around her. He didn't let himself think.

Charlie lowered his head to hers and kissed her. A soft, tender kiss, full of promise and hope and desire and love and longing.

All too soon, the perfect kiss ended and Charlie rested his forehead against hers. His hands moved to her shoulders where he let them rest.

"I have to go," she whispered.

"I know."

This time he kissed her forehead. "Be safe. Let us know when you get there?"

"I will." She took a step back and his hands trailed down her arms to grasp her hands.

Addie gave them a light squeeze, let go and walked out the doors.

And out of his life.

Addie stared out the window of the car as Mark drove her home. She could still feel the imprint of Charlie's lips on hers, the rush of feeling flooding through her as he gave her her first kiss ever. She relived every short second before her mind turned back to the situation at hand.

"Mark, do you have any more word on my father?"

"No, miss. All I know is there was a skiing accident. They have taken him to the palace rather than the hospital. I take that to be good news."

He had a point, but the medical facility in the palace was second to none. There were a few rooms set aside for the royal family. For sufficiently serious incidents, they would go to the nearby hospital, but most procedures, even surgery and birth, could take place without ever leaving the palace. The family physician was always on standby and had connections with many other doctors. None would refuse the opportunity to serve the royal family if called upon, even at the palace rather than the hospital.

Therefore, the knowledge of her father's location did little to quell the storm building inside her.

"When are we leaving?"

"There is not time to send the plane here, so we will fly a charter plane out of Springfield and board another plane in St. Louis about six hours from now. That plane has a layover in Atlanta and then flies onto Rome. From there, were will take the Montevarian plane home."

"How long until we arrive?"

"Nearly a full day most likely. We could board a plane sooner, but the traveling would be a bit more arduous."

Addie thanked him and sank back into the seat, trying not to let her fears overwhelm her. She had known from a very young age she would one day be queen of her homeland, but she had no desire to do so just yet, especially not if it meant the demise of her father.

The time at the house was a flurry of activity as she packed a few essentials then loaded two suitcases into the SUV.

As they pulled out of the driveway and turned onto the country road, she caught Mark's eye in the rear view mirror. "Will we be returning here?"

He gave a slight shake of his head. "I don't know, miss."

She looked back for a last glimpse of the house. Deep inside, she knew she would never live there again.

It had been a full day since Addie left and Charlie missed her more than he could have possibly expected. He and a despondent, feverish Lindsey attempted to play a game of ConnectFour, but neither of them were concentrating.

"Turn it up."

The shock in his daughter's voice caught him off-guard. "What?"

"It's Addie."

He looked up at the television to see a young woman, wearing the same thing he'd last seen Addie wearing, descend the stairs from an airplane. Unless his eyes were tricking him, Mark was in front of her and Todd trailed behind.

Since he hadn't reached for the remote, Lindsey did and turned the volume up.

"...earlier as Crown Princess Adeline of Montevaro returned from the U. S., where she's been attending college."

The blood drained from his face as he tried to assimilate the information, but the reporter droned on.

"The First Family has been in Montevaro for several days while the president is at the summit in Geneva. The First Lady and both First Sons are said to be just fine, but the king took a spill while skiing with the family. No one knows for sure where Princess Adeline has been, just that she is working on an advanced degree in International Relations somewhere in the Midwest. Reportedly, the heir to the throne and her two body-guards boarded a plane in St. Louis before heading to Atlanta then Rome where the Montevarian plane ferried them to the airport here."

The reporter continued for another minute saying they believed the king would be just fine, but Charlie tuned it all out.

When Lindsey put her hand on his arm, he turned to see her looking as shocked as he felt.

"Did they say Addie's a *princess?*"

Dumbfounded, he nodded. "I think so. And a Crown Princess."

"What's that mean?"

"The Crown Princes or Princess will be the next king or queen of a country. It means Addie's going to be queen of her country one day."

"Miss Addie's going to be a queen?"

"Looks like it."

"Why wouldn't she tell us?"

Charlie leaned back in his chair and stared at the television, though the news had moved onto something else. "Maybe she couldn't? Every time I tried to ask her about stuff, she would turn the conversation back to me. I knew she grew up in a small country in Europe, but I think she only mentioned the name of it once or twice. I knew she had to have been raised with money but..." He shook his head. "Royalty? I never would have guessed."

It explained Mark and Todd, though. Why they hardly ever let her go anywhere by herself. They were probably her bodyguards. Charlie reached over and brushed Lindsey's hair off her face. "Why don't you get some rest, sweetie? I'll watch for them to run the story again and see what I can find out."

He could tell her energy had been fading fast while they played their game. The high fever and infection were battling in her body and he was sure she would win the fight, but for now it was leaving her worn out.

Lindsey nodded against his hand where it still rested on her forehead. Her eyes closed and in minutes her even breathing told him she'd drifted off.

His mind reeled. Less than twenty-four hours earlier, he'd kissed a *princess*. And not just any princess - a gonna-be-a-queen princess.

That explained why she couldn't move to Serenity Landing permanently. It wasn't that she didn't want to. Maybe she didn't. But it didn't matter. She *couldn't*. He turned that over in his mind a few times.

Could there be hope for them yet?

Stop it! he ordered himself. He had no shot with a princess of any kind. He'd know that before he knew her true identity. In a few days, he would send her an email and offer his support and prayers, but the door was closed on the only woman he'd ever thought he could really fall for.

Adeline walked into one of three hospital rooms in the medical portion of the palace. Despite her mother's pleas for her to freshen up first, she had to see her father.

"Is that you, Adeline?" His voice was stronger than his appearance would suggest.

"It is, Papa." She had to take care how she spoke. While in the States, she often adopted some of the slang her few friends did, but it would never do here.

"I am glad you are here." Fingers, sticking out of a cast, patted the side of his bed. "Come sit by me."

After inspecting the blanket for wires or tubes, she perched next to him. "How are you?"

"I feel like I fell down a mountain."

She managed a weak smile. "You did."

"At least I am not imagining things. What is the media saying?"

Adeline shook her head. "I do not know. I have not seen anything. I can find out if you would like me to."

"It will not be necessary." He gave her the best smile he likely could given the bruising on his face. "However, I am sure you would like to freshen up some. You had a long day traveling. I am sorry you had to come, but I am very happy you are home."

"Have Ana and Rick made it home yet?"

"Ana has an exam she must take then will be home for a couple of days. Richard is in the Himalayas and they have not reached him yet, last I heard." His strength seemed to wane with just those few words.

The tears in her eyes overflowed. Just one or two on each side, but enough. She never cried in front of her father. No one did. He was the king. "I am glad I could come."

"We will need to talk soon, my dear, about your future, but until then, you shower and get some rest."

Adeline leaned over and brushed a kiss against the only spot on his forehead without scrapes or bruises. "I love you, Papa."

"I love you, too, sweet Adeline." His eyes closed and she knew the conversation had ended. The doctors had told her the medicine made him fall asleep mid-sentence sometimes.

She was glad she had worn soft soled shoes. The incessant clicking of heels would have pushed her sanity to the limit. When she left the medical section, she was joined by Gerald, her father's assistant.

"You are on the news in the States, miss," Gerald told her without preamble.

"I was hoping to avoid that."

"I know, but since the First Family was with your father and the press corp just a short ways away in Geneva... They came immediately when word got out but no one outside a select few knew for sure who was injured. The American press ran with it."

Of course. That meant Charlie and Lindsey and Mrs. Hart and all of the other girls and her schoolmates likely knew the truth by now. What would they think of her? She had heard some of her fellow students whispering about her a couple times. They seemed to think she was stand-offish. It was true, she supposed, but only because of who she was. It was dangerous to get too close to anyone.

Like Charlie.

He was the only one she really cared about. She would have to call him sometime in the next couple of days. For now, though, her parents were right. She needed to shower and sleep more than she needed anything now that she had assured herself her father would recover.

Gerlad peeled off into his office as they passed the hallway leading to it. Adeline continued, alone, through the maze of corridors and staircases until she reached her apartment. Her things had been moved from her parents' portion of the palace during her first semester abroad. When she returned, her room was no longer hers and she had her own staff when at home. How would things be different when she returned permanently?

She had gone over the list of things she would need to do after she graduated several times while she was home for Christmas, but now, she wanted a shower and her bed.

And not necessarily in that order.

13

"I need to talk to you." Charlie looked up from his textbook to see Dan walking in.

"Sure."

"It's about Addie."

The person Charlie had done his best to put out of his mind. They still showed pictures of her on the news networks. She had been seen around Montevaro a couple of times in the past week - at church and visiting an orphanage in her father's stead. "What about her?"

"Addie and Lindsey."

Lindsey had been home for two days and was pestering him to let her call the princess. "What did she do?"

Dan held out a card and Charlie took it, his brows pulling together when he realized it was...

"My credit card?"

"Lindsey had it." Dan handed it over. "She was online looking at travel sites."

Charlie's head snapped up. "What?"

"She was trying to find a bus trip to St. Louis and from there she was going to get a flight to Montevaro."

"Planes don't go from St. Louis to Montevaro." He said it before it registered.

The smile filling Dan's face said he hadn't missed a thing. "How do you know?"

Charlie ran a hand through his hair as exhaustion threatened to overwhelm him. "I looked. I knew Lindsey would want to go. I doubt we could actually see Addie but I wanted to be able to tell her exactly how long the trip would take and all that. And when she asked, I told her. There's no way she can travel like that so soon after surgery. Her doctor would kill me. If the trip didn't kill her, in which case the rest of you would have already ganged up on me and I would have let you."

He flipped the plastic over and over with his fingers much as he had that business card months earlier. "I should have known she'd try something like this."

"What're you going to do?"

"I can't afford to go. Even if she could, there's no way I can swing it for both of us to fly over there. I'd be paying it off until the end of time."

"Where there's a will, there's a way."

Charlie glared at his cousin. "This is no time to play the empty platitude game."

Dan sat in the chair across from him. "You love her, don't you?"

Deep inside, Charlie knew it was true, though he'd done his best to avoid it. If he closed his eyes, he could see her sitting on the couch, trying a big bite of barbecue chicken pizza and then proceeding to eat all of his until he was stuck with her cheese half. He saw her painting and trying so hard to prove she could do it. And if he wasn't careful, he'd be able to feel her in his arms, to feel her heart beating in time with his as he kissed her.

Finally, he looked up to see sympathy written all over Dan's face. "Yeah. I do."

"Then fight for her. Find a way to go see her."

Charlie let loose with a bark of laughter. "She's a *princess*, Dan. And not just any princess. The *Crown Princess*. There's no way she could want to be with me. And even if she could, there's probably some law against her marrying a commoner, much less a commoner with a kid and not even widowed."

"Maybe. But you'll never know unless you try."

A noncommittal shrug was the best he could do. "I don't see it happening."

Dan stood and started toward his room. "I understand where you're coming from. Really, I do. But I think if you don't even try, you're stupider than I give you credit for." His door closed behind him.

Charlie pulled his wallet out of his pocket and slid the card back in its slot. Addie was his one shot at love. He just knew it. At least until Lindsey was grown. He didn't dare risk his daughter's fragile heart again. She was devastated by Addie's departure and the idea there would be no future for them with Addie, no matter her royal status. His late night viewing of *Sleepless in Seattle*, driven by hospital boredom and sheer desperation for anything to do, had obviously made things worse.

He took a deep breath and blew it out slowly before standing to go see his daughter. If only he could figure out how to protect her and still get what they both wanted.

Addie.

Adeline walked down the hall, this time wearing her clicky-est heels. The ones she hated with a passion. But her mother told her to. And when the queen tells you what to wear, you wear it. Even in her sort-of-rebellious phase as a teen, Adeline had not dared to refuse when the queen made a specific request like that.

Her cream pantsuit and pale pink silk shell felt strange. After years of rarely dressing up, what would likely be her normal attire was far too dressy for her taste. She would get used to it again, but she did not have to like it just yet.

She entered the small formal dining room on the lower level and knew immediately why dinner was being held there rather than in her parents' suite.

"Princess Adeline." The smarmy count something or other from some other country took her offered hand and brought it to his lips.

Only years of training kept her from wiping the spittle off on her pants. "Good evening. So lovely of you to join us. How is your family?"

Her mother moved to her side. "You are late, Adeline. Count Bladvile has been waiting for you."

"My apologies, Mother, Count. I received a phone call." She nodded slightly toward the man. "I do hope you have not been waiting long, though my mother is an excellent conversationalist so you will not have been bored."

"You are correct, Princess Adeline. Your mother is never boring." His smile revealed a gold tooth peeking out near the corner of his mouth. How ostentatious when she knew precious few in his country could afford such a thing.

"Shall we be seated?" Her mother extended an arm toward the monstrous table and Adeline suddenly found herself wishing for the bar stool of her home in Serenity Landing - or, even better, the couch of Charlie's apartment sharing dinner they had made together.

The count did hold her chair for her. She would give a smidge of credit for that. "Mother, where is Ana?" Addie had not seen her sister since she arrived.

"Ana had another engagement and will not be joining us." The queen sat at the head of the table. "Count Bladvile, will you do us the honor of saying grace?"

Adeline watched closely and noticed a bit of fear skip through his eyes, but he nodded, bowed his head and said a lovely, if very generic, prayer over the food.

He did not mention her father at all.

The first course went fine. Small talk abounded. Mostly between the queen and the count. Adeline only answered when spoken to directly. Halfway through the second course, her mother's right hand lady came in and whispered in the queen's ear.

After patting her mouth with her napkin, her mother stood. The count hurried to do so as well. "I have some business I must attend to. I will return if I am able." She turned to look at Adeline. "Do be sure to make our guest feels welcome."

Adeline nodded slightly. "Of course, Mother."

When it was just the two of them in the room, the count turned a grin her way, one that could only be described as lecherous. "Alone at last, my darling."

And there it came out in the open. This dinner, the interruption, it was all a thinly-veiled attempt by her mother to get her to marry someone deemed acceptable to society. "We are not truly alone, Count Bladvile." The tight smile took all of her energy to muster. "There are always people around, including security staff. I am never without protection of some kind."

He leaned forward, one elbow resting on the table. "Why do you mention protection, dear princess?"

She looked him straight in the eye. "I merely wanted to make sure you know I am never truly alone. That is all."

The rest of that course and the rest of the meal she was mainly silent, allowing the count to talk incessantly about himself.

They were nearly done with dessert when she interrupted. "Pardon me, count. In your ideal world, what kind of wife would you like?"

He sputtered and started to say something, stopped, started, and stopped again. When he managed a coherent sentence, his words did not surprise her. "Why, a good countess, of course. Bear children. Entertain. The usual things."

She turned her most formal smile his direction. "Then why are you here, sir?"

"Pardon?"

"If you want a wife who is a good countess, why are you here? You and I both know I will never be a countess and my husband will never be king."

He spit and sputtered a bit more, but she pushed back from the table. "I will have someone see you out. I do hope you understand why there can never be anything more than cordiality between us." She turned, kept her steps measured and clicked her way to the large double doors at one end of the room. Before she reached them, he spun her around with a meaty hand on her arm.

"Do not walk away from me, princess."

Her insides quivered, but she showed no fear. She gave his hand a pointed glance then looked him straight in the eye. "Do not challenge me, sir. You will not win."

The count dropped his hands as the door next to her creaked open.

If she hadn't been trying so hard to keep her composure, she would have hugged Mark for the interruption. "Princess Adeline, you have a phone call in your office."

"Thank you, Mark." She nodded toward the count again. "Good evening, sir." Her heels clicked away as she heard Mark tell the count his car would be waiting when the ferry landed on the other side of the lake.

When she reached her office, there was no one on the phone, but her mother walked in a moment later.

"Why are you done already, Adeline?"

"I have no interest in that man, Mother, romantic or otherwise." Feeling bold, she sat in her desk chair and folded her hands on top of the blotter.

Her mother gave her most regal glare, but sat in one of the wingback chairs on the other side. "Who said anything about romantic interest?"

"He insinuated he may want to marry me, Mother. What else am I supposed to think?"

The queen waved the thought away with one elegant hand. "Marriage and romance do not necessarily have anything to do with each other."

"Maybe not for you..."

"You have spent too long among those who have no duty to anything beyond themselves. They can afford to marry for love and if it does not work out..." She gave a delicate shrug. "The monarch cannot be divorced, dear. You know that."

Her mother's words were not strictly accurate, but close enough. "You may not have married for love, mother, but I refuse to marry a man I have no attraction to."

"And if you do not find a man you are attracted to?"

"Then I will at least find a man I can respect to be by my side when I become queen someday. Not someone I feel is going to try to take over my kingdom once father is gone." Unease continued to whisper in the back of her mind. The count could not be an option. Period.

Her mother continued to press. "And if you do not meet someone you are attracted to or who you think you can respect and will also meet the requirements of Parliament and your father?"

Adeline did not respond and her mother was called away a minute later. She knew her father's feelings on the matter. Or thought she did. Her mother may not have married for love.

But her father had.

Jonathan walked down the jetway, overcoat over his arm and laptop bag in one hand. The small Montevarian airport held a definite chill. It was very early spring in the Alps, after all. He didn't know when it would warm up, but it hadn't yet.

He reached the gate area and saw a man in a dark suit holding a white board with his name on it. "That's me," he said, nodding at the board.

"Can I take your bag, sir?"

Jonathan shook his head. "I've got it, thanks."

The man tipped his head. "Very well. This way, sir."

They walked through the terminal, following the crowd to the baggage claim area. The man with him went to get the car when Jonathan told him he'd be fine and would meet him out front.

Sure enough, when he exited the terminal, the black Mercedes waited at the curb. Once his luggage was loaded in the trunk, he took his seat in the rear of the vehicle. After so long on his own, being chauffeured and catered to would take a bit of getting used to.

"Can you tell me where we're headed? And what's your name?"

The man nodded. "We're to head straight for the palace unless you'd like to take some time to freshen up at the Lydia House. And my name is James."

He turned it over in his head. A shower would be nice. "Lydia House, please, James. Unless the offer was made just to be polite, then I'm happy to head straight to the palace." He'd met any number of famous folks over the years and had even met Charles and Diana as a child, but Jonathan had never been to an actual palace before. He'd looked up pictures of it online. If he didn't get lost, it would be a miracle.

"No, sir. You're not expected for about ninety minutes."

"Okay. Lydia House it is."

The short trip wove down streets that likely belonged in a Dr. Seuss book, not a straight one among them. They pulled up to a gate set into stone pillars in a stone wall that had to be at least nine feet tall. The sentry in the guard house, snapped to attention as the gate opened.

They rolled to a stop in front of a building that rivaled any of the smaller castles he'd seen when touring England as a teen.

"Mrs. Castanella will show you to your room, sir. If you'd like to take a shower, your bags will be waiting when you're finished."

"Thanks, James." A lady who looked like every grandmother he'd ever seen showed him to his room, even as he amended the statement in his head. Neither of his grandmothers were so open and welcoming upon first meeting someone.

Ninety minutes later, he had crossed the lake and waited in a garden area for the princess to arrive. Would she be different here? More... princess-y? Would she welcome him? Sure, they'd gone out on several dates, but he hadn't kissed her. Hadn't even held her hand, much less defined their relationship.

He had nothing to worry about. Adeline took one look at him and her face brightened considerably. "Jonathan! How are you?"

He took her hands in his and gave her light kisses on both cheeks. "I am well, Princess Adeline." He'd known she was the princess for several weeks, but here, he didn't feel like he could be so familiar with her without permission here on palace grounds.

She rolled her eyes. "Please. I am Addie, my friend. What brings you to Montevaro? I know my mind is a bit fuzzy on the school schedule since I am finishing my coursework via email, but it is not spring break yet, is it?"

Jonathan tucked her arm into his elbow as they walked down the steps and into one of the palace gardens. "No, but I was asked to come."

"Asked?" He smiled down as she looked up at him. "By whom?"

"I don't know. My mother called me with the invitation to come see an old school friend."

Adeline laughed lightly. "Old school friend? I am not sure I like that description, especially since we were in class together less than a week ago."

"You are anything but old." He covered her hand with his other one. "And I'm glad to be here."

She sat on one of the benches in the garden. "We never defined our relationship, Jonathan."

He put a foot on the bench next to her and leaned a forearm on his knee. "No," he answered slowly. "We never did."

"My mother has been setting me up with different men since I returned. A count, others, though only one was so bold. I believe I have a trip to the hospital scheduled to visit the pediatric ward. No doubt there is a handsome doctor to show me around."

"Did you tell her we'd been dating?"

Addie shook her head. "No. I did not want to give her anything to work with and drag you all the way here while you should be studying."

Jonathan chuckled. "You and I both know our professors will work with us. You because of who you are and the reason for your absence with your father's failing health. Me? Because I'm a Langley-Cranston and I'm here with you. I do my best not to take advantage of it too often, but this is one time I will." He winked at her. "Besides, you can show me where your father was hidden during the kidnapping and I can call it a research trip."

That drew a smile from her. "I am glad you are here, Jonathan." For a moment, she seemed sad, but she took a deep breath and went on. "There is something we should discuss."

"Our relationship?" He turned and sat next to her, taking her hand in his.

"Yes. Your invitation to the palace means my mother believes Parliament would approve of you as my husband, as the Prince Consort, and holder of a seat on the Council."

There was something else. Something she must not want to tell him. "But...?" he urged.

Addie didn't look at him as she spoke. "I fear my heart may already belong to another."

Jonathan sank back into the bench. "Pardon?"

"Earlier this year, I dated another man for a few weeks. You heard me take the call for our first date."

"Of course." He remembered it all too well, thinking he'd missed his chance.

"Charlie is a wonderful man, but..." She shook her head. "While my father might approve, Parliament will not. He is what you Americans call solidly middle class, the son of an archaeologist and anthropologist. He will soon have his MBA, but currently works for Serenity Landing Hardware and Home Store. All of that might be overlooked by Parliament if the circumstances were right and I pushed them hard enough."

There had to be more and she went on.

"But he became a single father at sixteen. I do not condone the judgment that would come onto Charlie and Lindsey, but it is the reality." She looked up at him, her eyes bright with tears. "Do you think you could still court me, knowing I believe myself to be in love with another man?"

He thought for a moment. "What do you think? If we were to begin a real relationship, see where this goes with an eye toward marriage in the not-too-distant future, how would that work? I'm not in love with you, Princess. But I do admire and respect you. I like you and we get along. Is that enough of a basis for a relationship that would appease Parliament and my grandmothers? Is there enough attraction to fulfill what I'm sure is another part of your duties as future queen and that's produce an heir?"

That got him a small smile. "I believe, as time passed, my feelings for Charlie would recede and I would hope they would be replaced with feelings for another man. I concur with everything you said. I admire and respect you as well. I cannot say if it is enough for a lifetime." The tears had disappeared when she looked at him again. "If you are willing to try, I am. For the good of my country. I believe it is possible, in theory, to make it work - to spend life together, have a family, run my country - without being deeply in love at the start."

Jonathan stood and reached for her hand, pulling her into his arms as she stood. Addie rested her head against his chest and he felt an overwhelming desire to protect her, to take the pressures settling on her slender shoulders and bear them himself. He couldn't, of course, but he'd like to.

Could he go into a marriage knowing his wife could still love another man, though she'd never act on it? Knowing that, despite those feelings, she would do everything in her power to make sure their life together was both long and happy?

He didn't know, but holding Addie in his arms, he was willing to find out.

A knock on the door startled Charlie out of the book he was reading. The clock said it wasn't too late, but still. No one ever just stopped by. He peeked through the peephole, his brow furrowed as he opened the door.

"Dave?" Charlie stepped aside. "Come on in."

"I'm sorry to just drop by like this, but I tried to call. Guess I have the wrong number for you." Dave seemed nervous, uncomfortable. Charlie didn't know the other man well, just through Megan, but anyone could tell.

"What's going on?"

"You're a CPA or something right?" Dave sat on the couch, one leg twitching up and down.

If he hadn't been so serious, Charlie would have laughed. "I'm nearly done with my MBA, but I won't ever be a CPA. Is there something I can help you with though? Or find someone who can?"

Dave pulled something out of his pocket, a business size envelope stuffed to the brim. "You know I'm working at the comedy club, right?"

"Lindsey mentioned it." The girl was asleep in her room. For the moment. Until she tried to sneak out again.

"I'm just the janitor and do some handyman stuff, but I was emptying a trash can and saw a whole bunch of receipts that just seemed..." He shrugged. "I hadn't seen more than one or two any other time before this." Dave held out the envelope. "I wasn't trying to be nosy or anything, but when they all said 'refund' on the top of them I got curious. Something didn't seem right about it."

Charlie pulled a couple of the slips of paper out. Sure enough, they all said refund and all were within a few minutes of each other.

"I've only worked there a couple weeks and I have no idea who I can trust. It looks odd, but maybe it's not. Maybe they process all the refunds at once. But..." He shook his head. "It's not anything I can put my finger on, but something feels off about it."

A scan of one showed nothing too odd, except the time being so close to the others. By the time Charlie got to the fourth one something was niggling at the back of his mind, too.

"If someone's doing something wrong, who is it? Do I tell the big boss? He's got problems of his own right now. Or the sort of office manager? Or who? If I tell the wrong person and there is something wrong, it all gets covered up and I get fired. Right?" Dave ran his hands through his hair. "I can't afford to lose the job, but I can't not do anything either."

Charlie nodded. "I understand." He held up the envelope. "Can I hang onto these and see if I can figure out what it is that's bugging me about them, too?"

Dave hesitated then stood. "If you wouldn't mind looking at them? Maybe help me figure out who I can talk to?"

"Of course." Another thought flew through his mind. "Listen, if it wouldn't be weird, do you think you could get me something with signatures or employee numbers? Nothing that's not already in the trash. Even a photocopy of a letter sent out with a signature so I can see what they look like." The receipts had several different signatures on them, but...

"If I see something that might be helpful, I'll get it and bring it over." After talking for a few more minutes, Dave stood and headed for the door, glancing at the television as he did. Another news report from Montevaro flashed on the screen before Charlie could turn it off. "That's wild, isn't it? The girls' mentor being a real princess?"

All Charlie could do was nod and pray Dave wouldn't remember the rest of the story.

But he did. "Didn't you date her a few times?"

"Yeah. A couple dates and she came over for Lindsey's party. She's the one who took Lindsey to the ER that night."

"Guess we know why it didn't work out." Dave sighed. "Can't imagine a princess ending up with someone like one of us. Single dad. Struggling to make ends meet. We're not from that world and never will be."

Charlie walked him to the door and turned to stare at the television. The Montevaro story had changed to something else, but it wouldn't leave his mind. Dave was right. Geography was the least of their problems.

He'd never be good enough for a princess.

14

They hadn't shaken security entirely, but they were neither seen nor heard as Addie cantered through an open Alpine field in front of Jonathan. It had been years since she'd ridden with any regularity and she missed it. When they reached the other end of the field where the path reentered the woods, they slowed their horses to a walk.

"I haven't done that in years." Jonathan's voice drifted up to her. "I don't get to ride much."

"I have not ridden much either since I moved to Serenity Landing. We did not keep horses there and I often did not have time when I was home."

"Or too cold when you were home for Christmas, I'd imagine."

Addie laughed. "Quite true. Most of my Christmas vacations were spent at our mountain retreat and always too snow-filled by mid-December." She pulled her mount to a stop and looked through an opening in the trees to the valley below. "Richard would love to open a business here. Mountain climbing, horse-back riding, and survivalist camping during the summer and cross-country skiing during the winter."

"Your brother and sister are two years younger than you?"

"Eighteen months. My mother's job to have a spare, you know. She had two."

"I've not met Prince Richard, have I? I'd remember that and I know I met Princess Ana over the weekend." Addie had introduced Jonathan to most of her family and informed her mother they were something of an item.

"Richard is on an expedition in the Himalayas, I believe it is. They have limited reception but call to check in when they can. By the time they could reach him, the immediate danger had passed and he stayed to finish the trip. He may take one more short one on his way home, but that is yet to be determined. A..." She hesitated, deciding how to word her next sentence. "A relative of a friend in Serenity Landing works for a company much like the one he would like to have here and he may go on a short trip with them."

"A friend?" Jonathan's soft voice caused her to turn and look at him.

He knew there was something more. She sighed and nodded. "Charlie's cousin. Lindsey told me all about it one day."

"Lindsey?"

"Charlie's daughter."

"Right." He moved his horse around her and started back down the path. "Why don't we find another clearing and eat the snacks we brought?"

"Of course." It only took several minutes before they reached another clearing, this one also with a view of the valley below. Jonathan swung down and turned to help her, though she did not need it. They ground tied their horses as Jonathan pulled a blanket and package of food out of his saddlebags.

A minute later, Addie sat on the blanket with her legs tucked to the side. Jonathan stretched out and used his elbow to support his upper body as he reached for a piece of cheese. He handed her a Thermos full of hot chocolate, still warm thanks to the insulation. She watched as he opened containers and set them on the blanket between them. Finger chicken salad sandwiches, cheese, and grapes.

They talked about everything and nothing for about half an hour before Jonathan went silent and sat up, staring over the valley. "There's something we need to talk about, Addie."

She hugged her legs to her chest as he rested his forearms on his raised knees. "What is that?"

"The past." His head hung. "If we're trying to see if there could be a future, you need to know about my past."

"I assure you the security staff has already fully vetted you, no matter your name." But she had the impression what he planned to tell her went beyond what even the most thorough check could unearth.

"I'm sure they have, but there's a lot they couldn't find out. I've had investigators look to see before and they couldn't. Even knowing what they were looking for didn't help much."

"All right."

Over the next several minutes he told her about his high school years. The parties, the girls, the alcohol, and the rehab. He did not go into great detail, but enough to know they would need to have a serious discussion sometime when they were not in the middle of a meadow on a day too cool to stay outside for long.

"I thank you for telling me, Jonathan."

He turned to look her square in the eyes. "Can you live with my past, Addie? To know that I've been with a number of women, though none for several years?"

Could she? She believed she could have lived with Charlie's situation. From what he had told her, Lindsey was the result of a one-time indiscretion. What Jonathan spoke of was something completely different. Both showed great remorse for their decisions, but could she live with knowing Jonathan had such a past?

"I know my sins are tossed as far as the east is from the west but I also know those sins still have consequences." Jonathan stood and held his hands toward her. She grasped them, allowing him to help her to her feet. He pulled her close, keeping her hands in his.

When Addie looked up at him, she could see his green eyes up close, see the sincerity in them.

"I don't expect an answer right now, but can you tell me if it's a *possibility*? Or if you're certain the answer will be no?"

She shook her head. "I cannot give you an answer now, though I wish I could give an unequivocal yes. I need to think, to pray, before I can tell you for certain."

"I understand and thank you for being honest with me." When he tugged on her hands, she found herself as close to him as she had ever been except for the hug that day in the garden. "Addie, will you answer another question for me?" His breath feathered across her face as he whispered.

"If I can."

"Have you ever been kissed?"

Of course he would ask that, but she nodded. "Only once."

"Can I kiss you?"

Her insides churned, though she was not sure if it was a good-nervous churn or a bad-nervous churn, but she gave the barest inclination of her head.

Jonathan bent down as her eyes fluttered closed. He brushed her lips in the softest of touches before returning to press his lips more fully against hers. The ball of knots in her stomach released somewhat. By the time he moved away, she knew there was a physical attraction between them. She also knew she would have plenty to analyze as she considered the relationship.

She was not repulsed by Jonathan.

But he was not Charlie.

As Addie's escort, Jonathan entered the service with her, the next to last ones to enter. Protocol dictated the royal family be last to enter, with the most senior member and his or her escort leading the rest of the family. When they reached the end of the aisle, he and Addie stopped, leaving enough room for her little sister, Ana, to slip into the pew first. Addie took the aisle seat.

Their conversation from the night before came back to him as they waited for the service to start. The perfect romantic setting. One of the more intimate sitting areas in the palace, a fire burning brightly in the stone fireplace. Sitting on a fur rug with a glass of wine for her and one of sweet tea for him.

"Are you sure you want to attend church with me in the morning?" He watched Addie swirl the bit of red wine in the bottom of her glass.

"Of course. It's Easter Sunday."

"You realize the public and the press will take it as tantamount to an announcement of our engagement."

"I understand that." He took a sip out of his glass. "Are you okay with that?"

"I suppose it's inevitable." She stared into the fire rather than looking at him. "We have been seen in public already. It is likely there has already been mention of a pending marriage in the tabloid press. If not, there certainly will be after tomorrow, though I fail to understand the American fascination with overseas royals from a country most of them would be hard pressed to find on a map."

Jonathan chuckled. "You lived among us, Addie. A princess moving unobserved among the American people while working at, not just donating to, charities many Americans hold dear." He reached for her hand and debated whether or not to kiss her again. "The American public eat that kind of story up. Plus..." He *hated* sounding egotistical while stating fact! "...it's me we're talking about. I've lived my life in the public eye and they love my family, especially the younger generation they've watched grow up in *Humanity Magazine* spreads. My cousin stays out of the public eye because of his wife's fears and they love him all the more for it. But it does mean I tend to get more attention when they decide I'm doing something noteworthy. And, I'm afraid, dating you is the most noteworthy thing I've done in a long time."

The strains of music coming from the pipe organ brought Jonathan's attention back to the present. An unseen choir sang a song he didn't recognize in a language he didn't know, yet he still understood. He stared at the stained glass window depicting a risen Christ ascending into the heavens.

He'd grown up in the church and had accepted Christ as his Savior when he was young. High school rolled around and there was no room for God in his life. Not with the alcohol and the girls and everything else. Since college started, he attended church more often than not. He prayed, though probably not the kind of prayer he probably should. More of the "Dear God, a good parking spot would be great" or "God, it would be awesome if the rain would stop while I run inside so I'm not drenched for my presentation" variety, with the occasional plea to heal or protect a friend or family member.

And as he pulled his Bible out and opened to the verse the music leader asked them to, he realized he couldn't think of the last time he'd read it outside of church. As he read the words of Mark 16:5-7 and the angel told the women the one they sought was no longer there, Jonathan sorrowed in his heart. He knew he wasn't where he should be, where he needed to be, as a Christian.

Addie shifted beside him. He wasn't qualified to be her husband. Not because of his heritage or family tree. They were likely quite acceptable, but how could Jonathan claim to be a man of God, a man who wanted to support his wife in leading her country and praying over her, being her strength behind the scenes when she needed him, if he couldn't do something as simple as read his Bible regularly? And that's before adding any kids into the mix.

He stood with everyone else and sang several hymns, listened to a sermon that convicted him more than his own heart already did. Before anyone else left the building, he escorted Addie to with Ana trailing behind them. They all smiled and nodded at those gathered until they left the building. Addie ignored the press as he let both her and Ana precede him into the waiting car.

Jonathan spent the ride to the garrison in pensive silence. Addie and Ana spoke quietly in the seat beside him, neither interrupting his musing. As he exited the car inside the garrison, he whispered a prayer heavenward. "Help me find You." Peace settled over him, though he knew it would take hard work on his part to get where he needed to be.

Shaking off his melancholy, he followed the girls onto the yacht reserved for taking the royal family across the lake. He stood, leaning on the railing, letting the wind wash over him, when a gentle hand landed on his back.

"Are you all right, Jonathan?"

He turned to see Addie leaning next to him, wind whipping her hair. Jonathan took her hand in his, pulling her to his side. "Just doing some thinking. About us."

She took her hand from his and instead grasped his bicep as she leaned against him. "What about us?"

"Whether or not I could be the husband you need. Could I be a prince consort? Would I really be okay with my children not having my name? I read once that Prince Philip struggled with that for years since all of his children with Queen Elizabeth are Windsors not Mountbattans. I met him a few years ago and he's quite the man. I don't know that I could be him."

She squeezed his arm. "I would never ask you to be Prince Philip. I would ask you to be Jonathan, the best Jonathan you can be."

"You know what I mean. I don't know that I'm the right man for you, Addie."

Addie turned him to face her. "We do not need to answer those questions right now, Jonathan. We just see where we go, if this is working. We pray, seek God's guidance, together and separately. Then trust He will give us the answer we seek."

Jonathan pressed a kiss to her forehead. "That sounds like a good plan." The yacht came to a stop and he let her go. Praying. He needed to do a lot of that.

Charlie sat in Mrs. Hart's office with Dave at his side. If his heart nearly thumped out of his chest, he couldn't imagine how the other man felt. The worst thing that could happen to Charlie was for Lindsey to get kicked out of The Club. Dave could lose his job, making it even harder for him to find another one.

A minute later, Mrs. Hart walked in, closing the door behind her. One abstract part of his mind noticed it was one of the new ones donated by Serenity Landing Hardware and Home Store. "What can I help you with, gentlemen?" Mrs. Hart settled in behind her desk.

Dave shifted uncomfortably. "I can't thank you enough for helping me get a job."

"I sense a 'but' coming."

"I found something in the trash and took it to Charlie. We don't think your niece had anything to do with it, but her name is on some of the paperwork and, to be frank, I don't know anyone there well enough to know who to trust."

Mrs. Hart frowned. "I know almost everyone over there and I can't imagine anyone being untrustworthy, but why don't you tell me what you found?"

Charlie pulled out a manila envelope. "In here are copies of receipts and other documents, all found in the trash at the comedy club. Dave thought they looked weird and brought them to me. I looked through them and he's right. Something weird is going on." He walked her through everything they'd found. Receipts. Refunds. Too much that just didn't add up and lots of people's names on them.

Mrs. Hart studied them closely. Charlie had photocopied and highlighted so it would make the most sense. "What else do you have?"

Charlie handed over the other sheets. "Mostly just letters and so on with some of the signatures on them for comparison purposes. They don't all look like they match those receipts to us, but they're similar enough and we're not experts."

She looked through all of it for several more minutes, before linking her fingers and resting her arms on her desk. "What would you like me to do with this information?"

Dave leaned forward. "I don't think your niece is involved, but we both believe that, if she was, you would know who to talk to and not cover for her. You should be able to tell better than us if that's her handwriting or not. You'd have a much better idea than either of us what to do with the information to make sure the right people know about it. Someone seems to be stealing from them and that's not right."

"And you have the originals of all of these somewhere safe, I presume?"

Charlie and Dave nodded in unison.

"Very well. I'll look through them more carefully and decide where to go from here."

The three of them stood and exited the office, Mrs. Hart walking them to the front desk. "Thank you for bringing it to my attention." She shook hands good-bye with Dave then turned to Charlie. "How's Lindsey doing?"

"Much better. She should be back in a couple days." If he didn't end up chasing her to Montevaro.

"How's she doing with the news about Addie being a Crown Princess?" Mrs. Hart leaned one elbow on the counter.

Charlie shrugged. "She already wanted me and Addie to be

together. She's trying to go all *Sleepless in Seattle* on me." He felt his eyes narrow as he looked at her. "Did you know?"

She nodded. "She knew it would come out in the background check. No one else knew but me and she wanted it that way. I had to sign a nondisclosure agreement and everything." Mrs. Hart put a hand on his forearm. "When you see her, tell I said hello and we miss her?"

Before he could respond and tell her he doubted he'd ever see Addie again, she turned and walked off. With a sigh and a shake of his head, he turned and left the building. If only... No. No "if onlys." Only reality. And the reality was the sooner he forgot about Adeline, Crown Princess of Montevaro, the better.

Adeline kept a smile pasted on her face as she walked into the hospital. Her father lay in a bed much like the ones in this building. He was receiving the best care, but he had a long road ahead of him. Once the initial healing finished, he looked at months of physical and occupational therapy to get back to normal. She had an uneasy feeling she would be asked to take on more and more duties as the months went on. It would not have surprised her to hear he never planned to return to his life as king, but instead pass the crown on to her.

Once inside the building, she relaxed a bit, but not much. No press allowed, but cameras and camera phones were ubiquitous and she could not let her guard down. Those who knew her would likely see the strain she was under. First, the count she had no desire to ever see again. Then her mother paraded a string of men in front of her. Men her mother deemed acceptable, but Adeline had no interest in. This doctor was likely the latest on her mother's fishing line, despite her relationship with Jonathan. Either her mother had not believed her or, more likely, she did not care. Adeline had chosen to date Jonathan which meant her mother had not meddled. If there was one thing the queen loved to do, it was meddle in Adeline's life.

Dr. Fontaine was handsome, Adeline would give him that. And nice. And a doctor. With a Texas accent though he was Montevarian by birth.

And not Charlie.

That was what it boiled down to. For the moment, Adeline had no interest in anyone who was not Charlie Brewer.

But she was not here, officially, to meet handsome doctors with great accents. She was here to see the work being done in the children's wing her parents had donated significant amounts of money to. They walked around the ward for about fifteen minutes before she went into the day room.

She could not contain the tears when a dozen voices called at the same time. "Welcome home, Princess Adeline!" The older children held up a homemade sign with those words on it, signed by a number of people, some of who did not know how to write yet and scribbled instead. It meant all the more to her because of it.

"Thank you." Once the group quieted down, she continued. "Thank you all so very much. It is lovely of you to think of me while you are in the hospital. I do hope I will come back soon, but I also hope none of you are here when I do."

They laughed.

"How's the king?" one little boy asked. "Is he better?"

Adeline nodded. "The king is doing better. He is hurt badly but not so badly he will not recover, though it will take some time. My father is a strong man and he will work hard until he is back to his old self."

They were satisfied with that answer, which was the word coming out of the palace. She gave them nothing new, but she supposed it meant more coming from a member of the family rather than a press release.

For nearly two hours, she worked the room. She spoke with

every child, every parent, every doctor, nurse or other caregiver. Taking pictures. Signing autographs. Drawing a crown on one girl's leg cast. When she was done, she visited the rest of the floor. By the time they returned to the doctor's office, she felt both better and worse.

She perched on the edge of one chair as she took the bottle of water he offered her. "Dr. Fontaine, how is it those children are so happy? Some of them have lost their hair from chemotherapy. The one little boy lost his hand. Many of the others are simply ill, but how do they remain so upbeat?"

Dr. Jonah Fontaine sat in the chair behind his desk and shook his head. "I wish I knew. If I did, I'd bottle it up and give it to the grown-up patients. Maybe because they don't realize the severity, or potential severity, of their circumstances, but children tend to be happier overall, even in the most dire of circumstances. They see the good in everything."

Adeline nodded, though she was not quite sure what to make of his words. As hard as she tried, she could not see the good in her mother's attempts to find her a suitor. After talking for a few more minutes, Dr. Fontaine walked her back to the main doors where a car waited.

As he helped her with her coat, she mentioned something on her mind. "I understand you are to be our guest this evening for dinner."

"I am."

She turned and looked directly into his eyes. "I think you are a wonderful man, Dr. Fontaine, and the work you are doing with the children is wonderful, but I do hope you realize, no matter what my..." She stopped before mentioning her mother. "...anyone else may have said, I am not interested in you as a suitor or life partner or future prince at this point. I am already in a relationship."

He gave her what many would find to be a heart-stopping smile. "Of course not, Princess Adeline. I did get that impression from the invitation, but I would never presume you could not find your prince on your own. I will admit to wondering if we might hit it off, but no fear. You are a lovely and charming woman and will be a wonderful queen someday, but you are not the woman God has for me. I hope the invitation still stands?"

She gave a gracious, and relieved, smile. "Of course it does. I look forward to seeing you there."

Dr. Fontaine opened the rear door to the car driven by Mark. She slid in, waved to the assembled press corps then settled back for the short drive to the pier. It had been a long, if exhilarating, morning and promised to be a longer afternoon.

If he had to send that girl back to her room one more time...

Charlie took a deep breath and blew it out slowly. He would go stark raving mad if he had to take it easy for days and days after surgery, but she'd been in the hospital for five days fighting infection and since they'd been home she'd tried one scheme after another to get to Montevaro.

He shouldn't have let her watch *Sleepless in Seattle*.

So what if she'd drifted in and out late one night at the hospital and he was desperate for any non-infomercial to watch. He would have been better off learning how amazing some seventy dollar Great Dane sized dog-snuggle-blanket was. But wait! If he ordered now, he'd get two for the low, low price of only 39.95. For the dog he didn't have.

He needed sleep.

And it wouldn't come while he was sleeping on the couch. But if he slept in his room, he ran the risk of her sneaking out and trying to find a way to cross half a continent, an ocean, another continent and the Alps for a chance to see a Crown Princess she wouldn't be able to get close to.

He clicked the power button on the remote. It was still on the news channel Dan had been watching earlier while Charlie had a long talk with his daughter about staying put. But it wasn't a straight news hour in the middle of the night. No. This was a half-news, half-gossip show that ran overnight like SportsCenter did. Repeated over and over. Different anchors. Live delivery but same gossip repeated *ad nauseum.*

And the gossip at the moment had to do with some count going to dinner at the palace where the Crown Princess of Montevaro just happened to be holed up.

The first shot showed Addie walking into a building identified by the red plus sign in the background as a hospital. He watched as a man walked up to her. A good-looking guy if the cackling of the hostesses was any indication. The man didn't touch Addie but smiled at her and showed her which way they were going.

Right before she disappeared into the building, he got a good look at her face. Addie was exhausted. She put on a good front. Had a smile as she gave reporters a quick wave, but to anyone who knew her well, she looked tired and stressed. The stories said her father was banged up and bruised but would be fine so there had to be something more to it.

His answer came in the form of a still shot, close-up of an angry man bellowing at someone out of the shot. It was followed by another picture of him being driven off in a Rolls Royce.

The gossip-mongers wondered aloud if the princess was looking for a prince. They were especially interested because...

Another picture appeared on the screen. This one made Charlie sit up, bare feet on the floor and blanket falling off his knees. He knew that guy.

The woman's voice grated on his nerves, but he turned up the sound.

"This is, of course, one of *Humanity Magazine's* most eligible bachelors and one of last year's most beautiful people, number two in both categories. Jonathan William Langley-Cranston the

Fourth is the great-nephew of a former president and a distant cousin to two more. He also has connections to the Windsors, several centuries back. Reportedly, Jonathan attends school with Princess Adeline and he has come to Montevaro to offer his support during this difficult time."

The pretty-boy face of the man who had taken Addie out at least once, if Lindsey was to be believed, was the last straw.

They were going on a trip.

If it took the rest of his natural life to pay it off, he had to see her one more time.

15

Adeline longed for the day when she would not have so many public functions to attend on a regular basis. Even as she did, she knew the day would never come. Oh, she would have respite sometimes, but this was her life. As a teenager, she went to some public functions, appeared at a few charity events each year. In college, she did some when she returned home for visits.

Now, she was an adult and part of being an adult in the royal family meant making public appearances, attending charity functions, visiting sick children in the hospital, christening ships, and who knew what other kinds of things.

At least Jonathan was going with her to this ribbon cutting. His presence made it easier, though he did his best to blend into the background. If, someday, he were her husband, he would take a more central, but still supportive role. He would work the rope lines with her, shaking hands, kissing babies, all of those things. For now, knowing she was not alone was enough.

"So where is this we're going?" He took her hand. "You holding up okay? This is the second event today and you have two more after this. Then three tomorrow after four yesterday."

Adeline nodded. "I believe so. I am filling in for both of my parents and making appearances that were postponed after my father's injuries. Hopefully, things will slow down soon."

"They need to. You're falling behind in your schoolwork, aren't you?"

She shrugged.

"Plus, during your free time, you Skype with the girls back in Serenity Landing, helping them with homework and etiquette. Did you get the paper done last week?"

"No. I did not. I will be taking two days almost completely off after the Spring Festival next weekend. I should have no trouble catching up then. Tomorrow, we should both have the audio files of the last few classes. We can listen together in the car or at the palace and work on the projects." She looked over at him. "Did I tell you we were reassigned to work together since you are here and our other partners are still in Serenity Landing?"

Jonathan squeezed her hand. "No, you didn't, but I did get an email from Professor Putane about it."

The car turned into a parking lot and Adeline took a deep breath, putting on what Jonathan called her "game face." A smile that she did her best to let reach her eyes. They exited the car out of sight from the press and public, with Jonathan turning to help her out.

"Your Highness." A short, slender man bowed slight her direction. "I am the director of the facility, George Lawton. Thank you for coming."

Adeline held out a hand. "I am glad I could come. I know this is something my family has been very interested in for a number of years." The orphanage, in the small town of Viginio, served western Montevaro. For a long time, they only took in children for long term placement, until they might find an adoptive family. With help from her family and donations, they were opening an emergency shelter for children who needed a place to stay for a short period of time.

She and Jonathan followed Mr. Lawton into the building.

"We have facilities for up to twenty children in the emergency shelter," he told them as they walked into the first room.

"What kind of situations do you anticipate these children coming from?" Jonathan asked.

"Most of the time it's something where the children are left suddenly orphaned and they need a place to stay for a few days until family members can be located or make it to Viginio. They may be traveling or live in another country. If that's the case, it can take a week or more just to get a passport and other travel documents together. Or a single parent may be in a car accident and unable to take care of the children for a short time, but not have anyone who can step up. Generally, children will be limited to no more than thirty days without specific approval from the admissions coordinator. If the time is extended beyond ninety days, they'll be transferred into our long-term care facility and determine if they need to be put into foster care or up for adoption or what their status is."

They'd looked at several of the other rooms, including two with cribs. "Are there any accommodations made for sibling groups to stay in the same room together if they'd like to?" Adeline ran a hand over the bright comforter on the twin bed.

The next room seemed to be designed for just that with bunk beds on one wall. "We will do our best, though province law says opposite gender siblings can't stay in the same room over a certain age or if there is a certain gap in age."

Fifteen minutes later, they finished the tour of the building and exited onto the front porch. A crowd of reporters stood to one side with a group of onlookers in front of them.

Adeline walked to the podium as the crowd applauded. Her speech was in a binder waiting for her, flipped open to the first page. "Good afternoon, ladies and gentlemen." The speech was short, similar to many others she had given, but no less heartfelt. When she finished, she and Mr. Lawton took a giant set of scissors to the red ribbon strung across in front of the podium.

On the count of three, they cut it and it fell to the ground. With Mark and Todd flanking her, she went to "press the flesh" as it was called in the American political movies. She shook hands with more people than she could count, taking flowers and other little notes with her. If the past was any indication, some were for her and many more were well wishes for her father. As she reached the end of the line, she turned to go, only to be called back by a voice filled with desperation.

"Princess Adeline!"

Adeline stopped and pivoted to see a young man, perhaps her own age, running toward the line. Security moved to ensure he would not get through the rope, as Mark moved close enough for his jacket to brush her arm.

"I'm sorry, Princess Adeline," he huffed, out of breath. "I know you have a busy schedule but I have to try."

She held a hand up to the men guarding her and took a step closer. "Try what, sir?"

"My daughter. She's six and she's dreamed of meeting you her whole life, but I don't know..." Emotion clogged his face. "I don't know if she has enough time for us to try again. We don't live far, but our tire went flat about a half mile back and my spare is flat, too. My wife is on her way with my daughter, but I ran ahead, hoping I could get you to stay long enough." He collapsed until his hands rested on his knees. "Please?"

Adeline smiled at him. "Of course." She motioned to Todd. "Todd will go help your wife and daughter. Would you like to come inside and rest for a moment?"

The man nodded. "Thank you, Your Highness." He fell in a half-step behind her, but was stopped by security when they reached the door.

She gave him an apologetic look. "I do hope you understand. No one is allowed inside without being searched."

"I would be disappointed in our state security teams if I wasn't searched. Too many crazies in this world who would use a sob story to get close to you."

A minute later, they sat in the employee lounge with Jonathan. It was not long before Todd and a young lady arrived pushing a wheelchair. Tears filled Adeline's eyes as she looked at the little girl. Her head was covered with a bandana and she was obviously too frail to do much of anything.

The girl bowed her head. "I'm sorry I can't curtsy, Princess Adeline."

Addie knelt on the floor next to her. "There is no need for you to apologize, sweet girl." She took the small hand in her own. "I am so very glad we have met. What is your name?"

"Sara."

Addie smiled. "It is lovely to meet you, Sara."

"You, too, Your Highness."

Addie leaned closer and whispered. "You can call me Princess Addie." She held a finger to her lips. "But sh, do not tell anyone. I only let special little girls call me that and I can tell you are the most special little girl I have met in quite some time."

The smile nearly split the little girl's face in two. "I won't tell anyone, Princess Addie." Sara glanced over Addie's shoulder. "Are you gonna marry him? The telly says you are."

"I do not know. Jonathan is a wonderful man, but we have not decided if marriage is in our future." She squeezed the hand lightly. "But when I do get married, I want you to be in the front row, all right?" Addie tapped her finger against her mouth. "No. You know what? I believe I would prefer for you to be well enough to be one of my flower girls. Would you like that?"

Sara looked up at her parents. "Did you hear that, Mama?"

Addie pressed a kiss against the girl's forehead. "Get well,

Sara." She stood to see tears streaming down the faces of both of Sara's parents. "She is a lovely girl."

Sara's mother reached for Addie, then stopped herself before touching the princess. Instead she took a step away from the wheelchair. "I'm afraid Sara doesn't have much time, Your Highness. We've done all we can afford to do."

Adeline turned to Mark who held out a card and a pen. She wrote a note on the back of it. "Take this with you to Montevaro General Hospital and ask for Dr. Jonah Fontaine. If there is anything that can be done, he will see that it is."

Hope began to shine on the woman's face before it slid away. "We have no money, Your Highness. We've spent every penny we have and everything we could borrow."

"I understand. It will be taken care of." Adeline squeezed the young mother's shoulder. "If you will excuse me, I do need to get going, but please do send updates. The address on the card is for mail sent specifically to me and only given out to a few people. If you send an update there, I will get it quickly."

After several minutes of tears and "thank you" repeated over and over, Adeline and Jonathan were back in the limousine headed for the next stop. Peace filled her. She might not be able to help everyone, but every once in a while, she could turn someone's world around. She just hoped it was not too late for little Sara.

Charlie and Lindsey made their way out of the Montevarian airport. She had her backpack and favorite stuffed animal. He had two pilot cases and his laptop bag he was trying to manage successfully. The airport was much smaller than the Springfield airport with only six gates. There was a car rental place, but the hotel was, supposedly, right on a cable line and only a mile from the airport. He planned to just do that, but Lindsey's exhausted face made him change his mind.

He stopped an airport employee and asked where he could catch a cab. She told him where to go and fifteen minutes later, they had been deposited in front of the quaint building.

"This place is cool." Lindsey gazed up at the hotel.

According to the website, the building was a couple hundred years old, but thoroughly updated. The price was more than he would have liked, but cheaper than most of the others in the area - especially the ones with decent reviews.

Checking in went smoothly and they found their room. The excitement began to wear off and Lindsey couldn't muster the excitement over the room he would have expected. He pulled the curtains back on the window as she kicked her shoes by the door and peeled off the special stockings her doctor made her wear for the flights.

The view took his breath away. "Look at this, Linds."

The hotel was two streets from the lake, but on the side of a hill so each street was a fair bit lower than the next. In the middle of the lake was an island.

On the island sat a palace.

"Wow." Her word was barely a breath. "That's where Miss Addie lives?"

"I guess so, punkin."

"Why would she ever want to be with us then? We can't live anything like that."

Charlie had been asking himself that very question but he couldn't let his daughter know that. "I don't think that's what bothers Addie. But she couldn't move and I wasn't willing to so that had to be a big part of why nothing could ever happen with us."

"But I want her to be my mom and not because I'd get to be a princess." Even without looking at her, he knew she was close to tears.

He rested his hand on her back and moved her to the bed. "That's something else we need to talk about." How to tell her? "I don't know if anything's going to happen with me and Addie. In fact, if I had to guess, I'd guess it probably won't, but I had to come and try to see her one more time." His little girl's blue eyes nearly ripped his heart out. "But even if Addie and I got married, I don't think you'd be a princess."

The wheels were turning in her head as he watched her try to take it in. "Why not? You'd be a prince."

That was something he had a hard time even thinking about. "Well, yes. But *if* - and this is a big, giant, Jupiter-sized if - Addie and I got married, I'd be a prince *only* because I married her. And even though I bet she'd love you as much as her own daughter, you wouldn't actually be related to her and so you wouldn't be a princess. Does that make sense?"

Lindsey nodded. "I guess."

"But we're big giant moon steps ahead of ourselves. First, we have to find a way to see her. Then talk to her. Then see if she's even interested. There could be a lot of reasons why she's not." He pulled her close to him and wrapped his arms around her. "Sometimes princesses can't marry whoever they want, especially princesses who are going to be queen someday. There's rules about who they can and can't marry and no matter how much Addie might like us, she might not be able to and still be queen someday. It depends on Montevaro's laws and I have no idea what they are."

He crooked a finger under her chin until she looked at him. "Now, why don't you try to get some sleep? I know how tired you must be."

She might be eleven, but when she wanted to, Lindsey could turn on the whine. "But I didn't do anything but sit on a stupid plane all day long."

"And you had abdominal surgery less than two weeks ago. You're lucky the doctor let you come at all."

"I know," she muttered and moved to the other bed. "Do you know where my sleep mask went?"

"In your backpack."

Two minutes later, she was curled under the covers with the mask on. He pulled his laptop out, logged into the hotel's Wi-Fi, and tried to figure how to stalk the Crown Princess without getting arrested.

Adeline took one look at the visitor and her day brightened considerably. "Jonathan! How are you?"

He took her hands in his and gave her light kisses on both cheeks. She thought he would have kissed her. Really kissed her. But did she want him to? That question was too hard to answer. "Good. How are you?"

"I am fine. You know I am always happy to see you, but we did not have plans today, did we?" She had been sitting in the garden, enjoying being outside on a lovely day. Together, they started walking down one of the paths, her hand tucked in his arm.

Birds chirped in the nearby trees and if she listened carefully Addie could hear the waves lapping against the base of the island fortress. But right now, all she wanted to hear was what Jonathan had to say. "No, but I thought we needed to talk."

Addie sat on a nearby stone bench. Nearly as old as the palace itself, it had been surprisingly well-maintained. Most of the gardens had. "About what?" Tall shrubs surrounded them, blocking them from the view of anyone in the palace.

Jonathan sat about a foot away and stared at his folded hands. Butterflies filled Addie's stomach. What could he have to say?

Finally, he answered. "About us."

The butterflies sped up. "You do not beat around the bush, do you?"

He looked over at her. "They're shrubs, not bushes." His wink made her laugh.

"Very well. You do not beat around the shrub." Addie smoothed her hands over her skirt. "What about us?"

"What do you think about us, Addie?"

Thoughts of all sorts tumbled through her head. Uncertain what to make of them, she acquiesced. "I would like to know your thoughts." She refused to acknowledge he might be ending things with her. If he did, her mother would get even bolder. Addie did not want to deal with that.

Jonathan seemed to weigh his words, choosing them carefully. "I know I like you. I have since we took that first class on American government together nearly six years ago. I'm not in love with you, though I thought about asking you out for a long time. This spring, I decided to ignore the look Mark and Todd always seemed to give me to discourage me."

A tentative half-smile crossed her face. "You know why. They are bodyguards tasked with my physical, mental, and emotional well-being."

"I know."

The churning grew worse. "Have you decided you cannot accept being prince consort? Always being second to your wife?" She watched his face carefully for his reaction. "Your children never bearing your name?"

He walked a few steps away, his hands shoved deep in his pockets. "I think I could live with all of those things. But it's something more."

Something else was bothering him. "We are not in love?" Addie knew she sounded a bit desperate. But the alternative of someone like Count Bladvile... "I am not opposed to the idea of an arranged marriage. We have discussed that. I hoped to find someone Montevarian customs would find acceptable but who I also loved. Growing up that was my dream, but more and more I realize it may never be so." She clasped her hands in her lap, hoping if she squeezed tightly enough they would stop trembling. "I have always known my position and my people had to come before my own personal inclinations and desires. Since I was young, I knew I may not marry for love." She looked over at him. "But it is more than that, is it not?"

He sat down again, leaned forward, and rested his elbows on his knees. "It's my relationship with Christ. It's not what it should be. I admit that. I'm a Christian, but if I'm being honest, I'd probably be one of those lukewarm ones. It's something I keep meaning to change, but..."

"I understand. It is not always easy to maintain that relationship. I often struggle with it myself, but it is of utmost importance to me, regardless. Though I will be queen of my country, I want a husband who will be a scriptural head of our home without usurping my authority outside our apartment. It will be a difficult line to draw, but without Christ in the mix, it will be impossible."

Jonathan was quiet for several minutes. "Until that part of my life is straightened out, I can't be the person you need. If we're talking possible marriage, and I can't be the husband you would need me to be, I think we need to call it quits. At least for now. I promise to pray about it and do my best to grow that relationship, no matter what happens between us."

"I pray, for your own sake, your relationship with Christ becomes everything it needs to be. As for us... do you really believe we are meant to be together?" Deep inside, she did not think they were but she wanted to know what he thought.

"I don't know, but I would like to be your friend through the next few weeks. I have a feeling they could be difficult ones as you figure out what's going on with your father. And it would keep your mom off your back."

She turned that over in her mind. Not ideal. But not worst case scenario just yet. "Friends, but nothing more. In time, we may revisit the question of us, but for now, friends."

He stood and reached for her hand, helping her up. Once it

was safely tucked inside his elbow, he repeated the single word. "Friends."

Charlie checked the piece of paper again. They had to be close. "How much farther, Dad?"

"Not far," he assured her. *I hope.*

Crown Princess Adeline was scheduled to make an appearance at the hospital again, this time to visit the Neonatal Intensive Care Unit and see the latest advances in caring for preemies. The front desk clerk told him how to get there, said it was an easy walk, but Charlie hadn't taken his daughter's continued recovery into account. He checked the sheet one more time and they turned right at the corner.

He breathed a nearly audible sigh of relief as the hospital came into view. Right there was the entrance he'd seen Addie using on television a couple days earlier. Unfortunately, there was also a crowd. Not a huge one, but big enough that it would be hard to see Addie, much less get her attention.

Lindsey stopped, dropping his hand. "She'll never see us."

"We'll try."

Five minutes later, they were on the outskirts of the crowd as a black Rolls Royce with darkened windows pulled up in front of the hospital. Cameras started clicking as the front passenger door opened. Todd stepped out, looking more intimidating than ever in a dark suit with sunglasses on as he scanned the crowd. Charlie thought Todd looked right at him, but if he did, he gave no indication. A few seconds later, Todd opened the rear door.

Charlie's jaw nearly dropped when Jonathan William Langley-Cranston the Fourth climbed out. He turned and held out a hand to whoever was in the car. Charlie whispered a prayer for anyone but Addie to emerge, but no such luck. Addie's hand remained in

Jonathan's as they walked toward the hospital where the same doctor waited. Addie turned and waved at the crowds on both sides of the entrance, but didn't look anywhere near Charlie and Lindsey. Lindsey's cries of "Addie" couldn't be heard over the other people talking.

Addie, Jonathan, and the doctor disappeared inside. Charlie turned in time to see Lindsey's shoulders fall.

"She didn't see us."

He pulled his daughter to him and wrapped her in his arms. "We'll wait until she leaves and try again."

"Can we sneak in the hospital and try to find her?" Her voice was muffled by his coat.

"No, sweetie. But we'll wait."

The next two and a half hours were long ones, though they did find a stone bench to sit on. Charlie was starting to wonder whether or not Addie would ever emerge, or if she might go out a different entrance.

"Dad?"

He looked down to see Lindsey starting to shiver just a bit. It wasn't *cold* but it certainly wasn't a warm summer day either. Not this high in the Alps in early spring. "Are you ready to go back to the hotel and try again later?" But there wasn't anything on the palace website about her schedule for the rest of the week.

She shook her head. "No, I want to stay, but I have to go to the bathroom."

Charlie glanced at the door. No sign of activity. There was a café across the street. He'd been thinking about going to get a cup of hot chocolate for her, but hadn't wanted to leave their spot. "Okay. We'll get a drink and you can go to the bathroom."

It couldn't have taken more than ten minutes, but when they emerged from the café the car, driven by Mark with Todd next to him, was pulling away from the curb across the street.

"*Addie!*" Lindsey's scream tore through him, ripping his heart to pieces.

More than his own desire to remain unscathed from relationships turned sour, it reminded him of why he couldn't let a woman get too close.

Because in breaking his daughter's heart, his own shattered to pieces.

16

Adeline twisted in her seat to stare out the back window, her eyes scanning the crowd. She did not know what exactly she was looking for but she did not find it and returned to face forward.

"Is everything okay?"

Jonathan had been a God-send, keeping her mother from trying to play matchmaker with untold numbers of other men. Adeline gave him her best smile. "Yes. I thought I heard something, but I could not find its source so I must have been mistaken."

The drive back to the dock was short. She and Jonathan, along with Mark and Todd, were ferried across the lake to the palace. Adeline went to her office while Jonathan headed somewhere else. She would meet him again before dinner, after she went to see her father.

Her first order of business was to jot down a few notes about what she had seen in her tour at the hospital. Then it was time to head to the medical facilities, but as she walked across the plush carpeting to the door, she stopped.

"Do you really think it was them?" Todd was talking to someone.

Mark answered. "I think so."

"Why are they here?"

"There's only one reason I can think of."

She could not decide if Todd's answer was full of concern or fear or what might be coloring his words. "Princess Adeline."

Mark's one word answer made her blood run cold. "Exactly."

She turned and went back to the wingback chair. Who or what had they seen? A known threat to the royal family? There were not many. Her bodyguards were more a precaution than anything most of the time. That was why they were able to get their college degrees at the same time she did rather than *just* act as bodyguards.

The outer door opened and someone else walked in, though Adeline was not certain who it was. No matter. She took a deep breath, whispered a prayer for the safety of all those she cared about and went to see her father.

After two weeks, he looked better though Adeline knew it would be quite some time before he was back to his usual, robust self, if he ever would be again. Today, he was sitting up in a chair near his bed. The one window in the room overlooked one of several courtyards and he did not stop staring out it when she walked in.

When she reached his side, he finally looked up. "Hello, sweet Adeline."

She smiled at his affectionate tone. "Hello, Papa. How are you today?"

His movements were slow, but he stood and looked out the window, this time staring upward toward the Alps in the distance. "My body is healing, though more slowly than I would like. My mind is sharp. My family is nearby. My God is ever-present. What more can a man ask for?"

Adeline's brows knit together. "What is it, Papa?"

"Your mother and I have gone back and forth over a number of things since you arrived home, but now I am taking one matter into my own hands."

Part of her hoped he would call off the matchmaking, but the rest of her knew he had something much more serious in mind.

"'I will lift mine eyes unto the hills, from whence cometh my help.'"

"Psalm 121:1."

He smiled at her and started back for his bed. She slid a hand under his elbow and did her best to help him.

"That verse has been the cornerstone of our country for centuries. Not because the armies of our allies came over them, but because God is found in the mountains. He is found elsewhere of course, but nonetheless."

Adeline helped cover him with a blanket much nicer than the ones she had seen on her recent trip to the hospital.

"There is something I want to tell you. Something my father told me and his father told him. You will be the first woman, to my knowledge, to hear these words." His head lay back against the pillow and he seemed tired, but before she could tell him it could wait, he continued. "It was only a year or so before you were born that the rules of primogeniture were changed so the crown no longer passes from father to eldest son but father to eldest child regardless of gender."

She knew that and had been told as much from the time she was very young. One day, she would be Queen Adeline the First. The first queen to rule Montevaro.

"As much as I love your brother, I am glad you are the one who will be taking over for me. It is possible if he had known his whole life he would one day be king, he would be different, but as it is, I fear he would be stifled and trapped as monarch."

"I agree." She tucked the blanket more closely around him.

"I will be stepping down."

Adeline's head jerked up to see him watching her with serious eyes and a somber look on his face. "What?" she whispered.

"I will be stepping down soon. I do not know when yet, but you will be queen before the year is out, most likely much sooner than that."

Her stomach churned and her mind scrambled to make sense of it. "But why?"

"Recovery will take months with little time for anything but therapy and other things necessary to go along with it. But there is something we have kept from you." The king of Montevaro reached out and cradled her hand in both of his. "Several years ago, my physician diagnosed me with Parkinson's Disease."

Her mind overloaded. "But, Papa, you are not old enough..."

"But I am, sweet Adeline. The American actor from the time travel movie you loved so much growing up was diagnosed at thirty. I am well past that, though I am younger than most of those diagnosed with it." He closed his eyes and stroked the back of her hand. "It has progressed more quickly than any of us hoped and the medications will only last so much longer. Our plan had been for you to come home after graduation and spend a year with you, teaching you the rest of what you need to know and stepping down next summer, but my accident has sped the timetable up. The Parkinson's will complicate an already fairly difficult healing process. I do hope you will talk with me and let me advise you for at least the first couple of years, but I would not try to usurp your authority."

She took a deep, shuddering breath. "I..." She swallowed. "I will do my best to make you proud of me, Papa, but I am not ready to be queen."

He reached up with one hand and rested it against her cheek. "I am proud of you already, just for being you. And you will be ready. If you are not, I am still here to help you, if you will let me, but I have every confidence in you, or I would not make this decision." His hand fell back to the blanket. "I know I have dropped a heavy burden on you and I am willing to discuss it with you at length when you have had some time to absorb it all, but would you mind asking the nurse to come in? I am in need of pain medication and sleep."

Adeline bent over and brushed a kiss against his forehead before doing as he asked. She was supposed to go to dinner but sent word she was not feeling well. Instead, she went to her apartment and stared out the largest window in her bedroom. The mountains held resolute promise, but in front of them was the largest town in her small country.

There were three things she needed to do.

Read her Bible and ask God for His help and wisdom.

And talk to Charlie.

If only she could. But they were not to be and so she, as so many before her, would rely solely on God. Her life was about to get much lonelier than it already was.

One more day.

They only had one more day to find Princess Adeline.

Charlie tied his tennis shoes while Lindsey finished her shower. The water turned off and he heard her bumping around as she got dressed. When she emerged, she looked tired. He contemplated calling the whole thing off and resting in the room until their flight left the next evening.

Before he could say anything, a knock sounded at the door.

"Finish getting ready." He'd make a decision in a few minutes. There was no peep hole in the door, so he opened it just a touch. What he saw surprised him right down to his toes. "Mark? Todd?" An answer to prayer? Maybe?

Mark answered for both of them. "May we come in?"

Charlie nodded and opened the door all the way.

Lindsey sat on the bed and stared at them, but didn't say anything.

He didn't wait for them to speak. "How can we help you?"

Todd spoke this time. "We may be able to help you. You are here to see Princess Adeline?"

"Of course we are!" Lindsey jumped up and stared down the much larger man. "Why else would we fly all the way here? It wasn't to see you two!"

"Lindsey," Charlie started gently, but Todd interrupted him.

"It's okay. We saw you at the hospital yesterday and found out where you were staying. We will help you see Princess Adeline but there are a few things we need to discuss first."

Charlie felt himself deflate. They were going to confirm what he already suspected. "She won't be allowed to marry a man who isn't nobility of some sort, much less one who had a child at sixteen, so we shouldn't get our hopes up for some kind of relationship between me and Addie."

Mark nodded, though Charlie suspected he didn't agree with the rationale but there wouldn't be anything he could do about it. "As long as you're aware of that, we'll be happy to take you to the palace. I know Princess Adeline would be happy to see you. On the way we'll talk with you about some protocol things. For instance, you must never refer to her as 'Addie', unless she specifically gives you permission, and then never in public. She is Princess Adeline, Your Highness, or ma'am. I know it's very different from what you're used to, but..."

"But she's the princess," Lindsey finished for him. She had her coat on before she was done. "Let's go."

Charlie stopped her with one hand on her shoulder as she charged past. "Not so fast, hon. I'm sure there are some other things we need to talk about with Mark and Todd before we go."

Both men nodded. He and Lindsey sat back down to listen.

Adeline was wearing the heels she hated again. The clickety-click was enough to drive her crazy but there were not nearly enough runners in the halls or rugs in the rooms. Wall-to-wall carpet had not yet been invented when the palace was built and had not been added in many places except the bedrooms. Todd had been quite mysterious when he called and asked her to come down to one of the formal living areas where they often greeted dignitaries of some kind in a less formal setting than the throne room.

She heard voices coming from the other side of the door, though an impassive Mark stood outside it. He opened the door, cracking the smallest of smiles as he did.

Nothing could have prepared her for the sight that greeted her.

Her heart swelled as Lindsey started to run toward her, but stopped when Charlie rested a hand on her arm as she passed him.

Yet something else different here in her official capacity. Three weeks ago, Lindsey would have continued to run and give her a huge hug and Addie would have absorbed it in preparation for the day she would not see the girl anymore.

But now, a smile crossed her face and her spirit lifted. "Lindsey! Charlie! What a pleasant surprise."

Lindsey bit her bottom lip and tucked one foot behind her in an awkward attempt to curtsy.

It both warmed and broke her heart. "There is no need for that, sweet girl." She held her arms out and Lindsey ran to her. Addie enfolded the girl in her arms. It was a balm to her soul. She pressed a kiss to Lindsey's head. "I am so glad you are here." She met Charlie's eyes across the room. "I am glad both of you are here."

Lindsey moved back and Addie looked at her. Her cheeks were still a bit sunken and there were circles under her eyes. "How are you feeling? Have you fully recovered enough to travel so far?"

Charlie answered her question. "Her doctor didn't want her to and we wouldn't have except she kept trying to run away to get here."

He would not have come for her? For a brief moment, deep inside where she barely let herself believe in what her heart desired, she thought maybe he had come for her. She looked back down at Lindsey. "Running away so soon after surgery? That could be very hazardous to your health and I would have been deeply saddened to know you had a relapse of some kind trying to see me. Why did you not just call?"

"We tried but your number was disconnected." Charlie moved toward her but still stayed farther away than she would like. "Todd told us it was a security precaution."

She had not checked her phone much since she arrived, though when she had, she thought it was odd no one had called or texted her. There had been so much going on she had not had time to think about it too much though. But now, she needed to talk to Charlie.

"Lindsey, would you like to see my favorite place to play growing up?"

The girl's face lit up. "Yeah! Is it a turret or something?"

Addie laughed. "No. Do you have your coat?"

Lindsey grabbed it off one of the couches and slung it around her shoulders. "Let's go."

This time as she walked through the hallways toward her favorite courtyard, she barely noticed the clickety-clack of her shoes. All she could think about was the man walking beside her.

Charlie did his best to not get overwhelmed but it was impossible. Long corridors filled with paintings, each worth more than his annual salary - for several years or several decades. Coats of arms. Full bodies of armor complete with swords and spears lining part of one. Tapestries and expensive rugs that probably weren't called rugs but he didn't know what else to call them, lined the walls and floors. Through one of the doors, he could see portraits of people he guessed were kings and queens of the past.

"Through here, Lindsey."

As Todd and Mark had told them, he walked a bit behind Addie. No. Adeline. *Princess* Adeline. No one was supposed to walk in front of her or even beside her except a head of state or one of her siblings or her mother. Once she became queen even her family would walk a step behind.

But Lindsey must have forgotten because she skipped along next to Princess Adeline, holding her hand and chatting about the girls from her after school program. The princess didn't seem to mind, but he'd have to talk to her about it later.

They turned a corner and Charlie stifled a gasp. The doors in front of them were much larger than normal doors, with ornate glass work in them. They almost looked like stained glass windows - a design emerging from the metal in them - but with clear class instead of colored. Before he could figure out exactly what the design was, Adeline pushed one of them open.

Lindsey did gasp as a beautiful garden came into view.

"Go ahead," Adeline encouraged her. "See what you can find in the maze."

That was all the encouragement the girl needed. She ran down the steps and along the path into the row of shrubs. Where she came up with the energy after everything else, he didn't know except maybe adrenaline from seeing Addie - Adeline - again.

When he turned to look at Adeline, someone had handed her a coat and gloves. She buttoned it around her before pulling them on.

The princess gave him a soft smile. "I am glad you are here, Charlie. It is good to see you and Lindsey."

"It's good to see you, too, Princess Adeline." The unfamiliar title and name didn't roll easily off his tongue.

Something crossed her face. Disappointment maybe? But it was quickly replaced with a friendly, if somewhat distant, mask. Could this really be the same woman he had kissed right before she left?

"I am Addie when there is no one else around." She turned to look out over the garden. "Very few people will call me that and I am not comfortable enough around most people to let my guard down. You and Lindsey are two of the only ones. Please don't take that from me."

"Okay. Addie. How are you?"

"Things have been difficult in some respects but not so much in others. It is nice to be home. Being 'Princess Adeline' all the time can be tiring until I get used to it again." She started down the stairs, one hand resting on the wrought iron rail. "Why did you come, Charlie? Just to keep Lindsey from running off?"

He followed her until they reached the ground, hands shoved deep in the pockets of his coat. "Partly. I wanted to see you again, too." He stared at the intricate arch over the entrance to the maze. "I saw you on TV and wanted to check on you. You were walking into the hospital a few days ago and I could tell you were tired and stressed. They were talking about how they thought your father might end up stepping down. You looked like you could use a friend." They were also talking about her search for a husband, but he wouldn't mention that unless she did.

"You flew halfway around the world because I could use a friend?" Princess Adeline looked up at him and he was sure he saw tears in her eyes. "Thank you, Charlie."

"You're my friend," he said simply.

They heard Lindsey's giggles. "She must have found the wishing well." Addie smiled his way.

"There's a wishing well?"

"It is really a working well, though it has not been used as such in over a century. It was to make sure there was fresh water in case of a siege. There is little danger of that these days so it's been turned into a wishing well. At Easter, children from town come and have an egg hunt and make wishes."

Silence reigned as they waited for Lindsey to return.

At least until Addie broke it. "Is that all I am to you, Charlie? A friend?"

Where had the courage come from? Addie did not know, but she had and now she waited for the answer with bated breath.

"I think you know the answer to that, Princess Adeline." His voice was soft but the use of her title and name reminded her of all the reasons why they could not be more than friends.

"What if I gave up my claim to the throne?" The thought had flickered in and out of her head several times in the last few days, though she would not have mentioned it to anyone if he had not come to see her.

"What good would that do?"

She took a deep breath and blew it out slowly. Her next few words would bare her soul. "It would mean my parents and Parliament would have no say in who I marry."

"And you would be willing to give it all up so we could be together?"

Addie could not read the tone of his voice so she turned to look at him, to see if she could tell what he was thinking. Then her shoulders slumped and the weight of the world crashed back down on her. "I do not know. This is what I was raised to do. What I was born knowing I would do one day. But..."

He reached out and brushed a bit of hair away from her forehead, his finger trailing down the side of her cheek. How could he make her feel so much with such a simple gesture?

"But you don't want to lose a chance at someone who could love you for Addie, not just Princess Adeline." His insight into her should have surprised her but did not, so she simply nodded. "I saw some of the men who've been here. That count?" He shook his head. "Please tell me you're not considering him."

"No. There will be no future with him."

"What about Jonny-boy the 4th?"

"Who?"

"Jonathan William Langley-Cranston the Fourth. He was holding your hand yesterday."

"We tried dating, but there is nothing between us but friendship. He is keeping my mother from trying to set me up with anyone else. It was his idea to not tell her there would be no future for us either."

"What a guy." The sarcasm was not lost on her.

Lindsey chose that moment to walk out of the maze, the look on her face causing Addie concern. Charlie must have seen it, too, because he bolted toward his daughter. She could not hear what he said, but he scooped his girl into his arms.

"Do you have somewhere she can lay down?" Concern etched across his face made him look much older than he was.

"Of course." She trotted up the stairs and held the door open. "Do you want somewhere immediate or somewhere comfortable?"

"Comfortable, I think."

Her apartment was not too far away and there were plenty of extra bedrooms for Lindsey to rest in. She led him to a staircase that normally impressed even her with its ornate beauty, though she had walked it nearly every day since babyhood. Her hand trailed along the well-cared for banister, worn smooth over centuries of use but kept polished to a shine by people she never saw. This was one time, though, she wished for an elevator to whisk them up two stories. Not two regular stories either. Every floor was the equivalent of at least two normal ones.

By the time she pushed open the door to her apartment, she could hear Charlie breathing heavily a few steps behind her.

"In here." She stepped aside and let Charlie walk in ahead of her. "Head for the hall, second door on the right. It should be open."

A minute later, she watched him lay his daughter on the bed.

Addie just hoped the girl was okay.

Charlie pulled the door nearly closed behind him. Addie waited for him in her living room. He sank into one of the arm chairs as she sipped on something in a coffee mug.

"How is she?"

"The doctor said she's just been through too much the last couple weeks. He was surprised her doctor let her come, though we did take all the appropriate precautions." When he looked up, the care and concern on her face tugged at his heart strings. Almost made him want to ask her to walk away from this life she'd always known. But he knew he couldn't. So he settled for what he could say. "Thank you for calling the physician."

"It was the least I could do. He was here anyway to look in on my father. Perhaps we should have a pediatrician come visit as well." Her delicate brows pulled together. "I know one of the pediatricians at the hospital. I could call him."

"If he wouldn't mind, I would appreciate it." He looked down at his hands. "I don't know when I'll be able to pay him."

She waved him off with a wave of her hand. "Do not worry about that. He will likely do it simply as a favor to me, but if he does charge you, I will see it gets taken care of."

"I can't ask you to do that."

"You are not asking. I am giving. Those are two very different things."

The door behind him opened and he turned his head to see Todd walking in. He bowed slightly to Addie. "Your mother is on her way."

Addie's eyes closed and he whispered a prayer for both of them. He didn't know how to meet a queen, despite Todd and Mark's crash course earlier in the day.

"Thank you, Todd."

"You have about two and a half minutes, knowing how quickly your mother walks."

Addie smiled. "You mean how slowly?"

"Exactly." Todd walked through a different door, though Charlie didn't know where it went.

He stood and rubbed his hands on the front of his pants. "Now what?"

Addie stood up and walked toward him. She put her hands on his shoulders and straightened his shirt. "Do not worry. You will be fine. My mother is not an ogre."

A new voice entered the conversation. "How lovely of you to say so, darling."

Charlie's stomach dropped lower than the bottom of the wishing well in the garden. He couldn't do this.

Adeline stood next to Charlie and wanted to give his hand a squeeze to let him know it would be all right, but she did not dare. "Mother, this is Charlie Brewer, a friend of mine from the States. Charlie, this is my mother, Her Majesty, Queen Alexandra of Montevaro."

Charlie shifted next to her. "My apologies, Ma'am. I am not certain what the protocol is when meeting royalty. I don't want to offend you in any way, but I honestly don't know."

The queen waved a hand. "No matter. If you will be here more than a day or so, you will learn. I cannot imagine you will be able to stay long. Surely, you have duties that will call you home before long."

"Yes, ma'am, I do. We are supposed to leave tomorrow."

Adeline cringed as her mother raised one perfectly sculpted eyebrow. "We?"

"Yes, ma'am. My daughter and I."

The other eyebrow joined the first. "You have a daughter? How lovely. How old is she?"

"She's eleven."

"When do I get to meet her?"

Something was not quite right in her mother's tone but Adeline could not put her finger on what it was.

Charlie tilted his head toward the bedrooms. "She is asleep down the hall right now. She had surgery recently and tires easily still."

Adeline's mother nodded her head just slightly and she knew Charlie was being dismissed. She also knew Charlie would have no idea her mother was done with him. There would be a time and place for her to stand up to her, queen or not. This was not that time.

Turning to Charlie, she tried to convey a message with her eyes as well as her words. "Charlie, why do you not go check on Lindsey? We will speak later." She gave him a small nod and what she hoped was a reassuring smile.

He gave her a look she could not quite interpret but gave a slight bow their direction and went to check on his daughter.

When he was out of earshot, she shot a glare at her mother. "You were being rude."

Her mother gave her a half shrug. "I am the queen. I cannot be rude."

Adeline crossed her arms in front of her. "Oh, please. You can be rude and you know it. Why were you being rude to my friend?"

The queen came to stand in front of her, resting one hand on Adeline's arm. "What is your association with this man and his daughter?"

She did not flinch. "His daughter is one of the girls I worked with at the after school program. He is a man I dated a few times earlier this year and a friend."

"There can be no..." Her mother seemed to be searching for the right words. "...romantic entanglements with this man."

Addie's eyes narrowed. "Why not, Mother? He is a good man who has worked hard to make a good life for his daughter. What is wrong with him?"

One of those eyebrows raised again. "The first thing is his lack of title or even the American pedigree equivalent to a title like Jonathan. The second is a daughter without ever being married. Parliament might be willing to allow you to marry a widower but not a man with a child who has either divorced or never married."

"Parliament does *not* have the final say over who I marry."

"No. But they can prevent your husband from having a seat on the Council. When your father is no longer king, you will be queen and my seat on the Council will be empty. Your father may take it for a time, but if you do not marry someone Parliament approves of, you will lose a valuable ally on the Council and there will be an empty seat until you die or abdicate. Is that what you want?"

Adeline moved away. "I know my duty, Mother. I know better than you. I have been raised, my whole life, to know what my duty to my country is. But that does not mean I will marry some man just because *you* think he is acceptable. Stop trying to play matchmaker. I will marry who I want to marry and I fully understand the consequences if I marry someone Parliament does not approve of."

With one hand, her mother trailed a finger along the side of her face, much as Charlie had done earlier. "I do not think you do, sweet Adeline. I do not think you know how much easier having one person on the Council whom you can always depend. It makes a big difference. If you do not believe me, ask your father." She cupped Adeline's chin in her palm. "I love you, my sweet girl, and I only want what is best for you."

"I know, Mother." Adeline sighed. "Just trust me. Please."

"I will do my best."

It was the best Adeline could hope for and she knew it. If only she knew what she was going to do.

What exactly was going on out there? Charlie didn't know what he might have done to offend the queen - a rather severe and stiff looking woman if he'd ever seen one - but he must have done something pretty bad if Addie had asked him to leave.

Instead of trying to figure out what it could possibly be, he sank into one of the chairs in the opulent bedroom and stared at his daughter. She looked so small in the big bed - it had to be even bigger than a regular king sized bed. Compared to his twin bed back in Serenity Landing, it was ginormous.

He didn't know how long he'd sat there when there was a light knock on the door. Charlie crossed the room to find Mark on the other side.

"Princess Adeline has asked for you and Miss Lindsey to be her guests the rest of the time you are in Montevaro. Miss Lindsey can stay here if she would like and a suitable room will be found for you as it would not be seemly for you to remain in her apartment."

Charlie nodded. "Thank you."

"Lunch is in an hour. Someone will come get you." Mark hesitated and looked a bit uncomfortable. "It would be better if you remained here until someone did."

Another nod and Mark left. Charlie understood. Something about their presence made people uncomfortable or caused scandal of some kind. Because he wasn't nobility. He went back to his chair and covered his face with his hands. Why had God brought Addie into their lives, to get Lindsey's hopes up no matter how many times he told her not to, only to have everything be ripped away because of societal pressures in her country?

Addie came to get them a little over an hour later and they had a nice lunch together, though Lindsey obviously didn't feel great yet. Ten minutes after they finished eating, another doctor arrived.

He met them in the living room where Addie introduced them. "Dr. Jonah Fontaine, these are my friends, Charlie and his daughter, Lindsey. Her appendectomy was about two and a half weeks ago after it burst."

Charlie recognized the man as the one he'd seen at the hospital with Addie before deciding to visit Montevaro. He was a bit surprised by the man's accent but Lindsey loved it.

"Where are you from?" she asked him.

"I was born here in Montevaro, but my family moved to Texas right before I turned four and that's where I grew up. I moved back here about two years ago to be a doctor at the hospital." Dr. Fontaine put the ends of his stethoscope in his ears. "Now, let's take a listen."

After a few minutes of listening, poking and prodding, Dr. Fontaine stood and turned to Charlie. "Everything looks fine. She needs to take it easy for a few days, though. I wouldn't recommend traveling for at least another week. I'm surprised her doctor let her."

"She wouldn't take no for an answer," Charlie told him with a grim look directed toward his daughter. "She tried to run away several times to get here, but we stopped her. The doc gave her special socks. We walked around a bit every hour. Drank plenty of water. All the stuff he said to do."

The doctor nodded. "All sensible precautions, but just the same, her body isn't ready for another trans-Atlantic trip for at least a few more days."

Charlie nodded his agreement even as his insides quivered. Sure, he'd known Linds's teacher since they were kids. Sure Sam was sending work via email and video-chatting to keep Lindsey up with the class, but by the time he paid to have the tickets changed and the extra time off work...

His daughter's health came first. Period. And he should have remembered that better before traipsing around the world with her, no matter how much she insisted.

He'd just have to pray he'd have a job to go back to.

As she walked deliberately down one step and then another, Adeline wanted to turn and high-tail it back to her apartment, change into comfortable clothes and watch the movie marathon with Charlie and Lindsey. However, duty beckoned. Her mother had invited some other duke and duchess from somewhere. She was not even sure their country still officially had nobility, but their ancestry was all that mattered.

If only their boring son would not come with them. She had not been told he would be at dinner, but it would not surprise her if her mother had purposely not told her. At least this young man was not like the count from the week before. Count Bladvile still had not returned home and Mark had told her he was still seeking an audience with her father.

Her father was doing better, but he still was not receiving visitors on much official business. Only a few leaders of Parliament and a member or two of the Council had been allowed in.

One hand trailed along the ornate bannister and she wished, just once, she would have had the nerve to slide down it like her brother, Richard, had many times. Even Ana had been talked into it several times by her slightly-older twin brother. Adeline had never given in, no matter how many times Richard had tried to convince her.

The reality of her childhood had been in her mind since she had been spending time with Lindsey. Adeline had never, not once, had a slumber party with friends. She had never attended one. In fact, she had few friends growing up. It had not been a *bad* childhood, but it had not been much of a childhood at all. She vowed anew her own children would have more of one than she ever had - especially her oldest child who would be raised knowing one day he or she would inherit the crown.

"There you are, darling." Her mother's voice interrupted her thoughts as she reached the bottom of the staircase. "I do wish you would hurry. They are waiting on you."

"You are not there yet either."

The only response was a shrug of one shoulder that Adeline knew meant "I am the queen, I cannot be late." Another thing Adeline promised herself would change. If at all possible, she would arrive on time. Her time was not more valuable just because of her title. The queen typically was the last one to arrive but since Adeline was with her, the queen entered first, with Adeline trailing just behind her.

Just as she suspected, Peter was standing in front of the chair next to the one Adeline usually occupied. She groaned inwardly and tamped down on her desire to return to her friends or even to the States, away from the expectations threatening to crush her unless she found someone to come alongside her to help shoulder the load.

Peter held her chair for her and she gave him a slight smile. "Thank you."

"My pleasure, Princess Adeline."

"Please. Call me Adeline." She had told him that on more the one occasion, but he never seemed to remember or purposely did it. It *had* been nearly four years since she had seen him. Maybe his years at university had helped him become a bit more exciting.

And maybe she could find a wardrobe, climb in it, and emerge in the magical land of Narnia.

Charlie sat propped up on the bed next to his daughter. Her head rested on his chest as he gently stroked the hair near her temple. Even breathing told him she slept deeply, something she desperately needed. The princess movie with the British gal as the queen of a fictional country continued to play though he wasn't paying much attention. The two movies had been Lindsey's choice. Not too shocking given where they were.

Someone he didn't know had arrived with Lindsey's suitcase and told him his had been taken to Richard's apartment. The only problem was he didn't know who Richard was, where the apartment was located and if he wanted to be that far away from his sick little girl.

A light tapping sound drew his attention. He slid Lindsey to the side and she curled away from him, still sound asleep. The knock sounded again and he moved quickly across the plush carpet to open it. A tired looking Addie smiled up at him as he left the room and closed the door behind him.

"Are you okay?" He wanted to take her in his arms and hold her until the lines on her face eased away.

She gave a slight nod. "A tiresome dinner with another great-grandson of a duke in a country that no longer has nobility. My mother evidently was not convinced when Jonathan and I told her we were willing to see what developed between us." Addie walked next to him into the living area and motioned to a couch as she sank into a recliner. "I doubt it will be the last time either."

Charlie took his heart in his hands and spoke before he could stop himself. "Is it terribly presumptuous of me to wish I could help you with that problem?" He looked up, straight into her golden eyes. "Permanently?"

She gave him a sad smile. "It is presumptuous, though I would it could be so."

It took a second for her semi-foreign way of speaking to translate in his mind. By the time it sank in, she had reached across the gap between her chair and where his hand lay on the armrest of the couch. Her fingers curled around his and he brought it up to kiss it lightly though it meant she had to lean toward him a bit.

"I wish things could be different. Now that I know why you couldn't move to the States, I understand and I'd consider moving here, but I know what an impossibility that is." He squeezed her hand then released it.

She didn't need to tell him she understood. He knew.

Addie drew in a deep breath and blew it out slowly. "I will be staying in my sister's apartment while you are here, so you can be close to Lindsey."

She was moving for him? He wanted to tell her it wasn't necessary, but the need to be near his daughter overrode that desire. "Thank you."

They both stood. Charlie took a step toward her. He rested his hands on her hips and drew her to him. "I know there can't ever be a future for us, Addie." He hated the tears that filled her eyes. "But just once, I want to forget that and kiss you the way I would if you weren't the Crown Princess of a little country in the Alps."

At her nod, he didn't waste any time but lowered his head to hers, kissing first her forehead, then her eyelids as they fluttered closed. He tasted the saltiness of the tears that escaped before he kissed her. Her hands slid up his arms until they wrapped around the base of his neck. He pulled her closer and kissed her with everything in him, for everything he wished they could have together, for everything that would never be.

And then... when he never wanted to let her go... he moved away. "You should go."

Addie swiped at her cheeks as she nodded. "Thank you, Charlie. You will never know how much it meant to me to have someone I could be myself with. Not the Crown Princess or future queen. Just Addie. I will never forget that." She took a step back started for the door.

Charlie wanted to call her back, but he knew he couldn't. There could never be more between them than a few dates and a friendship that couldn't cross the Atlantic.

Hollow inside, he watched her go, then found his things and went to bed feeling more alone than ever.

Adeline had not cried herself to sleep in many years, not since her first nights away from home, living in another country, at seventeen. She had forgotten the pounding headache that followed the morning after the heart-rending lullaby. Thankful Ana was not at home, she headed for the kitchen in her sister's apartment and downed some pain medication. Once she was ready for the day, her next order of business was some school work. She still had to finish the semester out, though her professors were being more than understanding and letting her do the work from a distance. It would have surprised her if they would not - not once they knew who she was.

She did not like relying on her name and position for favoritism, but occasionally, it came in handy. They would not be so accommodating if not. The sledgehammers had been reduced to tiny chisels inside her head and her paper was nearly done by the time Todd came to get her. She was to spend some time with Charlie and Lindsey. She had a meeting and then lunch with her mother.

Adeline returned to her apartment to find Lindsey looking much better, though still a bit pale. The next hour was a lovely time, just talking with them, though she desperately wanted to kiss Charlie again. To change the customs of her country so they could be together. The time with them was too short and too bittersweet. She caught Charlie giving her the looks she longed to give him. It passed too quickly and she slid her feet back into another pair of heels she hated, but went with many of her outfits. After giving Lindsey a hug, she headed to her first ever council meeting.

She was the last one to arrive, though she was still a few minutes early. Everyone else stood and she walked to her father's seat. "Good morning, gentlemen." She sat and they followed suit.

"I am certain all of you know why my father is not here and this meeting is merely a formality on a number of items." She held up an envelope. "He has given me his proxy to vote in favor or against the items on today's agenda. The instructions are written on this piece of paper and I will not deviate from them. However, since this is my first meeting and I am not the monarch, I will defer to Councilman Martin to run the meeting."

There were ten seats at the table. Two were empty. One belonged to the hereditary Marquis of Montago who had died without an heir when she was young. The other belonged to her mother. Her mother rarely showed up to the meetings unless she was needed to break a potential tie or make certain the vote went her father's way. That would likely change when the Marquis's seat was filled and that was never how Adeline had wanted it to be. She wanted her husband to sit next to her, offer her counsel and ultimately honor her decision but to debate and play devil's advocate and allow her to be the monarch and support her. She did not want someone who would simply do what she told him to. No, she wanted - to borrow the American expression - a husband who wore the pants in the family but still supported her in her "profession" such as it would be. Someone who would question her in private if need be but be her staunchest supporter in public.

The meeting only lasted about half an hour, but the contentious nature of several of the Council members grated on her nerves. She began to understand what her mother had been talking about when she said having one guaranteed ally on the Council would be a benefit.

And that guaranteed she and Charlie could never be more than a "what might have been."

"Dad, can we go back to that garden?" Lindsey walked out of the room she'd slept in.

"Sure. If we can figure out where it is and no one tells us we can't." He sent her to her room to get her coat while he went to get his. A few minutes later, they were walking down that big staircase - about the only place he knew how to get to. A woman - presumably a maid given her black and white uniform - smiled at them as she walked by. He called after her. "Excuse me, ma'am?"

She turned. "Yes, sir? Can I help you?"

"I hope so. My daughter and I went to this garden with Addie yesterday, but we're not sure where we are."

The woman's forehead puckered. "Addie, sir?"

Charlie winced. "Sorry. Princess Adeline." The woman's pucker turned to a frown. "I know it's a major faux pas to call her that, but I've only known who she was for a few days." He gave the woman one of his best smiles. "I've known her as 'Addie' for months. I'm working on it."

The frown eased and she nodded. "You must be Charlie and Lindsey. We were told you would be staying with us for a few days. Any of us will be happy to help you in any way we can. My presumption is you'd like to see Princess Adeline's favorite garden, with the wishing well?"

Lindsey nodded. "That's it. She showed us but we're lost."

She laughed this time. "This place is a bit of a maze and it's easy to get lost if you're not familiar with it. This way." She started down a hall. "Are you enjoying your time in Montevaro?"

"We get to stay at the palace!" Lindsey gushed. "Are there any secret passages?"

The woman stopped and bent over slightly to be eye level with his daughter. "There are. But here's the thing. No one knows where they are. They used to know but somehow, over the years, the entrances have been forgotten. The only one anyone knows about for sure is into the wall behind the thrones in the throne room and then to the Council room so they could spy on people, but the Council room has long since been blocked off so no one can get to it."

Lindsey's face had fallen with each word. "So we can't go in them?"

Roberta smiled as she straightened. "I would imagine Princess Adeline would show you the one with the spy hole into the throne room. But the others? They are lost to time." She winked at him. "There's a reward if you were to find one of them, though. There are many, but one of them is particularly important and no one knows where to find it."

"A reward?" Lindsey bounced on her toes. "What kind of reward?"

"Kings and queens have been looking for this one for over a century but no one has found it. About fifteen years ago, a Marquis died with no heir and no matter how they tried to find someone with a hereditary link to the title, they could not, so the king offered the title and the land and the house and everything to the person who can find it. No one is permitted to look on the palace grounds without explicit permission and an escort. This passage led to a tunnel that led to the mainland and people have searched for the other entrance for years but no one has found it."

They reached the door Charlie remembered from the day before. "Thank you, Roberta, for the escort and the story." He rested a hand on Lindsey's shoulder. "I'm sure my daughter will spend the rest of her time here looking for one of those passages."

She laughed, bid them good day and turned. Charlie and Lindsey walked into the cold sunshine and down the steps. He smiled at a man sitting on the bench where he and Addie had been the day before.

"Walk this time," he admonished his daughter. "I don't want a repeat of yesterday."

"I'll be more careful." She walked through the arch and into the walkway beyond.

Adeline went to the same dining room where she took most of her meals with her parents.

Her mother was there, though her father was nowhere to be found. She took a seat to her mother's right, grateful no potential suitors were present.

"How are your friends?" Her mother sat up straight, her back not touching the seat behind her.

Adeline had no such compulsion and slumped back against the chair. "They are well. Lindsey seems to be feeling much better today."

"Very good." Her mother glanced at her watch, which struck Adeline as off.

"Will they be serving lunch soon?" She looked around but there was no one else in the room. Odd. Normally, as soon as the queen took her seat, the meal was brought in.

"Momentarily. We are waiting on someone else."

It could not be her father, as he would sit at the head of the table if he were coming. Instead, her mother sat there.

"Mother, who..." Before she could finish her question, the heavy door on one side of the room opened.

Count Bladvile entered, his quick steps sounding on the stone floor. "My deepest apologies, Queen Alexandra. My driver got stuck in traffic of all things. I did not know you had traffic in Montevaro."

The queen gave a slight nod. "It is the Spring Festival this weekend, Count. Something you would know if you were here more often instead of traipsing around Europe."

"This is not my home country, Your Majesty. I often travel around the world." He sat across from Adeline. "Good afternoon, Your Highness."

Adeline gave him a slight nod. He was doing more than just

"traipsing" around Europe. If her web search had any truth behind it, he was cavorting with more women than lived in her entire country. If his personality had not been a complete turn-off, his lifestyle would have been. How he convinced so many women he was worth their time was simply beyond her comprehension. Most likely he was on his best behavior and had already cast them aside by the time they realized what a pig he was.

Lunch was a strained affair at best. Adeline said little unless she was spoken to directly. Even the disapproving glares her mother sent her way when the count was not looking could not make her pretend to like the man.

Her mother's assistant walked in about the time dessert was served. It did not surprise Adeline in the slightest when her mother listened to a whispered message, stood and excused herself.

Once she left the room, the count dropped any pretense of civility. "I am tired of these games, Princess." The respect disappeared from his use of the title. "When shall we announce our engagement?"

Adeline picked her napkin up from her lap and very deliberately set it on the table. "We will not be, Count Bladvile. I made that perfectly clear the last time you were here." She stood and inclined her head his direction, just a tiny bit. "I do hope you have a good afternoon, Count. I will ensure your trip across the lake is quick but you will not return to the palace. Do I make myself clear?"

He shoved his chair back from the table, positioning himself between her and the main exit to the room. There were others, but they were farther from her position and he would easily be able to block her. The predatory gleam in his eyes could not be missed. She feared for her safety and was too far from the panic buttons hidden in nearly every room. Often she wore one on her person, but as she had no idea danger lurked at this particular luncheon, she did not.

The thick stone walls of the palace muted sounds in the enclosed rooms, just as they were magnified in the bigger rooms and down open hallways. Screaming would be pointless, show weakness and likely further enrage the man. For the second time in her life, she wished her mother had allowed her to learn self-defense like her brother. And both times involved this smarmy letch.

She hated that she backed away from him, knowing sooner or later she would get to the wall, but as much as she wanted to stand her ground, she did not want his hot breath on her. Adeline did not know how this would end, but the look in his eyes told her what he wanted.

If she had to fight him off, she would, but she would never just acquiesce to what he wanted. Taking a deep breath, she decided it was time to make her move.

18

Charlie watched the opening to the garden, feet braced shoulder width apart and hands shoved in his pockets. Before he could decide what he wanted to say to the man sitting there, the man spoke.

"They grow up too fast, don't they?"

Charlie turned to see him pat the bench and went to join him. "They do."

"She's ten?"

"Eleven."

"Almost a teenager."

He blew out a breath. "Don't remind me."

"Pardon my bluntness, but you don't look nearly old enough to have a child that age." The man wasn't old himself, but he seemed to have that grandpa-who-can-say-whatever-he-wants air about him.

Charlie leaned back and stretched his legs in front of him. "I wasn't much older than she is now when she was born. She's not a mistake but..."

The man nodded and held out a hand. "Jed."

"Charlie." He gave the hand a quick shake but noted the firm grip. This was not a man to be trifled with though he didn't look well. Maybe he'd been sick?

"You're visiting?"

"Princess Adeline asked us to stay while we're here. She volunteered at Lindsey's after school program in the States."

"That is how you met?"

He shook his head. "No. I ran into her car on an icy night. We had coffee waiting for a tow truck and her roommates-who-were-really-bodyguards to show up. Went out a couple times, but she couldn't move permanently, though she didn't say why, and I didn't want to uproot my daughter. A few weeks later, we ran into each other at the program's building."

Jed chuckled. "I heard about the accident. I am glad you're both okay but she got in a fair bit of trouble with Mark and Todd over taking the car."

The two of them sat there, alternately talking about the weather, travel, and daughters - Jed's may have found the man she wanted to marry and he worried about whether she was making the right choice or not - and sitting in silence.

Running footsteps shattered the silence and Lindsey burst through the arch.

Charlie jumped up ready to reprimand her, but the wild, scared look stopped him. "What is it?"

"Addie's in trouble." She leaned her hands on her knees as she huffed. "Some man..."

Charlie looked toward the palace. "Where is she?"

"A dining room of some sort."

He started toward the door but realized he had no way to know where she was. Jed stood there, with the help of a cane, and shouted directions - through the door, straight to the main room and the big wood doors on the right with carvings of fruit in them.

Before the instructions died out of the air, Charlie ran through halls that seldom saw such activity. It took more muscle than he expected to pull the heavy doors open, but when he did, the sight stopped him in his tracks for a split-second before he sprang into action.

A man, likely twice Addie's size, though the weight didn't come from muscle, had her pressed against a wall, wrists in his grip. Addie stared at the man, ever-defiant until she caught sight of Charlie.

"Let her go." Charlie walked as close as he dared, stopping when the man let go of one wrist to press against her windpipe with his forearm.

"Don't come any closer," the man snarled.

"You won't hurt her. If you do, the wrath of an entire country will come down on you. And not just Montevaro, I'm sure. She's been in the U.S. for several years, so I'd imagine the news programs would have something to say about it. If you make it out of here, out of a palace with more turns than the Daytona 500 surrounded by water, you'll never be able to show your face in polite society again."

Charlie hoped Jed sent help. Surely there was a way to ring for security, but he had no idea what it was. Addie caught his gaze with her own. Her eyes flickered toward the floor and her foot shifted. He shook his head. No need to make a move that might not work when back-up had to be coming.

Footsteps could be heard pounding through the open door, but they were still a ways away. Addie gave a long blink, brought her foot up and smashed the heel of her shoe into the man's foot.

He bellowed, let her go and Charlie tackled him hard enough to make his high school coach proud. Charlie's head was pillowed against the man's ample middle, but the cracking sound, followed by limpness in his muscles, said the assailant wouldn't be getting up.

Charlie scrambled to his feet and turned to see Addie standing there in the same spot. Her hands clutched her stomach and her breathing was shallow, bordering on hyperventilation. It only took two quick steps to reach her side. He didn't want to presume, but he wrapped his arms around her.

Her hands gripped his shirt as he sensed her struggle to maintain some semblance of composure.

Several doors flew open and the room flooded with security personnel, guns drawn, including Mark and Todd. The men came straight to their side.

"This way," Mark said quietly, his hand on Charlie's shoulder. Todd flanked Addie and they started toward the door.

Charlie's arm held Addie snug to his side. One of her hands still clung to his shirt, but the other held her blouse closed. He hadn't noticed it was torn open before but it made him want to go pound on that man a bit more. When they reached the large room on the other side, Jed stood there, looking serious and almost... indignant? The housekeeper was there, her arm around Lindsey's shoulder, but their little group of four didn't stop until they reached a sitting room on the other side.

Addie turned back into his arms as soon as they were safely in the room. "Thank you," she whispered, "for being my knight in shining armor."

"Oh, Addie," he breathed so only she could hear. "I wish I could be."

She had never felt so safe as she did at that moment. She had just been attacked by a vile man, her blouse was ripped, her hair disheveled, but here - in Charlie's arms - Addie felt safe.

But she could not stay and she knew that. She soaked up his strength for another moment before she felt him release one arm.

A signal to move away if there ever was one, but before she could she felt something around her shoulders.

"A blanket," he murmured. "To protect you from eyes."

"Thank you," she whispered again, knowing it was time to move away from him and face the music.

With a deep, steadying breath and a whispered prayer winging its way heavenward, she turned, clutching the blanket closed in front of her. There were more people there than she would have liked, but it could not be helped.

Her father was the first one to speak. "Are you all right?" When she nodded, he continued. "Did he hurt you?"

"Not really, Papa. He wanted to, but Charlie got there before he could." Something occurred to her and she looked up at her protector. "How did you know?"

His face had gone white. "I was in the garden talking to..." He nodded toward her father. "...Jed, there and Lindsey came running out of the garden yelling that you were in trouble."

Adeline looked around. "Where is Lindsey?"

Her father leaned heavily on his cane and sat in the wingback chair nearest him. "Roberta has taken her to get some hot chocolate. I did not think she needed to be here for this discussion, though she has our deepest gratitude." He motioned to the couch and she sat, perched on the edge while Charlie sat next to her, though too far away for her liking. "I will speak with her later."

But it still did not make sense. "How did Lindsey know?"

King Jedidiah shook his head. "We will discuss that at length later. For now, I need to know what happened."

Adeline nodded and told him in a few words what happened.

Her father frowned. "What did he hope to accomplish by forcing himself on you? Does he not know the penalties for assault on a member of the ruling family?"

She gave a small shrug. "I do not think he cared. He seemed to think if I was 'soiled', I would be forced into marrying him to save our reputation. His plan was to say I had initiated..." She felt the blood rush into her face. "...the encounter and use it as leverage to force a wedding."

"I cannot fathom why he would think we would believe him over you and you certainly would not go along with the story."

Adeline stared at the long, low table in front of her. "He said no one else would want me and I would have no choice but to go along with his plan."

Charlie stood so quickly, she startled. He shoved his hands in the pockets of the coat he still wore and walked away from her.

Could he believe that? Why was he leaving her when she needed him? He did not leave the room, but his presence no longer comforted her. His long legs carried him to an open area on the other side of the room and he began pacing. Fury, stress, and something else were etched all over his face. What could he be thinking?

"How did he end up here? I have never liked him and there are standing orders for him to be denied entrance to the property without explicit permission."

"I invited him." Another voice entered the conversation. Adeline did not look up to see her mother walk in. She could sense the queen's confidence without seeing it.

"Why would you do such a thing?"

Her mother took a seat on the couch opposite Adeline, across that long, low table and its ornate ivy centerpiece. "Adeline needs to meet *acceptable* men. She needs to be settled before she inherits the throne and should have her children before then if at all possible."

Compassion filled Adeline as her father stood, drawing himself to his full height and looking down at his wife. "My daughter would *never* marry that man if he was the last bachelor on earth. She does not need your interference with her life to find a husband."

If anything, her mother looked intimidated and, for the first time in a long time, Adeline felt sorry for her. "Sit down, Father. You are still recovering." She fixed her stare on her mother. "Mother has only my best interests at heart. The problem is she fails to understand what those interests are."

Her father sat, though the lines on his face would become permanent if they did not leave it soon. "We will discuss this later, Alexandra. In the meantime, your matchmaking days are over. I do not know what other men you have paraded Adeline in front of, but it ends now. You have taken advantage of my weakened state and recovery to go behind my back and it will not happen again." His steely glare locked with her mother's eyes and her mother seemed to wilt as she nodded.

"Yes, Your Majesty. I understand." Normally, the queen reserved the title for introductions, formal settings or teasing behind doors, but this time, Adeline sensed something she never had before. Her mother acknowledging her father's rightful place not only as the head of his country, but of his household.

Charlie stalked from one side of the room to the other, hands in his pockets to prevent anyone else from seeing they were balled into fists. If he could bleed off some of his desire to pummel the man through stalking, he would. Addie didn't need to see how affected he was.

After about his fifteenth trek across the room, he noticed Todd move into his path at one end. The other man caught his gaze and held it, until Charlie stopped and turned to face the room. Everyone stared at him now that the showdown between the king - the king! - and queen had apparently ended.

He turned to look at Addie's father. "Sir, I hope you'll forgive any breech of propriety in our conversation or my abrupt departure."

The king waved a hand dismissively. "Charlie, if you had not left so abruptly, we would have a problem. Indeed, you have my utmost gratitude and I will be thinking of a way to properly thank you for protecting my daughter's person and her virtue. As for our conversation, you had no idea who I was and I wanted it that way. How else could I have had a real conversation with the man my daughter loves?"

Charlie felt his eyes go wide as he looked at Adeline. Her shocked face mirrored his own. "Sir, I promise..."

He stopped when the king held up a hand. "I know the bind you are both in. Though Parliament does not have veto power over who the monarch, or future monarch in this case, marries, they do have power to seat the Council, including the spot reserved for the monarch's spouse or the abdicating monarch. They cannot forbid Adeline from marrying whoever she chooses, but they *can* make her ascension to the throne much more contentious than necessary and, under the right circumstances, prevent it all together."

The king finished his pronouncement with a sad shake of his head. "Unfortunately, at the moment, we have an old-guard in control of Parliament. Though they adore Adeline, they also hold to some of the old ways, including the one that says the future monarch must marry aristocracy or nobility. Someone such as Jonathan William Langley-Cranston the Fourth is close enough for their taste, given his connections to the American presidency, but..." He sighed. "Especially given your status as a single, non-widowed father, I am afraid they will fall back on an ancient law that allows them to forbid Adeline's husband take a seat on the Council and perhaps strip her of her rights as Crown Princess."

A heaviness settled over the room as the king stood, leaning heavily on his cane. "I am sorry, Adeline and Charlie, but for the moment I cannot bless a potential union until other concerns have been addressed." Charlie watched him close his eyes for a long moment and both hands gripped the cane in front of him more tightly. "Especially as I will be abdicating before summer."

Adeline felt the breath leave her body in a whoosh. "What?" she whispered, looking up at the weakened man who stood in her father's place. She had known it was coming soon, but in a month? How could he toss this on her now of all times?

"We discussed it, Adeline." The compassion in his eyes made her nearly forget everything else. "We had not discussed this time table, but given everything else, it will be best. Once you have finished your studies next month, we will formalize the time line for your takeover and ascension to the throne before fall. That is why I cannot give my blessing. If there was more time to convince Parliament, perhaps but..."

Something she could not define crossed his face, but it fled before she could analyze it. "I am going to rest, daughter. That man will not bother you any longer and will likely not see the outside of the prison for some time. We will discuss this again at a later time."

Mark opened the door and bowed his head as her father passed through, followed by her mother. Before the door closed, she saw him sink into a waiting wheelchair and his valet helped him get situated. Her heart cracked further at the signs of his failing health.

She opened her mouth but no sound came out. After clearing her throat, she tried again. "Mark, Todd, can you leave us for a moment?"

They did not protest or throw any threatening glances toward Charlie. He had proven himself in their eyes. Now that it was too late for them.

"Are you really okay, Addie?" He still stood too far away for her liking, but she knew he would not come closer. Not after her father's pronouncement.

A single tear leaked down her cheek, followed by another from the other eye. She closed them, desperate to keep the rest from spilling over. Instead, she felt the phantoms of Charlie's soft kisses against her eyelids the night before.

"My heart is breaking." She had to be honest with him. "I thought, perhaps, we could find a way. We could convince Parliament, get my father on our side, and be together. I thought of stepping aside and allowing my brother to take the throne instead, but I cannot let my father down like that. My brother is not monarch material at this point in his life. He is young, makes too many grievous errors in judgment that would be written off to youth if he was not a prince, and does not take life - or responsibility - seriously enough for me to follow through with that idea. He has not even come home since Papa's accident, though he is in the Himalayas so it is possible he has not heard. But even if I could, I could not marry you without my father's blessing." Adeline looked at him, blurred as he was by her tears, and prayed he would understand her heart.

Charlie sat next to her and tugged the blanket more closely around her shoulders. He leaned over and pressed a kiss to her forehead. "I understand." She heard his shuddering breath. "It is for the best." Was he trying to convince her or himself? "We will never have to deal with Lindsey feeling slighted when her half-siblings are treated as royalty by well-meaning though unfeeling media or others. She and I had talked about how, even if I were to marry you, she wouldn't be a princess. It disappointed her but she said she'd rather we be together. She can't understand the full ramifications and I didn't know if I'd be able to put her in that position anyway. It's for the best," he repeated before kissing her forehead again. "We'll be out of your apartment and back to our hotel as soon as we can. No sense in prolonging things."

Her breaking heart shattered into a million pieces as he stood and walked away. Despite her efforts, she could not help but watch him. He stopped with one hand on the door.

"Addie, no matter what that man said, even if he had done what he wanted to, I want you to know I still would have married you."

Without looking back, he left.

19

Walking away from Addie was the hardest thing Charlie had ever done. Even harder than taking on a baby at sixteen. That had been easy. Lindsey had stolen his heart at first sight and taking care of her was something he'd do again in a heartbeat.

But leaving a heartbroken Addie behind?

He didn't know if he could do that again.

As he left the room, he'd jerked his head back toward it, giving sentries Mark and Todd the signal Addie needed them. With the staircase there, he knew where to go to get back to her apartment. He was packing their things when Lindsey walked in, tears streaming down her face.

"We're really leaving?"

He nodded. "I'm sorry, punkin, but we have to. We'll stay at the hotel until you can go home. I'm behind on my school work as it is so I can use the time to get caught up before we get back."

"But I want..." She didn't finish her sentence but broke down instead. Charlie wrapped his arms around her as they sat on the bed.

"Sometimes what we want can't be."

"I know, but I thought *this*..."

His heart was too heavy to offer her the assurance that someday, maybe, she'd be able to visit Addie. Her sobs had quieted before he spoke again. "We need to pack and I need you to not fight me on this, okay?"

Lindsey nodded but didn't say anything and after a minute she moved to begin, swiping at her cheeks with the back of her hand. They were nearly done before she broke the silence. "I wish the tunnel I found was the one that lady told us about."

Charlie looked at her, confused. "What tunnel?"

"I was by the wishing well and wondered if maybe one of the passages was near there since it's a real well and all. Around the outside of the well are these stones with this poem on it. There's one word per stone and like fifty stones. They're all loose, but I think they're supposed to be. Like it's not supposed to be solid."

"Okay. But what..."

She gave a characteristic roll of her eyes. "Just listen. On the palace wall right there is this verse from Psalms. Something about lifting eyes to the hills where help comes."

"Psalm 121:1," Charlie answered softly.

"Sure. But when I was reading the poem and looked up it was *right there* and I thought it had to mean something. When I read the poem again, I noticed some of the same words, like 'whence.' So I pushed on them in the order they were in the verse. The whole verse was there and when I pressed the stone with cometh' on it, this door opened."

Charlie's heart stopped. "And you just walked into this passage you know had been lost for years, that no one knew about, without coming to get me? What if you'd gotten shut in there? We never would have found you!" His voice grew louder and louder and Lindsey started to look scared. He took a deep breath to calm himself down. "Okay. You made it out fine but don't ever do that again, understand?"

She nodded. "I knew I should go get you, but it was right there and I found it. Me! But I didn't want to get locked in so I moved this big rock in the opening so it wouldn't shut all the way. I'm not totally stupid, Dad. I've seen enough movies to know that's how you get in trouble in secret passages."

He relaxed just a bit at the knowledge his daughter did have a good head on her shoulders.

"So I went in and walked along. It's pretty wide, and not even cobwebby so it must be sealed up pretty good if there's no spiders in there. There were some stairs going down and a hall going straight. I wasn't going to go down the stairs without a flashlight, so I went down the hall. The door stayed open so I had some light, and I could see light ahead." She folded a shirt and stuck it in her suitcase with a shrug. "I followed it and went up some stairs. Almost a full flight's worth. When I got to the light, it was the stained glass window in that dining room and I saw that man threatening Addie. So I ran back and got you."

Lindsey sank back to the bed. "I just wish it had been the one Roberta told us about so we could get that title and stuff and you could marry Addie."

Charlie pulled her to his side and kissed her head. "I know and I'm proud of you for being smart about it and for getting Addie help. I wish things were different but they're not."

There was a knock on the door. A man Charlie didn't recognize stood there and said he'd been told they were ready to leave. He would help them to the boat that would take them off the island.

Ten minutes later, Lindsey was safely in the cabin, but Charlie stood on the bow and stared at the dock on the other side of the lake as it grew larger. He didn't look back.

He couldn't.

"They are really gone?" Adeline, freshly showered and dressed in untainted clothes, sat in a chair next to her father's bed, looking up at Todd as he reported in.

He nodded. "The boat left a few minutes ago." His report given, Todd left her alone with her father.

The king grasped her hand. "I am sorry, my sweet Adeline."

"I know, Papa, but I knew months ago Charlie and I were never to be." Tears threatened again, but she blinked them back. Maybe she'd be a dowager queen. Not the widow kind of dowager but the dignified, elderly woman. Once she got elderly anyway. Her brother's children would inherit the throne if she lived longer than he did. If not, by the time she died or abdicated, he'd be mature enough to handle it for a time.

"It does not stop the pain."

She shook her head. "How did you know I loved him?"

He inclined his head toward the window. "I saw you with him yesterday. The way he touched your face and the way you leaned into it, I knew."

Adeline asked the question that had been bothering her for hours. "How did he know I was in trouble?"

"I wish I had more time to talk with his daughter. Lindsey came flying out of the garden to tell us. Charlie ran off to help you and she helped me up the stairs." He grinned at her. "It was kind of nice, them not knowing who I was. I could tell she wanted to run after her father, but she did not want to leave me either when I am so obviously frail at the moment. She is a good child and a credit to her father. As we walked, she told me how she had found a secret passage near the well."

Adeline's eyes blinked rapidly. "She found one of the secret passages? At the well? How? Where?"

He shook his head sadly. "I did not have a chance to ask her. Perhaps, once I decide on a proper way to thank both of them, they will come back for a ceremony of some kind and she will tell us then. Otherwise, I will have to ask someone to go talk to them, I suppose."

She slumped back in her chair. "I do not suppose you can make him the marquis can you?"

"No, child. I wish I could, but that title has been promised to whoever finds *the* passage and the hidden chamber. Last I heard, a team from the States had a new theory, but I have heard nothing of them in months."

"And there is no chance this is the other end of that tunnel?" She clung to the slight hope until he shook his head again.

"I do not see how it could be. It is an interior wall of the palace and she said it stopped at the landing where she looked through the stained glass into the dining room, but she bumped the rock she used to prop it open when she ran out and it shut behind her. Even if it was, she would be the Marchioness, not her father."

"But if his daughter was titled, then, maybe..."

"If wishes were horses..."

Adeline leaned over and pressed her lips to his forehead. "I know, Papa. I think I am going to go rest for a while. I doubt I will be at dinner." She could not stomach another meal with her mother at the moment.

"Your mother apologized to me but is afraid to talk to you. She was the reason no one else was in the area. Even security had been moved to another area to go over plans for some ball she wants to hold. I believe her when she says she had no idea what kind of man he is. She thought with a bit more time together, you might grow to like him some."

She clamped her lips shut. Her mother was either incredibly stupid or easily manipulated. Adeline did not know which was the better option.

"It's a festival of some kind." Lindsey turned away from the window. "Looks like the streets are blocked off and everything. People in costumes are wandering around." She flopped on the bed in front of him. "Can we go, Dad? Please?"

Charlie looked out the window to see a number of people wandering around in the streets. If he had to guess, he'd say the clothing was from the Italian Renaissance period. And given what his parents did for a living, he was probably right. "We don't have costumes," he reminded her.

"So? Not everyone had costumes on." She turned on her pouty voice. "Please, Daddy?"

With a chuckle, Charlie nodded. "Okay. Why don't you take a shower and get dressed? I'll go down to the front desk and see what I can find out."

Twenty minutes later, they emerged onto the streets armed with informational flyers and maps. "Why don't we go to the café and get some hot chocolate and figure out what we want to see at the different stages in the pavilions so we know when to be where?"

Lindsey liked that idea and he had to keep her headed the right direction as she read through the booklet. "'The Festival is a celebration of the Montevarian defeat of invaders during the Italian renaissance. A splinter group of Italians from across the Montevarian-Italian border sought to capture the smaller country and bring it into the fold of Italy. The Montevarian army, under the leadership of Crown Prince Richard, who would later become King Richard II, drove back the invaders. Every year, the country celebrates with costumes, dances, and traditional Montevarian food.'"

"Head up, kiddo." It wasn't the first time she'd nearly walked into a pole while reading and walking at the same time. She stuck her finger in the booklet as he opened the door to the café. The crowd filled the room wall-to-wall and they had to inch their way through people in costume to get to the counter. The regular menu was covered with a vinyl sign advertising the special menu for the weekend.

"Hello, Charlie and Lindsey!" The same woman who had waited on them every day they'd been there stood behind the counter, looking like someone misplaced from a Renaissance Faire. "What can I get you today?"

Charlie stared at the unfamiliar items on the sign. "I have no idea."

She laughed. "Trust me?"

"Sure."

Two minutes later, Lindsey squeezed into a suddenly vacant table as Charlie carried the plates of pastries. She'd set their drinks on the table by the time he sunk into the chair.

"What are these?" Lindsey held up one of the vaguely-croissant looking pastries.

"I'm not sure, but they have cheese in them." He leaned toward her. "Do you really need to know anything else?"

"Nope." They spent half an hour savoring their breakfast and hot chocolate while looking through the brochure. Demonstrations of how things were done in Renaissance time period. A fashion show with clothing from all walks of life. A fireworks show set off on the lake with the palace as a backdrop. A church service. Three weddings - one royal, one aristocratic, and one peasant. A marketplace. It was overwhelming.

The crowd had thinned out some by the time the employee stopped at their table. "Are you trying to figure out where to go?"

Lindsey held out the schedule for the day. "What do you recommend?"

The woman scanned it. "One thing I always make sure to go to is the Dance of the Victors in front of the Cathedral. Usually the king and queen will be there leading the dance, but I haven't heard if the king is well enough to be there today."

Lindsey bit her lip for a second then looked up. "Who would take their place if he can't?"

She shrugged. "I'd guess Princess Adeline since she's home from wherever she's been going to school. Maybe with that American hunk since Prince Richard still out of the country doing whatever it is he does when he disappears for months at a time. Or maybe one of the Council members or members of Parliament. I really don't know."

Charlie knew what was going through Lindsey's mind. Even though there was no future, she still adored Addie, and would want to see the Dance of the Victors, just in case.

The waitress leaned over and whispered conspiratorially. "In fact, they usually pick at least two people out of the crowd to dance with the king and queen. I'd imagine Princess Adeline would do the same."

Opening the map up across the table, Charlie looked for the Cathedral. When he found it, his heart dropped. "I don't know, Linds. It's a long way from here." Nearly two miles. She couldn't walk that. Not after the last few days she'd had.

"You know what?" He looked up to see the waitress deep in thought. "I can get off in a few minutes. I think we can get there, if we go the back ways. It'll cut half the distance off. I'd be happy to go with you and show you the way." Her finger traced along what looked to be alleyways and a marketplace. Charlie knew he couldn't figure it out on his own, even if she marked it on the map for him. "I'll be right back." Her long skirt swished as she hurried off through the café.

He looked at Lindsey's hopeful face and sighed. "Okay. But if it's too much for you..." He let the warning trail off. "You'll never get better if you keep overdoing it."

"I *know*, Dad. I'll tell you." She hurried through the last couple of bites and threw their trash away. About the time she finished, the waitress returned.

The woman held her hand out to Charlie. "I realized that in the week you've been here, I don't think I've introduced myself. I'm Sherry."

Charlie shook her hand. "You already know I'm Charlie and that's Lindsey." He had no intention of telling this woman about his connection to Addie and hoped Lindsey would keep her mouth shut too.

Sherry tugged a shawl around her. "All right. We're going to walk fast so we can try to get there for the first couple rounds of the dance competition." She smiled at Lindsey. "You up for this, kiddo? Your dad told me the other day you've been sick."

Lindsey nodded. "I'm ready."

After handing Charlie a slip of paper with her phone number on it in case they got separated, Sherry went out the door, Charlie and Lindsey in her wake. The cobblestones of the street were rough under their feet as they hurried down the center of it. Sherry called over her shoulder. "The roads are closed for about a three mile section of Old Towne. You'll see some carriages and horse-drawn wagons, but no cars except emergency vehicles and official Festival vehicles. The trolleys still run, but it would take us too long to get there taking them."

She turned down a narrow alleyway that twisted and turned behind buildings that may have been around during the actual battles. Sherry took them through the regular marketplace where Charlie and Lindsey had visited a few days earlier. Beyond that, one of the streets was filled with a Renaissance marketplace. They weaved through the stalls until they came out the other end and into another alleyway.

Twenty minutes later, they'd talked little in their efforts to speed through town. Lindsey seemed a bit winded but not enough to worry Charlie. The crowd gathered around the dance stage area near the Cathedral surprised him, but Sherry had a trick up her sleeve. She sidled up to a member of the security team - a police officer, maybe? - and rested a hand on his arm. Charlie thought she was flirting with the man, but a minute later all three of them were allowed through the rope line into an area sectioned off for VIP viewers.

"How'd you get us in here?" Lindsey asked as she took a seat on the front of the bleachers.

Sherry laughed. "That's my husband. I texted him earlier. He usually works around here during the contest."

"How cool! Thank you!"

Charlie sat on the other side of Lindsey from Sherry as the first group of dancers took the floor.

"Most of the VIP people won't show up until closer to time for the royal dance," she explained. "But I can tell you all about how the Montevarian Victor Dance works." Sherry pointed to one of the couples near them. "I happen to know this couple is married. They come into the café sometimes. See how far apart they're standing?"

The couples' hands were flat against each other, but there was nearly a foot and a half of daylight between them.

"The way this dance works, the more serious a couple is about each other, the further apart they are while they dance. Many couples over the years would wait until after the Festival to go public with their relationship so they could dance closer." She pointed to a couple across the floor from them. "See how close they are?"

Lindsey nodded.

"They're cousins. So there's no romantic relationship which means they'll dance close enough for their torsos to touch sometimes."

The competition intrigued Charlie and Lindsey loved the costumes and the tidbits Sherry shared about the history of Montevaro and the Montevarian royal family.

"What's the tunnel?" Lindsey asked, munching on some popcorn Charlie had bought.

Sherry smiled. "I see you've heard about the long-lost secret tunnel used to get into and out of the palace in case of a siege, like the one during the war. It had been built over the century prior as the palace was being built. So I guess you know that whoever finds the tunnel will be granted the March about an hour's drive from here. The last Marquis died about thirty years ago with no heir found. My brother and I spent lots of time looking for the end of it when we were teens."

Lindsey opened her mouth to say something, but Charlie stopped her with a jab of his elbow as the winning couple was chosen to sit on the dais. The host of the contest, decked out in tights, billowy shorts and a funny looking hat, spoke into the microphone. "Ladies and gentlemen, we ask that you keep the king in your thoughts and prayers as he continues his recovery from the skiing accident several weeks ago." A murmur of assent swept through the crowd. "King Jedediah sends his regrets and his commendation for our winning couple. In his place, we have Crown Princess Adeline -" Charlie heard Lindsey's quick intake of breath. "- and her escort, Jonathan William Langley-Cranston the Fourth of the United States of America."

The applause kicked up a notch as Addie and Jonathan stepped to the middle of the dance floor. Charlie held his breath, waiting to see how close they moved to each other. He knew it wasn't a definitive answer, but it would give him some clue about their relationship, but he had to know.

As they turned to wave to the whole crowd, his eyes connected with Addie's and time stood still.

He is here? Adeline saw Charlie and Lindsey sitting on the bottom bleacher seat next to someone who looked to be a Montevarian native given her clothing. She longed to step close to Jonathan as they danced, so Charlie would know she had not moved on quite so quickly. But if she gave the impression she and Jonathan were not an item... her mother would be trying to set her up with, quite literally, Lord only knew who. *Lord, please help*

me. Help Charlie and Lindsey. I don't know if there's way for us to be together, but I trust You.

Adeline glanced up at the hills beyond Charlie. If only...if onlies were not real life. She would not marry Jonathan, but she would not marry someone her father, and Parliament, could not approve of.

Her arm ached from being outstretched at shoulder height for so long as she and Jonathan completed their circuit around the dance floor. He led her to the center and turned to face her. They had spent the better part of the last several days practicing, while she had also spent the time trying not to cry in front of him over the finality of the end of her relationship with Charlie.

"You can do this, Princess Adeline." Jonathan looked straight into her eyes as he held his hands up for her to place her palms flat against. "I know you'd rather be here with him and maybe, someday, there will be a way, but for now, you can do this. You can be the symbol your people need while your father recovers."

Adeline took a deep, fortifying breath and gave him a slight nod as she placed her hands against his. They remained about eight inches apart, a sign of courtship in this ritual.

The unseen string quartet started to play. Adeline followed Jonathan's lead as they moved around the floor. The crowd clapped in time to the music, but she could not bring herself to smile. This was a courtship dance, yes, but also a solemn remembrance of those who fought and died to protect their country. Not just those who repelled invaders a thousand years earlier, but also those who had served throughout the ages.

The dance was both too short and too long. Adeline kept her eyes fixed on Jonathan's eyebrows, close enough to his eyes that no one but him would notice. As the music reached a crescendo then stopped, she and Jonathan backed away from each other. He bowed and she curtsied, though as Crown Princess she was not technically required to.

The emcee for the event announced their names again, as though they needed to be reintroduced.

"And now, for the part many of us have been waiting for. Mr. Langley-Cranston will choose two people to dance the next dance with himself and Princess Adeline."

Adeline's stomach dropped. He would not. Would he? A barely perceptible wink told her he would as the announcer went on. "These two and their families will be invited to the ball at the palace this evening." Jonathan turned in one spot, taking in the whole crowd as he pretended to ponder his decision. It came as no surprise when he stopped facing the bleachers.

She watched his long, purposeful strides as he headed straight for Charlie and Lindsey. He bowed to Lindsey, asking, Adeline knew, if he could have the pleasure of the next dance. Once Lindsey agreed, he turned to Charlie. She could not hear the words, but could see the play of emotions on Charlie's face. He nodded, knowing, perhaps to turn down the offer would create more attention than accepting it would.

And then he was there. In front of her, bowing at the waist then holding up his hands. "I don't know this dance, Princess Adeline. Perhaps you can help me?"

Swallowing hard past the lump in her throat, she nodded, resting her hands on his and moving as close to him as she could. For just this moment, she could close her eyes, thank God for the odd rules of the dance, and enjoy Charlie's closeness.

"Thank you for taking care of my daughter, Your Highness." His stiff formality unnerved her. "Your kind gestures of paying for our hotel and arranging our flight home is above and beyond."

"I would tell you it is my pleasure, Charlie, but we both know I wish things were different and I were arranging your flight home to pack and move back here."

"With you."

She nodded as the music started again. "With me."

They started moving in time to the music, with Adeline using gentle pressure to help him know how to lead.

"Your father sent word this morning that I'll be receiving the Knighthood of the Royal Order of King Richard, for bravery and service to the crown above and beyond the call of duty." His mouth twisted into a wry grin. "But apparently even that doesn't mean Parliament would accept me."

"I want you, and only you, to know there is nothing but friendship between Jonathan and I. We are keeping up appearances to keep my mother from playing matchmaker." She hated the tears in her eyes. "I could not bear to even pretend to be interested in a date with anyone else. Jonathan is making public appearances with me while I cry my heart out behind closed doors." It was too much of an admission and she prayed, belatedly, no one had a long distance microphone pointed at her.

"I'm glad you have someone to lean on, Princess Adeline." Their last spin around the floor came to an end. Charlie stepped away. "You will always have a special place in my heart, Princess."

"And you mine, Charlie." She watched as a member of security walked them over to the side and, presumably, took down their contact information so their official invitation to the ball would be waiting for them when they returned to the hotel.

Jonathan returned to her side and tucked her hand into his elbow, leading her backstage once more. "Would you like to stay and see the Festival?" She did not, but this was Jonathan's first time and she knew he wanted to. With a nod, she sank into one of the green room chairs.

"In a few minutes." She looked around. Only Mark and Todd were near. "Why did you choose them Jonathan?"

A smile played about his lips. "I couldn't choose anyone else. I know how you feel about him, Addie. I know how he feels about you. It would have killed him if I'd chosen anyone else who would then get to come to the ball instead of them. It was the right choice."

It was a painful choice. A reminder of what they would never have together.

But it was the right choice. And she was glad he had made it.

Jonathan kept Adeline's hand tucked in his elbow as they wandered down the streets of the capital city of Montero. As they walked, she pointed out architectural details in the old buildings that lined the cobblestone streets. The people gave them - or more likely their bodyguards - a fairly wide berth, though many waved and a few children broke through the invisible bubble to see their Crown Princess. Addie took time to talk to each one, learning their names and at least one special thing about them. He noticed Mark making notes in a small notebook. If Jonathan were a betting man, he'd bet Mark was noting the things she learned and Addie would use the information at a later date to mail out Christmas or birthday cards or something.

Several hours later, they walked toward the garrison at the lake to take the yacht back to the palace. The ridiculous outfit he wore for the dance contest had nothing on the one he'd been told he'd be wearing to the ball. Addie's likely would be the same. She looked beautiful in the Renaissance dress, but she always looked beautiful. Several times throughout the day, he'd found himself half-wishing there really could be something between the two of them. Not because it would make him the Prince Consort someday but because he really did like Addie and he liked spending time with her.

They rested their forearms on the top rail of the boat as it took them toward the palace. "How do I do it, Jonathan? How do I spend this evening at the ball with you as my escort when the man I love, who saved me from certain harm the other day, is standing across the room? And how do I not let the whole room know how I feel?"

Jonathan reached over and squeezed her hand. "You hold your head high, smile, and be who you are."

She nodded. "I am the Crown Princess of Montevaro and, before long, I will be the first Queen of Montevaro."

Though she didn't say it, he knew what that meant. It meant she wouldn't let her feelings show. She would pretend to be taken with him, while longing to be with Charlie. She wouldn't let anyone see how much her heart broke each time she saw Charlie dance with another woman. He prayed she would eventually be able to do as she hoped, put her feelings for Charlie in a place in her heart that would allow her to love another man fully.

Her heart had to rest heavy in her chest. He didn't envy her. Jonathan himself was under pressure to marry well, but if he married someone his grandmothers didn't approve of it wouldn't be the end of the world. They'd hem and haw and give him a hard time sometimes, but the odds were against him being disowned or losing his position in the family business. If Addie didn't marry the right man, she could lose her crown, be essentially disowned by her entire country.

The boat docked at the palace and he helped Addie onto the gangplank. As they reached the staircase leading to her apartment, he stopped her. "You will be wonderful, Princess Adeline." Jonathan gave her his best grin. "You keep telling me God has a plan for everything. I'm sure He has a plan for this as well." He leaned over and pressed a kiss onto her cheek. "Pray about it. I will, too. Whatever the plan is, He'll reveal it in His time."

Addie nodded. "Thank you, Jonathan. I know you speak the truth, but that does not make it any easier to wait on Him."

"Waiting on Him isn't easy, but I believe you can do it. He has someone amazing for you and you'll find the man of your dreams when the time is right."

"I know." She squeezed his arm and walked sedately up the steps, the train of her skirt trailing behind her.

Jonathan shook his head and went to the room he'd been given to use while he was in the palace. He'd been spending the night at the Lydia House, but when he was here, there was a place for him to change or relax if he needed to.

When he arrived, his temporary assistant, Danica, was just leaving. "Mr. Langley-Cranston, I left your costume for this evening hanging in the closet. Someone will be by in about an hour and a half to see if you need any help with it." She grimaced slightly. "It's a bit complicated. If you need anything before then, you know how to reach me."

Jonathan murmured his thanks and closed the door behind him. After snapping the lock, he stripped out of the costume he'd worn most of the day. For the next ninety minutes, he'd wear the comfortable pajama pants he'd brought for just this purpose and try to take a bit of a nap. If the schedule was right for how long the ball was supposed to run - and as the Crown Princess's escort, he'd be required to attend the whole thing - it was going to be a late night.

After nearly an hour playing a mindless shoot-em-up game on his smart phone, Jonathan hopped in the shower before standing in front of the ridiculous costume wondering if he could figure it out for himself.

But when he pulled it out of his closet, he just stared. He'd need help. Knee high butter-soft leather boots with a matching belt and... they weren't gloves but arm things that would cover from his wrists to his sleeves, but he had no clue what they were called. The pants could only be called black leggings and he whispered a prayer of thanksgiving that the... doublet? Whatever the vest-looking thing was called would come to mid-thigh. The Montevarian royal crest covered the chest and there was a deep red cape with white fur trim. All of that he might have figured out, but the rest of the undergarments and such? Then it hit him.

The only thing missing was a crown.

Just what was Queen Alexandra up to?

20

Charlie stood in front of the five-way mirror. "Is this really what everyone else will be wearing?" He looked ridiculous, but all of the costumes in the giant room were medieval or renaissance in nature, so he'd fit right in. Wouldn't he?

The fairly plain long-sleeved white shirt was covered with a vest of some kind, black and edged in fake fur and gold trim. A purple satin cape attached to the back of it and a chain made of inch-and-a-half gold links ran from shoulder to shoulder. Black stretch pants and knee length black boots, folded over at the top completed the look. Until he put the hat on - complete with giant purple feather.

"You look *awesome*, Dad!"

He turned to see Lindsey hurrying toward him. "You think so?"

"Yep. Miss Ad..., Princess Adeline will love it." He heard the catch in her voice and he hated the pain she'd go through when they finally left the country. Until they left Montevarian airspace, she would hold out hope and he didn't blame her a bit. She whirled around. "What do you think?"

The pink shimmery fabric had that renaissance look to it. Gold ribbons criss-crossed from the neckline down to a bow tied at her waist in front of a light pink panel. Darker pink went around the back and the sleeves to the either side in front. The sleeves were wide and fell in a bell shape around her wrists. A slender headband circled her crown with a flimsy bit of the material veils were made from dangling from one side and going under her chin to the other side.

"You look lovely, kiddo." He gave her a big hug. "I'm gonna have to fight the boys off sooner than I'd like."

She rolled her eyes at him. "Whatever."

"Mr. Brewer?" Charlie turned to see the woman who helped them both find something to wear. "If you're ready to go, someone is here to take you to the ballroom."

Charlie held out his elbow for Lindsey to slip her arm in but she didn't. "Dad, didn't you see Addie and Jonathan earlier?" She held her hand straight out at shoulder height as he chuckled. "You go like this."

He took her hand in his as they walked to the entrance of the costume room. When they exited, Mark stood there, waiting. He bowed to Lindsey. "You look lovely tonight, Miss Brewer."

She dropped in a slight curtsy. "Thank you, Mr. Mark."

They followed him through the hallways of the palace until they reached the ballroom where Mark turned them over to another member of the staff who led them to the large double doors. The woman smiled at Lindsey and bent slightly to be eye-to-eye with his little girl. "Are you ready, sweetheart?"

Lindsey nodded and the woman motioned to two men in Renaissance garb who pulled the doors open. From somewhere unseen a voice called out, "Mr. Charlie Brewer and Miss Lindsey Brewer of Serenity Landing, Missouri, United States of America."

He escorted his daughter into the room to a smattering of

applause, something he'd learn they did for everyone announced. Charlie pulled a small card out of his pocket. "We're at table 36, kiddo."

They wove their way among the tables, smiling at those who smiled at them. When they reached theirs, he held Lindsey's chair out for her. Most of the other people in the room seemed to know each other and were sitting in clusters talking. Another announcement was made and the applause sounded again. Charlie watched Lindsey look around, her eyes wide in awe as she tried to take it all in.

A few minutes, and a few announcements later, another girl, about Lindsey's age, and her parents came to sit with them. Lindsey and the girl, Emily, hit it off right away exclaiming over each other's clothes as Emily's father held out a hand to Charlie.

"I can't believe we're here," Emily's mother gushed. "We happened to be on the same street as Princess Adeline and that handsome American earlier today. Emily managed to meet her and when we got home, there was an invitation waiting for us to come tonight." She looked around. "We've never been to the palace or even a real ball before." She squeezed her husband's arm. "Can you believe it?"

"It is pretty amazing." Charlie was underwhelmed. Not because it wasn't pretty incredible, it was, but because he'd have to watch the love of his life dancing with another man. A man everyone expected her to marry.

"So where are you from?" The man, who'd introduced himself as Rob, took a sip of his water. "Your accent is American?"

Charlie shifted in his seat. "Yes. We're from Serenity Landing, Missouri."

Rob's wife, Marianne, jumped back in. "Isn't that where Princess Adeline had been attending school? No one knew for sure where she was except in the States, but I thought I heard that on the news the other day and that's where the American she's been seen with is from."

"Yes. We met there several months ago. I, um, sort of ran into her car with mine during an ice storm and we had coffee."

Whatever their response would have been, it was swallowed by Emily's exclamation. "You called Princess Adeline Addie! No one does that!"

Poor Lindsey looked like she wanted the earth to open up and swallow her. Charlie rested his hand on hers and squeezed lightly. "Princess Adeline volunteered at Lindsey's after school program. She told everyone to call her Miss Addie. We're working on remembering to call her Princess Adeline."

"You know Princess Adeline?" Emily's amazement came through loud and clear.

Lindsey nodded. "She came to my birthday party." The two of them went back to their hushed conversation.

Rob and Marianne's eyes were as wide as their daughter's. "You actually know her?" Marianne asked.

"Yes. She's a very nice lady, but none of us knew who she was until she came home after the skiing accident." Oh, how he wished for the dancing or dinner to start. Then, maybe, he wouldn't be subjected to the grilling he felt sure was coming.

"Have you met the rest of the royal family?" Marianne leaned as close as she could with her husband in the way.

"We met Princess Ana the other day and I spoke briefly with the king."

"But not Queen Alexandra?" Marianne looked disappointed.

"Not really. Someone introduced us but barely. She was on her way to a meeting." A meeting with Addie to tell her just how unsuitable Charlie was as a potential husband.

Whatever else they were going to ask was interrupted by horns blowing and the scraping of chairs as everyone stood.

"Ladies and gentleman! Her Royal Highness, Princess Anastasia and her escort, Mr. Isaac Graham of Montevaro." The polite applause increased as they walked in a different door from everyone else. As Princess Ana and Isaac reached the bottom of the staircase, the next couple was announced. "Crown Princess Adeline and her escort, Mr. Jonathan Langley-Cranston the Fourth from the United States."

Charlie's heart tightened in his chest as he joined the applause. Addie took his breath away. A long white gown with sheer, flowing sleeves. Deep royal purple ribbons around the back from the neckline to her waist where they tied with the ends trailing to the floor. Jonathan looked like he was already a member of the royal family. Had he chosen the costume? Or had it been chosen for him once the queen knew Charlie and Lindsey would be at the ball? A way to make sure Charlie knew, as though he didn't already, there was no hope. Like he needed reminding.

When they reached the bottom of the stairs, the trumpet sounded again and any of the remaining whispers stopped. "Ladies and gentlemen, His Majesty King Jedediah and Her Royal Highness, Queen Alexandra of Montevaro." The loudest applause filled the room as the couple descended the stairs. Immediately, the band struck up a song and the king and queen began to dance as everyone else took a seat.

"He looks better than I expected," Rob whispered.

Charlie took a good look at the king. "He looks better than he did when I met him the other day. He seems to be healing well." He watched closely for the telltale shake he'd seen in the other man's hand, but it was nowhere to be seen at the moment. About halfway through the dance, Addie and Jonathan joined them on the floor, followed by Ana and her date a minute later.

Once the first dance ended, all three of the couples broke apart and any number of others joined them on the dance floor. After a couple of dances went by, Charlie stood and bowed Lindsey's direction. "May I have this dance?"

She nodded and took his hand. He twirled her around as they reached the dance floor. Both of them concentrated on not running into other people until someone tapped Charlie on the shoulder. He turned to see Jonathan standing there.

The other man smiled. "May I cut in?"

Jonathan took Lindsey's hand in his as Charlie nodded. She seemed a bit intimidated but did her best to keep up with him as he led her through the dance.

"Are you enjoying your trip?" he asked.

She nodded. "Yeah."

"But you wish your dad and Addie had a chance?"

"Yeah."

He leaned closer. "Want to help me get them together? At least for a few minutes tonight?"

Lindsey's eyes lit up. "How?"

"The next to last dance before dinner, I'll dance with you and your dad with Addie. It's part of the tradition since we danced with you earlier."

"Okay."

"After the dance ends, I'll dance with Addie again and you'll go back with your dad. Tell him you want to go out on the terrace. Since it's almost dinner time, there shouldn't be anyone out there. I'll get Addie out there for a minute after our dance is finished and then we can disappear. They can have at least a few minutes alone together."

"I can do that."

The dance ended all too soon. Lindsey was a lovely young girl and he hoped Addie would end up being her step-mom someway. One dance after another with women he didn't know, but before long, he was with Lindsey again.

"Did you make a new friend?" he asked, nodding toward a girl he'd seen Lindsey talking to.

"Her name is Emily. She met Addie while you were walking

around with her this morning. When they got home, there was an invitation waiting."

Jonathan looked a bit more closely. Sure enough. He remembered Addie talking with her and Mark making a note of her name. Surely, that also explained the other pre-teens he'd seen. Addie had gone out of her way to make sure Lindsey wouldn't be the only one her age at the ball.

He handed the girl back off to her father and found Addie before the last pre-dinner dance began. As they twirled around the floor, he noticed she was oddly quiet. "What is it?"

"It has been a long week."

"You miss Charlie?"

She nodded. "Thank you for being such a good friend, Jonathan."

He nodded toward the open terrace doors. "We have a few minutes. Why don't we get some fresh air?"

"That would be lovely. Thank you, Jonathan."

The cool air felt good after an hour dancing in the costume get up. As he suspected, the terrace was empty except for Lindsey and Charlie.

Addie stopped when she saw them. "We should go back inside, Jonathan."

He refused. "Talk to him, Adeline. You're both miserable. Get some closure."

"We already said our good-byes."

Jonathan stepped away from her. "Then say them again."

Adeline glared at Jonathan as he pulled away, motioning for Lindsey to follow him. With her slippers gliding over the stone floor, she kept her eyes on Charlie.

"I guess we're outnumbered." His voice floated toward her though he hadn't turned.

"Outmaneuvered, anyway." Her hands came to rest on the ornate stone railing. "I am glad you are here. Lindsey should get to experience this."

"I'm glad she's here so she can. And thank you for making sure there were other children her age here."

Adeline waved her hand. "Of course. I would not want Lindsey to be uncomfortable as the only one under the age of eighteen."

She saw his hand reach for hers, hesitate, then come to rest a hair's breadth away on the railing. "She's going to miss you. *I* am going to miss you."

"And I will miss both of you." But she would miss him more. Miss what they could have become.

"I should go back inside. I'm sure your parents won't be happy about us being outside alone. Be well, Princess Adeline. I'll be praying for you." He turned to walk away and she nearly let him.

Grasping his forearm before he moved out of reach, she looked up into his beautiful eyes. "There is one other thing I would like from you, Charlie."

Her fingers burned where they touched his sleeve, tingles running up her arm. The goosebumps had nothing to do with the chill in the air.

"What is it, Princess Adeline?"

She moved a half step closer until his breath mingled with her own. "This."

Feeling more bold than she had in her entire life, Adeline placed both hands on his face and leaned into him, her lips brushing against his. She swayed against him, struggling not to lose her balance.

Charlie groaned and wrapped his arms around her, pulling her tight against him as he kissed her again. This kiss was different than the few others they had shared, or the one Jonathan had given her. Her arms wound around his neck as the intensity of the kiss grew. This was not a gentle kiss, but one full of passion, of need, of longing. Not just hers, but his.

First one tear, then another, streaked down her face as her fingers threaded through his hair, knocking his hat askew. When he pulled back, his mouth was mere millimeters from hers.

"This is wrong, Adeline. I love you, but we can't be together." He tried to set her away but she grabbed hold tighter. "Only one man should kiss you like that." Charlie pressed his lips to hers, a hard, final kiss. "Your husband."

She sagged against him, knowing he spoke the truth. "I do not believe I will ever find a man who stirs me like you do, Charlie Brewer."

His thumbs stroked her cheeks, wiping away her tears. "You will find love, Adeline. I believe that. A man who adores you, heart and soul, no matter the crown you wear." With a final brush of his lips against her forehead, he moved back and this time she let him go. "Lindsey and I are going to leave. I can't stay."

Adeline nodded, unable to trust her voice. She sank backwards against the railing as she watched him walk away. Once Charlie was inside, Jonathan returned.

"Are you all right?"

She shook her head. "Will you let Mark and Todd know that I will be in my room?"

He glanced around. "Can you get there without going through the ballroom?"

"Yes." Determined, she walked around a large column, nearly four feet around. On the other side was a door. Few knew of its existence, hidden as it was. She walked through the door with Jonathan's assurance he would notify her security team. As the door closed behind her, she knew, deep inside, Charlie was now a chapter in her past.

She threw herself, in her crushed white velvet gown - the one that symbolized the purity of the unmarried Crown Princess - onto her bed, heart-wrenching sobs shaking her body. Having used a security code that would lock out everyone except in a true emergency, she released it all. Everything she thought she had a few days before, everything she wished for. All of it she sent into the hands of her Father.

When she finally slipped out of the beautiful renaissance gown and into a pair of her most comfortable pajamas from Serenity Landing, she went to sit in a comfortable wingback chair looking out the window. The moon hung low over the Alps as the Psalm came back to her.

Her help would come.

It was just a matter of time.

Charlie sat on the side of his bed, having listened to his daughter cry herself to sleep. He wished he could comfort her, tell her it would be all right, but as emotionally drained as he was, there was no way. The vest of his costume hung open, his hat left on the terrace, where Addie had knocked it off as they kissed.

Outside the window, a large nearly blue moon hung low over the mountain tops. It looked like something out of a renaissance painting with the palace lit up in the middle of the lake in front of the evergreens and snow-capped peaks.

I will lift mine eyes unto the hills, from whence my help cometh.

What did that mean? God had all of this in His hands. Charlie believed that with his entire being, but he failed to see how this would end up being a good thing. *All things work together? God, ya gotta help me see how, because I just don't...*

Trust Me.

The voice reverberated in the room, not just his soul. Just saying, "God, I trust you" wouldn't work. He needed to find a way to actually put Addie out of his mind.

Something niggled at the back of his consciousness. They

couldn't attend church in the morning. No way he was up for running into Addie or seeing her sit next to Jonathan, no matter her claims that there was nothing between them.

Maybe they could take a hike in the mountains. Nothing too hard. Or he could go by himself. A hike until he was tired enough to not think sounded like just what the doctor ordered and Lindsey could stay at the hotel. Charlie knew the hotel had been instructed to give them whatever he needed. Surely they could help him find a babysitter or companion for the day for Lindsey.

But maybe, just maybe, they'd come across something no one had ever noticed before. Maybe God was telling him to trust Him because Charlie would be the one to find the tunnel.

Then he would be a Marquis. And the Parliament wouldn't be able to find fault with him then, would they?

He'd still be the same Charlie, but maybe they'd finally see him as good enough.

"Is there anything else we need to go over?"

Monday morning dawned too early, with Adeline still attempting to recover from the headache she woke up with on Sunday. An early morning meeting with one of the charities she sponsored in Montevaro could not be avoided.

"No, ma'am. I believe that's it."

Adeline nodded at the director who stood and left, though she remained seated.

Mark walked in as the other woman left. "How are you?"

She gave a slight shrug. "About as well as you would guess, I suppose. Jonathan remains a good friend, keeping my mother away, but Charlie is the man I love but will never be able to marry."

When she looked up, there was an unusual twinkle in his eye.

"I imagine there's good news just around the corner. Don't ask me what, because I don't know, but I can feel it."

With a tight smile, she stood. "The meeting with my father is still on?"

"Ten minutes."

"I will head that way now." She clicked her way through the halls until she reached his well-appointed personal office. His secretary, on the phone, motioned her into his office.

She sat in one of the leather chairs across the desk from him. Without a word, Adeline knew he knew exactly how she felt and wished he could make it better.

But since he could not, they spent the next hour going over assorted business as he started telling her things she would need to know when she took over as queen. The meeting ended without mentioning the elephant in the room. She gave her father a kiss on the cheek and turned toward the outer office.

Before Adeline could leave, there was a sharp knock at the door.

"Come," the king called.

His assistant entered the room. "My apologies, sir, but you said you wanted to know immediately when I got this news."

"What news is that, Gerald?"

"The team from the States believes they have found the other entrance to the tunnel and the treasure room."

Adeline's eyes went wide and she turned to her father to see the same look on his face.

"Thank you, Gerald. Have they documented this?"

He nodded. "They have video tape of the site and the tunnel which apparently very well-preserved in most areas. They know of your health and knew you would not be able to visit the site yourself, so they have the video evidence, though they expect you to send a team to verify it, of course. They said the seal on the treasure room is cracked but mostly intact and they did not touch it."

The king closed his eyes and a smile settled on his face. "Very well. Arrange for them to come to the palace and present their findings to me."

"Yes, sir."

Gerald gave a small bow at the waist and left.

Her father's eyes grew sad once more. "If they did find it, then there is no chance Charlie could even if he were to get some idea no one else had. I am sorry, Adeline."

She nodded but did not speak as she left the room and fled to her apartment, flung herself on the bed and cried.

Charlie and Lindsey stood in front of the hotel once more. This time it didn't seem nearly as impressive as it had when they first arrived. They went in and were given the same room they had vacated. Charlie didn't have the desire to unpack or do anything more than flip on the television and see if he could find some American sports of some kind. Or maybe a good rugby match or some mindless action movie he wouldn't normally let Lindsey watch.

"Can I get a soda, Dad?"

He hadn't settled on anything when she asked. Tossing his wallet onto her bed, he nodded. "Go ahead. There's some Euros in there. Should be enough. Ask the clerk if you need help figuring out the machine."

She dug some bills out and went out the door. He had just about decided on some movie he'd never seen but seemed to have lots of explosions when he heard her chattering her way down the hall. He frowned. Lindsey knew better than to talk to strangers. Could it be Todd or Mark coming to tell them something?

The key scraped in the door and it opened to excited prattle.

"Dad! Look who I found!"

It took everything in him to muster up enough excitement to look toward the door. Even then, it took several rapid blinks to register who was there. "Mom? Dad?"

"Charlie!" His mom opened her arms and he stood to embrace her.

"What are you doing here?" He moved to hug his dad. "I thought you were on a dig in Greece or something."

His dad chuckled. "Nope. But Linds didn't tell us what you were doing here either. This is much more our neck of the woods than yours."

"We're..." Charlie looked at Lindsey's crestfallen face. She tried to hide it but couldn't. Not from him. "...visiting a friend," he finally finished. "We stayed with her family for a couple days but they had something come up so we're back here until it's time for us to head home. We'll do some site seeing before we go back to Serenity Landing." There had been a note waiting for him saying Addie had taken care of their hotel and flight change expenses, but that was cold comfort to losing the woman he loved.

"We'll be here for a couple of days, I'm sure." His dad sat in the desk chair. "We're supposed to have a meeting with someone, but the time hasn't been set yet." As soon as he said it, his phone buzzed and he excused himself to the hallway.

Charlie looked at his mom. "What have you guys been doing then?"

She waved him off. "We'll talk about it later, but I want to know why you dragged my granddaughter across the Atlantic and half the Continent so soon after surgery." She sat next to Lindsey and took her hand. "How are you feeling, sweetie?"

Lindsey shrugged. "I'm okay but I get tired easily still. It's been a long day already. I might take a nap."

She went from asking to go get a soda to wanting to take a nap? He'd never understand preteens. His dad walked in before he could say anything.

"I hope you don't want to take that nap right now, princess. Grandma and I have a meeting to go to in a cool old building and I bet I can get you guys a tour if you come with us." He grinned. "Trust me. You'll love this building."

Lindsey looked at him and shrugged. "Do you want to go, Dad?"

What Charlie really wanted to do was wallow. He'd never understood the whole eat-ice-cream-from-the-carton thing until now. "Can you guys take Linds? I'm pretty beat."

His mom shook her head. "Sorry, honey. Dad and I will both be in the meeting and she'll need a grown-up with her."

His daughter had been disappointed enough for one day. She pretended nonchalance, but he knew she wanted to go. Especially since they'd been denied a tour of the palace. Finally, he nodded. "Okay." He stood. "Let's go."

With a raised brow, his mother looked him up and down. "I hate to be a pill, but I think you both need to change into something a bit nicer. We have time?" She looked askance at his father who nodded.

Ten minutes later, Charlie was dressed in Dockers, a collared shirt and his "church shoes" - a pair of two-tone brown Sketchers his mother had reluctantly approved. A car waited for them outside the hotel. His dad rode in front and he rode in the back with his mom and Lindsey. He stared unseeing out the window for the short trip. When his mother announced, they'd arrived, he looked to the other side of the car.

His jaw dropped when he saw where they were. "We're going to the palace?"

Adeline sat in the conference room in her father's office suite. Everything they needed for a presentation was in there. Except something to fill the void inside. When she had been told of the meeting, she had to hurry to pull herself together enough to look presentable. Hopefully, the lights would be off for most of the presentation and no one would notice her puffy eyes.

Her father entered the room, but she did not bother standing like Gerald did. "Are they not here yet?" he asked.

Gerald answered. "They have arrived with their son and granddaughter in tow. They asked if the two of them could meet you and then be given a tour. Apparently, they ran into each other on the way here."

Her father nodded and sank into the deep, leather chair at the head of the table. Silence reigned until footsteps were heard in the hall. Adeline took a deep breath and stood to greet their guests. The king remained seated, likely due to how he felt more so than anything else. The door opened and a man and woman entered, followed by...

Adeline's breath caught in her throat. "Charlie?" she whispered.

He shifted uncomfortably. "Princess Adeline." He nodded to the king. "Your Majesty."

Adeline did not dare look at her father. Before she could ask what he was doing there, the woman spoke.

"Charlie, you know the princess?" Surprise colored the woman's voice.

"Yes, Mom. We've met. She volunteered at Lindsey's after school program for a while this spring." Charlie looked at her but before Addie could convey her feelings, he looked at the floor.

The woman - his mother - clapped her hands together. "What a small world!" But rather than questioning further. "Your Majesty, we had planned to introduce you to our son and grand-daughter, but it appears you already know them." She turned. "Lindsey, are you going to say hello?" the woman whispered loudly.

Lindsey came around Charlie and looked straight at Adeline.

"Hi, Addie." Charlie nudged her and she corrected herself. "Princess Adeline."

Adeline's heart broke fresh at the pain written on the girl's face. How hard must this be for her? To come back to the place where her dreams had been ripped out.

Charlie's dad spoke up. "Your Majesty, at the risk of sounding presumptuous, is there someone who could take our son and granddaughter on a tour?"

The king shook his head. "No. I would prefer they stay for your presentation." He looked at Lindsey. "Do you know what they will be talking to me about, young lady?"

Lindsey shook her head.

The king smiled. "I think you will find it most interesting, Miss Brewer. If you change your mind at any time, please let me know and I will have someone take you for hot chocolate again. I heard you quite enjoyed it."

"Thank you, sir."

To Adeline's great discomfort, and Charlie's too, she was sure, the king directed everyone to their seats. Charlie was at her right side. The implications were not lost on her. Neither were they lost on her father, if the wink he gave her was any indication. Gerald sat across from Adeline, pen poised to take notes and Lindsey sat at his side while Charlie's parents set their computer up on a lectern off to one side and hooked it up to the projector.

Charlie's dad spoke first when they were done. "Your Majesty, we have met several times, but we have not had the pleasure of meeting your daughter in a number of years." He bowed slightly. "I am Randall Brewer and this is my wife, Suzanne. We are here to tell you what we discovered."

He turned off the lights and a PowerPoint presentation filled the wall. Randall gave a brief history of the origins of the tunnel, complete with images of recovered drawings and sketches Adeline had seen a number of times before. But the *way* he presented them was new to her.

After he finished giving an overview, an ancient map came up on the wall. The top left corner was blown up as an inset.

"This section here is what we looked at most closely," Randall told them. "Everyone has taken this map at face value." With his pointer, he traced the line of the tunnel. "But here, in this corner, the document has been torn. On all of the Montevarian maps we've studied from this era, the compass rose has been in this corner." The red dot lit on the top right of the map. "If there isn't one, it seems they would have expected the reader to know what direction it was facing. The island where the palace is isn't perfectly round, though it's fairly close to an oval." He pointed to several spots on the map. "Given these points, it's seems to show which way the map is supposed to go."

Suzanne took over. "Or is it? About two years ago, I wondered what this smudge was." She pointed back to that corner and clicked to the next slide where it was enlarged even more.

Adeline squinted. It was not just a smudge but a point of some sort.

"When comparing this tiny bit of something to a compass rose on a map from this same era, this fancy point is similar, but on the bottom left instead of the top right. When you flip it to make that the top right..." The next slide reoriented the map. "Now, the island is somewhat wrong, but this here..." She pointed to the end of the tunnel within the palace. "Using satellite images readily available online, we overlaid the two and came up with this." A satellite image appeared with the map superimposed on it. "The island doesn't quite match up but this courtyard matches with a different one."

Lindsey jumped in. "That's where the wishing well is!"

Suzanne looked surprised, but nodded. "That's right. It looks like the tunnel ends in or near the courtyard with the well." Another click and a bright green line appeared on the screen. "This is the tunnel as shown on the map. If this orientation of the map is correct, the tunnel won't come out to the east where everyone has been looking for the last hundred years or so, but to the north, in this area of the mountains."

It was Randall's turn again. "That's where we've been looking for the last year, but even so the map isn't entirely accurate. Our assumption is that if it fell into the wrong hands, even knowing the compass rose was in the wrong corner wouldn't be enough." Another slide had dots around several slight bends in the tunnel. "These points are backwards. Not all of them, but some. When you take those and turn them around..." A blue line appeared, similar but different and leading to a completely different location. "And at the end of this line is this odd mark on the map that doesn't mean anything in common map making legends. Unless you suspected it was something more, you would never think twice about it."

Adeline's father spoke up. "This is a wonderful theory and I would love to hear more about how you determined those spots were the ones that were backwards, but this does not prove anything except there is a new place to look."

Suzanne nodded. "Of course. As we mentioned, we have spent the last year working on this, trying different combinations of changes until we got to this one. At this location, there is what in the States we'd call a ghost town. It was never very large. Through a total of two years of research and another year of excavation, we found the tunnel." The picture changed to one of Suzanne and Randall perched next to an opening in a stone wall. "More accurately, we found a dry well, crumbled over with debris. Handholds lead down several stories before it turns into a tunnel." The next slide had a black circle with a play triangle in the middle. "Before we start the video, are there any questions?"

Charlie surprised her when he asked one. "What does this have to do with me and Lindsey?"

He'd never been fond of his parents' presentations. They would come back from one of their expeditions and make him, his aunt and uncle, and his cousins watch slide shows. The technology had improved over the years, but the content hadn't changed much. He struggled to stay awake and really, the only reason he could was Adeline's presence.

His mom looked at him. "I'm not sure, Charlie, but when the king asks you to stay for a presentation, you stay and don't ask questions." He couldn't miss the warning tone in her voice.

Charlie gave a slight nod and tuned out the rest of the presentation. There was a tunnel. With rock walls and beams helping support it. Small phone booth sized slots in the walls were spots where provisions had been stored. Eventually, they came to one with an emblem over it. It looked like the others, but when his video-father reached up and pressed the emblem, the wall slid open.

The video paused. "Inside this door, is another one. That one has the seal around it." He pushed play and they saw the red wax sealing up another opening with a the royal crest pressed into it. "You can see where the seal is cracked but not broken. We have not entered this room and have no idea what, if anything, is in it. We would be honored to help in the excavation, if you would accept our assistance. Our presumption is the artifacts you have been looking for are in there, but we do not *know*."

His father turned the lights back on. "Any questions?"

Charlie turned to look at Addie's father. He sat back in his chair, his fingers steepled and tapping against his chin. "I am convinced to this point. It will be independently verified and we go from there. If it checks out, we will discuss the reward."

Addie surprised him when she leaned forward to look at the wall where the presentation was. "Can you go back to the slide with the green and blue lines on it?" His father obliged and Addie asked another question. "Can you explain to me how you came to these conclusions about which bends were incorrect?" As his father did so, pulling up another presentation explaining some of the different theories they tried, she surprised Charlie again when her forefinger slid around his pinky and squeezed.

He schooled his features but curled his finger around hers. She was trying to convey something to him, but he had no idea what it was.

Once his father was done, Addie moved back in her seat, releasing his finger. "Father, if this information is accurate as it seems to be and there are no complaints or anyone who comes along claiming the Brewers stole their information and so on." His mother opened her mouth to protest their innocence, but Addie held up a hand. "I am not trying to insinuate you would do such a thing, but there are those out there who would. If this all proves out, Mr. and Mrs. Brewer would be offered the title of Marquis and Marchioness, yes?"

The implication of what she was saying began to sink in and Charlie looked at the king who had a smirk on his face.

"Yes, Adeline, they would."

"I see."

His father answered for his parents. "I believe I speak for my wife when I say we didn't do this for a title. Not too much further beyond this alcove, the tunnel is blocked, but we don't believe it is caved in. It almost seems walled off with a pile of rocks. Not an actual wall, but there's something about it that seems man-made. We still have not determined where or how you can get to the tunnel from the palace."

Lindsey piped up. "I know how."

Everyone but Charlie and the king looked surprised, but Addie asked the question for all of them. "How do you know?"

Eyes bubbling with excitement, Lindsey told them about how she opened the secret passage to find Addie and the staircase leading downward.

The king stood. "It is settled. Once this is confirmed and we have excavated the room Mr. and Mrs. Brewer found, the title of

Marquis and Marchioness of Montago will be bestowed upon them. However, if Miss Lindsey is correct, I believe she has earned the right to inherit the title on her own without it going through her father."

Charlie's father looked puzzled. "But, sir, isn't that most unusual? To have a title skip a generation?"

Addie's father nodded. "It is. But if her find checks out as the other end of the tunnel, it will skip Charlie and go to Lindsey when the time comes. That will likely be one condition of conferring the title." He looked straight at Charlie and unless he was mistaken, the king winked at him. "Thank you for your time and efforts on our behalf, Mr. and Mrs. Brewer. I look forward to hearing the findings of our team and I do hope you will work closely with them. I do not believe you have ever been on a tour of the palace and I know Charlie and Lindsey have not been. I am sure my daughter would be happy to take you on a personal tour very few will ever get. As much as I wish we could talk more, it is time for me to get some rest."

Everyone, including Addie, stood as the king left with Gerald in his wake.

Charlie turned to Addie and caught the twinkle in her eye as she spoke. "Shall we go? I would be happy to give you a tour and I would love to see how Lindsey opened the passage." She motioned for everyone to go, telling his parents their equipment would be waiting for them when they left. Once the rest of his family had left the room she turned to him. "I pray it turns out to be true, Charlie." She lifted a hand to his cheek. "We will talk later. You and me."

He nodded, not trusting his voice, and followed her out of the room with his hope beginning to soar.

Addie tucked Lindsey into bed in the room she had stayed in before. The girl had shown them how to open the hidden door, but they had only peeked inside. Charlie's parents were staying in her apartment as well, meaning she could stay in her own room. Charlie could still be near his daughter and they would be properly chaperoned. But once she covered Lindsey and told her goodnight, Addie returned to the living room to find Charlie seated on the couch.

"My parents have already turned in," he said before she had the chance to say anything.

She arched an eyebrow his direction. "So we are alone?"

"I believe so."

A smile crossed her face and she sat next to him, his arm wrapped around her shoulder tugging her close. "This has been quite a day, has it not?"

"I don't think I've ever had a day full of so many ups and downs and emotions on complete opposite ends of the spectrum. From realizing I had to walk away to being told there's a good chance I won't have to..." She felt rather than saw him shake his head. "It's a lot to take in."

"I came back up here when you left and cried out to God on my bed. He met me there. I know it sounds odd, but He did. I could feel His Spirit wash over me and tell me honoring my father was the right thing to do and He had me in the palm of His hand. The verse my father has quoted to me many times came to me. Psalm 121:1, the same verse Lindsey used to open the passageway." She nodded to the windows across from them. "My bedroom faces the same way this room does and when I sat up and looked out the window, I could see the Alps. I whispered that verse and not two minutes later, my assistant told me about the meeting with your parents. I did not know how my help would come from those hills, but that is where your parents say the entrance is. You cannot see it now because it is dark out, but right out the window is the exact location."

"Amazing how God works, isn't it?"

"Just when I told God I trusted Him, He came through. I just knew, deep inside, that either you were the man I was meant to love until the day I die, or I just thought you were and He would bring someone better into both our lives."

He kissed the side of her head. "I'm glad He seems to think we belong together."

"We have a lot of things to talk through, Charlie, before we formally announce our intentions."

"I know."

"I will be queen of my country and therefore, I will be the final answer on many subjects and you may not always agree with me, but my decision is final."

"I understand that."

"But at the end of the day, when it is us and our family, I want to be Addie again. Just Addie, with my husband who is the head of my house, but is willing to let me lead my country."

Addie let him tip her face toward him with a finger crooked under her chin. "I know, Addie. I want to be that for you."

"You cannot ask me to marry you yet, Charlie."

"I won't. But I will. Someday soon. Lindsey and I need to go home and finish out the school year. Plan a move to Europe. You need to finish your degree and take over your country. Once those things settle down, then we will make it official."

He moved closer to her, brushing a kiss on her forehead and again on her eyelids. "You're crying."

"These are happy..." She could not finish her sentence, because he silenced her very effectively. Once she was snuggled back in next to him, she mentioned something she'd thought about earlier, when Todd walked part of the way down the staircase Lindsey showed them. "You know why my father insists the Marquis title skip to Lindsey?"

She felt him shake his head.

"Because you will have a title of your own by then."

His low chuckle warmed her insides like nothing else could. "I will?"

"By then you will be Prince Consort Charles of Montevaro." She smiled at the thought of Charlie as her husband.

He shifted behind her. "Uh, there's one problem with that."

She looked up at him to see a grimace on his face. "What could be the problem?"

"My name isn't Charles."

Addie moved away from him, tucking one leg under her. "It is not? What else is Charlie short for? Is your name just Charlie?"

"No. It's not just Charlie, but it's not Charles either." He winced and told her. "It's Charlemagne."

Both of her eyebrows shot sky high, though she did her best to control her surprise. "Your name is Charlemagne?"

He nodded. "You've met my parents now. Their favorite time period is Charlemagne's kingdom so they named me after him but always called me Charlie."

Addie took his face in her hands. "Prince Consort Charlemagne of Montevaro?"

His face looked a bit pathetic as he gave a single nod.

She could not help it. She laughed.

"What?"

"Charlemagne controlled this area. There was a... delicate situation with the daughter of an important Englishman. An exceptionally large area of land was given to this Englishman who passed it on to his daughter. His daughter and her husband had three sons. The three sons split the land into what became Montevaro, Mevendia, and Ravenzario. Today, the three countries still make up the Royal Commonwealth of Bellas Montagne. He hated giving up the land, but apparently, he believed it was the right thing to do."

By the time she finished, Charlie had joined her laughter. "Just promise me none of our sons will be named after me."

She gave him a smirk. "If our first child is a boy, I think we should name him Charlemagne. Then there will be a King Charlemagne in Montevaro."

Charlie kissed her until she could not remember what they were discussing. Here, in the arms of the man she loved, the names of their children did not matter. The only thing that mattered was Charlie and that she had finally proven he was good enough for a princess.

EPILOGUE

Charlie waited for the call to go through, using the small window on the bottom of his screen to straighten his tie.

"Is she here yet?" Lindsey's bright purple satin dress had been completely paid for by the program Addie had set up. He was proud of his daughter - for her hard work and for choosing a modest ankle length dress with spaghetti straps. Addie could probably describe it better, but all he knew was that she looked lovely.

At that moment, Addie's face filled the screen. Lindsey pushed him out of the way. "Addie! Why aren't you here?"

Charlie winced, though he knew the excitement that filled his daughter. She just wanted to see the woman who would be the only mother she'd ever know. In person. It had been nearly two months since they left Montevaro. They texted daily. Spoke on the phone nearly as often and Skyped when they could, though the time difference made it hard at times.

"I am sorry, Lindsey. I will not be able to go to the banquet with you and your father."

Lindsey's shoulders slumped. "I figured. You said you'd try, though. I knew it was a long shot."

Charlie rested his hands on his daughter's upper arms. "Why don't you go finish getting ready, sweetheart?" He'd finished his finals and turned his notice in at work. Lindsey had two more weeks of school left. Once the banquet was over, his attention would be turned to packing up the apartment. They wouldn't leave for Montevaro until after Dan and CeCe's wedding, but it was only three weeks away. King Jedediah had insisted they stay at the palace until his parents were given their titles in June. The day before the king had told Charlie he'd be knighted at the same time - for service to the crown and protection of the royal family above and beyond the call of duty.

He sat in the chair Lindsey vacated. "How are you?"

Addie sighed. "Missing both of you."

"Anything interesting happen yesterday?"

She gave him a small half-smile. "The Council meeting with the leaders of Parliament went very well, if a bit long and tedious. They indicated their tentative approval of our relationship, but until your parents are officially the Marquis and Marchioness and you receive your knighthood..." Her voice trailed off.

As they expected. The continued uncertainty wore on both of them, but there didn't seem to be any anything in the way except time.

"We have a coronation date. September fourth. We talked about July fourth, but I did not want to share the day with the anniversary of American independence." Humor colored her voice.

Charlie leaned forward until he could get a closer look at her eyes. "I don't blame you."

If only she would be at the banquet. The velvet box lay heavy in the inside pocket of his suit coat. They could make their engagement official and begin to plan their life together before the coronation planning took over.

So much for his plans.

But God's plans were best, something Charlie was learning every day.

He reached out and traced his finger down the side of her face. "I miss you."

Addie reached toward him. "I miss you. I love you, Charlie."

"I love you." He glanced at the clock on the bottom of the screen. "But I have a lovely young lady to escort to dinner tonight and it's time for us to go."

He could see the tears in her eyes. "Have a wonderful time. Text me pictures of all the girls?"

"Of course." The days until he could hold her again couldn't go quickly enough. It had already been an eternity. "I thank my God..."

"Upon every remembrance of you." She looked up to one side. "It's time for me to say good-bye, too." Neither one wanted to end the call, but both knew they had to.

He closed his eyes as the screen went dark. Soon.

Half an hour later, he escorted his first love into their first non-Renaissance formal event. Given his girlfriend, it wouldn't be their last, but this one would always be special because it was just the two of them.

The red carpet had been rolled out - literally - and a valet parked their cars. Most of the girls were already there and he called them together with the help of Mrs. Hart to get a couple of pictures to send Addie. She hadn't replied when it was time for the group to be seated. He and Lindsey were at a table with three other girls and their fathers when Mrs. Hart walked to the podium.

"Good evening! And welcome to the first Father-Daughter Banquet in our newly renovated facilities! I cannot begin to tell you how proud I am of all of you for your hard work and someone else wants to tell you, too."

Two large screens flanked the podium. Throughout the night,

they'd have pictures of fathers and daughters and who knew what else. They'd been part of his plan to propose, but he'd have to come up with another way. Maybe once they got back to Montevaro.

Addie sat in one of the chairs in the sitting room in Montevaro. The room where they'd escaped after the incident with the count. "Good evening, ladies! I cannot begin to tell you how proud I am of all of you." Her dark blue pantsuit and bright pink top were elegant and understated, as she always was. "I miss all of you more than words can say and I do hope to stop in sometime to see you all." She spoke for a few more minutes before smiling as though she had a secret. "I do have a surprise for all of you. Someone I hope you recognize will be emceeing the event this evening. If you'd turn your attention to the right of the podium..."

Dark curtains covered the walls of the room, giving it a more elegant feel than the painted white would have. Someone unseen drew two of them aside and in between...

Gasps filled the room. Lindsey was out of her seat and halfway across the room before Charlie could stop her.

"Addie!"

Lindsey wrapped her arms around the princess who held her tightly in return. Addie's pale pink dress spoke of class and elegance. Charlie couldn't stop the tears that filled his eyes. He wanted nothing more than to take Lindsey's place and kiss Addie until neither of them could see straight.

Instead, he remained seated, the box burning a hole in his pocket. The box the king had given him before they'd returned to the States. An heirloom passed down from several generations earlier. A box that led Charlie to get his first ever safe deposit box.

Lindsey returned to her seat. Addie made the rounds as the first course was served. Their table was last. The tension he felt, wishing she was closer bled away as Addie rested her hand on his shoulder.

"You lied to me, Miss Addie." Lindsey's tone held disapproval.

"No." Addie laid her other hand on his daughter's head. "I told you I would not be able to *go* to the banquet with you. I did not say I would not be here. I do hope the surprise was worth it."

"Oh, yes. I'm glad you're here. How long will you stay?" Charlie knew his daughter was hoping for a few days with her.

"Only until tomorrow afternoon. I have many things on my calendar early next week."

After another moment, Addie moved on, promising to accompany them home before returning to her hotel and to attend church with them in the morning.

The rest of the night went both too quickly and too slowly at the same time. Charlie shared his first dance with his daughter and realized just how quickly she was growing up. Before he knew it, he'd be dancing with her at her wedding. Time passed too fast when one had a daughter to raise.

By the end of the night, he could see exhaustion written all over her face, though he doubted anyone else would. The girls left, one by one, after spending a few minutes with her. He knew they were going along with the plan though. They'd be hiding in the kitchen to see if he could pull it off.

Lindsey and Mrs. Hart disappeared, leaving them alone at last. Charlie held out his hand. "May I have this dance?"

Music began to play softly as she put her hand in his. Tugging her much closer than Lindsey had been, they moved slowly to the music. The curls of her dark hair teased his chin as he tightened his arm around her waist.

"I have missed this," Addie whispered.

"We haven't ever done this," he whispered back.

"I know. I miss being with you." She sighed. "Your move cannot come soon enough. I miss your presence and your strength when I need it, your comfort, your support. Your arms around me."

"Soon," he promised. The pictures he'd planned to show on the big screens had never started, evidently forgotten or deleted when he said Addie wouldn't be there.

"I wish we could be married before the coronation," she blurted out. "I want you there, not just as a new resident of Montevaro but as my husband."

She couldn't have given him a more perfect opening. Charlie stepped back and reached into his pocket as he dropped to one knee.

"Then say you'll marry me."

Addie's hands flew to her mouth as the box popped open. "Charlie!"

"Adeline Julianne Elizabeth, will you do me the honor of being my wife?" He knew her answer before he asked, but his heart still stuck in his throat.

Tears began streaming down her cheeks. "Yes." The word was barely more than a breath, but it was enough. He took the ring and slid it on her outstretched finger. When he stood, she threw her arms around his neck and kissed him, sealing the engagement with that promise, telling him without words she meant to spend her life with him.

But before he could truly kiss her the way he wanted, he remembered their audience and, sure enough, as they parted, the door to the kitchen opened and a dozen girls streamed out dressed in their best. Lindsey led the charge, hugging first Addie, then him as she greeted the other girls.

They oohed and aahed over her ring, a sapphire and diamond combination that had belonged to her great-grandmother and her great-great-great-grandmother. Her grace and poise never ceased to amaze him. Could he live up to the example she set? A whispered prayer went heavenward, but when she looked at him with those brilliant hazel eyes, he knew it would be all right.

With God's help, they'd proven to Parliament he was good enough for their Crown Princess. And with God's grace, he'd be the husband she deserved.

As Addie moved away from the girls and back into his arms, he knew, beyond a shadow of a doubt, that he'd made the right decision. Finding themselves suddenly alone again, he brushed the hair back off her face. "I love you, Adeline Julianne Elizabeth."

A wicked grin crossed her face. "And I love you, Charlemagne. For the rest of my life, and beyond, you'll always been good enough for this princess."

Before he could protest, she kissed him, proving once again, they belonged together. For the rest of their lives.

LETTER TO READERS

Dear Reader,

Thank you for joining Addie and Charlie in *Good Enough for a Princess*! I appreciate you and hope you enjoyed it! Addie's younger siblings, Rick and Ana, will be getting their own stories beginning with *Along Came a Prince* and *More than a Princess*, both releasing in December 2014. There will be more of Jonathan and the cast of characters will also travel in the other two countries of the Royal Commonwealth of Bellas Montagnes. Following the acknowledgments, you will find a preview of *Along Came a Prince*, as well as a preview for *Grace to Save*.

I see a meme floating around Facebook from time to time that tells readers what they can do to help their favorite authors. Buying their next book or giving a copy away is kind of a no-brainer, but the biggest thing you can do is write a review. If you enjoyed *Good Enough for a Princess* would you consider doing just that? You can do so by going to the Amazon page and scrolling down until you get to the button that asks if you'd like to write a review of your own.

I would LOVE to hear from you! My email address is books@candidpublications.com. You can find my website and blog at www.carolmoncado.com. I blog most Sundays and about once more each month at www.InspyRomance.com. And, of course, there's Facebook and my Facebook page, Carol Moncado Books.

Thanks again! I hope to see you soon!

ACKNOWLEDGMENTS

They say writing is a solitary endeavor and it absolutely can be. Sitting in front of the computer for hours on end, talking to imaginary people.

And having them talk back ;).

But the reality is no one walks alone. Since I began this writing journey five years ago, I can't begin to name all of those who've helped me along the way. From my husband, Matt, who has always, *always* believed in me and my best friend, Penny, who has brainstormed and critiqued and made me stop using passive voice more times than I can count. Others like Becki, Allen, Tina, Bobbie, Candice, the fitting room attendant at my local Wal-Mart, and so many others who encouraged, cheered, and cried with me. My mother-in-love, Andrea, who has prayed over us for years. All of the rest of my family and in-loves who never once looked at me like I was nuts for wanting to be a writer, including Gloria, my avid-reader sister, who has watched my kids countless times so I could work. Jan Christiansen (my "other mother") has always believed in me and Stacy Christiansen Spangler who has been my dearest friend for longer than I can remember.

Then there's my writer friends. My NovelSistas, Jessica Keller Koschnitzky and Kristy Cambron, both sisters of my heart. They're part of my BritCrit gals. Joanna Politano (who has talked me down off more virtual ledges than anyone), Jen Cvelvar (the best case of misidentification *ever*), and Stacey Zink (who never, ever fails to have a fabulous encouraging word) are BritCritters, too. We do a lot more living than we do critting, and I wouldn't have it any other way. All five of them are beyond gifted as writers and I thank God they're in my life. There's my MozArks ACFW peeps who laugh with me, critique, and encourage to no end. Christina Rich and Laurie Tomlinson who have often stepped in when I needed them most.

Then there's the Seekers, the AlleyCats, the InspyRomance crew, the CIA, my TSG peeps (you know who you are!) and all of the others who've helped me along on this journey.

I could go on for days about beloved mentors like Janice Thompson who has poured her time and energy into this newbie, going above and beyond for me. People like one of my spiciest friends, Pepper Basham, who inspired Charlie's name, or Julie Lessman, who has prayed me to this point - and inspired Julie Harders (whose son, Travis, will eventually get his own book). And, of course, there's Tamela Hancock Murray, agent extraordinaire, who believed in me enough to want to be my agent.

Good Enough for a Princess began as a NaNoWriMo project in 2012. Super special thanks go to everyone who helped it get to this point - I know I could never name all of you! And especially to Jerenda C., Tory U., and Amanda who helped proofread.

I said I could go on for days and I could keep going. On and on. I know I've forgotten many people and I hate that. But you, dear reader, would quickly get bored.

So THANK YOU to all of those who have helped me along they way. I couldn't have done this without you and you have my eternal gratitude.

And, of course, last but never least, to Jesus Christ, without whom none of this would be possible - or worth it.

Along Came a Prince

"**W**hat do you think they're arguing over?"

Richard Antonio David Nicklaus, spare to the heir of Montevaro, didn't take his eyes off the two trail guides while he answered Dennis. "Probably us." Rick hitched his backpack a bit higher. "Writing me off as another pretty boy and you two as my best-friend-tagalongs living off trust funds. Same as always." It wasn't the first time. It wouldn't be the last.

Dennis, Rick's bodyguard-turned-friend, moved to stand next to his backpack outside the headquarters of Ozark Outdoors as they watched the two leaders in a heated discussion.

Rick had spent the last four years seeing the world on his own terms, doing things just like this around the globe. If only he could convince his parents - and his sister, once she took the throne in a few months - something like this would thrive in their corner of the Alps. With Italy to the south and Switzerland to the northeast, they had a prime tourist area to work with. Directly north lay Montevaro's sister country, Mevendia. Between them they could create something spectacular.

"Maybe next time you should go buy the same clothes everyone else wears." Steve, his other bodyguard, brought Rick's attention back to the trail head in Missouri. "Try to blend in."

"Off the rack? I don't think so."

"And you wonder why people think you're a pretty boy," Dennis muttered.

"Don't start." For all his outdoor-loving, Rick didn't like wearing off the rack. His height made it hard to find clothes his size in the first place, but his proportions were off for a guy as tall as he was. Tailor-made was the only way to go.

"Okay, everyone!" The guy leader walked toward the two groups of three. Richard and his two bodyguards/best friends stood together. A woman stood to one side and another woman and a man seemed to be a couple. "I'm Trent and the cranky gal back there is Ellie. You've all been told the basics of what's going to happen. We'll be together most of the time, but you'll also be in groups of three that stick together no matter what." He nodded toward Richard and his friends. "Since you booked together, you'll be one group." That was good. Dennis and Steve wouldn't have let it happen any other way. Trent looked at the other three. "You're with me."

"That means you guys are with me." The girl introduced as Ellie pointed at Richard and his two friends. "Who's Richard?"

Rick stepped forward. "I am."

He heard her muttered, "Of course." Then louder, "Then who's Dennis?" His friend to his right raised a hand. She nodded to Richard's left. "Then you're Steve." He nodded. "We've got a long way to go today so let's move out." She pointed to the path. "Get started. Wait at the first tree you come to."

Rick raised a brow at Dennis, who shrugged. They started off, his friends trailing behind him. He turned to walk backwards, eyeing Ellie in the distance. She'd snapped at him, made judgments about him based on the quality of his clothes, and wanted nothing to do with him, but all he could notice was how the sun gave her brown hair gold highlights from this angle.

"So, Ellie," Rick called as he walked backward toward the trail. "I take it there's no orientation meeting about how far we plan to go today or how many different camps we'll set up over the next few days."

"No." The one word answer told him everything he needed to know - for the moment at least - about how this week was going to go. She'd be bitter and snappy until he could prove he really did know what he was doing when it came to camping out and surviving in the wilderness.

A wicked grin crossed his face. Or maybe he'd feign ignorance and let her help him with everything. It wouldn't get him on her good side, but it sure would be fun.

All six of them set off down the brown dirt trail through the field next to the Outdoor Ozarks building. It was narrow enough the thigh-high weeds on either side brushed his legs as he caught up to and passed Dennis and Steve. He reached the tree she'd indicated, walked a few feet further into the woods of the Mark Twain National Forest, and stopped to wait.

Another pretty boy. Just what I need. Ellie Brewer stuck another protein bar in her pack before surveying the group of six as they walked away for the next several days of survival training in the Missouri Ozarks. Three of them looked ready for the trek. Two women and one man with appropriate gear who wore it well.

The other three...She stifled a sigh, knowing Trent would catch on immediately and, as the senior guide, he'd assigned them to her. The tall one - Richard? - was the pretty boy. The other two looked comfortable enough but none looked like they were ready for this.

Unless she was really honest with herself. But then she'd have to admit the pretty boy actually wore his gear well, too. His boots were sturdy but worn. There were scratches and scrapes on his pack showing it had been well-used, but still in good enough condition it wouldn't fall apart the first time he tossed it on the ground. The camouflage pants had pockets on top of pockets stuffed with additional supplies to be kept on his person at all times.

But even though the clothes were worn, when new, they had to have cost more than her monthly salary. Not that she made much.

"You about ready, Ellie?" Trent slung his pack on one shoulder before sliding his other arm in and buckling it around his middle.

"As ready as I'll ever be." She yanked the zipper shut and winced when it stuck. She'd need a new one soon but that wouldn't happen until her parents realized this wasn't just a whim or until one of her survivalists decided to give her a big tip for helping him survive in the wilderness because he wasn't smart enough to realize he wasn't the ourdoorsy type. A face flashed through her mind, but she shoved it out of the way as she situated her pack. If only Trent would help that memory stay gone. "You get the pretty boys."

Her efforts to walk off before Trent could protest didn't matter, because his laugh followed right after her. "Not on your life. Assignments are already made, and I didn't make them. Not this time."

Ellie swiveled on one heel and her eyes met Trent's in a stare down for the ages. "You would do that to me? After everything I went through, you won't trade me?"

Trent shrugged. "You know what they say to do when you get bucked off a horse."

"This isn't like falling off a horse or a bike or anything else. This is getting your heart broken, and you like me too much to watch me go through that again."

His trademark grin in place, he walked past her, whispering in her ear as he did. "Then don't fall in love with this one."

They started down the trail watching to see if those in front of them could follow the very basic instruction of "stop at the tree."

Ellie stifled a sigh. Five of them had. The pretty boy was six feet further in and grinning like the Cheshire cat. Of course.

After Trent lectured all six of them about listening to your guide and doing what you're told, they took off again. Only four more days and she could ditch this guy. As much as she loved the outdoors, this was one time she'd rather be home sick.

An hour later, the pretty boy behind her didn't bother to lower his voice. "I can't believe Maddie talked me into this."

"Your sister hates it when you call her that," one of the other guys told him.

"My sister's not here."

"Don't let her hear about it," the other guy said.

"Then don't tell her."

"And she didn't have to try hard to talk you into it."

"I'm just a glutton for punishment."

Right. Of course he was. He was too good looking not only for his own good but to be traipsing around the woods. Sure, the clothes looked worn in, but maybe he'd borrowed them from a friend who hiked a lot. Never mind that her traitorous brain had taken note of not only his height, but the broad shoulders, lean waist, and long legs. He wouldn't be able to borrow clothes from just anyone. Her rebellious mind had also noted his easy smile and thick, dark hair.

Ellie wasn't going to fall for another pretty boy. Even as she thought it, she knew it didn't really apply. Yes, he was good-looking, but not in a sissy-pretty-boy way. Yet she knew, no matter how ruggedly handsome other women might find him, she needed to keep her distance. Instead, she focused on the trail in front of her as they neared a clearing. Four days with these three yahoos and she'd be asking for a raise. She wouldn't get it, but she'd ask.

The next three hours passed both too quickly and too slowly. Too quickly because the sooner they reached their camp site, the sooner she'd have to help them set up shelters. Too slowly because of the incessant stream of chatter from Pretty Boy and the somewhat amused replies of his friends. At least they'd kept up. Trent and his group had fallen a fair bit behind, but she wasn't worried about them. Every half hour, he checked in over their radios. There was no cell phone service in the middle of nowhere, but if they needed help they could get a hold of the home base.

They stopped for a quick lunch. Protein bars and trail mix along with the allotment of water were downed by all of the men as they sat on a group of rocks. Ellie sat off to the side, against her favorite tree at this particular rest spot. She let them sit for about twenty minutes before she stood.

"Time to move out." She hoisted her pack up and moved to the trail out of the small clearing, waiting there for them to pick up the trash. As soon as they had their backpacks on, she started down the trail.

"Hey!" Rick stopped a couple feet away, forcing her to stare up at him. "I know we're doing the whole minimalist thing, but there'll be a cabin nearby right? Just in case."

Deep breath in. And out. In. And out. She counted to ten. Then twenty. Then in Latin. "No, Ricky. There won't be any cabin. Just what we can carry or find or kill." Spinning on one heel, she started up the trail. She sent up a prayer - or two - and tried to tune out the chuckle she was sure she heard coming from behind her.

"You're not being very nice." Dennis walked next to Richard for a few feet where the trail widened. "You know all this stuff. We lived in the Amazon for three months with less than we have now. What're you doing?"

Richard shrugged and made sure Ellie was far enough ahead

she wouldn't hear. "She made snap judgments about us. I didn't want to disappoint her."

"Don't do it. I get why. I know how sick you are of being written off as a pretty face or a spare - and not in the fun sense of the word - but playing up to that role isn't going endear you to her. Once she finds out you're not as helpless as a newborn kitten out here, she's going to be madder than the rhino on that safari."

"I know." But he wouldn't be able to help himself. He knew that. Dennis knew that. Or maybe he'd just tell - or show - her the truth.

Steve called from behind him. "How much farther? I'm not complaining, just curious."

Ellie turned around and Rick caught a glimpse of a scowl that disappeared almost before it began. She walked backwards as she called out. "About two more hours to the campsite, where there are no cabins and no facilities of any kind - except a nearby stream."

Rick hid his smirk until she turned around then let it break loose. Dennis just shook his head.

The next two hours went quickly and before they knew it, the forest opened up into a clearing. He dropped his pack and took a deep breath of clean air. The clearing wasn't too big, but also not too far from a drop. The incline wasn't nearly steep enough to be called a cliff, but it did allow them a decent look over the Ozark Mountains. The view wasn't as awe-inspiring as some he'd seen in other places around the world - including his home country - but...

He started softly and grew louder with each word, not caring who was around to hear it. "'The heavens declare the glory of God; and the skies proclaim the work of his hands!'" Rick's arms spread wide over his head as he yelled the last.

"Are you done?"

Rick turned to see Ellie standing there, arms folded across her chest and eyes snapping. A slow grin crossed his face. "For now.

But look..." One arm swept across the expanse toward the hills. "How can you look at this and *not* shout about God's glory? If we're silent, 'the stones would immediately cry out!'"

Ellie rolled her eyes. "Luke 19:40? Really? That's not exactly what Christ was talking about, and I'm sure you know it."

"You're right," he conceded, "but..." With his eyes closed, he drew in another deep breath. "I can't help it."

With another glance heavenward, she turned and went to start unpacking. Dennis moved to his side and mimicked the deep breathing.

"You know you don't have to yell everywhere." His friend put his hands on his hips and inhaled again. "I know it's your thing but..."

Rick let out a chuckle. "When you see the world from the top of Kilimanjaro, what else are you supposed to yell?"

"Nothing?" Dennis shrugged. "Most of us are happy enough with a quiet moment of reflection."

With a slap to Dennis's back, Rick took a few more steps forward, coming close enough to the edge to make his body-guards-slash-friends look at him twice, but it couldn't be helped. Whenever he had a moment to stop and reflect, he took it. Especially when confronted by the glorious tapestry spread out in front of him. Maybe it had something to do with growing up in the shadow of the Alps or in the middle of one of the clearest lakes in Europe. Surrounded by those during his formative years likely affected his perspective.

Chuckling to himself, he turned back to the campsite and started to set his things up.

He'd be on her last nerve before the day was out.

Ellie did her best to be patient, but some men just made it

impossible. The only consolation she had was to watch Trent and his crew - two of whom, despite how they'd appeared at head-quarters, were less experienced than her Pretty Boy and hadn't kept up nearly as well on the hike.

Just a few days and they'd get back to the trail head, and she could ditch all of this for a long-overdue vacation. The tall, unfor-tunately handsome one she was trying to ignore had even brought his camera with him. Who did that on a minimalist trip? And a very nice camera at that. He'd get some great shots, she admitted, although grudgingly and only to herself. She sighed and looked around the camp. The bear bags were hung. Water bladders were filled and purified. Trent was helping his people finish their shel-ters. Her team had finished much more quickly than she would have expected. Ellie tried not to remember how Rick's fingers felt under hers as she helped him with the knots. Or the feeling of his breath on her cheek as he asked one astute question after another.

Ellie finally turned her back to the man filling way too many of her thoughts. She poked at the campfire with a stick. The stove was off to the side and had a pot on it. The water would boil soon and they'd use it to mix with their dehydrated meals for dinner. She'd bet her three boys had packed their own then been forced to take the ones Trent provided when he disapproved.

A nudge to her gut made her rescind her internal criticism. They had outperformed her expectations today. Even the pretty boy only had to be shown once how to tie the knots.

Normally, Trent enforced a fairly early bedtime, but Ellie saw the sly look he was giving her as the stars began to appear. He tilted his head toward Rick. She just rolled her eyes and went to sit on her favorite rock.

"Is this seat taken?"

Ellie looked up to see Rick standing there. "If I say it is?"

He gave her a cocky grin. "Then I'd guess you were saving it for me."

"Don't be so sure," she muttered when he sat down anyway.

A crunching sound caught her attention but she refused to give into her curiosity. "You do this all the time?" he asked around whatever it was he was eating.

"Sit and watch stars?"

"Lead groups of people who have no clue what they're doing into the middle of nowhere and hope you all survive."

The comment stung. "Glad to know you think we're incompetent."

"I don't think you're incompetent."

"Then why would we only *hope* to survive? If Trent and I are any good at our jobs, and we're very good at our jobs, then everyone will survive just fine, thank you very much."

"I didn't mean to insult you. You seem quite competent." This time she saw him take a rather large bite of an apple.

Ellie should have brought some fresh fruit along but she hadn't wanted the extra weight in her pack this trip.

He held it out to her. "Would you like a bite?"

"No, thank you." She didn't need anything from him.

Even if the next crunch of his apple made her mouth water. The crunch after that made it even worse.

"So, what is on the agenda for tomorrow?"

"Weren't you paying attention?" Did he expect her to repeat everything over and over just for him?

"Yes. I was hoping you could give me a bit more detail. Pack up camp, hike for a while, and set up camp again isn't much in the way of information."

She'd give him that. Trent was pretty sparse with details. "If you and your buddies keep up the way you did today, we'll hike for about three hours, break for lunch, hike for two more hours then set up camp. We'll stay there tomorrow night and the next night then pack up again. Another day hike to our last campsite. After a night there, we'll retrace our steps."

"Why two nights at the one spot?"

"We'll practice some more survival skills. You'll set out your own snares and dress the squirrel or rabbit then cook it yourself. No stove."

"Sounds easy enough."

He would think that.

"I'll even share my rabbit with you." That cocksure grin was back.

And made her traitorous stomach do slow flips as he took the last bite of his apple.

Rick knew he shouldn't try so hard to irritate her, but it was so easy.

And so fun.

His mother would tan his hide. Well, not really. Hide tanning wasn't in his mother's genteel nature, but he'd be grounded for a month.

A shrill whistle behind them caught his attention. "Lights out. We gotta pack up early." Trent's voice carried to where he and Ellie sat.

"That's our cue." She stood and brushed the back of her pants off with her hands. "Dawn comes early and we have a big day."

"Sleep well, Ellie." He watched her walk away, one corner of his mind wishing she wore shorts so he could appreciate the long legs hidden under her cargo pants. The rest of his mind felt guilty for his deception. Tomorrow, he'd have to come clean.

That had been his plan but Ellie woke up on the wrong side of the bedroll. When she started snapping at all three of them first thing after dawn, he fumbled his way through packing up his part of camp. He could have done it with his eyes closed, or in his sleep, but instead she had to help him get everything folded and packed right.

A hand on his shoulder as they started off stopped him. "This is going to backfire, sir."

Dennis's voice wouldn't carry far enough for anyone else to hear him, but Rick glared at him anyway. "Don't call me that."

"Then stop the charade. I've got a bad feeling about this."

Those words stopped Rick in his tracks. "What kind of bad feeling, Dennis?"

The bodyguard-turned-friend shook his head. "I don't know, but nothing good can come of it, and something is churning in my gut. It won't end well."

"I won't do anything stupid. You know me better than that."

"I know you won't do anything *you* think is stupid." Dennis stepped directly in front of him. "You *will* listen to me, to Steve, and to Ellie. Understand, Your Highness?"

The barb struck where it was supposed to. "Don't call me that."

"Then behave yourself. Do as you're told, and don't pretend you're incompetent." One more withering look and Dennis turned to follow Steve and Ellie.

Rick sighed and trudged after them. He knew Dennis was right. He just needed to remember that the next time the opportunity arose to annoy her.

"Rick! Get back here!" Ellie charged after him as fast as she could through the dense underbrush.

"We won't go far!" His long legs carried him further and further away from her faster than she could follow him.

This was what happened when you took arrogant, self-centered pretty boys on hikes. They didn't listen, did their best to get lost, and she had to save them. It wasn't the first time. It probably wouldn't be the last. This time she wouldn't rescue the guy from being hopelessly lost, lose her heart in the process then get it broken again. She'd shove him, hard, and watch him land on his backside.

"This is the coolest cave around, right?" Rick called back.

"Yeah, but this isn't the best way to get there." Like that would stop him.

"But we can't get to the best way to get there from here, right?"

"Rick, we can't go this way. Stop!" She hurried as fast as she could, but his long legs carried him further away from her.

His two buddies weren't being much help. They'd yelled after him when he'd first taken off, but once he'd insisted, they'd exchanged a look she couldn't interpret and followed in his wake.

She thought about grabbing the walkie-talkie and calling Trent, but what could Trent do? They were only checking in every ninety minutes during this hike and Rick had waited until just after the last call to make his move into the woods. Besides, if she stopped to get the walkie out of her backpack, Rick would be long gone. He had grabbed her map and compass, so he wouldn't need her. Instead of wasting time, she followed him, hollering at him to stop every few minutes.

But he just kept going.

After almost an hour, they broke through the rugged forest onto the trail that would lead directly to the cave. Ten minutes after that, they stood in front of the entrance.

"We won't be in here long," Rick promised looking up at the mountain above the opening.

Ellie crossed her arms in front of her. "That's because we're not going in at all. We don't have the equipment for wandering around in the cave."

"We won't wander around." Rick hiked his backpack a bit higher. "We'll just go in and look around for a few minutes then get back to where we're supposed to be." He headed for the entrance. "Come on."

She heard Dennis and Steve muttering behind her, but they

didn't try to stop him. If they didn't go far, they'd be fine, but she didn't trust Rick not to push the limits.

With a frustrated growl, Ellie ran after him until she could grab him by the arm and spin him around. "Okay. Fine. Look. It's my job to keep you safe. You won't listen to me and turn around, and I won't let you go on by yourself. So you're going to listen. You'll stop when I tell you to stop, and we'll leave when I say to leave, understand?"

Rick's smug grin was more than she could handle. She put both hands on his chest and shoved. Just like she'd planned.

He didn't move.

Annoying pretty boy.

She turned and stalked into the mouth of the cave, pulling her flashlight out of its spot on her backpack.

The sound of water trickling in the distance caught her attention first. Cool air greeted them as they moved further in. Stalactites and stalagmites reached for each other, glistening as their headlamps illuminated the space.

"This is amazing," Rick whispered. He tilted his head down toward the opening in front of them. "How far down does that go?"

"Not too far. I forget exactly but maybe fifteen feet or so." She turned and crossed her arms across her chest. "We are *not* going down there."

His eyes narrowed. "I wasn't suggesting it."

"You were thinking about it."

He sighed. "Okay. I was. But you're right. We don't have the equipment." In the dim lighting she could see a gleam in his eyes. "But we *can* explore this way a bit more." He turned toward the path that led along the side of the cavern.

Ellie smothered her frustration and started after him.

But her boot slipped on the loose gravel.

A scream ripped from her as she dropped her flashlight and plummeted into the darkness.

Available Now!

Richard Antonio David Nicklaus is Montevaro's spare - and he likes it that way. He prefers traipsing through mountains and rafting down rivers to board rooms and state dinners. After one more trip through the Ozark Mountains, he'll have to head home and help his sister prepare for her wedding and coronation, taking over more official duties because of their father's ailing health.

Trail guide Ellie Brewer is sick of rich, pretty boys, but she's assigned one on her last trip before heading to Montevaro to spend time with her aunt, uncle, and cousin, Charlie, before he marries a princess. She admits Rick does okay - until he fails to follow instructions and she ends up injured miles from where they're supposed to be.

After Rick takes her on a once-in-a-lifetime trip on their way to Europe, Ellie spends her recovery in Montevaro. When Rick takes off for weeks at a time, and is seen dancing with other women, Ellie wonders if she really meant anything to him. Ellie finds herself drawn to another man, but knows he can't compare to the one she misses. Rick wants to be with Ellie but official duties have him flying around the world and concern for his distant cousin - Queen Christiana of Ravenzario - preoccupies him when he's home. Somehow, he'll have to convince Ellie not to regret the day Along Came a Prince.

GRACE TO SAVE PREVIEW

SEPTEMBER 11, 2001

A ringing jolted Travis Harders from a deep sleep. He cursed as the phone knocked to the floor with a clatter. "This better be good," he snapped when he got the handset in place.

A glance at the clock nearly made him groan.

4:07.

"You'll be hearing from the police soon."

He rubbed the sleep out of his eyes with the heel of one hand and tried to process the statement. The words didn't really register as the guy, whoever he was, kept talking until Travis interrupted. "What? Who is this?"

"Mark's dad." Right. Travis's best friend. "You remember us? The ones who treated you like family? Let you live with us?"

Travis's stomach sank. Mark's family had practically adopted him when he moved from southwest Missouri to the Big Apple. They had filled the gap in his life left by parents who disapproved of Travis's choice to move to New York. Mark's parents let him spend holidays and birthdays with them, with Travis making only the obligatory phone calls back home.

But none of that explained why Mark's dad would be calling the police.

"Who is it?" a sleepy Jennifer asked.

Travis covered the mouthpiece and whispered to his girlfriend, "No one." His feet hit the cool floor, and he headed for the other room. At least he had a place to escape to. Being an out-of-work-actor-turned-barista didn't pay much, but he'd lucked into a fabulous apartment. Closing the French door behind him, he tried to focus on the voice yelling from the other end of the line.

But he only caught "my daughter" and "spring break" and "drugged."

If possible, Travis's stomach clenched further as that night flooded back to him. Memories of bringing her back to this very apartment when she was in no condition to go home without risking the wrath of her parents. But after what happened between them...it was only right for him to be on the receiving end of her dad's anger. "I don't know what she told you sir, but..."

"I know all I need to know," he bellowed.

Even though he was in the other room, Travis lowered the volume on the handset. "I take full responsibility for..."

"You're right, you do!" He let loose a string of obscenities. "You'll spend years in prison! Drugging a girl! Sleeping with her!"

"What?" His whole world spun. Travis regretted every minute of that night after they got back to the apartment, but he hadn't drugged her. He didn't even know where to get those kinds of drugs. They weren't in love, never had been, but to place the blame solely on him? The next morning, they'd talked about it enough to know she hadn't blamed him.

What changed? Feeling sucker punched, Travis hung up on the man. What he said didn't matter. Travis would find out when he was on trial for something he didn't do. On autopilot, he dressed for his five a.m. shift. Coffees of the World wasn't the best job, but it had flexible hours and had led to finding this sublet. There was no shortage of interesting characters to populate his imagination. Like the skinny brunette with the shoulder length bob who worked for Morgan Stanley and always ordered a short nonfat mocha, decaf, no foam, no sugar, no whip. She could be the heroine in one of his screenplays even if he never knew her name.

He kissed Jennifer's hair and told her he'd call after work. Five flights of stairs later, the sounds of the city waking up greeted him as he walked toward the train that would take him to the Trade Center. Standing at the top of the subway steps, he changed his mind. Travis headed for his car parked a couple streets over and called in.

Two hours later, he stopped in McLean for gas about seven thirty, filling up the tank of his Toyota Corolla hatchback. Three hours after that, he could still drive for a while longer before he'd need to stop again. He contemplated leaving the state, but decided not to, instead turning northward before leaving Allegany County.

He'd gone through more emotions than he knew he had, none of them good. Anger. Fear. Frustration. Blame. Worry. Intimidation. In western New York, things were more peaceful than they ever were in downtown Manhattan, but his insides were in utter turmoil at the thought of an arrest and trial.

His favorite heavy metal CD blared from the speakers. During the lull between songs, Travis could hear his cell phone vibrating on the passenger seat where he'd tossed it. After an hour and a half of the stupid thing ringing nearly nonstop, he finally snatched it up.

"What?" Travis growled.

"Are you okay?" Though he only talked to her twice a year, there was no mistaking his mother's voice.

Or the panic in it.

The tremor set him on edge. "Yeah. Why?"

"Thank you, Jesus," she whispered, though Travis couldn't figure out what she was thanking Him for. "Where are you? You got out okay? Were you working? There was no answer at your apartment."

Why was Mom calling just to ask if he was okay? Why was she frantic? "I'm in western New York State. Out for a drive. Get out of where?" Could Mark's dad have called already?

"You don't know?" Frenzy changed to disbelief.

"Know what?" Travis held the phone against his shoulder as he downshifted into a turn.

He could hear the tears over the static-filled line. "Two planes, Trav. They hit the Towers. Both of the buildings are on fire."

His heart thudded to a stop. "What?" Hadn't a bomber hit the Empire State Building in WWII? But two planes? On a brilliantly clear day? No weather in sight. "How bad is it?" he croaked.

"They're saying it's a terror attack. The Pentagon is on fire. There's another plane out there somewhere. Big jets, Travis. I saw the second one hit. The explosion. Papers flying everywhere. The people..." Her voice broke. "You really weren't there?" she confirmed.

"No, Mom. I'm not anywhere near there." But he needed to find a place to stop. A television. He had to see for himself. Tens of thousands of people would be dead and dying. Did he know any of them?

"There are people jumping, falling, out of the upper stories. I can't imagine." He could almost see her pacing around the kitchen alternately running her hands through her hair and wringing them together. "They're jumping from a hundred stories up. What could be so bad to make that the better option?" Her voice caught. "I don't know how I can watch this, Trav, but I can't turn away. All I can do is pray."

Pray. Right. A face flashed before Travis. The uptight former-football-player-turned-businessman from the 102nd floor of the North Tower with his caramel macchiato and corny joke of the day. Was he one of those jumping?

She gasped then whispered. "Dear God, no. No!" Her scream made him move the phone even as his stomach sank.

He pulled into a café parking lot near Danville. "What?"

"The tower. It's gone. Just gone. The south one, I think." Her voice trailed off in prayer.

The shock he'd felt after the phone call from Mark's dad paled compared to what he felt now. "Mom, I gotta go." Jen. His friends. His coworkers. He needed to make calls of his own. Find out if they were okay. And Mark. His best friend had been a firefighter for a year. He'd be down there. Inside one of the Towers. Travis hadn't talked to him since that night, the March before, but part of him, the part that still believed there was a God in heaven, whispered a prayer that Mark was somewhere safe as faces of customers and friends flashed through Travis's mind.

The blonde. The cute, petite one who ordered a crunchy, cinnamon pastry and half caf, double tall, easy hazelnut, non-fat, no foam with whip extra hot latte on Tuesdays. She flirted shamelessly, though he knew she was recently and happily engaged to some guy in Tower Seven. Her family lived near his in Serenity Landing, Missouri, and she worked at the Marriot World Trade Center in the shadow of the Towers. Could it have survived the collapse? Was Joanna now buried underneath the rubble?

"Be safe, Travis. Do you have somewhere you can go? They're evacuating Manhattan."

"I'll be okay." He hesitated. "I love you, Mom. You, Dad, Jay. I love all of you. I'll call when I can, but I have to try to find out about my friends, about my girlfriend. I'll talk to you soon."

His mom's "I love you," came through the line as he clicked his phone off.

He started his first call as he walked into the café. Call after call failed as he stood with others, watching the screen in horror as the second tower crashed down. His problems. Mark's dad. Mark's sister. All of it fled as the enormity of what was happening sunk in.

The whole world had changed.

December 18, 2001

"It's a girl."

Abi Connealy collapsed back onto the bed, tears streaming down her cheeks as a newborn squawk filled the delivery room.

A girl.

A million thoughts flew through her mind, few of them happy, as a nurse laid the baby on her chest. So small. So scrunched up and red. Dark hair. Abi couldn't see her eyes as she wrapped her arms around the tiny bundle. "Hi, baby," she whispered. "I'm so glad you're here."

"How are you?"

Abi looked up at Brenda Wardman. Her brother's girlfriend had been a rock the last few months. She didn't need to clarify, because Abi knew what she meant. "I don't know." The voice mail she'd left her parents on the way to the hospital remained unanswered unless Brenda knew something she didn't.

Her fingers brushed over the cheek of the tiny girl. "She's perfect, Bren." Another tear fell, this one landing on her new daughter's face as Abi closed her eyes.

The nurse took the baby to the warmer and did whatever it was nurses did, but Abi didn't see any of it. Her eyes remained closed, and she clasped Brenda's hand as more hot tears streaked into her ears. Just under twenty-four hours of labor meant she didn't have the energy to wipe them away. She knew she didn't have the will to do so even if she could have.

"Do you know what you're going to do?"

Abi wanted to yell at her friend for bringing up the most difficult decision of her life just moments after the birth of her daughter. But since Abi hadn't made up her mind beforehand, Brenda needed to know to help make the arrangements.

Except Abi didn't know.

Not for sure. She knew what the smart decision was, though her head and her heart didn't agree. But she had to put her baby first. "I'll have them call."

"It's going to be fine," Brenda tried to reassure her, but Abi heard the doubt in her friend's voice.

Right.

Fine.

Once the social worker arrived, she'd never be fine again.

Somehow, Abi managed to doze for several hours during the afternoon, but after listening to the message from her parents, the one that told her all she needed to know without really saying anything, her eyes refused to close. Instead, she stared at the bracelet encircling her wrist, rotating it around time and time again.

A knock sounded half a second before the door pushed open. "Hi, there, Abi. Someone's looking for her mama." The nurse compared the baby's bracelet to Abi's before lifting the blanketed bundle out of the clear bassinet. "The card says you're giving her formula?"

There was no judgment in the woman's voice, but Abi felt her own condemnation eating away at her. All she could do was nod.

After a few minutes of helping them get situated, the nurse started to leave, but stopped before walking out the door. "The emotions are normal, honey. They get everyone at one point or another."

Abi nodded but didn't take her eyes off the little cheeks sucking in and out. She memorized the sounds, the smells, the essence of the tiny bundle in her arms. Or tried to. Even as she did, she knew it would never work. In the morning, a social worker would come and Abi would sign the papers put in front of her.

And she'd never see her daughter again.

But when the social worker sat in the chair by the window, asking the questions, one tripped Abi up.

"Do you know who her father is?"

The night was burned in Abi's memory banks. Part of it anyway. When she hesitated too long, the worker prompted her again. Abi nodded. "Yes. I know who the father is."

"Then we'll need his signature, too."

"He doesn't know," she whispered. "I haven't talked to him since. I was going to, but then 9/11..." Her voice trailed off.

"Was he in the Towers?" the social worker asked as gently as she could.

Abi shook her head. "I don't he was. I mean, I know he wasn't one of the three thousand, but I don't know if he was there or not." She'd called his apartment from a pay phone a few weeks later. When he answered, she hung up.

"If you know who he is, we have to have him sign away his parental rights, sweetie."

Something she hadn't considered when she made this plan.

The nurse walked in, once again pushing the bassinet. Her face fell when she saw the social worker. "I'm sorry. I didn't realize you were..."

With a swipe of the overused Kleenex, Abi wiped her face. "I wasn't sure, but now I can't anyway."

The social worker left a couple of fliers and walked out with a sympathetic smile. The nurse awkwardly helped Abi get situated to feed her daughter one more time.

"Do you have a name you like?" The woman sat on the edge of the bed holding Abi's empty water bottle.

"Cassandra."

"That's beautiful."

"It was my grandmother's name. She died this past summer." The grandmother who would have adored meeting her great-granddaughter, who would have taken Abi and the baby in when she needed somewhere to turn. Had given Abi hope she'd do just that before succumbing to a sudden, massive stroke.

Abi didn't have anyone else like that in her life. Brenda would if she could, but there was no way. Abi had no other family. No one else in her life who would support her no matter what.

Darkness descended, but Abi refused to send little Cassie back to the nursery. She didn't know what she planned to do about adoption, but she wouldn't give up another minute with her baby.

Yet another round of tears leaked down her face as Abi cuddled the tiny bundle against her chest. With all but one light turned out, the desperate whisper ripped from her throat. "God? Are you there?" She'd never prayed before, but this seemed like the time to start if there ever was one. "I don't know what to do."

Baby Cassandra yawned and blinked her eyes open, staring up at her mother. The light caught them just right and struck Abi with the bright blue.

Then it hit her.

The one place she could take her daughter where she'd be safe. And loved.

December 23, 2001

Two days before Christmas, Abi sat in a coffee shop on Long Island and waited. Calling him had taken every ounce of courage she had. Leaving the voicemail took more.

Sitting there, Abi didn't know if she could go through with it. The stroller with her little girl sat to her right. On the other side of it, Brenda sat with her back to the door. Diners nearby sipped on gourmet coffee, but Abi focused on the stationary in front of her. She arrived early so she could write the note, but the paper remained nearly blank.

When she'd arrived at her parents' Long Island home after leaving the hospital, a note reiterated her father's threat. Since then, Abi had planned what to say, but realized she'd never make it through even the shortest speech. She'd planned the words to write, but now the time had come to put pen to paper, and she only managed his name. A glance at her watch told her she didn't have much time. If she didn't write it now, she'd have to make the speech. No way could she do that.

She picked up the Mont Blanc knock-off she'd received for graduation from her grandmother and scribbled a few lines. Her heart squeezed as she reread the note. She couldn't be a student and a mom. But *this*? Abi had her suitcase packed. She wouldn't return to her parents' home but would crash at Brenda's for a few days while her friend went out of town. Brenda knew most of what happened, but not everything. Abi's fingers furrowed through her hair, and she turned to stare out the window. There he stood. His six-foot frame seemed shorter with his shoulders slumped and hands shoved deep in the pockets of his coat. He looked at his watch and trudged across the street.

The bell over the door jangled. Abi crossed through the unfinished sentence, scribbled a last sentiment and her name, and shoved the note in her purse as he sat down across from her.

"Hi." At the sound of his voice, the knots in her gut tightened.

Abi looked up, knowing he'd see the remnants of her tears. She twisted the napkin in her hands and tried not the think about the weight she'd gained. And if he'd notice.

"Thanks for coming. I wanted to try to explain, but..." Abi shrugged. "After 9/11, after Mark..." The thoughts of her brother nearly overwhelmed her already overwrought emotions. "Daddy isn't going to pursue anything. I tried to tell him you weren't guilty, but he didn't believe me at first. He found your name in my journal on 9/11-before it was '9/11.' I'd left it lying out by accident." This time the shrug was a mere halfhearted lift of one shoulder.

"Mark?" he interrupted. "I read the list of firefighters a bunch of times to make sure he wasn't there."

"He wasn't on the lists. He was killed at a fire on 9/11. Not at the Trade Center. Another fire where they didn't have enough manpower because of everything else. They think he died right around the time the first tower fell."

Were those tears in his eyes? He and Mark hadn't spoken in months. "I'm so sorry."

Cassandra let out a cry. The disguised Brenda made a shushing sound, but Abi didn't look. She couldn't. It was too much. She had to get out. "Can you excuse me for a minute?"

She didn't wait for a reply but motioned toward the back, leaving before he had a chance to stop her. Brenda went out the front door. Abi dug the paper out and waved the barista over. "Can you give this to that guy?"

The woman nodded. Abi fled to the other side of the street and collapsed in Brenda's arms.

Travis read the note three times before it began to sink in.

Dear Travis,

She had to have written it earlier. There hadn't been time since she excused herself.

I hate doing this to you, especially like this. I tried to handle it on my own. I thought I could, but this semester was so hard. Even more than just everything on 9/11 and Mark. I can't do it. I can't be a college student and a mom.

It took several minutes for that to really register.

A mom?

He read on, his disbelief growing with each word.

The baby in the stroller is yours. From that night. I hate that I haven't told you sooner, but I didn't know how. I couldn't tell my parents what happened, not all of it. They would blame you, and it wasn't your fault. I know this is the coward's way out, but I can't tell you to your face. Everything you need for a couple of days is in the diaper bag and the duffel on the bottom of the stroller. So is her birth certificate.

Her name is Cassandra. She's only a few days old. Please take good care of her for me. I won't be home for a while so you can't reach me. My parents left for vacation out of the country, so they wouldn't be here when she was born.

I wish things had worked out the way we planned. The way we talked about all those times. I wish

Whatever she wished, she didn't finish the thought before scribbling through it. About like their relationship had been. A wish that was never finished. He went back to the letter.

Tell Cassandra I love her.

I'm sorry.

Abi

He read it two more times, starting to come to grips with what it meant.

And then the baby began to fuss.

Taking a deep, steadying breath to fortify himself, he turned to the blanket tented over the handle of the car seat. Lifting up one corner, he saw pink. Fuzzy bunnies on the toes of a sleeper. A tiny foot kicking those bunnies in the air. He looked further and saw the bluest eyes he'd ever seen staring back at him, almost as though she knew who he was.

Her father.

Her daddy.

The one responsible for her from here on out.

And in that moment, he fell helplessly in love.

December 25, 2001

Christmas night, the little gray Toyota turned off I-44, south towards Serenity Landing, as the wailing in the backseat reached a new level.

"I'm sorry, Cassandra. We're almost there. I'll get you something to eat in a ten minutes, I promise." Jennifer kicked him out the moment he tried to explain his arrival at the apartment with a baby. Instead, he'd boxed up all his worldly belongings along with the things Abi had left for the baby and packed it in his car. They headed for the only place he knew he could get the help he needed until he had a better handle on things.

Over twelve hundred miles. Stopping every two or three hours to feed his daughter or change her diaper. Sometimes more often than that. Always taking much longer than it should. Failing to take into account how many things would be closed on Christmas Day, he ran out of the bottled water when he needed to make one more meal for his daughter. He pressed the pedal a little closer to the floor in an effort to reach Serenity Landing a little faster.

The newborn squalling had quieted a bit when Travis finally pulled to a stop in front of the house where he'd grown up. In the front window, a Christmas tree stood, multi-colored lights twinkling. In the window next to it, he could see Mom and Dad sitting at the dining room table, though he knew they wouldn't be able to see him. His brother walked in with a platter, piled high with a turkey way too big for the three of them. They'd be eating leftovers for a month.

Another squeak came from the back. "Okay, baby. We're here."

Somehow, Travis managed to get the diaper bag and the baby seat out of the car and headed toward the door, snow crunching under his boots with each step. The smell of oak burning in the fireplace both comforted him and heightened his anxiety. What if they turned him away? Then what?

Should he knock?

He hadn't been home in two and a half years. Did he just walk in?

Even with his hands full, Travis managed to press the doorbell. He took a deep breath and blew it out slowly, finishing as the door opened.

Mom stood there, her jaw hanging down for a second before her hands covered her mouth. "Travis!"

He tried to smile but failed miserably. "Hi, Mom." In the space of a heartbeat, he saw what he needed to in her eyes. Forgiveness. Acceptance. Love. Grace. With a prayer tossed heavenward, he tried again to smile, this time successfully. "There's someone I want you to meet."

Available Now!

Travis Harders has been a single dad since the day he learned he had a daughter with his only one-night stand. Fifteen years later, he and Cassie are getting along just fine and he's even fallen in love. The last thing he expects to find on his doorstep one Tuesday morning is Cassie's mom - the one person he thought he'd never see again - and she's asking the impossible.

Circumstances, including her firefighter brother's death on 9/11, forced Abi Connealy into a decision she's spent years regretting and her daughter grew up without her. But now, a family crisis compels her to do the one thing she swore she never would: find the daughter she'd abandoned just a few days after birth.

Shocked when Travis doesn't send her packing, Abi prays to a

God she doesn't believe in that her relationship with her daughter will be restored. Travis plans to propose to his girlfriend, but their relationship hits the rocks as he and Abi both struggle with the long-dormant feelings that never had the chance to develop.

When Cassie demonstrates incredible grace toward the grandfather who refuses to acknowledge her existence, Abi begins to learn the love of a Savior - a Savior who has more than enough Grace to Save.

ABOUT THE AUTHOR

When she's not writing about her imaginary friends, USA Today Bestselling Author Carol Moncado prefers binge watching pretty much anything to working out. She believes peanut butter M&Ms are the perfect food and Dr. Pepper should come in an IV. When not hanging out with her hubby, four kids, and two dogs who weigh less than most hard cover books, she's probably reading in her Southwest Missouri home.

Summers find her at the local aquatic center with her four fish, er, kids. Fall finds her doing the band mom thing. Winters find her snuggled into a blanket in front of a fire with the dogs. Spring finds her sneezing and recovering from the rest of the year.

She used to teach American Government at a community college, but her indie career, with over twenty titles released, has allowed her to write full time. She's a founding member and former President of MozArks ACFW, blogger at InspyRomance, and is represented by Tamela Hancock Murray of the Steve Laube Agency.

www.carolmoncado.com
books@candidpublications.com

OTHER BOOKS BY CAROL MONCADO

The CANDID Romance Series

Finding Mr. Write
Finally Mr. Write
Falling for Mr. Write

The Monarchies of Belles Montagnes Series
(Previously titled The Montevaro Monarchy
and The Brides of Belles Montagnes series)

Good Enough for a Princess
Along Came a Prince
More than a Princess
Hand-Me-Down Princess
Winning the Queen's Heart
Protecting the Prince (Novella)
Prince from her Past

Serenity Landing Second Chances

CAROL MONCADO

Discovering Home
Glimpsing Hope
Reclaiming Hearts

Crowns & Courtships

Heart of a Prince
The Inadvertent Princess
A Royally Beautiful Mess

Crowns & Courtships Novellas

Dare You
A Kaerasti for Clari

Serenity Landing Tuesdays of Grace
9/11 Tribute Series

Grace to Save

Serenity Landing Lifeguards
Summer Novellas

The Lifeguard, the New Guy, & Frozen Custard
(previously titled: The Lifeguards, the Swim Team, & Frozen Custard)
The Lifeguard, the Abandoned Heiress, & Frozen Custard

Serenity Landing Teachers
Christmas Novellas

Gifts of Love
Manuscripts & Mistletoe
Premieres & Paparazzi

Mallard Lake Township

Ballots, Bargains, & the Bakery (novella)

Timeline/Order for Crowns & Courtships and Novellas
1. *A Kaerasti for Clari*
2. *Dare You*
(the first two can be read in either order, but technically this is the timeline)
3. *Heart of a Prince*
4. *The Inadvertent Princess*
5. *A Royally Beautiful Mess*